CHORUS OF WITCHES

Nothing is known about PAUL BUCKLAND, the author of *Chorus of Witches* (1959). The name may well be a pseudonym, and there are no other works credited to Buckland. No copy of the contract or other correspondence with the author was to be found in the archives of the original publisher, W. H. Allen, meaning Buckland's identity may never be known unless a relative or someone who knew him comes forward with information.

D1091199

PAUL BUCKLAND

Chorus of Witches

VALANCOURT BOOKS

Chorus of Witches by Paul Buckland
Originally published in Great Britain by W. H. Allen in 1959
First Valancourt Books edition 2021

Published by Valancourt Books, Richmond, Virginia
http://www.valancourtbooks.com

ISBN 978-1-954321-51-9 (trade paperback)
ISBN 978-1-954321-52-6 (trade hardcover)

Also available as an electronic book.

Set in Dante MT

With the exception of 'Duncan',
all the characters in this story are
fictitious.

CHAPTER 1

"All down for the finale! All down for the finale!" The call-boy's mocking voice piped shrilly along the empty corridor; he pushed open the battered-looking door marked CHORUS and poked his angelic little head into the room. "Come on, girls! Get down them stairs!"

A loud scream pierced the babel; bright pink clouds of powder wafted in the air, and sickly-sweet perfumes mingled with the sharp odour of perspiration. Faces were patted, eyelashes curled, carmined mouths were twisted grotesquely and flashing white teeth leered back from mirrors. There was a flurry of fans, a rustle of crinolines, a vulgar expletive and a hurried concealment of a gin bottle. Laughing gaily they swept past the boy, some pausing a moment to pinch his smooth cheeks or his small rounded bottom, which, as it was Saturday night and a good tip was in the offing, bravely bore the indignity. He liked this show and the chorus were generous and made a great fuss of him, unlike some of the bags who had been here and carried on as though they owned the theatre. He gave an extra-wide grin, wriggled appreciatively and sped back to the stage manager.

"My feet," complained a voice, mournfully.

"You and your feet, Netta. What's the matter?"

"It's me Louis heels. They're killing me."

"Take your shoes off, dear. No one will notice. Did you see what happened to Tessa tonight? She got the end of her train wet in a fire bucket."

"That's what *she* says," someone remarked kindly. "More likely pissed herself singing."

"My God, where is she?" asked Netta, rushing back to the dressing-room door.

"Oh, leave her alone, she's in there crying."

"The poor thing."

"She'll get over it."

"You're hard, Josie. And your coronet's slipping."

"You have to be hard in this game." Josie gave a tug at the coronet and one of the pointed glass beads broke off. "Oh God, these diamonds! Come on."

But Netta had already gone over to the hunched-up figure at the dressing-table, who sat staring into the mirror, eyes blurred with tears and cheeks stained with thin trickling rivers of mascara.

"Tessa! Now come along, dear, you can't let the show down like this. You'll ruin your voice if you keep on crying, and I don't suppose anyone out front noticed your train anyway. Just look at your face!" A cleansing tissue was grabbed, and quick, deft hands began to repair the ravaged make-up. "That's better. Now—a bit of slap——" A dab of powder followed and a dash of lipstick was hastily applied to the trembling lips. "There. Come on, or we shall miss our entrance. You're not to worry about that train."

"It's not the train!" Tessa shrieked, with another crumpling of the face. "Leave me alone! I'm not going on! You none of you understand me! You all hate me!"

"Look, dear . . ." A soothing hand was laid on the heaving shoulders.

"I know what people say!" Tessa's voice had become thick and hoarse and the mascara had started to run again. "Just because I have four numbers in the first half——"

"Three," Josie quietly corrected.

"It's four—with the opening. And I get just as much applause as Magda."

"Huh! Magda," Josie dismissed Magda and looked down at the stupid, pretty little face. "You silly cow. You silly great cow. Magda's jealous, that's all. Don't take any notice of her."

"But she's pinched my ear-rings and won't give them back!" wailed Tessa.

"Is that all?" Josie said witheringly. "You wait until she starts pinching your men. That'll be the time to worry, girl."

"Oh, do come on," urged Netta, giving up Tessa as a bad job and tottering painfully in the Louis heels towards the corridor.

"You pull yourself together, darling," Josie advised Tessa. "We can soon have those ear-rings off Magda." Vivid red lips drew back into an acid smile, displaying two even rows of large, white teeth. Someone once said that Josie resembled an evil edition of Gloria Swanson.

Then, while Tessa continued to weep, Netta and Josie breathlessly rushed down three flights of stairs to the stage, where the assembled company awaited their entrance in the Finale.

"Quiet, please!" commanded the stage manager.

"Get you, Mabel," said someone.

The comedy double act dashed from the stage into the quick-change room. Roars of laughter and applause came from the auditorium ... the orchestra blared and the gold-spangled tabs parted.

"Oh, my feet," groaned Netta, "if only we could walk on from the wings instead of down that bloody great staircase."

With a flick of a black lace fan, and for the twelfth time that week, Netta began the regal descent, praying with each step for a safe arrival at the right side of the footlights.

On the other side of the footlights a huge Saturday night audience packed the theatre from stalls to gallery. It had been 'standing room only' for both houses and the vast auditorium glowed with the warmth and friendliness from a crowd which had obviously come to enjoy itself. This was no polite teacup entertainment; it was an occasion for full-throated, happy, astonished and sometimes coarse laughter. So astonishing, in fact, that one of the occupants of a stage box, who had viewed the entire performance with sheer amazement, had considerable difficulty in controlling a rapidly growing feeling of suspicion and alarm. Notwithstanding the photographs in the foyer, even the most lurid posters outside the theatre had given scant indication of the ensuing 'extravaganza' which so outrageously graced the boards of the Palace Music Hall.

Gertrude Ford and her husband Eric were paying one of their rare visits to the Palace, which in the past had usually meant two centre seats in the front row of the dress circle for the Christmas pantomime. The habit had persisted from earlier days when they had taken their children, Colin and Laura, and wholeheartedly revelled in the innocent delights of *Mother Goose* or *Sinbad the Sailor*. These days, of course, the pantomime was not always the safe 'family' affair it once used to be, although to Gertrude it seemed, in spite of its failings, infinitely preferable to the type of show they were now witnessing.

Barely two minutes after the curtain had gone up she had regretted their decision to book seats, and deplored even more their embarrassing nearness to the stage. She realised it was probably silly and prudish to be so shocked, but was extremely thankful that they had not after all invited anyone to join them. It was going to be difficult enough explaining her reactions to her next-door neighbour, Mrs. Wellington, without appearing stuffy and old-fashioned. It was she who had suggested they should go to the Palace and see *Merrie Belles*—as it really was a scream, terribly funny and you'll love it . . . and Olive Wellington wouldn't be content with a noncommittal "Yes, very amusing." She would demand a detailed account of the whole evening and be fully prepared to exchange notes. The mere thought of discussing anything so distasteful was bad enough, but even worse was the growing feeling of alarm which kept her tensely on the edge of her seat as the evening progressed.

Nervously clutching her gloves she gave a worried glance at her husband, but he seemed unaware of her agitation. Perhaps he hadn't noticed anything, and perhaps after all her imagination was playing tricks with her . . . She sighed and brought her mind back to the brilliantly lighted stage. The last turn had finished and it was the finale. She watched the curtains part, revealing a glittering silver and black staircase gracefully curving from the wings into the centre of the stage. The scene was slightly marred, however, by two dusty-looking bamboo baskets, clumsily filled with artificial hydrangea, standing one each side of the bottom step and bearing unmistakable signs of much travel. This could be said, too, of some members of the company who now, one by one, began their parade down the stairs. First came the chorus in red, blue and yellow off-the-shoulder crinoline dresses. Each moved identically: the back arched, the head high, arrogant, disdainful, the lace fans delicately undulating, the coronets winking and flashing like diamonds as a low curtsy was executed, impeccably, centre stage. The applause was loud and long, increasing in volume as the principals made their entrance. Dresses were more lavish, more fantastic ... down they came—comedians, dancers, singers, a pianist, and a negro knife-thrower with naked torso and skin-tight sequin trousers. Last of all came Tessa, light as thistledown, gay as a butterfly.

"Oh! The *cow*!" Josie murmured indignantly.

The crimson plush curtain swished into the footlights, rose again. Bold smiles were thrown from the stage to the nearest boxes and front-row stalls.

"Well, I suppose it's very clever," said Eric Ford, turning to his wife. "A change. Something different. Funny thing is—I wondered if you'd noticed or not—but one of the chorus—the one in blue——"

"Yes, Eric, I did," Gertrude spoke quickly. "Come along—we'll go before the crowd——"

"Better wait for the Anthem. Do you think Colin's seen this show up in Liverpool? A bit embarrassing if he has."

"I don't suppose they look alike at all, really. I didn't think much of the show, it's rather loud and vulgar, although some of the costumes are beautiful. I suppose I'm old-fashioned, but ..."

Once more the curtain rose, and with a flourish from the orchestra the entire *Merrie Belles* company doffed their wigs and coronets and bowed to an admiring audience, revealing above their painted faces the incongruous spectacle of short masculine hair-cuts, with here and there a defenceless bald head. Gertrude stared in horror at the stage, her eyes on the blue crinoline. "Eric—Eric—it *is* Colin!"

She was forced into silence as the curtain cut off her view and the orchestra vigorously struck up 'God Save The Queen.' The whole theatre, with its gilded plasterwork and amber lights, seemed to be falling on top of her. Eric dragged her from the low edge of the box, and she crumpled limply into his arms.

In the stalls, a young woman said to her escort: "It's not *quite* what you'd expect, is it? Taking off their wigs like that. Somehow it spoils the illusion."

CHAPTER 2

Gertrude and Eric Ford had reason to be proud of their son Colin, if only for the fact that he arrived long after all ideas of another child had regretfully been abandoned as an obstetrical impossibility and undue wishful thinking. His late appearance, therefore, was the cause of much rejoicing and inconvenience on the part of his mother, a gratifying sense of rejuvenated virility in his father and, providing that she could avoid any pram-pushing, a faintly sceptical tolerance of the whole affair from his eleven-year-old sister Laura.

This was in 1935, when they were living in a big and old-fashioned semi-detached house in South London, a few minutes' walk from Wandsworth Common. There was nothing to distinguish it from the other houses in the neighbourhood, which all wore the same placid and inoffensive air of respectability. This suited Gertrude, who had never demanded an exciting or adventurous life and was satisfied with her home and reasonably content with her sensible husband who had a safe, comfortable job in the City. Her life would have been uneventful, but for the children, and even then inclined to the ordinary if the natural process of their growing up had followed the average pattern of development. Unfortunately it had not. There seemed nothing to worry about at first. As far as Colin was concerned, he had grown from a sweet and tractable baby into a nice-looking and affectionate little boy. Occasionally he was secretive and dreamy—or 'imaginative,' as his mother liked to put it—and although this sensitive, withdrawn and solitary side of his nature more often than not baffled his parents, it was usually followed by more understandable, if violent and obstreperous behaviour. "A real, high-spirited boy," Eric remarked to his mother-in-law, who privately thought the child's temperament was more akin to hysteria than to high spirits.

"You want to watch that boy," she advised her daughter. "He's too highly strung, if you ask me."

"He's just excitable," said Gertrude.

"You said exactly the same thing about Laura," her mother replied crisply, "and she's certainly been more than a handful. Did you ever find out what really happened at that boarding school? . . ."

Now, years later and Colin approaching his twentieth birthday, Gertrude sadly reflected that she had never understood her children. Laura had always been difficult; aggressive and jealous—particularly after Colin was born—and often a cause for anxiety during her years at boarding school. Even the following period at a select finishing school had not effected a complete transformation of character and behaviour. Laura had been altogether too assertive, and seemed to resent the presence of her young brother. Heaven knows why, for there had never been any lessening of affection and love from her parents, any favouritism towards Colin because he was the 'baby' of the family. Why, then, this antagonism between the children? Had Laura imagined herself neglected, unwanted because she had been sent away to boarding school while Colin remained at home? Had she, as their mother, failed somewhere? Perhaps the war years were to blame; in a sense they had been a divided family, growing away from one another and not finding it easy to adjust their relationships on the infrequent occasions when they gathered under the same roof. At that time, Eric had decided that she and Colin would be safer living in the country, and while he remained working in London she had moved into a rented cottage on the outskirts of a village in Hampshire. She had found a school for Colin and a place for herself as a voluntary helper at the church canteen, where she spent many hours industriously cutting sandwiches, making and serving cups of tea, and being left by some of the grander village 'ladies' to do most of the washing up afterwards. She felt she was 'doing her bit,' and enjoyed ministering to the gigantic appetites of young soldiers who demanded sustenance after their hours of rigorous training at the hutted army camp, half a mile away along the main road.

After a while, noticing how lonely and bored some of them were, she invited several of these young men to the cottage, and they became regular visitors. She supplied hot baths and cosy high teas, and her efforts to impart a few home comforts into their lives were rewarded by kind offers to guard the cottage and keep an eye on Colin whenever she was at the church hall. She could safely leave him at home, knowing that the boys would give him his supper, see that he went to bed at the proper time, and also keep the fire stoked up during the cold winter evenings.

Colin was eight years old, a sensible boy, rather independent and grown up for his age, and she could trust him not to get into mischief while she was away from the cottage. She was, however, a little worried at times by his lack of interest in the other schoolchildren, and by his unenthusiastic response to their cheerful, boisterous games. (Miss Hudders, the sports mistress, was terribly keen on 'character-building' recreation, and expressed herself as 'absolutely stumped' when Colin told her that cricket bored him. Being a jolly good bat herself, she couldn't understand it at all.) He seemed not to mind this absence of close friendship with any of his schoolfellows, and when at home appeared happy enough on his own, showing no desire to go out and play with the other boys. Instead, he would spend hours sitting at the dining-room table, contentedly drawing or painting. Although she knew nothing whatever about art, she could see that there was something unusual and imaginative in his work. He would never copy anything, preferring to invent his own designs. Eric, on one of his week-end visits, had been sceptical about any signs of real talent emerging from the boy's efforts—dismissing them as daubs and scribbles, and overlooking the strong element of fantasy which the young art master, a visiting lecturer, had found so intensely interesting and extraordinary.

She had met Mr. Foley, and it was gratifying to hear her son's work praised, even if she hadn't altogether understood his explanations; he was rather 'modern' and 'advanced,' and seemed to attach a great deal of importance to the 'psychological manifestations in Art.' She hadn't the faintest idea what he meant by that, and although she knew it was fashionable to drag 'psychology' into everything, she wondered if it was really necessary to make a child's natural aptitude appear so suspect. To her, Colin's fanciful little paintings were simply the outcome of a lively imagination, which he brought to everything that he did. Perhaps that was why he preferred to be alone and invent his own amusements, finding the village children rather dull and unoriginal. He didn't need to be told *how* to amuse himself. Without playmates he could people his games with imaginary characters, becoming, himself, each one in turn. A favourite game was pretending to be Kings and Queens, parading up and down the stairs, draped in a bedspread and carrying a rubber ball and a brass poker; this represented the Coronation in Westminster Abbey.

On one occasion there was a troublesome incident when Laura came home from the finishing school at the beginning of the summer holiday and found him in one of her old dresses, his face smeared with lipstick and a pair of her ear-rings dangling from his ears. She had made a terrible fuss about it, treating a childish game as if it were a direct insult to herself. It hadn't helped matters when Colin flew into a rage and spat at her. To be quite truthful Laura caused far more trouble than her brother. There was that time, for instance, at the cottage . . .

Laura was on her first leave from the W.R.N.S., extremely smart in her uniform, and also, it must be admitted, very full of herself. Nor could it be denied that after three months' training she had become remarkably 'bossy' and behaved as if she were already a high-ranking officer at the Admiralty. Eric was proud of her, but apart from taking her out to lunch one day in the City he had only seen her at the week-end when he came to the cottage. He had not known, and neither had she told him, that although she was equally pleased by Laura's wartime role in the Navy, she was not altogether sorry to see the end of her daughter's seven days' leave. Laura had become a stranger; hardened. She smoked and drank too much and, worse still, vented her bad temper on Colin. She seemed actively to hate her brother. On top of everything, there had been that evening when she slapped his face and accused him of lying.

It was one of the 'canteen' nights, and Laura had stayed in with Colin. As usual, several of the boys from the camp had called, and Laura made tea for them. Presumably, as on previous occasions, they talked and played cards while Colin sat by the fire with his drawing-book and pencils. They were well-behaved young men and there had never been any trouble from them.

They were so good with Colin, too, often including him in their amusing banter and making him feel quite grown up. "The kid's all there," said one of them, and it was obvious that the boy was not shy or awkward in the company of older people; he liked being with them. His particular friend was the red-headed Sergeant Kendrick, who was so kind and patient with him. Alan was different from the others. Quieter, more sensitive; and although he couldn't have been all that much older—perhaps twenty-three at the most—he appeared to have a greater maturity and, without being domineering, an authority which singled him out from the rest. He was really better than Eric in his handling of Colin— far gentler and persuasive and it was a blessing to have someone so reliable to hand at a time when the boy's own father could give only perfunctory attention to his upbringing. One couldn't be grateful enough to Alan for all his help, and it was a pity that Laura had behaved as she did and spoilt the future chances for a happy continuance of these open-house evenings at the cottage.

However blameless Laura might have been, and however justified in her anger—her "outrage," as she herself described it—it was unforgivable to involve a boy of Colin's age in a situation which was, to put it mildly, not for children. Laura had stated, with alarming frankness, that Alan Kendrick had assaulted her— molested her while she was making tea in the kitchen—and also been guilty of using bad language in front of Colin. Threatening to inform the camp's commanding officer, she had ordered Alan and his friends to leave. Later, during the heated telling of this episode, when Colin came to the defence of his friend and swore that Alan hadn't done anything, she smacked his face and called him a liar.

Gertrude clearly remembered that evening, and wondered whether she had been wrong in not saying anything about it to Eric; but he would have blamed her for being so trusting and taking strangers into the house, and she could not believe that her judgment had been at fault over any one of those boys, least of all Alan Kendrick. The others were pleasant enough; he was different and obviously—well . . . a gentleman. She did not despise that description. And yet, after the Laura business, why hadn't he come to see her? Laura had returned to her training establishment on the following day, and Alan must have known that he was considered one of the family and would not be met by reproaches or any unpleasantness. They could have straightened out any misunderstandings which, she felt sure, existed more in exaggerated imagination than in actual fact. (Hearing Laura talk, one would think she had been attacked by a sex-maniac and raped.) Whatever had happened, Alan owed some explanation. If he were innocent, surely he would wish to vindicate himself? But he had not come. Instead, he had written to her, saying how sorry he was that the warm friendship between them all had caused an element of friction which could be resolved only by his staying away. He would always, the letter continued, remember her and Colin with deep affection and gratitude, and would no doubt see them again in the not too distant future. That was all. A week later a convoy of army lorries and trucks passed along the main road, and by dawn the camp was deserted.

Poor Colin had shed bitter tears, and for a long time afterwards remained inconsolable. Alan's departure upset him terribly, adding to the confusion in his mind over Laura's accusations against his friend. Frankly, Gertrude was puzzled herself, not having been there when the alleged incident occurred, and it was quite impossible even to think of questioning her son as to how much he had seen and heard. Laura had shut up like a clam, directly afterwards, and Alan had retreated, sending that ambiguous letter which neither confirmed nor denied his position in the matter. Did his failure to come forward indicate a sense of guilt? Was Laura telling the truth? And *had* Colin lied, that evening? It remained a mystery to her. One simply didn't know what went on in their minds—what sort of impression it would have, for instance, on a boy of that age ...

He could have told his mother quite a lot; but ever since Laura's nasty behaviour over his Kings and Queens game, he had learned to keep quiet and avoid his sister's spiteful tongue whenever possible. Everything he did she criticised and complained about. He had heard her saying to Mother, "Colin ought to go to boarding school, it would do him good," and "He's getting soft, he's not like a real boy." And his mother's reply: "Just because he's not rough . . ." At which Laura said grimly, "Father ought to take a firm hand with him." She had called him 'a cissy,' too. He hated her. She was jealous if anyone paid him attention, wanting it all for herself; she didn't like it because Mother allowed him to mix with the grown-ups—the soldiers who came to tea. But she didn't know everything, and he wasn't going to tell *her* that one of them was his special friend, Sergeant Kendrick. He had two friends really, because Sergeant Bill Burton was Alan's friend too, and they always came to the house together. 'Big Bill' was very nice, although he was older and a 'regular,' which meant he was in the Army all the time, even when there wasn't a war. And he was very kind, always doing things for Alan—which everybody ought to do because Alan was better than anyone. They had great fun together.

Sometimes, though, Alan was very serious, gazing into the fire and not saying much, and Big Bill would be quiet instead of laughing and jolly. When they were like this he wanted to ask why they were sad and what was the matter. Perhaps they were thinking about the war; perhaps they might have to go away and get killed. It frightened him. He loved Sergeant Kendrick more than his father, and he had said so, to Big Bill. Bill had told him not to say anything about it to anyone, because it might upset people, and he had promised he wouldn't. It was a great secret— something of his own that he could keep for himself, something that Laura wouldn't know about and try to spoil. He would never say *anything* about Alan, and Laura would never guess that he was a special friend of his. It would serve her right.

So, on that night when she said terrible things, he kept his promise—although he almost didn't when he started to say that Alan hadn't done what she said. He had stopped himself in time. Nobody but himself and Alan knew about Laura, and Alan told him to forget what he had seen. Both Alan and Big Bill were angry about it, but wouldn't let him hear what they said because he was only a child. He knew that the things he had seen were something to do with being grown up—older people kissed and hugged each other, only it was different, not like his mother kissing him. They made 'love.' He supposed Laura was making love; but there were other things, too, not just the kissing . . . something which puzzled him. He had never seen anyone older, and he wondered about it. He hadn't known that a grown-up person was like that; it seemed funny somehow and he was afraid to ask questions about it. If he asked his mother or his father, perhaps they would want to know how he had found out, and make him tell them about Laura and Corporal Ellis. Laura was always being silly when the soldiers came to tea—laughing and showing off and making them dance with her to the wireless. They all made a terrible noise, except Alan and Big Bill, who didn't dance with her, although she tried to make them and was rude because they wouldn't. But Corporal Ellis was always dancing with her. And then there had been the row . . . Alan said something to the corporal, and Laura lost her temper and went into the kitchen, slamming the door. Alan followed her, and when they came back she ordered them all to go. Then later she said things about Alan to Mother—but not about Corporal Ellis. She didn't tell Mother about going into the bathroom when the corporal was having a bath.

He had seen her go in, because he was just coming out of his bedroom with the new paint-box Alan had given him. Laura took a clean towel into the bathroom, which was silly because there were some there. But she didn't come out at once, and he heard them laughing and heard water splashing about. The door wasn't properly shut and he could see in. Corporal Ellis was standing up in the bath without anything on, trying to grab the towel from Laura. Then he climbed out, still showing himself, and she threw the towel at him. He held it in front of him and kissed her. They stood there a long time. Suddenly there was a noise on the stairs, and he heard Alan saying "What are you doing?" The door opened a bit more and Laura came out, seeing them. Her face went red, then she started shouting something about spying, and Corporal Ellis shut the door. "I was taking in a clean towel," Laura said, then went downstairs. He tried to tell Alan about seeing them in the bathroom, but Alan put his arm round him and told him to forget about it and not worry. When they were in the living-room again, Alan talked quietly to Big Bill, and Bill said "Good God." The other soldiers were playing cards. Laura came in; then Corporal Ellis—and after a little while the row started.

He could never understand why Laura said those things about Alan and not about the corporal. And why hadn't Alan come to see them afterwards? He couldn't have known what Laura said, because she hadn't spoken until *after* he'd gone. And now perhaps they'd never see him again, because all the soldiers in the camp had left. Sometimes in the night he cried a lot about Alan, who had often tucked him up in bed and put out the light when Mother wasn't there. He was so nice, a very special friend, and he loved him and would never forget him. It was silly that Laura didn't like Alan. Why didn't she like him? . . .

She was sick to death of the whole thing and thankful to see the end of her leave, vowing never to spend any future seven days at home—or anyway not if her brother were still there. It was ridiculous the way Colin was allowed to do exactly as he pleased, monopolising everyone's attention and being spoiled and pampered and getting away with God knew what. All that favouritism and petting from an uncouth bunch of soldiers, as if he were a little Shirley Temple or someone; which was not far short of the mark, either. Dressing up in Mother's clothes—even in *her* clothes once—and pretending to be a girl. If Father knew what was going on, he'd have something to say, but he was hardly ever at home and Mother couldn't or wouldn't see that Colin needed stricter discipline. It was nonsense to imagine that Alan Kendrick was the person to control and guide the boy—Colin just twisted him round his finger and could do no wrong. Admittedly, Alan was a cut above the others—but so damned superior. Attractive, too, if you liked the red-haired type; but insular, you couldn't get anything out of him. She had tried to, at first, because it was a challenge and she was curious about his reserve. She had wanted to penetrate his armour and expose some vulnerable spot, but nothing would weaken him. He remained behind a barrier, secret and strange.

This failure had riled her so much, bringing with it an overwhelming desire to say or do something which would sting him into life, even if it meant making him angry. It was humiliating to be ignored, and she began to retaliate . . . he was sensitive and it excited her to be a little cruel and to watch him flinch. But there was never an opportunity to be alone with him. That Bill Burton creature was always there, hanging at Alan's heels like a dog, and worst of all was Colin's smug taken-for-granted attitude that he was included in everything they did. She had warned him, too, about making a nuisance of himself and pestering Alan, but it had no effect; Alan seemed to encourage the wretched boy even more, and Colin was exhibitionist enough without adding to it by constant praise and admiration for his 'clever' drawings and paintings—which as any sensible person could see were nothing more than childish scrawls and daubs. She had put herself out to be charming to Alan; she had tolerated Bill Burton's almost 'animal' roughness; but she had been made to feel a stranger by Alan's disinterested politeness, and an intruder by Bill's unconcealed dislike of her. With Colin, they appeared to be in league against her. And those scruffy-looking soldiers, clumping about in their boots and khaki . . . so gangling and awkward compared with the smart boys of the Navy. Physically, Peter Ellis wasn't too bad; he was a bit young, but well built and had a cheerful, easy-going manner. She didn't mind dancing with him, although it was obvious that it was not just the pleasure of dancing which made him partner her in almost every number played on the radio. It was a sort of harmless flirtation, and since Alan so churlishly refused to dance, better than nothing.

Still, Peter got a bit too carried away. The bath-towel incident began as a joke, she hadn't meant it to go so far, and everything would have been all right but for that little beast spying on them and telling Alan. She could have strangled him. And Alan, having the cheek to criticise . . . Well, she had soon settled that. One or two things hadn't escaped her notice. It was quite easy, breaking up the happy little home, and Alan had been powerless to stop her. He hadn't the guts, and didn't dare to open his mouth. Good riddance to him anyway—he could go to hell for all she cared.

He was aware of his cowardice in evading the issue, in not returning to see Gertrude and Colin during the remaining days before leaving the camp. Even if he had risked facing the possible consequences of Laura's threats and abuse, would it have done any good? She was capable of saying anything to spite him, and of taking revenge; not only because she was jealous and frustrated but, more dangerous to him, because she was thwarted and hostile. She had wanted to pay him out for his criticism of the Corporal Ellis incident, in which his only concern had been for Colin's moral protection. When he spoke to her, her cold brutality had appalled him, and he would never forget the scornful triumph of her voice and the hard glitter of her eyes as she ruthlessly maligned her brother. Deceitful . . . vain . . . girlish . . . Her words uttered with icy contempt. And darker hints emerging as the attack became sharper and more pointed—involving himself and Bill Burton. It was the first warning of danger. He was startled and shocked by her alarming accusation: "Both of you, pampering the boy—like a couple of dirty old uncles with a favourite niece" . . . and then, bitingly, "or should I have said 'favourite nephew'?" He was too taken aback to answer immediately, and she went on: "I'm not blind. Don't think I can't see what's going on." Angrily he tried to interrupt, but she continued in a sneering tone, "Deny *that,* if you like—but you've got a damned cheek, criticising Pete Ellis and me, and smugly talking about being moral in front of the child. Oh, yes—" she made her final thrust, "I got your number all right—you and that fetch-and-carry oaf Bill Burton. Fine example—a couple of bloody queers about the place . . ."

Furiously he had grabbed her arm as she turned away. "Take your dirty hands off. Don't blame me if the pair of you finish up in the glasshouse. It'd be a damned good job and the best place for you. Now get out of here. We don't want you. Don't come back here, otherwise there might be trouble."

It was his first experience of open hostility; the first time he had been made to feel an outcast because he did not 'conform.' He had known that it was a situation he might one day have to face, but to be accused also of a corrupting influence on Colin was something he never envisaged. It was completely untrue; impossible. As an unofficial 'guardian' to the boy, he had always been mindful of the trust which Gertrude placed in him, and he would never have done anything to jeopardise his acceptance within the family circle. There was no evidence to justify Laura's monstrous suggestions. Unless . . . unless, perhaps, she had misinterpreted Colin's innocent demonstrations of affection. It was true that the boy had shown a loving regard for his friends, but surely at that age it was merely a natural form of 'hero-worship.' There was nothing at all unhealthy about it, and by their friendly but deliberately impersonal response he and Bill had, or so he thought, succeeded in conveying to him that they attached no special importance to his fond embraces. Because of that, and because of his own association with Bill, Laura had arbitrarily denounced him, and with sweeping condemnation sought to link his conduct with a form of behaviour utterly repugnant to him. Perhaps he should not expect otherwise. To her, it would be all the same—"that sort of thing" . . .

It was hard to bear, and in the present situation difficult to see a way out. If he had gone to see Gertrude, and Laura *had* said anything about him, it would have been a ghastly business. He wished he had Bill's strength; Bill didn't care what anybody thought, and had offered to go to the cottage to find out what had happened. In fact they had a heated argument about it, with Bill swearing his head off in the best parade-ground manner. Eventually he simmered down, with a final warning that they must not go through life always weakly giving in and accepting defeat as inevitable. "It's fight, fight, fight all the time," Bill said. "Not only the bleedin' war, but the bleedin' what-do-you-call-'em's—people who are against everything and everyone, except themselves."

But Bill came from a tougher school altogether. At sixteen Bill had known everything there was to know, and had courageously faced up to it; unlike himself, who now, in his early twenties, had to orientate himself in a world only recently discovered and still so new to him. For a long time he had been conscious of his inclinations, and had tried to suppress such tendencies, even deluding himself that marriage would solve the problem. He was nineteen then, and Myra a few years older. Without pausing to consider his inexperience of women, or indeed that it was better to 'look round' a bit first before taking such a step, he had rashly plunged into disaster. The marriage was a complete failure. Not because he was cold, unemotional or under-sexed, as she had once stated, but because he had discovered almost from the start that he was married to a nymphomaniac. In a way, of course, they had both cheated; and perhaps he was the more to blame. Myra had simply followed her instincts, and accepted the most available male offering. He had tried to avoid the truth of his own nature, and out of desperation sought a 'cure' in marriage. Not exactly flattering to any woman . . .

Eventually, after his call-up into the Army, she left him and—true to type but hardly original—lived with an American Air Force officer stationed in Norfolk. Although released from the misery and pretence of his existence with Myra, he remained plagued by feelings of guilt and anxiety, further heightened by the imposed conditions of service life. The all-masculine atmosphere in which he moved served only to increase the forbidden thoughts and desires, which once had come to him in dreams but now proclaimed their reality in his waking hours. He found it more and more difficult to keep up a disguise—to force himself into acting a part no longer fitted to him.

And then Bill Burton entered his life. Sensing his dilemma, and with the gentleness so often concealed beneath a rough-hewn exterior, Bill had compassionately befriended him. His understanding and sympathy soon led to a deep affection, and in Bill's regard for him there came a lessening of the conflicts and uncertainties in his own mind. They had been discreet in their behaviour and welcomed the opportunity to share the quiet, homely pleasures of family life at the cottage. Everything had gone smoothly and peaceably until Laura's arrival on the scene. She had made short work of reminding him that he and his kind could expect no sympathy or tolerance from the 'righteous' majority.

In a way their departure from the camp was a relief, although he would sorely miss the two people who had come to mean so much to him. He hoped that in some way, however small, his genuine devotion to them would not entirely be forgotten. If they were ever to meet in the future, he did not want it to be as strangers to one another. Without being mawkish or sentimental about it, he couldn't help wondering how Colin would fare, and in what way his personality would develop. He imagined it would be far from negligible, whatever he became. On mentioning this, Bill had replied. "Let's hope the poor kid turns out better than his sister—because with two of 'em like that it'll be hell for their mother."

Into the small hours Gertrude lay awake in bed, reliving the past and trying, without success, to find some explanation for the alarming state of the present. At the theatre last night, the shock and surprise at seeing Colin like that on the stage had left her feeling numbed and helpless. And matters had not been improved by her fainting during the National Anthem, and having to wait while Eric searched for a taxi to take them home. All she could remember about the journey was Eric's set face and the way he sat stiffly on the edge of the seat. Neither of them spoke until they were indoors, with Eric grimly pouring out two glasses of brandy. She knew it was irritating, the way she kept saying "I can't believe it. What does it mean? I can't understand. What are we going to do?" But Eric's silence bewildered her, and she had to say *something*. His reaction was puzzling; she expected some terrible outburst from him—he had often been rather strict in his treatment of Colin—and now, when there was justification for anger and disapproval, he had only stared into his drink and murmured "I don't know. *I* don't know at all." He made it sound as if she were to blame for everything. How *could* she be blamed for something like this, something completely beyond her understanding? He was the boy's father, and it was up to him to handle this—this thing . . . whatever it meant. He must see Colin. Talk to him. Oh, it was all so confusing. As if Laura hadn't been enough trouble in the past . . . and now Colin. She just couldn't believe it. What was he doing in the theatre, in a show of that sort? When all the time she thought he was in Liverpool, working at designing for a textiles factory. It didn't make sense. And how long had this been going on? What kind of life was he leading? It all seemed so cheap and sordid—and unlike Colin. Of course, he had always been secretive, but there had never been the slightest indication that he would even contemplate doing a thing like this. It frightened her to think that anything could be wrong with Colin; that he could be influenced to *do* wrong. They ought to have kept him at home, instead of allowing him complete freedom, although if they had done so it would have been inconsistent with their wanting him to stand on his own feet and achieve independence and success by his own efforts. And he had made good progress, too, after leaving art school.

From his letters, she understood him to be getting on well in Liverpool, and he seemed to like the work and be happy up there. This theatre business was something new; a foolish idea— probably someone had egged him on and dared him to do it. He could be impulsive, she knew, and yet he was not irresponsible; he had always given the impression of knowing exactly what he wanted—to be an artist—and having become one, why should he want to throw everything away and lower himself by appearing on the stage in such an unedifying type of entertainment? From where and from whom had he got this fantastic notion? What- ever sort of people were they, to go around in a show like that, imitating and dressed as women? She just couldn't imagine Colin being associated with anything so vulgar and tasteless, and as she possessed little knowledge of theatrical life, except that it was a precarious profession, it was difficult for her to envisage the kind of existence he was leading. Surely, by what she had seen, it could not be other than artificial and perhaps even squalid; attracting all manner of riff-raff, not in the least suitable as companions for Colin. He must be made to see what folly it was, and how distressing for his family.

Of course it would have to be done tactfully, without putting him against them. No hysterical pleading or storming would be of use, any more than advising him to do something for his own good. Most people resented that, anyway. If only Eric would discuss this properly with her . . . naturally, he was upset, but this brooding silence of his was most disconcerting. *She* would prob- ably have to make the first move in approaching Colin, but how could one find him? They should have gone round to the stage door last night, but it never occurred to her then. Perhaps she could telephone the theatre today, although it was Sunday and there might not be anybody there. In any case, Colin wouldn't be. As far as she knew, the show was visiting a different town every week, and he must already be on his way to the next place. She must find out somehow . . . it was dreadful enough to think of his being in the show at all, but it would worry her too much not to know where he was. She supposed he lived in lodgings most of the time . . . "I must try to get some sleep," she thought . . . but what could it be like, with those people, and working at a theatre every night? She couldn't picture it at all. The theatre was another world entirely. A sort of dream world in which the people weren't quite real.

CHAPTER 3

"Finale Act One! Finale Act One!" This time the voice was thin and tired and belonged to an ageing call-'girl' whose pinched and raddled face sadly belied the youthful frizz of peroxided hair above it. Nothing, not even the hopeful fringe and Alice-in-Wonderland ribbon, could transform the careworn features; neither could the generous lower dorsal curves, coquettishly quivering with each step of the high-heeled shoes, convince anyone that Maisie Minter looked her best in gay tartan trousers.

However, although Maisie looked and sounded tired, she still retained the indomitable spirit of a real theatrical 'trouper,' and she had been at the Hippodrome, apart from a brief spell in munitions during the war, ever since leaving the chorus of *Who's Dancing Tonight?* in 1941. She had retired from the stage (so she informed friends) because the bright, saucy 'soubrette' type was no longer fashionable and, unless you were a show-girl, an 'individual' personality was wasted on the gymnastics which comprised the average chorus routine of the day. Musical comedy had gone to the dogs; it wasn't like the good old times when she was in the original Number One tours of *A Racing Romance* and *The Honeymoon Girl* . . . marvellous shows, especially *Honeymoon,* with the Battle of Flowers at Nice, and the ballroom of Hotel Splendide . . . Of course, latterly, she had been aware of one or two catty references to her age, but that was just jealousy and they resented her experience. She might have been a little older than some of them, but she'd been able to high-kick as well as any—*and* do the splits.

Unfortunately it was this last achievement which precipitated the end of her career, for she had been unwise enough to show off during an audition, and apart from embarrassing everyone present had seriously strained herself with the effort. She'd been forced to 'rest,' and having to take things quietly naturally stiffened her up a good deal. Then with the new craze for 'ballet' in all the shows, she'd found it impossible to get into a decent tour again, let alone into the West End. She couldn't stand about and sing, either, for she had no voice to speak of, and in any case the money wouldn't have been enough. It was a great wrench having to give up like that, when she loved the theatre so much; but in a way she'd been lucky, and able to stay in the theatre somehow—first of all as an usherette till the Hippodrome went over to repertory and closed, and then as a call-girl when it had reopened for variety on her return from six months' factory work. Sometimes, though, she wished she'd stayed 'front of house' instead of getting herself mixed up in all the backstage excitement. It reminded her too much of the old days, all those wonderful times . . . At first she'd always been talking about it, but now nobody seemed interested. The way some of them looked at her you'd think she'd retired on the last night of *The Merry Widow* at Daly's.

At any rate this was one of her good weeks; there were no chits of girls to snigger behind her back or make her needlessly run up and down stairs on stupid errands. She was welcomed in the dressing-rooms, sometimes ribaldly but always kindly, and there was no denying the laughs she'd had! There was generally a drop of gin going, too—strictly against orders, of course. Naturally she had to shut her eyes to a thing or two, but then you couldn't expect otherwise in this kind of show, and after all life was life (as her mother had always told her) and it was no good pretending it wasn't.

Broad-mindedly she pushed open the door marked LADIES CHORUS, and entered. "Oh, my Gawd! Sorry!"

"It's all right, dear, I'm *fully* dressed."

The one they called 'Josie' was standing in the centre of the room in Louis heels, black fish-net nylons, a pink brassiere and a jockstrap. "Are you going on the stage like that?" Maisie asked.

"Do you think I'm overdoing it? What shall I take off? The shoes?"

"Oh, you are awful!" Maisie shrieked.

"The show could do with a bit of livening up—especially first house in this God-awful dump of a town. That audience! What are they doing out there, anyway? Sheltering from the rain? Netta! Have you pinched my skirt?"

"No, dear." 'Netta' zipped himself into his can-can ruffles and winced his way towards the door. His feet were still bad and it was agony in the Louis heels.

"There's a thieving bitch somewhere." 'Josie's' eyes narrowed.

"Oh, pipe down," a voice growled from the end of the room. "Who the hell wants a tatty bit of drag like that?"

"Tatty?" 'Josie' flared. "Did you say tatty?"

"Yes. You heard. Tatty. TATTY DRAG."

"That dress is pure nylon. Also, I wore it for the last Vic-Wells Ball—and won a prize for it."

"Runner-up for the Campest Costume, I suppose?"

"Don't you sit there sending me up, Stanley Butcher. You might call yourself 'Butch' and put on that tough manly act, but everyone knows you're Queen of the Fairies and the biggest belle in the business!"

"Why—you bloody little whore!" 'Butch' rose menacingly, looking like a prize-fighter in fancy dress. He had a short, stocky figure and the muscles bulged in his thighs and arms. His face underneath the shoulder-length wig and the thick layers of makeup, was coarse and leathery, with a flattened, pugilistic nose and small slitty eyes.

"Whore I may be," 'Josie' replied, "but at least I look the part and don't pretend otherwise. But *you* . . . you're just a *travesty*!"

Maisie began to feel alarmed. She had heard that fights sometimes broke out in the dressing-rooms between the 'girls,' some of whom, in spite of their daintiness, seemed as strong as road labourers when it came to a show-down. In fact, Mrs. Plunkett, who ran the dress circle bar, had told her that one of them actually had a cut-throat razor—"Tho' mind you," said Mrs. P., "that doesn't prove anything—most of 'em have to shave their legs. Not to mention their armpits," she added unnecessarily. Maisie

hoped it wasn't 'Butch' who had the razor, or there might be a
nasty mess at any moment, and she couldn't stand the sight of
blood. Of course she wasn't quite sure what it was that 'Josie' had
called him, but she had to admit that he did look very unpleasant
with his ugly face all painted up, standing there with his thick
body almost nude and not caring what he was showing, either. It
was disgusting. The other boys all looked so lovely, even close to.
"Don't start a fight now, dear," she begged 'Josie', "you've only
got a few minutes. I expect Mrs. Oldham has your dress in the
wardrobe room, for repairs or something."

'Josie' haughtily threw back his head, and with a vulgar two-
fingered gesture at 'Butch's' face ran with long, graceful legs out
into the corridor. 'Butch' gave Maisie a sour look and began struggling into his costume. No one else had taken much notice of the
incident, they were all too busy with their last-minute primping
and preening. Maisie watched them hurry from the room, and as
she teetered after them she saw 'Josie' doing up his skirt and swishing towards the stairs. It was going to be dreary next week, she
decided, with ordinary variety, and a low comedian and a troupe
of performing dogs sharing top of the bill. Nothing glamorous or
different about that; although perhaps the 'Merrie Belles' weren't
always glamorous *all* the time. Not on a Sunday morning train-
call, anyway. She thought she'd have a look at the first-half finale
from the wings, and following the highly perfumed trail made
her way down as fast as her heels would allow.

In the orchestra pit the players dashed recklessly into Offen-
bach's 'Can-Can,' and the drop curtain, which vaguely depicted
a glass of bubbling champagne and the Eiffel Tower (or was it
Blackpool?) shuddered uneasily as it creaked up to the 'flies.' The
scene was supposed to be a gay Parisian night club; but, apart
from the tables and chairs, more nearly resembled the entrance
hall of the local Odeon cinema. Three or four bored-looking
girls were sitting about in slinky evening gowns, and a couple
of men in white dinner-jackets ogled a pert 'cigarette girl' who
tripped back and forth between the tables. Eventually, tired of
approaching the same few customers, she gave it up as a bad job
and sat down with them.

The cabaret began.

In a frenzied frou-frou the dancers pranced on and leered evilly across the footlights. And well they might, thought Maisie; the conductor was taking the number much too fast. She drew back a little as they returned to the wings, swearing and perspiring.

"My God, I nearly ruptured myself," 'Josie' gasped.

"Borrow my truss, darling!" cried 'Netta.'

"I'd like to throw it at the conductor."

The lights dimmed and a dazzling 'spot' hit the curtained archway, back centre. Maisie leaned forward expectantly . . . but it was only 'Magda,' in black velvet, with a neck-line plunging to the navel, a dead-white face and ear-rings like chandeliers. He sang 'Parlez moi d'amour' in a yearning contralto and departed whence he came.

"Lucienne Boyer's mother," 'Josie' observed acidly.

Next came an Apache tango by the comedy double act, which was brilliant and really funny. Then the Can-Can dancers again, with 'Netta' triumphantly achieving the triple-splits in record time. There was nothing like the old 'triple,' Maisie thought wistfully. Suddenly a drum roll thundered and a half-naked man, disguised as a negro, leaped on to the stage, his arms aloft and his hands bearing two sinister, glittering knives. He began to spin rapidly in the spotlight, his eyes glinting and the steel flashing above his head. A cymbal clashed. He stopped, poised beside the curtained archway. A young, slim creature in a white jewelled turban and a shimmering dress of lamé stepped out from the shadows. He waited, still and serene, as two of the chorus placed behind him a large board covered in red baize. They withdrew and the 'negro' approached the boy and pinned the white arms against the baize, tying the wrists on to the hooks which were screwed to the board. Maisie sensed the rising tension from out front, and from those watching on the stage. She held her breath and nervously dug her nails into the palms of her hands; she always felt a bit frightened of this kind of thing. After all, it was highly dangerous throwing knives at someone, and you never *knew* . . . and the way that 'negro' looked, with his eyes gleaming! The orchestra had stopped playing and a taut silence gripped the whole theatre; there was not a cough or a rustling programme anywhere. Even Mrs. Plunkett in the dress circle bar had ceased rattling her bottles and glasses.

Zing! the first knife shivered in the red baize, just above the right shoulder. *Zing!* again, this time close to the left shoulder. One of the chorus ran forward with a basket of knives and placed it at the 'negro's' feet. Now, with increasing speed, the pointed shafts of steel winged towards the slender lamé-clad figure, tracing the outline of the body from shoulders to feet; only the white-turbaned head remained free from the bristling silhouette of knives.

"Now for the head," Maisie heard 'Josie' whisper, and she shuddered at the mere thought of it. If she had any sense she'd close her eyes, but she couldn't bear to miss anything! Anyway, the boy seemed to be quite calm, standing stock-still and gazing straight ahead.

"I should want danger money to do anything like that," 'Josie' said. "One slip of the hand and you're a human pin-cushion."

"Torture," 'Netta' gulped.

"Sshh!" Maisie hissed.

Zing! Zing! . . . and *Zing!* The first two knives spiked the board, one each side of the head, almost glancing the ears. The final knife completed the triangle, skimming the topmost point of the jewelled turban. A sustained chord crashed out from the orchestra but was drowned by the surge of applause. Quick as lightning the boy's wrists were released and, hand in hand, he and his partner bowed low to the audience. Then they ran from the stage, brushing past 'Netta' and 'Josie,' and stood for a moment behind one of the large floodlamps. Maisie turned to look at them. The 'negro's' arms and chest glistened with perspiration, and he was peering intently at the boy's face. Maisie of course knew that the man wasn't really coloured, and she'd heard him speak before, but she couldn't get over how funny it sounded; it just didn't seem to go at all with that 'darkie' make-up.

"Did ye no' feel frightened *that* time?" he demanded in an accent peculiar to Glasgow, and even there not always recognisable out of its precise locality. He went on, as the boy smiled and shook his head. "Ye must hae got a wee fright." Another amused shake of the head. "Och," the man insisted, frowning, "ye must hae. Ye're pretending."

Maisie heard 'Netta' whispering to 'Josie': "Does Jock *want* the kid to be scared?"

"I shouldn't be surprised," said 'Josie.'

"But why does the kid go through with it?"

"Netta, dear, I hate to enlighten you, you're such a cosy old auntie, but that child probably *likes* Jock to throw knives at him."

"My *dear!*" 'Netta' let out a strangled squeak. "And to think I shared 'digs' with Jock only the other week."

"Oh *you're* quite safe," 'Josie' replied cattily. "Quick! We're on in a minute. Tessa's finished her number."

Maisie, absorbed by this strange conversation, had been vaguely conscious of some shrill top notes and hastily turned her eyes again to the stage, just in time to see 'Tessa,' in a head-dress of ostrich plumes, disappear through the archway. A mad scramble followed and the entire company danced on for the finale.

The curtain fell, rose, and fell again. There was no time to waste, the interval was only six minutes, worse luck. "Too short for the audience to go to the lavatory *and* have a drink," Mrs. P. always grumbled. Above Maisie's head the blaze of pink and amber lights went out and all colour and life was suddenly drained from the scene. In a second the stage had emptied and she was alone in a grey, shadowy world of flimsy canvas and wood. She heard the iron safety curtain rumbling down, cutting off the sound of voices and movement in the auditorium, but almost at once the feeling of quietness and desertion was broken as the scene-shifters noisily began their work. The stage became a ship; ropes slewed, pulleys whirred and canvas 'drops' and curtains soared into the air, billowing like gigantic sails.

"Look out, Maisie!" one of the men warned, and she hastily ducked her head from a flying rope. She heard the stage manager calling for her, and carefully picking her way over struts and cables, made for the door marked SILENCE, which led to the main corridor and staircase. A pale-faced young man with a permanently harassed expression and baggy corduroy trousers pushed an envelope into her hand and told her to run up with it to No. 5 dressing-room. She glanced at the letter but had no idea whom it was for; nobody seemed to be called by their real name. Rather out of breath she reached the second floor and tapped on the door marked 5. Beneath the numeral was a blank name-card in a brass frame. During last week's variety show a printed card had announced Desirée La Fleur, who was down on the bill as a French contortionist, but whom Maisie knew damn well came from Huddersfield. The door opened and she was confronted by Jock, still in his 'negro' make-up and wearing a dressing-gown. He was smoking a cigarette and holding a glass of whisky.

"Oh—excuse me, dear. I've brought this up. It's just come," she handed over the letter. "Is that right?" She felt him looking at her suspiciously. "The name, I mean."

"Aye."

"Well—I hope it's not bad news!" she went on brightly. "I did enjoy your turn tonight. I was watching from the wings. It was quite exciting."

"Aye."

"I suppose it's not really as dangerous as it looks? I mean——" She broke off, embarrassed by his persistent stare.

He regarded her doubtfully. "Are ye Scottish?"

"No, I'm not. I was born in Scunthorpe—on tour—and I was brought up in London, mostly. Why?"

"D'ye ken it's an offence to wear tartan trews when ye shouldna?"

"Well, I like that!" Maisie shook indignantly. "I bought these slacks in Aberdeen last summer. And I wore them up there, too— it was cold enough! Nobody objected to them."

"Ye've no sense of the fitness of things. A woman shouldna wear a man's trews. It's verra undignified."

"It's no worse than all you boys in this show wearing women's clothes!" Maisie snapped.

"And ye should no' call them *slacks*."

Maisie was about to retort "Oh, go and blow your bagpipes" when her eyes suddenly caught a glimpse of the dressing-table behind him. Lying on it was a white, jewelled turban, and in the big wall-mirror, framed by naked electric bulbs, she could see reflected a corner of the room. The arms of a youthful barebacked figure in brief pale blue trunks were reaching up to replace a dress of lamé on its hook.

"I'll be wishing to close the door," Jock said quietly but firmly, and before she could reply Maisie found herself staring at the blank name-card again. With strong disapproval she pursed her lips and went downstairs.

In the dressing-room Jock turned to its other occupant. "This'll be for yersel'."

"Leave it on the table, Jock, will you? I must wash my hands, they're filthy." The water flowed and gurgled in the wash-basin.

Jock held the letter in his hand, his mouth tightening. "Are ye expecting to hear from someone?"

"No. Why? Another silly fan letter, I expect."

"Perhaps."

"If it's addressed to me here, at the theatre, I don't see what else it could be. Why should it worry *you*, Jock? Don't you like it when I get letters?"

"Ye get far too many."

"Oh yes, sackfuls every week. Hundreds of proposals."

"I shouldna be surprised."

"Don't be so *dour*, Jock. Where's your sense of humour?"

"I havena any."

"Not just a 'wee drappie'?"

"Ye've no call to laugh at me."

"What do you want me to do, then?"

"Ye could be more serious for a start. Ye're too frivolous, and ye waste yer time wi' yon silly creatures upstairs. They're no good to ye."

"We're all in this show together and I'm no better than they are." The boy turned from Jock's surly gaze and took down another costume. "If it comes to that, what about you? If you don't like the people in the company why be in the show?"

"That's ma own business. I wouldna be in it if I had to dress up like that."

"I suppose you'd rather I didn't?"

"I would prefer it—but I'm no' objecting to it. Ye're no' cheap and common like the rest. Ye're young and ye're beautiful and ye dinna flaunt and parade yersel' like the others. Ye're more innocent-looking in those clothes than any girl could be."

"Oh dear!" the boy said in mock surprise. "How very Freudian. I'm surprised at you."

"Och, shut up," Jock spoke abruptly and downed the remains of the whisky. For a moment they were silent, and Jock stared at the boy, as if trying to make up his mind about something.

The boy smiled and crossed to the door. "I must go."

"I'll no' object to ye talking to the others sometimes," Jock said grudgingly, "but I've no liking to see ye have yer head turned by a lot of disgusting old gentlemen sitting in yon stalls."

"The poor old things, it's the only pleasure that's left to them. We bring a little colour into those tired, grey cheeks. We're almost a public service—like blood donors." The boy laughed and went into the corridor.

Jock crushed out his cigarette and jealously stared at the unopened letter on the dressing-table.

After she'd called "Curtain going up!" Maisie popped into the 'wardrobe' for a few minutes to have a chat and a cigarette with Mrs. Oldham, who travelled with the company and was a useful source of information, gossip, guesswork and scandal.

"Come in," Mrs. Oldham said. "There's some tea in the pot on the window-ledge; you can help yourself and sit on that basket."

Maisie did as she was told and Mrs. Oldham went on with her work: she was making use of the amenities and ironing one of her own blouses. The board creaked heavily as she smoothed her way over the elaborately fussy tucks and frills of pink crêpe de Chine. As usual she was wearing a hat; in fact nobody had ever seen her without one, and it conveyed a discouraging impression that she was always just about to go home. Maisie was inclined to distrust people who kept on their hats in an indoor job. However, it was not her place to criticise or show disapproval—at any rate not when there were cups of tea going—and if she wanted to find out a thing or two it was better to overlook Mrs. Oldham's little failings. "Well, the show seems to be going all right," she remarked, feeling this would be a good opening to the conversation.

Mrs. Oldham gave a pitying look and shook her head sadly. "I'm afraid it's a very poor date. Very. A great mistake to play a date like this. With a Number One show."

"What do you mean?" Maisie stiffened, prepared to defend the Hippodrome's reputation. "This may not *officially* be a Number One house—but it's always considered Number One *standard*."

"There's just that difference. You can tell."

Maisie was livid: "Of course if the show's not up to class the audiences don't come." For two pins she'd knock the silly bitch's hat off and jump on it.

"There's nothing wrong with the show," Mrs. Oldham went on irritatingly. "We've always been packed out. No, it's a depressing theatre. Always has been. Cold. Damp. The auditorium never gets really warm in the winter—and in the summer it's badly ventilated. Then again, look at the position. Not near enough to the centre of the town."

"Well, it's very close and convenient for the station," Maisie sharply retorted.

"Too close if you ask me. You can hear the trains shunting and the whole place shakes when an express passes. There, that's better." Mrs. Oldham switched off the iron and hung the blouse on a coat-hanger. Maisie thought it looked terrible. Common.

"Now last week we were full both houses every night." Mrs. Oldham poured herself a cup of tea. "A lovely date. London. Wandsworth Palace. Sold out for the week. And mind you, that's London; there's plenty of competition. But up here ... what do you get? Panto from Christmas till Easter—then you might just as well close down till the next one. Waste of time putting on anything sophisticated. Still, there you are. It'll be better next week; we're playing Newcastle. The industrial towns are the best—they like a colourful show. As a rule we don't go farther north, but this time we're doing Edinburgh and Glasgow. Of course Edinburgh's not really industrial, but since the Festival and everything it's like being in London—full of foreigners. There's a drop more tea in this pot; would you like it?"

"No, thank you," Maisie sounded perfectly polite, but by a shake of the head and an upward swivel of the eyeballs clearly expressed her opinion of the tea. Then, as Mrs. Oldham's monologue seemed to have landed them in Scotland, she seized the opportunity to carry out the intention of her visit: namely, to ask a few questions. "Funny thing you should mention Scotland. I've just taken in a letter to that 'Jock.' You know, the knife-thrower one."

Mrs. Oldham gave her a genuinely surprised glance. "Oh? That's very unusual, that is. Jock doesn't as a rule get letters. Not at the theatre. All the others get fan letters, and you'd be surprised at some of them, I can tell you—even from women . . . well, I suppose they feel motherly or something . . . but with Jock just being ordinary and disguised as a negro—though of course it might appeal to some people—it doesn't attract the same sort of attention. Fancy him having a letter."

"What's his name?" Maisie asked.

"Calls himself 'Barbuda Jackson' on the stage—West Indian or something—but I think his real name's Macmillan."

"That wasn't the name on the envelope."

"Oh." Mrs. Oldham was disappointed. "I expect it was for the other one, he's always having letters. You know, lots of people don't believe they're not real girls. And then with him being so pretty . . . on the stage, I mean, though he's good-looking off it too, but not so *artificial* as some of the others. There are one or two of 'em who wear almost as much make-up in the street as they do on the stage. After a bit they begin to think they really *are* women. Sad—really . . . but there you are. I always say it takes all sorts. Now what was I talking about? Oh yes . . . I expect that letter was for the other one. Adrian Graye."

Maisie shook her head. "No, that wasn't the name, either."

"That's his stage name, of course. The real one is—now let me see . . . what is it? Cyril something. No, not Cyril . . . Colin. That's it. Colin Ford."

"Yes, that's it," said Maisie.

"Of course a lot of them don't use their real names in the programme. Well, I mean, it might be embarrassing, mightn't it? Maisie agreed that it might be.

"I wouldn't care," Mrs. Oldham ventured her opinion, "to have a boy of mine doing anything like that. Though it would be even worse if it was your husband. That did happen in the company some time ago—a man joined the show to get away from his wife."

"Fancy." Maisie clicked her tongue. "I suppose all sorts of funny things happen?"

"Bound to," Mrs. Oldham assured her. "Well, it's a mixed lot, after all; some are worse than others. But there's not been anything really terrible lately. Mind you, the management are strict and they won't allow any nonsense—you've got to behave yourself while you're in the theatre. And if anyone gets a bad name when they're off the premises it means they're on the carpet in front of the boss and as likely as not 'rested' for a bit, if not pushed out altogether."

"Is it true," Maisie asked, "that one of them has a cut-throat razor?"

"As likely as not. I can't swear to it exactly or mention names."

"It wouldn't surprise me," said Maisie, a faint crack sounding from her knees as she rose from the basket. She skittered youthfully towards the door, but not quickly enough to avoid Mrs. Oldham's gloomy observation about the damp finding you out and how glad she'd be when they got into a warm, comfortable theatre again in Newcastle.

Well, really, thought Maisie, on her way down to the stage, it's not surprising that woman feels the cold, just standing about in a hat doing nothing all the evening. Some people were the limit, never satisfied. Oh well . . . it *did* take all sorts, you couldn't deny *that,* and she had certainly found out a thing or two. It was a pity, though, that the show wasn't on for longer than a week. After this those performing dogs were going to seem damned dull.

When he picked up the letter on the dressing-table and saw the writing on the envelope, Colin experienced what is usually described as 'a sinking feeling.' The letter was from his mother. Obviously, she had discovered that he was no longer in Liverpool, but how on earth had she tracked him down so quickly? This was only his fifth week with the company; either someone had given her the information, or she had seen him last week at the Wandsworth Palace, and surely that was highly unlikely, as she never went near the place except for the Christmas pantomime. He noticed that the letter was addressed to 'Colin Ford' and not to 'Adrian Graye.' His reaction, after the initial shock of seeing her neat handwriting, was to tear it up, unread . . . and yet he couldn't entirely suppress his curiosity . . . besides, it might be some urgent news; an accident or illness at home. Although if it were that she would have sent a telegram. Still, perhaps he'd better open it. It had been on the dressing-table since the interval of the first house, and it was now ten-fifty, with the second show over five minutes ago. He was aware, too, of the silence in the room; a sort of questioning silence, inescapable as Jock's accusing eyes.

He looked into the mirror and saw Jock standing in front of the wash-basin, apparently intent on the messy business of removing his 'negro' make-up. A naked, domino figure of black and white, the back ebony and glistening to the waist, and the sharp contrast of the pale flesh of the firm buttocks and smoothly muscled legs giving him the appearance of a half-cleaned piece of statuary. It was certainly a finely proportioned body, Colin thought, reminding him of his art school days when he had sat for hours in front of plaster models and tried to reproduce on paper a classical purity of form. One day he must get Jock to pose for him, although he knew he would not easily gain his consent. Jock, in his brusque way, would dismiss the idea as rubbish; also there would be no time to spare for it at the theatre, and out of working hours the man kept himself aloof from his colleagues. Colin had only known him a few weeks and their friendship had not progressed as smoothly as he had hoped. He was still unsure of Jock, whose possessiveness and jealousy seemed to turn inwards and deny a natural intimacy and trust. If only his mind and spirit could match that physical perfection! Hastily he averted his eyes from the image in the mirror, but it did nothing to lessen the waves of suspicion which flowed, almost visibly, from the opposite corner of the room. He knew Jock was waiting for him to open the letter.

With the sharp point of a nail file he slit the envelope.

"Dear Colin,
    "This is a very difficult letter for me to write, as I am sure

you realise. I think you know that I have always had your welfare at heart, and I hope I can say that I have helped and encouraged you to follow your own choice of career as an artist. It is not an easy profession, but I have always had faith in your talent—and it has been justified by the excellent beginning you have made. Securing such a splendid first job seemed to augur well for a promising future. Can you now wonder at my bewilderment and dismay? Colin, dear, what has gone wrong? I can't begin to understand why you have thrown everything away. I have tried very hard not to interfere too much in your life, but you are still under age and until that time must remain your father's and my concern. However much we may have failed, we want to help you.

"I know you can sometimes be impulsive, and perhaps in this instance you have been too easily persuaded into doing something you may later regret. I don't want to sound like an old-fashioned parent—if I were I would have equally strong feelings about your becoming an artist—and although the stage, at its best, can be distinguished and ennobling, it can also be cheap and unworthy of its great traditions. Even if some people have to earn their livings in a touring revue of that sort (which your father and I would never have seen but for Mrs. Wellington's recommendation) I cannot imagine that they feel a real sense of achievement. I suspect, too, that I may be right in thinking that you have done this as an amusing, rather daring joke; for what future can there possibly be in it for you? Can you really be happy, touring up and down the country and living in lodgings, without all the comforts you've been used to? And I am not forgetting that you were in a boarding house in Liverpool—although, according to your letters, you were exceptionally well looked after. There is also the matter of finances. You were getting a very good salary in Liverpool, which enabled you to put money into savings. I am sure you are not being paid enough now, to do that, and theatrical engagements do not last for ever.

"I beg you to think over the whole matter very seriously—not just for yourself, but for our sakes, too. I know you want us to be proud of you, and I am sure, deep down, you realise how wasteful it is to neglect your true talent—a gift which already promises so much. In the meantime, please write and assure me that you are keeping well and able to 'manage.' Remember, darling, that I am writing this because I *do* care what happens to you, and because I love you and want you to be happy.

"As always,

"Mother."

Colin thoughtfully folded the letter and replaced it in the envelope. Then he began to remove his make-up, conscious once more of Jock's presence and the unvoiced questions which hung between them. It would do Jock good to wait. He stared at his own face in the mirror. His mother had let him down fairly lightly; she had not written angrily or hysterically—or threatened him with an immediate visitation from his father, although it might have been easier if the balloon had really gone up. The very reasonableness of her arguments made it difficult for him convincingly to explain his actions. All that she said was perfectly true, but had she any idea of the real truth? Did she really think the whole thing had been done as a joke? If so, perhaps it would be better to let her go on thinking that. He could not go to her and say: "Mother, I have no talent whatever as an actor—I did this simply because I love dressing up as a woman, and revel in the excitement, the applause and the admiration." She would never understand. And as for explaining the situation to his father ... it just wasn't possible! They would never believe that such things could happen in *their* family—or in any other respectable family. People like 'Netta' and 'Josie' and 'Tessa' weren't real. They were freaks—something for circuses and morbid curiosity—but far less understandable than dwarfs, and 'fat' ladies, and giraffe-necked women, all of whom were physically classifiable and merited consideration.

He smiled grimly and finished cleaning his face. At the moment he had no idea how to answer his mother's letter; she would be horrified by the truth, as so many people were, and in any case it was such a complicated business if one tried to explain everything to somebody who didn't want to believe it anyway. All this hypocrisy and nonsense ... why couldn't people be honest about life? God knows it was short enough, and nobody benefited by plunging into a vortex of misery and guilt. It did not remove or lessen an inescapable fact. Besides, he enjoyed his work in the theatre, and away from it he had no desire to behave brazenly or shamelessly; one could draw the line somewhere.

Jock cleared his throat and looked over his shoulder. "Ye've no' spoken for ten minutes."

"I've been thinking."

"Aye."

"You needn't sound so doubtful. I do think occasionally, in spite of being so frivolous." Colin rose as Jock merely grunted in reply. "Do you want me to clean your back, Jock?"

"I can manage, thank ye."

"Just as you like." Colin, annoyed, began to get dressed. Jock was always snubbing him, sometimes by abrupt refusals of help but more often by wordlessly implied censure; and yet he was possessive and jealous. Guarded, too, in his friendship. But why? There had never been the slightest cause for Jock to imagine that he, Colin, was making 'advances' or 'overtures.' The thought had never entered his head—he was far too strong-minded to get involved in *that* kind of situation! He was perfectly willing to be friends with Jock, but there was no need to get sentimental and silly about it . . . it would only interfere with one's work. And Jock was so moody and peculiar.

There was a knock on the door and 'Josie's' mask-like face peered in. "Coleen! Not dressed yet? You've had enough time to get ready for a Court ball. Nett and I are going over to the Swiss Buttery—so madly Continental! We just can't face dried haddock again at the digs. Hurry up and we'll wait for you downstairs."

"I can't, Jo. Thanks all the same." Colin smiled. "I must write some letters tonight."

"Fiddledeedee—*and* Pish! Don't be affected. Come on."

"Och, ye heard what he said. Take yersel' awa'." Jock glared at the intruder.

"The Monarch of the Glen," said 'Josie,' unperturbed. "Well, perhaps tomorrow night—if your friend has no objection." He flashed a brilliant smile at Colin and joined 'Netta' in the corridor. "Mmm . . ." 'Josie' nodded musingly, "I wonder what's going on there? Your mother is curious. Mmm . . ."

"What do you mean?" 'Netta' frowned impatiently at the nodding mask. "Tell me! Don't just stand there like Mata Hari!"

"All in good time, my pet. I may be wrong, but . . ."

"But what? *Is* there something going on?"

"Well, Jock couldn't wait to get me out of the room—and you can't tell me that people go home and write letters at this time of night."

"Oh, but I don't think——"

"Sshh!" 'Josie' warned. "Look out." He pulled 'Netta' towards the stairs as descending footsteps sounded from the floor above. They hurriedly disappeared round the corner as 'Butch' came into sight, crafty and comfortable in a luxurious camel-hair coat. He paused to take out a cigarette from a gold case, which matched the gold wrist-strap of his gold watch, and proceeded to light the cigarette from an elegant lighter—unfortunately silver. If he played his cards properly a gold lighter would complete the hat trick. He padded sleekly down the corridor in his thick crêpe-soled suèdes. He should worry! A shining new car was waiting for him across the road.

Next came 'Magda,' soulful and pale, clasping a bottle of sherry, a dozen new-laid eggs in a bag ("Regular every week—I'm sure she lays them herself," was 'Josie's' opinion), another bottle containing milk of magnesia, and a neatly packaged supply of phenobarbitone tablets ('Magda' found it difficult to get off to sleep). It was going to be awkward boarding the tram and he really shouldn't have started on the sherry before getting home . . . well, perhaps this awful depression would lift when they got to Newcastle, he kidded himself. He would have to see a doctor. Some day. Muzzily he weaved towards the stairs . . .

The rest had all gone, except 'Tessa,' who had limped around the dressing-room for ten minutes, minus one shoe and painfully smarting under the cruel indifference of the others. Nobody cared. Eventually he found it, unlaced, in someone's suitcase, and there wasn't a piece of string anywhere with which to tie it. He dried his tears and slipped the shoe on loosely, hoping it wouldn't fall off in the street. Poor 'Tessa'! Life was dreadfully hard and no one realised what he had to endure. His voice was liable to go at any minute, and if that happened it meant being pushed back into the chorus again . . . and 'Magda' would get all his numbers. 'Magda,' who constantly poured down the sherry and by rights ought to have a voice like a fog-horn. But hadn't. It wasn't fair. Then on top of that for six weeks he hadn't heard a word from his friend in the Parachute Regiment . . . That's what you got for falling in love with a married man. You couldn't trust them. The tears started to well up again as he scraped his way down to the stage door.

In No. 5, Colin finished dressing and Jock thrust the whisky bottle into the deep pocket of his overcoat. Neither of them had spoken since 'Josie's' intrusion, and Jock's black mood darkened the brightly lighted room. Colin suddenly felt tired and depressed, an unusual experience for him when normally he was elated and keyed up after the show. He wished now that he had gone to the Swiss Buttery; at least there would be cheerful company there. His hand was on the door-knob when Jock spoke:

"Who have ye to write to in such a hurry?"

"My mother."

"That'll be nice for her." Jock's mouth twisted sarcastically.

"I don't know about that, but it's certainly not going to be very nice for *me*. That letter was from her." It might have been a trick . of the light, but he thought he saw a flicker of relief in Jock's eyes. "She—she didn't know about my being in the show, until last week."

"What will ye say to her?"

"I don't know. What *can* I say?"

"Ye've told me nothing aboot yer family, so I've no idea how to advise ye."

"I didn't think you were particularly interested." Colin was exasperated by Jock's unhelpfulness. "Are you?"

"No." Jock's mouth set in a firm line, which might have deceived others, but Colin had come to know this expression very well during the last few weeks and no longer mistook it for a typically Scottish indication of pride and strength. It was a sure sign that Jock was going to brood and sulk for days—he was childishly obdurate and unreasonable. All this fuss about a letter . . . what the hell was the matter with him?

Colin heard Jock following him down the stairs, but did not

look back; deliberately he stopped to have a few words with the stage-door keeper, letting Jock pass him, and knowing very well that he would hang about near the door, waiting for him. The telephone bell rang, and Mr. Hammers went to answer it. As Colin approached the swing door, Jock held it open for him.

Outside, the pavement was patched with wet, after a heavy shower, and a raw wind rippled the pools of water in the gutter. It was a bleak, ill-lit and unprotected road, without buildings on the opposite side, and iron railings divided it from the steeply sloping embankment of the railway. The back wall of the theatre was grimed with soot, and the large posters which advertised the Hippodrome's weekly attractions (just in case somebody happened to be looking out of a train window) soon bore the ravages of smoke and climate. This narrow road, or passage, also served the trade entrances of the adjoining shops, and dustbins of all shapes and sizes and varying degrees of salubrity were standing only a few feet apart along the entire length of the pavement.

Colin shuddered at the force and sting of the wind which whipped at his coat tails and sent the scattered contents of the dustbins flurrying around his legs. He felt half inclined to go to the Buttery after all. The prospect of trudging back alone to his bed-sitting-room seemed a dismal one, and Jock, in his present mood, would almost certainly refuse to accompany him even if he had been going in the same direction. He hesitated, wondering whether he should ask Jock, but decided against it. Had he but known it, they were both affected by indecision, and Jock was unhappily struggling with his conscience, knowing that he had been unreasonable and yet not daring to become a slave to his own weakness. Jock feared a rebuff from this boy who was beginning to enter and disturb his thoughts rather more than was comfortable.

Behind them the swing door emitted a small, teetering figure in a scarlet coat and tartan trousers. It was Maisie, whose bird-like face was almost lost beneath a head-scarf which depicted the Street Cries of London. "My goodness, what a night!" she addressed them cheerily, not at first recognising them until Colin turned his head. Then she realised that the man standing beside him was Jock and that he had not even bothered to look round.

It was hardly surprising, though, when she remembered how rudely he'd shut the dressing-room door in her face. However, she'd got nothing against the other one, who at least was a gentleman, so she gave him an encouraging smile.

"Hullo, Maisie." Colin was glad of the interruption.

"Has it stopped raining, dear?"

"Yes, but there's a hell of a wind."

"Just my luck. Awful when you're waiting for the tram. Goes right through you. If you miss one, the next isn't for over ten minutes and there's no shelter. Well—" she peered suspiciously along the deserted street—"this won't get me home. I wonder, dear—if you don't mind my asking—would you walk with me just to the corner? I'm a bit scared of this road, to tell you the truth, and generally there's somebody to go along with—only they must have all gone by now."

"Yes, of course I will," said Colin. "Which way do you go?"

"Up to the bridge. I get a No. 3, to Boundary Park, then it's only a few seconds. Don't have to cross the park, thank God!"

Colin was willing to go along with her; it would be someone to talk to and was partly on his way. He'd go by tram instead of walking.

"That's ever so nice of you. Sure you don't mind? I mean— what about your friend?"

"He goes the other way," said Colin firmly.

"Oh well, that's all right." Maisie was relieved by the information. She didn't fancy walking even the shortest distance with a man like Jock, who only opened his mouth to criticise or say something irritating like "aye" or "noo." Funny lot, the Scots, you never knew where you were with them. She stepped forward on to the pavement and a furious gust of wind almost blew her off her feet.

"Stormy weather!" She laughed and waited for Colin to join her, her eyes darting from the youthful figure to the stern, unyielding face of the Scotsman. She was aware of a strange tension between them. Jock looked bitter and accusing—the boy withdrawn and still. She hoped there wasn't going to be a quarrel or anything unpleasant. She wished now that she hadn't asked Colin to go with her; there might be quite a long argument, and she would miss the last tram.

But it was all over in a moment. Jock could not break through his hard, unhappy silence. Instead of asking to go with them, he remained miserably by the door as, with a calm "Good night," Colin left him and walked up the street with Maisie. It was his own fault that the boy was so offhand with him—paying him back for his churlish behaviour in the dressing-room. "Och, ye bloody fool!" he swore inwardly, raging against his stupidity and his persistent failure to free himself from the guilt and shame of his past conduct. Because his whole life was smirched and unclean, he was afraid to claim any rights to friendship or love. How could he expect either from a boy of Colin's upbringing and background? Whatever reasons Colin had for joining the show, he could not be placed in the same category as the others.

His anger ebbed, leaving a hollow despair. Slowly he began the long walk home. After a while he quickened his pace as the rain started to fall sharply, blowing towards him and drenching his trouser legs as it spattered from the uneven stones of the pavement. He hurried on, keeping his head down and trying to avoid the larger puddles. It seemed as if he had been walking for hours when eventually he came to the street leading to Balfour Square. Desolate stretches of shadow lay between the flickering gas light of the lamp standards; he was completely alone in the tearing wind and agitated sibilance of rain—the houses were dark, their windows curtained, shuttered and unfriendly. Swiftly he turned the corner, into the square, almost colliding with a black-macintoshed figure which suddenly loomed in front of him. Abruptly he stopped, as if rooted to the pavement. The black macintosh dripped and gleamed snakily, and above it a prominent thrusting jaw was emphasised by the leather strap which flanked the heavy cheeks and rested firmly in the cleft of the chin. The eyes beneath the tall, rigid helmet were uncompromising. He stared at the moving lips, scarcely registering what the rumbling voice was saying.

"A fine night for ducks, young fellow." The simple statement was uttered with incontestable solemnity, and before he could find a reply the policeman had moved on.

Feeling sick and weak, he remained still for a moment. The rain was beating down, choking the drains at the kerbside and streaming monotonously from window-ledges, balconies and top-floor coping-stones. His clothes were sodden and heavy, but their weight and coldness was nothing to the chill of fear in his heart; a feeling of dread which he had never been able to cast off, and which would perhaps always be with him.

On the other side of the town, in a 'modern' suburban villa (permeated with the odours of fried fish and vinegar) Colin sat at a pickled-oak table and listened to the torrential rain outside, thankful that he had just got back in time. He had finished supper —a repellent piece of rock salmon and soggy chips—and had cleared a place among the plates, sauce bottles and cruet with the intention of replying to his mother's letter, but somehow he was unable to concentrate. Everything distracted him; the rain, the smell of fish, the acrid smoke which blew back down the chimney and made him wonder whether the coal would be of better quality next week, in Newcastle. Worse than anything, however, was the hideousness of the room: the bilious shade of the artificially grained woodwork, the dirty-pink wallpaper with its corner clusters of faded roses and mimosa, the cheap plastic lampshade of the centre light, the chromium ornaments on the mantelpiece and—most horrible of all—a bowl of coloured glass fruits which lighted up inside and gave and overripe appearance to several bananas, two apples, two pears and a bunch of straw-berries.

Regretfully he wished he'd been more experienced in the matter of selecting accommodation, as there seemed to be no connection whatever with the landlady's enticing advertisement: *Single bed-sit. Modern. Comfortable. Sunny. All amenities. Home cooking. No children. Reasonable. Spcl. facilities theatricals.* Single bed-sitting-room it certainly was, for the narrow divan held one person with difficulty, and the rest of the furniture left free only a small area of floor. The lack of sunshine was merely an unfortunate caprice of the climate, but the amenities, comfort and home cooking were elusive as the 'sea views' of many back-street lodging-houses in a coastal holiday resort. There were no children, much to his relief, although they would have been preferable to Topsy, a bad-tempered little dog who yapped outside his door every morning and tried to bite his ankles when he went to the bathroom. What had attracted him in the advertisement was the *Spcl. facilities theatricals*—cosily suggesting delicious after-theatre suppers, hot baths at night and leisurely, late breakfasts with perhaps some amusing gossip and shop talk from the landlady (an ex-'pro,' of course!). He was doomed to disappointment. Mrs. Carswell, a stringy, pallid woman dressed always in beige or grey, had never been on the stage, and as far as he could make out seldom went to the theatre. Any tickets given to her were passed on to her sister, who lived in the next street and called regularly every Tuesday to inspect the boarders. She didn't think much of them, either, as she watched from behind the net curtains, whenever they left the house. Mrs. Carswell, though, had fixed ideas about 'theatricals'—they were easygoing, uncomplaining, would eat anything that was put down in front of them, and offered her drinks and cigarettes *ad lib.* It was money for jam.

Colin could hear her coming up the stairs now and scuffing along the landing in her feathered mules, which for some strange reason were worn only while cooking the lodgers' supper. With a shock he realised how late it was, and that he had made no attempt to write a single word of his letter. He stared at the blank sheet of paper. What could he say to his mother? An absurd rhyme came into his head:

> "Mother, dear,
> I am queer,
> Whatever shall
> I do?
> Blank blank
> Blank,
> And blank blank
> Blank,
> While sitting on
> The loo."

No, not quite the reply she'd expect. Well what? He sighed, got up and went over to the window. The street lamps had gone out and it was still raining. He wondered if the others had escaped the rain, and whether they were all back in their various rooms. So far, he'd elected to live on his own during the tour and not share digs with any of the company. It was much better that way, and it reduced temperament and strained relations to the minimum; there was quite enough of it at the theatre. But tonight he would have welcomed someone—someone to talk to. It had been a difficult evening, leaving him depressed, and the teeming rain and the ghastly bed-sitting-room lowered his spirits still further.

He knew there wasn't anybody he *could* talk to; it seemed not to matter before, but it did now. Perhaps it was his own fault that nobody thought he could be serious—he'd always given the impression of being frivolous and light-hearted. Jock had said so. Jock was serious all right, but too steeped in gloom and twisted up inside to be of any comfort, and some of the others were sweet and meant well, although they usually over-dramatised their problems, or became excessively sentimental. He prided himself on being clear-cut and realistic about things (which was easy enough when they were going the right way), but now his assurance was rapidly dwindling and there was no one to whom he could turn for help. But why, he reasoned, should he need help? Was it because of his mother's letter, and because he wanted somebody to tell him how to answer it? After several months of independence in a life fraught with complications above the average—and now, in a profession in which only the strongest could survive—surely one didn't weaken so easily?

Then suddenly it came to him; it wasn't weakness at all. It was disappointment. Disappointment that Jock was not stronger, not able to match him and not willing to accept a challenge. Also, he remembered with anger that Jock had dismissed the incident of the letter once he'd discovered it was a family matter and not likely to concern him personally. For several minutes he inwardly denounced Jock for being a coward, self-centred, worthless. After that he felt better. Almost charitably he admitted that people were as they were; that is, maddening, difficult and unreliable (except himself, of course). In the morning he would write and tell his mother that he was perfectly all right, that he knew what he was doing, and that he could manage quite well on his own.

Well, why not? It was much better to be on one's own, to be self-sufficient, to watch the little comedies under one's nose and to be wise and serene and detached. Having come to this conclusion, he saw no reasons why he shouldn't adhere to it.

Briskly he turned back the divan cover and began preparing for bed. At the last minute before getting in he opened the window a few inches at the top and watched the pale green curtains flap and shudder in the wind. Then he switched off the light and slid between the cold sheets of the divan, closing his eyes and trying to empty his mind before drifting into sleep. He had no premonition of the dreams which lay waiting to claim him and disturb him by their strange truths.

He was in a railway carriage, and the train was in Crewe station. The compartment was full of elderly business gentlemen, except for another woman sitting in the opposite corner. She gave a confident smile and showed her big, white teeth.

"I'm Dame Josie of the British Theatre," she announced. "Who are you? Are you an actress?"

"Yes, I suppose so. In a sort of way," he answered.

"I imagined you were," the woman said. "You have such poise. That's a Dior model you're wearing, isn't it?"

"Yes," he replied.

"I thought it was," the woman said knowingly. "You can't deceive *me*."

"I'm not trying to deceive anyone," he said.

"We all deceive ourselves in time," she said. "You can't always get away with it."

"Get away with what?" he asked.

"Travelling about in drag, my dear!"

"What do you mean?" He was indignant.

"You can't fool me—let alone all these gentlemen here."

"Yes, I can," he said. "They all stood up when I entered."

"You could be arrested for travelling like that." The woman's smile had changed.

"With *my* poise?" he laughed. "Nonsense. It's a complete transformation. Every detail is perfect. The dress, the shoes, the wig, the hat. The make-up is a work of art. So is my false bust!"

"It looks," said the woman, "as if Picasso designed it."

"You're just trying to send me up," he said.

"*Send* you up?" the woman shrieked. "You're up there already!"

"Please control yourself," he said icily. The train began to move, leaving the shadows of the station and coming into bright sunlight. He took out a powder compact and glanced in the mirror. A two days' growth of beard showed through the alabaster make-up. He looked down nervously at his feet and found that he was wearing army boots. The business gentlemen were all staring at him.

"Some people," said one of them disapprovingly, "refer to that sort of thing as transvestism or cross-dressing. I know. I manufacture ladies' corsets, and sometimes gentlemen order the same garments."

"We frown on that kind of thing in the City," said another. "It's very irregular."

"It needs looking into," said the first man.

"We must *examine* him," the others chorused, closing in upon him.

"You fools!" Dame Josie suddenly cried. "What do you expect to *see*? Don't you realise that all men have female as well as male elements in their nature? Don't think it can't happen to *you*! Or to me!" Dame Josie's skirts were hitched up above a pair of hairy legs, and unmistakably revealed a well-known brand of X-front briefs.

"This is insupportable!" exclaimed the corset man.

"On the contrary," said Dame Josie. "It's the best support I've had in any play."

"Disgraceful! Supposing *I* went around wearing *this*!" cried another man, producing a straw cartwheel hat and placing it on his head.

"Or *these*!" said a staid bank manager, clipping on a pair of diamond ear-rings.

"And *these*!" A chartered accountant drew on some lace elbow-length gloves.

"*This*!" A mink stole swathed a company director's shoulders.

"And . . ." A beaded dorothy bag.

"*Or*..." A silk parasol.

"Gentlemen!" roared the corset manufacturer. "Must I send for the police?"

"No!" cried Dame Josie. "Pull the communication cord!"

With resignation the corset man did so, and then slipped a nylon girdle over his blue pin-stripe. The carriage and its occupants disappeared.

He found himself wandering along a sea wall, with the wind blowing the spray into his face. Jock was beside him. "If I were to fall into the water, would you rescue me, Jock?" he asked. But there was no answer, and as he slipped into the green depths it was a stranger and not Jock who came to his aid. And when at last he was safe, he embraced his rescuer, feeling the drops of salt water splashing on to his brow, as the strong sea wind raced over their heads, tangling and tugging their hair, and driving the foam and sand into their eyes. He felt the stranger's face touching his own and a blurred image swam before his eyes. He raised his hand to touch the stranger's head and run his fingers through the damp, red hair. The wind grew fiercer and colder. With a shock he found that his clothes had vanished. "This is terrible," he thought. "What will people say?" A crowd was already gathering on the beach. "Please help me," he said to the stranger; but it was Jock who was standing with him, and who answered: "No one can help us. We're lost." Everything around them was fading ... he must try to escape from this place ... Leaving Jock, he began to run. Darkness was overtaking him, but a faint glimmer of light showed in the distance ... somehow he must reach it. He ran on and on, not moving ... crying out, soundlessly ... the wind was forcing him back, and the far-away light was shrinking. He fell, caught in a swirling mass of white gauze, and struggled desperately to free himself. A strange, rattling noise sounded in his ears as he gasped for breath.

He awoke, terrified, his legs and arms thrashing, entangled with the sheet which he hastily pulled from his face. The blankets and eiderdown had slipped to the floor, and the wind from the partly lowered top pane blew coldly over him. The curtains were ballooning from the window, noisily jerking apart on their rings.

Shivering, he retrieved the bedclothes and wrapped them tightly around himself. For several minutes he felt shaken and possessed by the dream. Then, as the warmth returned to his chilled body, the vivid impressions of the dream stirred his memory. The stranger with red hair, his rescuer . . . why had he dreamt of Alan Kendrick? Someone he had not thought of for years. It was all so long ago. Alan . . . he lay still, thinking, his mind recalling incidents of the past. Alan, during the war. Yes, that was the time when they were in Hampshire—it was coming back to him now, more clearly. But what exactly *had* happened then? He could remember the trouble over Laura and that soldier, and Alan being involved in some way, but he never really discovered what it was all about. Typical of Laura to make trouble, anyway. One thing he did remember, though, was Alan giving him a paint-box, which he still had. Now that he came to think of it, it struck him that he must have had quite a schoolboy 'crush' on Alan—for how else could one explain his behaviour of nearly two years later, when Captain Kendrick, recently promoted, suddenly appeared out of the blue and had tea with them one afternoon? As it was, Alan had been considerably surprised to find him looking so grown up, and must have been even more astonished to receive such an emotional demonstration from him when the time came for departure. He had flung his arms round Alan's neck and kissed him (really, what youthful indiscretion! Surely he hadn't started so early in life?). However, Alan hadn't repulsed him or been disapproving; actually he had laughed and patted his face. And then they never saw him again. After a while he forgot about him; although perhaps not completely—the memory of his physical appearance must have remained strong enough for him to recognise the stranger in his dream.

For a long time he lay awake, listening to the wind and rain beating on the window. Sleep eluded him, and he couldn't get Alan out of his mind. He wondered what had become of him, what sort of life he was leading, and where; whether he had changed very much . . . he must be getting on a bit, he thought . . . but it was all rather vague speculation. He had known nothing whatever about Alan, and as far as he could remember had never heard him mention anything about his life away from the Army.

He must surely have some family background. Parents, brothers and sisters—perhaps even a wife and children by now. But this is ridiculous, he protested, a guessing game to which there were no answers. Damn the dream, whatever it meant. He wasn't going to let his sleep keep him awake! Alan must be middle-aged now . . . at least forty . . . and perhaps that red hair was going grey . . . or do red-heads go white . . . ? And do cats eat bats? he wondered drowsily. Of course, for all he knew, Alan might even be dead . . .

CHAPTER 4

From the precinct of Edinburgh Castle, where he leaned against the waist-high outer wall beside Argyll Battery, Alan Kendrick gazed across the rooftops of the 'New' town. The Firth of Forth shone brightly in the morning sun, and he could just see the bridge, rising above the trees. In the light, everything was sharp and clear—the islands of Inchkeith and Inchcolm, the far green shore of Fife, and the distant mountains. Nearer to him, spread out like a pictorial map, lay the formal, eighteenth-century elegance and symmetry of broad streets, dignified squares and crescents, and the weathered grey stone of church towers and steeples.

It was a magnificent panorama, and never ceased to inspire him, for after passing through the enclosed area of the Old town he always felt astonishment and elation at finding this breath-taking scene. Years before, during the war, he had experienced the wonder of standing on the mountain ridges of Italy and looking down upon terraced, vine-clad hills and the dusty grey-green olive trees in the plains which, ribboned with silver rivers, extended to the blue Tyrrhenian Sea. The sea where islands of volcanic rock rose sheer from the glassy surface of the water—Pontine, Ischia, Capri—like precious stones broken from the fabulous, jewelled coastline of Campania. Over that vast land and seascape, dominated by the twin cones of Vesuvius, he had gazed with awe and felt the heartache of a stranger who knows that he might never again see such beauty. It had been a momentary interlude during the terror and carnage which raged across the mountain peaks; something infinitely lovely, sad and remote.

Now, from this other eminence, he could linger and watch in peace. The familiar sights and sounds were comforting and reassuring; he felt as if he had come 'home,' after years of upheaval and restless wanderings. It was a deeply satisfying return, for although he might be dubbed a 'London Scottish' his father had been born here and a great deal of his own childhood and youth had been spent in the city and near by. He 'belonged,' and perhaps, now, would stay. He smiled to himself, thinking that this desire to settle down must surely be a sign of age. He was thirty-seven—but that was nothing, these days, and he certainly didn't feel it or, according to others, even look it. He was far from decrepit! His body was fit, and hard, and his weight and figure had remained the same for ten years. No unsightly 'paunch,' thank God. He still had his teeth, good sight, and the same thick crop of red hair. But that was only the outward appearance; within himself he had changed—he was no longer the intense, unhappy person who had once fled from the truth, and in so doing had been guilty on either count of 'going against nature.' After his disastrous marriage, he had lost confidence and all hope of ever finding happiness (what a gloomy, depressing creature he must have been in those days!). But fortunately Bill Burton had entered his life and changed everything. Their friendship had eased his troubled mind and helped him through the early stages of his delayed initiation. Without that experience, he might still be floundering in a miserable state of indecision, becoming more and more inhibited, and unable to form any kind of relationship for fear of making a mistake or inviting disillusion. Bill had simplified the whole problem of transition, and a great burden had been lifted from him. However short-lived their happiness, it gave him the courage and determination which he was so soon to need ... when the ill fortunes of war separated them—and Bill had reached the end of Time on the stricken sands of Battapaglia. With an empty, desolate heart he had mourned for Bill, and at first his own life seemed nothing to him; but after a while he realised how defeatist it was to let his grief turn to waste. However sorrowful his loss, it was not what Bill would have wanted. "Fight, fight, fight all the time—and not only the bleedin' war," Bill said. That's how it was to be, and he would not disappoint him.

And now ... there were still difficulties to face, sometimes pain and despair to receive, but always a renewed rising of hope to stir him. More than ever, caught in the inspiration of the charmed city, he was aware of illimitable possibilities, of sublime experiences awaiting him! The vital quality of clear, keen air lifted his heart, as the North Sea wind went singing across the battlements, on its way like a boisterous chorus, to the Pentland Hills. The sunlight, pouring from the rim of a golden-edged cloud, flooded the gardened valley below him, gilding the jubilant trumpets of daffodils, proud in their April glory. Princes Street was alive with the humming of tramcars; a faint bugle call sounded in the distance, muted whistling and clanking came from the direction of Waverley Station, and he could see puffs of smoke hanging over a train as it emerged from its tunnel and traversed the ravine at the foot of Castle Rock. Fascinated, he watched these everyday signs of activity, content for a while with an aerial view of life. Presently he must return to the clamour and bustle of the streets, but for the moment he tasted freedom, as a king of all he surveyed.

The minutes passed, then, as he watched, the swiftly moving shadow of a cloud drew across the gardens and streets, and swept like a grey curtain towards the river. As if to cheat Spring of its gentle birth, the sudden veiling of the sun brought back the lingering fingers of Winter. Abruptly his exalted reverie was broken, and he shivered slightly in the chill wind. Turning from the wall he glanced up at the massive citadel of the Castle; then slowly he began climbing the cobbled slope to the King's Bastion and the shelter of the Palace Yard. Apart from a gaunt-looking woman wearing a raincoat, tam-o'-shanter and stout shoes, there were no visitors in evidence, and the courtyard seemed silent and remote from the outside world. Fearing that she might engage him in conversation he remained at some distance from her, but she merely gave him a resentful look, as if she, too, wished to avoid intrusion, and with a frowning intensity resumed her contemplation of an unaesthetic but necessary drainpipe, which was fixed to an otherwise bare section of wall.

Facing him was the entrance porch of the War Memorial, with its severe façade and niched and windowed walls of ashlar. Standing here, looking at the simple, dignified building, his thoughts again went back to those grim years of struggle—to the early days of training camps, the constant moving from one place to another, the unsettling 'leaves,' the making and parting of friends. Already he had forgotten many of them, but there were still the few who stayed in his memory, and of whom he would always be reminded when recalling the brief period of his happiness with Bill. There were some, too, who were on his conscience—not so much guiltily as lazily. The Fords ... Gertrude and Colin ... he had fully intended seeing them again directly after the war. And how long was it now since that afternoon visit in Hampshire? Ten years? He could still remember his surprise on seeing Colin in long trousers; much taller and thinner, with a faun-like grace of limb and head. Somehow, in spite of his fair hair and complexion, he hadn't looked like an English boy. There was an awareness about him, a latent sophistication which he had since seen in the faces and behaviour of many Italian children. Nor had he forgotten the somewhat Latin ardour and naturalness of the fond embrace which Colin had given him. The boy had, in the past, always been eager to show affection, innocently and certainly without the emotional intensity of that last demonstration. He had wondered about it for some time.

Ten years ago ... the boy would now be a young man of nineteen or twenty, and if the promise had been fulfilled undoubtedly good-looking. It would be interesting to see him again and discover how he had developed, for the youngster had shown definite artistic ability, which even at that early age had the stamp of an individual personality. He really must write to Gertrude and ask for news of them all—Laura included!—and also apologise for his long silence. He should have got in touch with her when he came out of the Army, but kept putting it off. He was living in London then, and working at the Regent Street branch of the travel agency—a firm to which he still belonged and was now working for in Edinburgh. He had done a great deal of travelling for them, and frequent trips abroad had prevented him from becoming desk-bound, as well as supplying him with romantic opportunities. His eyes had been opened wide to the realistic European acceptance of the unconventional. As an onlooker he had found amusement in the diversities of human behaviour; as a participant he had merely skimmed the surface, unharmed. Only once, during a month at the Rome office, had he been swayed by the allure of beauty and corruption, which like the hot Italian sun had drugged his senses. He had escaped to England, with relief, exhausted by the unreal, operatic drama which had passionately resounded about his head.

His life in London was pleasant. He had his own flat and was able to entertain his friends, go to theatres and concerts, and live an untroubled 'bachelor' existence. Regularly he went to see his parents in Eastbourne, and sometimes they came to stay with him for a week or ten days in the early summer. Their visits had not been entirely successful. For one thing, so much unnecessary preparation went on beforehand—minutely detailed letters and telephone calls about clothes and luggage—that the whole thing assumed the proportions of a complicated world tour, and by the time they arrived his initial enthusiasm had evaporated. Getting them 'settled down' had been a problem, too, with his father inclined to be cantankerous over the change of normal daily routine, and his mother unable to relax her rigid domestic habitude. Not for a moment had her strong sense of duty allowed her to admit that she would far rather be back in her own surroundings in Eastbourne. "You mustn't mind Father, you know what he is," was what she had always said, but he had instinctively known her real thoughts on the matter—that it was all wrong for a man to live alone like this, doing his own housework and cooking (and what about washing and mending?). Even his protest that he was quite a good cook and found no difficulty in darning socks or washing shirts hadn't convinced her. She had been wise enough not to drop any further hints, but her expression plainly conveyed her long-cherished hopes: that he would marry again—some nice girl who would make him happy, look after him, and present her with grandchildren. How disappointed she must have been, perhaps unhappy about him, worried, and in her old-fashioned way bewildered by him. It must have hurt her, not knowing him at all, not having any share in his life. She hadn't always approved of his friends, either, even when they were on their best behaviour and anxious to make a good impression. This wasn't because they were outrageously camp or anything like that—he had never been mixed up with that type anyway—but she was surprised by his choice of so many who were, according to her standards, "not quite gentlemen." And how could he explain to her the charm and attraction of the slightly rough and unpolished? What, he wondered, would she have thought of Bill Burton?

His sojourn in London was over. The agency had recently taken premises in Edinburgh, just off George Street, and opened a travellers' club, for the use of visitors to Britain. In an atmosphere of discreet luxury members relaxed, ate and drank, and without lifting a finger had all their sightseeing and entertainments arranged for them—of which service he was in sole charge. He thoroughly enjoyed his work, and there had been a tremendous amount of it while getting his particular department organised and running smoothly. At the moment, however, it was early in the season and things were fairly quiet, but he could foresee a strenuous time ahead during the summer months, especially in the three weeks' pandemonium of the Festival. Already he was inundated with inquiries and requests for tickets to the various events.

He was fortunate, also, in having solved his domestic problems. No mean feat. It had seemed at first that he would have to 'live in' at the club, and it was not an arrangement he favoured. Off duty he wanted to get right away from the job, and from the impersonal hotel-like atmosphere of the place. But where could he go? To relations? There were plenty of them about, although he hadn't seen them for years. The Scottish members of the family, on his father's side, were rather forbidding and clannish, and memories of long-ago visits discouraged him from approaching them. They all resided in pretentiously turreted granite villas, whose draughty rooms bristled with antlers, spearheads, and unread volumes of Walter Scott. The mere thought of a wet Sunday in Corstorphine or Liberton filled him with dismay. What he had really wanted was a small flat with a good address—preferably in the New town—but so did a vast number of other people, and with the exception of a few dank catacombs in the wrong quarters of the city, the agents had nothing to offer at a price within his means. Having too hastily rejected the club accommodation, which was immediately seized by another member of the staff, he had found himself homeless and faced with the prospect of having to move into a boarding house or a 'private' hotel. He had chosen the latter, a modest little place within easy reach of Princes Street and the club. It had been a very depressing experience. Apart from the guests, who had all been well over eighty, his room had never been free from the smell of kippers. Enduring it for a couple of weeks, he made up his mind to leave and go elsewhere, even reconsidering the idea of staying with relations. He telephoned Eastbourne for advice on the matter, and his father had snorted contemptuously: "You'd be a damned fool if you did. No patience with that lot. Have you tried Julia? Harry Douglas's widow. They hate her. She'd put you up."

He had completely forgotten about 'Aunt' Julia, an English-woman who had married into one of the lesser branches of the family and, because she had consistently ignored all attempts at drawing her into their exclusive circle, was looked down upon with strong disapproval as being freakish and unsociable. Julia Douglas, as he now knew, had been wise in electing to remain free from family conclaves, bickerings, petty jealousies and interference, and he admired her independence and frankness of mind. She was completely honest and straightforward in her opinions; and because she had never given them an opening, by being downright rude and offensive, the others found her calm self-sufficiency very irritating indeed. After all, they protested, 'poor Harry' had been one of *theirs*, and but for their astute finan-cial advising when he was alive Julia wouldn't have a roof over her head today; nor would she have had the means to go gallivanting all over the place the moment he had gone. (And with such zest, too, for a widow of sixty. It was almost indecent!) A short trip for her health, directly after the funeral, would have been reasonable enough—but to prolong it into a world-wide tour seemed need-lessly extravagant. In their opinion, a few children of the mar-riage might have given her a greater sense of responsibility and also a closer understanding and appreciation of the family values which so united the rest of the Edinburgh Kendricks. They were positively biblical in their disparagement of Julia's barrenness—and in their extreme partisanship attributed to Harry a somewhat embarrassingly mythological potency.

Taking his father's advice, he had written to her, suggesting they should meet, and she had replied immediately, without frills: "Yes, by all means. Many thanks. Wednesday, 12.30, will be fine. I don't think we've met since you were at school. Yrs. J. Douglas."

She had lunch with him at the club, and he had taken to her at once. Her vitality was amazing but not exhausting to others, and she made no pretence at being younger than her sixty-six years. She was tall, good-looking, with fine eyes and softly waved grey hair, and she favoured expensive, well-tailored costumes, antique jewellery, and enormous handbags which seemed equipped for every possible emergency. Their main topics of conversation had been travel, which they were able to discuss knowledgeably, cooking and interior decoration—she was particularly interested in old china and glass. He had told her briefly about his work and she had nodded approvingly; no mention was made of family affairs and relations. After lunch, which had been an unhurried meal and eventually terminated by the reproachful glances of the one remaining waiter, he had accompanied her to the entrance hall, still without having broached the urgent matter of his future domestic arrangements. He had followed her through the revolving door, cursing himself for being so backward, when on the steps outside she had suddenly turned to him and spoken: "Look here—if you're not doing anything, why don't you come back with me and have tea?"

Recalling that afternoon, he hoped she hadn't regretted her invitation, although he felt fairly certain that she wouldn't have asked him unless she had really liked him. He had gone back with her, to the solid grey-stoned house overlooking the Meadows and the Royal Infirmary. Unremarkable from the outside, it contained large, finely proportioned rooms with tall windows and exquisitely decorated ceilings and fireplaces. The ground-floor rooms opened on to a square, white-panelled hall, and beyond a pillared archway a staircase curved gracefully out of sight. In the drawing-room there were tapestry-covered chairs and settee, heavy damask curtains and a lovely old rosewood grand piano; on the wall above it, richly glowing against the pale ivory-tinted paper, an Italian landscape painting in oils held in one small area of canvas all the brilliant sunlight and warmth of Tuscany. The Italian influence was prominent also in the collection of Venetian glass and Florentine silver.

Julia had given him tea and deliciously crisp brandy-snaps, and they had sat in front of the fire and talked, oblivious to time until he glanced at the clock and saw how late it was—long past his hotel's dinner hour. She had been surprised on hearing that he was not living at the club. "It sounds ghastly," she said, when he told her about the hotel. "Have dinner with me. No, it's no trouble at all. Quite simple. Omelettes. French bread, and cheese. A bottle of wine—and coffee afterwards. How's that? It won't take a moment. Help yourself to cigarettes. Magazines on the table. Cloakroom in the hall, through the arch, first left. Shan't be long!"

She had whisked out of the room, and twenty minutes later they were enjoying their meal, set on a small table in front of the fire. Then, over coffee and cigarettes, and after a few gentle hints from himself, she began talking about 'the family' . . . "Why should I have anything to do with *them?* They opposed Harry's marriage in the first place, presumably because they didn't want *me.* They've never got over the fact that he went against their wishes, married a 'foreigner,' did a damn' sight better than most of them and left everything to me when he died. *Me,* a childless widow . . . and all those nephews and nieces completely forgotten in the will. Of course, the final straw, in their opinion, was when I tossed my bonnet over a whole row of windmills and went off on a leisurely tour. Just squandering Harry's money on amusement! I've never disillusioned them—and it was worth every penny—except that the money happened to be my own and Harry's is still untouched, and I hope accumulating a little interest. I haven't decided yet who's to have it when I'm gone. It might even be you. That would surprise them! More coffee?"

He had left the house very late, but still no nearer to solving the problem of bed and board. After her remarks about the rest of the family, he doubted that she would want him as a lodger, however well they had got on together at this first meeting. Several days went by before he heard from her again, and then she had telephoned and asked him to lunch. When they were having coffee, which seemed to be Julia's favourite time for plain speaking, she had come straight to the point.

"I've been thinking. Here am I, in a large house—there are five bedrooms and two bathrooms—and there are you, stuck in some miserable hotel and very likely paying through the nose for it. It's not a *home* for you. After all, you're not a commercial traveller. If you'd like to live here you're very welcome. If you'd rather not, say so, and I won't be offended. You can even have your own sitting-room—you haven't got to act as my 'companion' just because you're living in the same house—and of course you would get good food and drinkable coffee. You'd have somewhere nice to bring your friends—better than an hotel lounge, and no tiresome bills for 'extras.' Do think it over. You needn't feel that it has to be a lifelong arrangement; you could stay here for a short while if you like, to see how we get on. Let me see— you don't like kippers for breakfast, do you? . . ."

He gratefully accepted her offer. Two days later he moved in. Julia had given him a charming room, on the first floor at the back of the house, and the window overlooked a walled garden. In the middle of the lawn was a lily pond, and beyond it a flagged path, passing between two yew trees, led to a group of statuary placed in front of a curved, latticed wood screen. A blossoming creeper trailed over the screen, and against it the shapely figure of Apollo stood naked and unabashed between draped and demure canephori. A most affecting sight, whenever he looked out of his window.

He had settled down quickly, delighted with his room and with the whole house. He appreciated the quiet and the comfort, and the way Julia never intruded upon his privacy. She appeared to enjoy his company, on an easy and friendly basis, but had never embarrassed him by personal and intimate questions, or by hints that he might be a little more communicative about his past. Thank God she wasn't the type who made coy references to marriage and 'eligible' men. He told her that he liked her because she wasn't in the least 'nosy,' and she had frankly replied: "My dear boy, if people really want you to know something, they'll eventually tell you, whether you like it or not. So why bother to worm it out of them?" Many women would have made such a remark with the express intention of inviting confidences, but there had been no ulterior motive in Julia's words. Even if he had wanted to talk about himself, there would be little to divulge beyond what she already knew—his work, his travels, family concerns—for the other side of himself must remain secret. All the same, he could not help feeling puzzled and slightly apprehensive; Julia's exemplary tact and lack of inquisitiveness made it impossible for him to know what she thought, or to gauge what her reactions might be to some of the details of his private life.

Since he had been living with her, his work had occupied most of his time, and his hours of leisure were spent in thoroughly re-exploring the city. Social life, of the kind he had known in London, seemed to be at a standstill, although they went to theatres and concerts together, but he had yet to find his own circle of friends, reliable companions whom he could entertain at the house without resorting to caution and subterfuge. He would have to do something about it, for it certainly appeared odd for someone like himself not to have any friends. That was not the least of his problems, either. Delightful as it was to have congenial and interesting companions, it was equally necessary to fulfil one's need for a deeper, emotional stimulus. And lately this need had grown worse. Whatever the reason—spring, the sap rising, or not being completely congealed by the cold—he was conscious of a tension, an inward excitement which quickened his response to the subtle undercurrents which existed, for himself and others, in the life of the city. Wherever one went, in all parts of the world, there was an awareness and recognition between the many who shared a different and secret life from the rest. Sometimes, more openly, it could be found in the crowded pubs—expressed in the knowing smile of a sailor, the conscious physical pride of a soldier in kilts . . . in the shy smile of the lonely . . . in other smiles, too, less endearing—from the bitter old 'queens' who watched and waited . . . Gathered in a single bar were the beautiful and the sordid, the tender and the vicious, gaily or tragically seeking forgetfulness of the hostile world outside.

For a moment a bitter sense of frustration overcame him. Because he was 'different,' he must be denied the love and happiness which others accepted as their right. No matter what suffering it caused, there were inflexible rules and regulations, which took no account of nature's inconstancy. He remembered an argument during a party at his flat in London, when one of his guests had committed the indiscretion of bringing along two 'outsiders': a man and a woman who, before proceeding to belittle his friends, had taken full advantage of his hospitality by generously sampling the food and drink without even being asked. Appropriating the best seats, they had surveyed the room with an air of nauseous contempt, exchanging glances of impatient disgust and flicking cigarette ash on to his carpet. Handing them a large ash-tray, he had politely asked them if they were all right—implying, of course, that he was attentive to their comfort and wants.

"Frankly, I'd like to be sick," the man said. The woman merely smirked. "Some of these people ought to be locked up. All these degenerates and queers ought to be put into a gas chamber."

At this point, fortunately, the steely voice of George Hatfield intervened. "Why?"

"Eh?" The man looked startled. "Who are you?"

"Never mind who I am. *Why?*" George towered above them, his strong face like an angry avenger. Over six feet tall, with distinguished greying hair, he wasn't going to let anyone get the better of him. "Why, any more than you, should they be put in a gas chamber?"

"To make the world a better place for decent people, that's why."

"Oh," George said, "you're one of the decent people, are you?"

"Is there anything wrong in that? I'm not ashamed of having principles, and sticking to them."

"I'm sure you must be completely gummed up."

"Are you making fun of me?" The man flushed. "I suppose you think it amusing and clever not to have any morals?"

"I certainly don't, but I think you have a limited appreciation of what morality means."

"Everybody knows what morality is!" The woman indignantly chimed in.

George warmed to the subject. "Do they? I think you'll find that a great number of people imagine it solely to be connected with sex."

"I've heard that clever talk before," the man sneered, "but you can't tell me that all this homosexual business isn't just a dirty form of sex."

"Dirty?"

"What else is it? It's all wrong, and against nature. It's perverting the whole meaning of life."

"Because it's non-reproductive?"

"Yes, the function of sex is to——"

"Oh. It's just 'functional,' is it? I see. And would you consider sterility and barrenness against nature?"

"Not if it's a natural disability."

"My dear man, in many ways the whole of life is a natural disability—we're still grovelling but we have to put up with it. What do *you* mean by 'natural,' anyway? Nakedness is natural to certain races of people—until they are taught by others to regard it with a sense of shame. All sexual impulses are natural, or shall we say 'of nature,' whether reproductive or not. When you say 'against nature,' what you really mean is against society and man-made laws. God had seen fit to bless or curse us, and if you knew anything at all about biology you'd soon discover that nature isn't tied up in separate, dainty little parcels of black or white. And now I must go. Forgive me, Alan, if I've embarrassed you—but I feel very strongly about it."

"Well!" exclaimed the woman, as George left them. "Can you understand what all that was about?"

"A lot of twaddle," the man snorted. "Just a pouff trying to justify himself. They all do."

"George Hatfield is a married man with five children," he quietly informed them, adding casually: "He works at Scotland Yard."

"Scotland Yard! And he winks at this sort of thing. No wonder crime's increasing."

"He is not a criminal investigator—and neither are these people here criminals. Would you like to go?"

They left without a word. For a long time afterwards he had felt angry and frustrated; grateful, of course, to George, for his outspokenness, but resentful at the whole stupid business, at the necessity of always having to defend oneself, to pretend, to lie.

He gazed towards the wall of the Palace. The tam-o'-shanter woman had turned round, and their eyes met. He smiled at her, and saw her thin lips draw back and quiver for a moment over two, long, rabbit's teeth. He wondered ruefully what she would have done had he spoken his thoughts aloud. Recoil in terror? Stare blankly in disbelief? Or chase him from the Yard, screaming "Pariah! Pariah!"? However, there was no need for this alarming conjecture; she had already smiled at him, a little timidly perhaps, but hardly suggestive of prescience or telepathy, and was now leaving the courtyard after nodding pleasantly to him.

It was time, too, for him to be going. He had spent long enough up here, wallowing in self-pity, and also he was beginning to feel hungry. Probably a good meal would restore the earlier mood of hopefulness and expectancy. In a more cheerful frame of mind he returned to the Battery, joining a stream of people who were passing under the portcullis gate, on their way down to the Guard House and main entrance of the Castle.

For more than a week the city had lain under a pall of rain-clouds. Occasionally the bleak sky lightened, and towards sundown a fitful gleam would play across the wet and shining rooftops, quickly fading as the clouds over the North Sea gathered again and pushed their way inland. The lengthening twilight was shortened with a deluge, and daybreak was heralded by that optimistically termed understatement, a 'Scotch mist.' ... In a dank, mournful drizzle, Alan left for work each morning, boarding a crowded tramcar which carried him to Princes Street. In the rush hour there was something ruthless about the trams, almost tip to tail as they went grinding through the streets, one following the other on a seemingly endless conveyor belt. The discomforts of travel were not mitigated by the climate, either. The absence of sunlight altered the whole appearance and feeling of the city, which crouched under a grey tent of sky, isolated from the surrounding hills, now curtained in a drifting haze of rain.

On days like these his work at the club seemed ludicrous;
there were few visitors and little to offer them in the way of
entertainment. Some of the hardier ones braved the weather,
returning later with squelching shoes, sodden macintoshes and
dripping umbrellas. The more sensible ones stayed in the lounge
and waited for the bar to open. He felt restless and depressed. It
was a miserable outcome to that promise of spring which had
drawn him to the Castle heights, nearly two weeks ago.

Then, as if they had never been, the dreary succession of
clouded days vanished. Waking up one Sunday morning, he
was astonished by the brightness in his room, and thinking it
was later than his usual time of rising hastily sat up in bed and
looked at his watch. It was eight o'clock. The distant rattle of
tramcars and gentle pealing of church bells came to him faintly;
a shrill chatter of birds sounded from the garden. Expectantly,
but still partially suspicious, he crossed to the window and
drew aside the curtains. A clear blue sky greeted him, and in the
garden the warmth of the sun was already drawing moisture
from the humid earth. The lawn—a green breakfast-table for
the comic starlings—was watched by two pairs of eyes: his own
and a plump blackbird's, who with tail aloft perched on Apollo's
head. Liquid, fluting notes of song poured from his throat, rising
clearly above the sharp chirpings of sparrows and starlings. The
god and his attendant nymphs appeared entranced—as if listening to a joyous aubade in some enchanted grove. The tramcars
and grey streets of the city seemed far away from the tender,
vernal prospect of the garden. He waited at the window, not
daring to open it wider for fear of disturbing the blackbird, and
basked in the sun through glass, feeling the warmth seductively
caress him. Dreamily he thought of grapes and wine and the
heavy pine-scent of Mediterranean summer.

From the house next door, the sudden clanging of a dustbin
lid startled the birds on the lawn. He left the window and went
off to the bathroom, pausing on the landing for a second to
sniff a pleasing mixture of aromas, which indicated that Julia
had been out of bed for some time; lilac bath-cubes, upstairs,
and freshly-brewed coffee, downstairs. After taking a shower,
he dressed and went down to breakfast, with the agreeable and

relaxed feeling which comes on the first morning of a long holiday.

Alan listened patiently and with, he hoped, a suitable expression of sympathy and concern on his face to the involved and baffling account of Gavin Jamieson's tortured love-life; or rather, he half listened, for his real interest lay with the occupants of the next table—an obviously 'gay' group of uninhibited American tourists, who for the sake of culture and education were making the best of Edinburgh after a fortnight in Paris. The French capital had certainly impressed them.

"Sheer Babylon! After Paris, this is like coming to the Holy City." The speaker was a vivacious young man with a crew cut, and facing him was an older, balding man in rimless glasses, whose mouth seemed permanently curled from the taste of sour fruit. There were two other young men—the coltish, careless, blue jeans type—and two women, one who looked delicate and pretty, and the other who looked as if she'd be quite at home in the old corral. Alan expected her at any moment to turn round and spit.

He brought his attention back to Gavin. Gavin was his assistant at the club, and occasionally during a lunch hour they came to this intimate bar which opened on to Waverley Steps. He was not particularly drawn towards his companion, but it had become a habit, and as the bar was invariably interesting he was able to tolerate the dismal outpourings of Gavin's inmost heart. A somewhat mistrustful organ, which turned itself inside out and attributed oblique motives to the very simplest expressions of affection. He felt sorry for the girl in question, a Jean Anstruther, who apparently had only to say "Thank you," or "What lovely flowers" or even "Please pass the pickles," with every likelihood of these innocuous remarks being carefully scrutinised and analysed for possible hidden meanings.

"What do you think she meant by that?" Gavin asked in his refined Edinburgh accent (peculiar to Princes Street teashops and the like).

"I don't know," he replied; which was true enough, for by now he had lost the gist of the story. Anyway, it didn't really matter, as

Gavin mostly supplied the answers himself, often at great length, and his listener's interjections served as a kind of springboard for the next sentence.

"Do you think she wants me to seduce her?"

"I thought you had."

"Not in the ordinary way. No."

"Oh." Was there some other way? Something he didn't know about? Had Gavin appeared to Jean in a shower of gold? As a swan? Or a bull, perhaps? But no—— Gavin had now launched into a symposium of erotic symbolism (or it could have been symbolic eroticism!) culled, surely, from the most abstruse sources, and in no way connected with classical examples of adaptability among the gods. That Scotch teacake voice made it sound like an unseemly conversation in church.

He glanced at the Americans again, who were now looking towards the bar, where a sturdy young soldier in a kilt, rosy-faced and slightly tipsy, stood flexing his muscular calves, enjoying in a detached sort of way the diversion he was creating.

"Don't you adore that outfit, Mel?" 'Crew-cut' asked the older man.

"Better watch out, Mel," the younger woman warned, "or he'll have you ordering tartan by the square mile."

"Holy smoke," said one of the blue jeans boys, "are you figuring on getting arrested? Why, if you wore a thing like that back home ... Do you know, they don't even wear drawers underneath. Isn't that so?"

"Well, *I* would."

"You're darn right you would," the older woman rumbled. "Pink lace. With *your* legs and cross-ventilation you'd look mighty pretty."

"Oh, Ed's got a fetish about clothes. Remember those sailor's pants—and the patrolman breeches and the cowboy ..."

The rest of this illuminating conversation was drowned by Gavin's insistent voice, determinedly raised against all opposition, while continuing to expound the sexual subconscious.

Alan gave him polite attention for a few minutes, then at the first available pause briskly suggested "I think we ought to have something to eat," and had risen from his chair before

Gavin could reply. They crossed to the bar, where, along the wall behind the counter, a pyramid of glass shelves contained all the ingredients for a cold banquet. Glossy pink hams and galantines and briskets of beef, interspersed with formal groups of daffodils and maidenhair fern comprised an edible monument which rose to a triumphant apex of parsley and sausage rolls. As he gave his order Alan glanced discreetly at the soldier, who was steadily growing redder in the face and collecting tiny drops of perspiration on his brow and upper lip. The boy winked at him, but somehow continued to remain disinterested.

The bar began to fill, and during their meal, in which Gavin was mercifully silent, Alan tried to resist the urge to turn round and see what was going on at the bar counter. The Americans were still seated near by, and above the noise of the crowded room the lyrical tones of Ed's voice indicated all kinds of fascinating possibilities... "Oh, now look at that ... what the hell could you do with *that*—even for money? ..."

Alan felt compelled to find out. Deliberately putting down his knife and fork, he turned and looked at the standing customers now occupying the entire length of the counter. His eyes went immediately to the soldier, who was swaying backwards and forwards a little from the waist and fixing a cock-eyed gaze on the man next to him. The man was a repulsive sight, and owing to his drink-sodden appearance it was difficult to specify his age. His ruined features were purple and pock-marked; the nose a flaming beacon, and the eyes yellowed and blood-shot. Far worse, however, than the bibulous expression on this wrecked visage was the grotesque attempt to be provocative and alluring. The man's head shook continuously, and the fluttering lashes over the dead eyes looked like the worn-down bristles of a toothbrush. A glass of whisky trembled in his hand as, with swollen-jointed fingers, it was raised in toast to the soldier. The other hand automatically smoothed down a few remaining strands of hair at the back of his head. Alan felt a mingling of disgust and pity for this sorrowing spectacle, and hoped that the soldier would not be too cruel in his rejection of such unbecoming advances.

"What's up?" inquired Gavin, suddenly aware of losing his companion's attention.

"Nothing—I was trying to see the time." Alan hastily turned round.

"You've got a watch, haven't you? We'll have to go in a minute."

"Yes."

"Of course, Jean can be awfully prudish about sex, but ..." Gavin began.

Alan forced himself to listen, until distracted once more by Ed's voice: "Well, that's that, thank God ... poor old thing ... but I mean you really couldn't, could you?"

Out of the corner of his eye he saw the man approach the swing doors, reaching them with uncertain gait and disappearing from view after a moment's confusion over the 'pull' and 'push' signs below the brass handles. He heard the Americans rise from their table, like an audience at the conclusion of a play or film, and gather up their cameras and guide-books. Gavin was also preparing to leave, and they followed in the tourists' wake. Alan gave one more quick look towards the bar, and the soldier winked at him again.

On the Steps, outside, the Americans were planning the next move in their full programme of sightseeing. A strong wind was blowing down from Princes Street, and anyone descending to Waverley Station had difficulty in negotiating the long flight of steps. Dust, paper and people were all swept forcibly down in undignified haste. It was even harder work for those coming up. Alan watched a panting trio laboriously climbing; a heavily built man and woman and a strapping girl of about twelve, each holding a suitcase and a carrier bag. The man appeared to be quivering from head to foot—from the fleshy folds around his chin and neck to the flapping columns of his trouser legs. The woman, Junoesque in figure if not in bearing, struggled against the impeding wind, in a skirt which unflatteringly outlined her formidable, well-rounded thighs. The girl, with pigtails and wearing a youthful dress and short socks, was already on the way to exceeding her mother's bust and hip measurements.

"Nearly there, Moother," the man gasped, in a broad Lancashire accent.

"Don't talk. Save breath. Coom on, Shirley."

They reached the level stretch of paving which made a half-way break in the Steps. At the same time the door from the bar swung open and the young soldier swaggered out, his eyes glinting with mischief as the Americans turned to look at him.

"Oh, the Gay Gordons!" Ed exclaimed audibly.

As if responding to cue, the soldier rapidly stamped his boots, like a Spanish dancer, and wickedly screwing up his face lifted his kilt and twisted from side to side.

"Jesus!" Mel croaked.

"Eee—what the 'ell's going on?" The big man staggered with his suitcase. The soldier dropped his kilt, and with a merry laugh darted away down the Steps towards the station. Astonishment, amusement and outrage broke forth among the spectators.

"Well! I don't know—I never did . . ." the woman heaved indignantly. "'Ow disgoosting! Stop giggling, Shirley, there's nothing to laugh about. It's disgraceful, in front of a child, too . . . Ee, I'm boiling! It's very oopsetting. Let's get to 'otel." And then, accusingly to her husband: "If you'd listened to what I said we would've 'ad taxi."

Hot and flustered, the family trio resumed their climb.

"Well, get that," said Ed. "I'll bet not so little Shirley wetted her panties in excitement."

"We never saw anything like this in Paris," laughed a blue jeans boy.

"Aw c'mon," the older woman said gruffly, "what's so funny about it?"

Alan and Gavin followed them up the Steps.

"I must say," said Gavin, unexpectedly prim, "I think it was a bit much, don't you?"

"Enough, anyway," Alan replied dryly.

Reaching Princes Street, the Americans ambled off towards the gardens, in quest of further culture and education. Alan had just recovered a suitable frame of mind in which to approach the afternoon's work at the club when something even more startling occurred. Glancing casually in the direction of the shadowed pavement near the corner of the North British Hotel, he received a sudden shock, and stared in amazement. A young man with a head of fair curls and a man with dark hair emerged into the sunlight and turned to go down the Steps. He had only a brief glimpse of their faces, but it was enough to recognise that blond head and youthful face. He could swear he wasn't mistaken.

"Wait a minute . . ." he managed to get the words out, and Gavin stopped and looked at him. "I've left my cigarettes behind. You go on. I'll see you at the club."

Swiftly he broke away from Gavin, and with a wild thumping in his chest almost fell down the steps. Below him the two figures were just going into the bar. He grazed a heel on a ledge of sharp stone, but ignored the pain. The pain didn't matter. Nothing mattered except the moment before him, when he would re-enter the bar and at last discover the answer to a question so often asked in his mind but never resolved by any practical and active inquiry. Well, his speed and eagerness made up for it now . . .

He came to the door, and pushed it open. Whatever happened, Colin would be very surprised to see him!

CHAPTER 5

"Quarter of an hour, please. Quarter of an hour, please." A voice issued from a loudspeaker on the wall above the doorframe. There was no feeling of urgency and none of the excitement of a call-boy rapping on each door to summon the players to the stage; and how could the sensitive artist respond under such impersonal conditions to that hollow-sounding announcement? Its tones seemed more in keeping with the departure platforms of a busy railway terminus and lacked the emotional impetus so necessary to the theatre. In one dressing-room, however, the reaction was typical.

"Netta! You cow! Where are my drawers?" 'Josie' screeched bawdily to the far end of the long and brilliantly lighted dressing-table, where sat a cascade of satin and lace topped with jewelled combs and crimson roses—a rare vision of Iberian glamour.

"Dulling!" cooed 'Netta,' jangling an armful of slave bangles. "I haven't a clue. They're probably lying on the railway lines somewhere between here and Newcastle."

'Josie' flung open the door and shouted imperiously: "Mrs. Oldham! Wardrobe! Knickers!"

Mrs. Oldham, in a modish hat of crushed velvet and Parma violets, eventually appeared and promised to find something, although, she explained, she was rushed off her feet and couldn't be in two places at once. It was the Monday night opening at Edinburgh and the skips had arrived late and the backstage staff were being truculent. What's more, she added, she'd had a blazing row with the stage manager, who had accused her of incompetence, thus forcing her to remind him rather sharply of her ten years with Emile Littler—and *there* was a management if you like. Kind, helpful, always considerate whether you were a big star or a scene-shifter—and a wardrobe mistress was just as important as any of these. It was a responsible job, when you had hundreds of costumes to look after; she had handled, unassisted, the entire wardrobe for *The Venetian Princess* (the ballroom scene alone having over eighty dresses and uniforms) and not a single complaint during a twelve months' run thank you very much. It certainly wouldn't be *her* fault tonight if the whole chorus went on without their knickers. She delved into the 'spares' hamper and produced a shapeless garment which, in all but its flaming colour, suspiciously resembled a pair of dyed 'regulation' bloomers.

"What the hell are these?" 'Josie' roared. "About as Spanish as a Girl Guides' gymkhana."

"It's all I've got," said Mrs. Oldham. "They won't show."

"They'd better not, I might have friends out front tonight." 'Josie' returned to the dressing-room and scrambled into the offending article, swearing loudly and ignoring 'Netta's' shrieks of mirth. After donning a black wig with centre parting, lace mantilla, brass hoop ear-rings and a gigantic posy of yellow tea roses at the waist, he smiled brittly at his reflection in the mirror.

"Oh, oh, oh, Dolores!" Then, turning to 'Netta.' "Come on, you bloody old gipsy, don't forget your tambourine."

"Overture and beginners, please," the loudspeaker cut in harshly. Seizing a tambourine, 'Netta' tottered to the door. 'Josie' followed, clicking a pair of castanets. In the corridor they met 'Butch,' returning from the lavatory, and who shared the dressing-room with them. The enormous theatre had ample accommodation for the company, there was no overcrowding, and the other three members of the chorus had a room of their own on the same floor. 'Tessa' had been 'promoted' and dressed alone, likewise 'Magda'—their names inserted in the card-holders on the doors.

"Come on, Butch, you'll be late."

Half dressed and looking more aggressive than ever, 'Butch' frowned crossly at them and went into the dressing-room. 'Josie' shrugged and pulled a face.

"Well, really," said 'Netta.' "Did you notice that black eye? All puffy underneath."

"It was worse yesterday. That's why he didn't come up on the same train," said 'Josie.' They hurried down the stairs.

'Butch,' staring into the mirror, dabbed some powder under his eye. It was still painful and swollen. A Saturday-night souvenir. He was glad to get out of Newcastle. A narrow escape all right; he'd certainly made a mistake that time. A black eye instead of a gold cigarette lighter.

"Curtain going up," said the loudspeaker.

He savagely rammed on his wig and left the room.

On the stage, behind the drop curtain, the chorus whispered together during the overture. In spite of the blazing lights above, the atmosphere backstage was decidedly chilly; the scene-shifters were dour and unamused, the electricians temperamental, the stage manager apprehensive. The auditorium was even colder, and half empty. It was rumoured, too, that the Management were in front—that omnipotent body which controlled their destinies (usually operating remotely from a suite of offices near Charing Cross Road). But why were they here tonight? Wasn't the show running smoothly? Were there to be alterations or cuts? Changes in the cast? Surely the closing notice wouldn't go up—this was the only really bad house they'd had; it couldn't be like this for the rest of the week. Then, after anxious moments of doubt, each freezing heart thawed at a new thought: perhaps this would be the time when one's own brilliance would be rewarded, when one's star quality was recognised and given its due. To be 'discovered' in the chorus wasn't exactly unheard of . . . you'd only got to think of Jessie Matthews and Anna Neagle, or Audrey Hepburn . . . you'd only got to think, too, of a couple of weeks back and poor old Maisie Minter . . .

"Quiet, please!"

Lips smiled, teeth sparkled, eyes flashed; tambourines and castanets were raised expectantly above poised heads. Up went the curtain . . . and here, swaying to the rhythm of 'Lady of Spain,' were the fiery señoritas, the passionate, pulsating Barcelona Belles expressively stamping their red-heeled shoes in the sunlit *plaza*. ("Ouch! The poor old plates," 'Netta' inwardly groaned.) This was *fiesta*—or as near to it as one could get on a Monday night in Edinburgh—and the dancers, turning and twisting into dizzy evolutions, filled the stage with a dazzling riot of colour and movement. Whirr! Whirr! Bang! Bang! went the tambourines. Clickityclickityclickityclack! the castanets snapped. How gay it all was! And who were these two, coming on now? The gipsy and the orange seller . . . Mad Magda of Madrid and Tessa the Toast of Toledo . . . the rich contralto, the piercing coloratura . . . (Was 'Tessa' frowning with the effort of reaching those top notes, or counting the empty seats in the stalls?) The music throbbed; lips stretched into wider smiles, and eyes took on a frenzied, despairing glaze as the silence in the auditorium deepened. A deathly hush, like the disapproval of a Watch Committee, filled the theatre. They weren't even coughing. The final *Bang!* on the tambourines echoed from the rococo heights of the domed roof, as if someone had committed suicide above the heads of the audience, and the curtain descended to tepid, far-away applause, up in the gallery.

"My dear!" gasped 'Netta,' as the chorus hurried from the stage. "That SILENCE! You'd think we were in a religious pageant at the Albert Hall."

"Or on trial at the Old Bailey." 'Josie' scrabbled for the flame drawers, which had slipped down during the dance and were now flapping around his knees. "Blast these things!" A sharp tug released them and they dropped on to his feet.

"There wasn't even a laugh," 'Netta' went on. "Do you suppose they thought we were just ordinary chorus girls? I mean . . ."

"Don't be funny, darling. You've only got to look at Butch to know that we aren't. Listen—was that a laugh?" It was. The comedy double act were doing their famous sketch, 'Madame ZaZa the Palmist.' Fantastically garbed as a fortune-teller—the Mystery Woman of Ten Continents—Peter Hutton gloated with fiendish delight over the hands of Charles Keen, his partner, who wore a shapeless gown of jet beads and a bright red wig with a fringe and coiled 'earphones.' Slowly, but surely, the laughs were coming. The torpid audience was at last aroused, and even the orchestra permitted itself a few guarded chuckles.

"You've got to hand it to Betty and Charlotte," said 'Josie.' "They certainly know their stuff. They were wonderful as the Ugly Sisters at the Hackney Empire last year."

"No talking, please," the stage manager hissed.

"You dreary thing," said 'Netta,' "get back into your dirty old corner. Honestly—" his voice dropped to a loud whisper, "he ought to be at the Old Vic."

"My God!" cried 'Josie,' waving the discarded knickers. "Look at these. Black! This floor is filthy; it can't have been swept for years."

A nearby stage hand, hearing this remark, glared at them so fiercely that 'Netta,' in over-anxious haste, caught his Spanish heels on a thick piece of cable, and in the wild, plunging movements to regain his balance dragged a floodlamp out of its position in the wings. With a terrible rattling sound, the metal stand and container jerked across the floor and fell at a perilous angle against a supporting strut of the scenery. The amber gelatine slipped out of its frame, and a harsh white light streaked over the backcloth, revealing in its glare several patched holes in the canvas and a large crease in the plumed jet of a Spanish fountain. The stage hand leaped to retrieve the lamp and an angry "Sshh!" came from the prompt corner. 'Netta' and 'Josie' fled to the corridor. It was one of those nights when everything went wrong.

Two floors up, 'Tessa' was noisily weeping into his make-up tray, his face smeared with running colours, which congregated in a sticky blob on his chin. Attempting to stem the flow, he dabbed his cheeks with pink powder until the puff became saturated and useless. 'Netta' and 'Josie,' who had entered the room, thinking that someone was being strangled to death, anxiously waited for the paroxysm to subside, but 'Tessa' grew even more hysterical when they tried to question him.

"But what *is* it?" they begged.

"Oh God . . . oh God . . . oh God . . ." 'Tessa' moaned.

'Netta,' calm and compassionate as Florence Nightingale, dispatched 'Josie' for some brandy. "You'll make yourself ill if you go on like this."

"I don't care . . . I don't care . . . I don't care if I kill myself!" 'Tessa's' bewigged head rolled from side to side among the greasepaints. 'Josie' returned, and with some difficulty a little brandy was administered. Gradually the sobs died and 'Tessa' spoke in a husky exhausted voice. "It's Jimmy . . . he's written . . . he's on leave . . ."

"But aren't you pleased?"

"He's not coming to see me."

"Why not?"

"He's gone back to his wife. She's going to have a baby! Oh God . . ."

"Well, you can't give him *that*," said 'Josie.'

"Sshh! Be quiet." 'Netta' frowned.

"I wish I'd never been born. I wish I was dead."

"No, you don't. That's silly."

"I've nothing to live for." 'Tessa' wearily closed his eyes.

"Look, dear, you've got ten minutes before your next number . . ."

"I can't go on . . ."

"Yes, you can. You must. I'll see that you get on. Now, have another sip of brandy." 'Netta' signalled to 'Josie' and together they went into the corridor. "I'd better bring my things down here and use this room, in case she does something silly. You go up and change—I'll have to miss my next entrance."

"I'll get Mrs. Oldham to bring them down," said 'Josie.' "My God, that poor cow, she must be in love."

"Of course she is—you know what it's like."

"Not me." 'Josie's' lips curled.

"You're not as hard as you make out, so don't try to kid me."

For a moment 'Josie' became serious. "What a bloody, hopeless life we lead."

"We're all God's creatures and we must make the best of it."

"Well, get you. Salvation Nell." And 'Josie,' still holding the disreputable knickers, ran the length of the corridor and disappeared upstairs. 'Netta' returned to the dressing-room and shut the door. The room was empty.

"Tessa . . ." No answer. The silence was frightening. "Tessa! Tessa!" The window was open; the brandy bottle and glass stood on the table, dusty with drifts of pink powder. "Tessa! Oh Christ . . ."

"What . . . ?" 'Tessa' appeared from the curtained alcove, holding a gown of white organdie.

"My God, Tessa, you cow! How you frightened me. Oh, my God, I must have a sip of brandy, then I'll do your face." 'Netta' poured out a good glassful.

"Jimmy's promised to call the baby 'Tessa,' if it's a girl."

"Oh my God . . ."

During the interval, Colin hastily swallowed a codeine tablet before changing into his next costume. He had a splitting headache, and with the heat from the radiator the room was stifling and airless. Also, the window was jammed and wouldn't open, which meant leaving the door ajar, thus inviting every passerby to take an inquisitive peek into the room. Neither was he immune from the nervous tension backstage. The first half of the show had taken a long time to warm up; several things had gone wrong—'Tessa' in a complete daze, singing flat; the 'tabs' sticking and spoiling the opening of the cabaret scene; 'spots' and 'floods' coming on late, or not at all; and one or two rather nasty tempers being lost—a thorough mess, and with the Management sitting out front, too. It seemed doubly unfair that the audience was meagre and so grudging with its applause. The company had never previously experienced such a disheartening Monday night. Perversely enough, now that he had a dressing-room to himself, he missed Jock's company—or rather, it would be truer to say that he missed the advantages which went with it—for during the past week, in Newcastle, Jock had been remarkably subdued. Although withdrawn, he had been submissive and obliging, and this change of mood was welcome, and perhaps sufficient reparation for all past misunderstandings. It would certainly be churlish to complain of this new phase in their relationship, especially when it included such practicalities as Jock's offer to clean his shoes for him and fetch him coffee and sandwiches between performances.

About to bang on the wall, to summon Jock from the next room, he was surprised to hear a rapid thumping on the other side of the partition. A reversal of procedure. Really, he hadn't got time to go running in and out to Jock, there were far too many costume changes to make . . . it was all very well for Jock, who only changed his clothes once . . . The thumping was repeated, more urgently. Damn . . . but it did seem a bit odd. Perhaps he'd better go. Quickly he entered Jock's room.

"Jock—what is it?"

"Och, I've just been sick. I feel terrible." Jock leaned against the wall near the wash-basin. His negro make-up glistened with sweat.

"Oh Lord. Come and sit down." He helped Jock into the big arm-chair.

"I'm sae hot." Jock closed his eyes.

"Are you? You're shivering. Here—put this on." Colin picked up a dressing-gown and covered Jock's bare shoulders and chest. "I'll give you some codeine. I'll ring down to the stage manager on the house phone, and he can send for the doctor."

"There's no need to do that," Jock weakly protested. "I'll be all right."

"Don't be silly. We don't want you collapsing on the stage. Quite enough has gone wrong tonight, already. I hope you're not sickening for 'flu or anything." Colin ran to his room and returned with the codeine tablets. Then, warning Jock not to move, left the room and telephoned the stage manager. Hurriedly he finished dressing. The second half was due to begin in two minutes. Would anything else go wrong, he wondered?

Meanwhile the stage manager, in resigned agony, hastily consulted the musical director about alterations in the programme—a suggestion not happily received by a man whom even the Musicians' Union found obstructive (at the band call that morning he had placed an alarm clock in front of the footlights, calculated and set for the split second when rehearsal ended and overtime began). The stage manager attempted to ease the situation by pointing out that if Jock's numbers were cut, the curtain would fall sooner and the orchestra would be able to go home several minutes earlier than usual—with the same rates of pay. Fuming, the musical director returned to the orchestra pit and began conducting 'The Dolls Dance' as if it were the 'Ride of the Valkyries.'

After the curtain had fallen on the first house, Colin encountered Mrs. Oldham on the stairs, where she was on her way down for a quick Guinness at the adjoining pub.

"Yes," she said, "the doctor's been. Took Jock's temperature and everything. Told him it was dangerous to hang about and he must go to bed at once—so he's given him a lift home in his car—wouldn't let him go on his own. Well, you never know, do you?" This was delivered with considerable relish, and she was quite prepared to elaborate on it, but Colin impatiently interrupted.

"Did he say what was wrong?"

"Not to me he didn't," and Mrs. Oldham's tone indicated her approval of the professional etiquette which conceals the patient's dangerous condition from all but the next-of-kin. "No," she shook her head, "I didn't like the look of Jock. I didn't like the look of him at all. I've seen it before."

"Seen what?"

"My brother was just the same. Couldn't stop him sweating. Had to change the bed four times in the night. Everything. Sheets, blankets and pyjamas. Wringing. He was feverish—hot and cold alternately; my sister-in-law had a terrible time with him and she wasn't any too strong herself . . ."

Colin hurried to his room, irritated by Mrs. Oldham's gloomy and exaggerated forebodings and by his own weakness in half believing them. On the dressing-table was a brief message: 'Have gone home. Sorry I couldn't get your sandwiches. I shall be all right. Jock.' He stared at the large, rather childlike handwriting, suddenly feeling oddly moved and disturbed. Jock was ill and alone, in some dreary boarding house, and there was no knowing whether he'd be looked after properly or not. It would be a poor look-out for him if his landlady was like that Mrs. Carswell the other week. Poor Jock . . .

He sat down, feeling breathless and shaken. This was absurd; he was being sentimental. Jock was ill, certainly, but there was no need to become sloppy about it. He wasn't 'Tessa.' And it was no good sitting here when he ought to be changing into his Spanish costume. Briskly he began preparing for the next performance, but his concern for Jock increased. Ought he to go to him? It was impossible to leave during the show, which was complicated enough by Jock's absence—on the very night when the Management was here, and when his own most effective appearances would be deleted—for already there was a nerve-racking atmosphere behind the scenes, and it wouldn't help matters to have two people out of the cast. He would have to go to Jock after the show, although it would be rather late.

"Overture and beginners, please," the stage manager's voice rasped through the loudspeaker.

He went into the corridor. The chorus was on its way down to the stage, and unusually silent. There were no screams and cackles from the gaudy procession which swished towards the stairs.

"What a ghastly night," 'Netta' murmured. "Everything going wrong when *they're* out front. The stage manager said they were watching *both* houses . . . God knows what this performance will be like . . . I only hope poor Tessa stays upright; she's been knocking back brandies by the dozen and crying her eyes out in between . . . and did you see those two men at the stage door? I'm sure they were the Management, they looked grim enough . . . and that orchestra . . . you'd think they had to catch a train or something. And what about Jock? Is it true he was taken out on a stretcher?"

"What?" Colin stopped, alarmed. "Who told you that?"

"Well, Mrs. Oldham said . . ."

"But she told me he'd gone in the doctor's car."

"I don't know, dear, I didn't actually hear her, but Magda distinctly said—— Colin, where are you going?"

"To Mrs. Oldham. You go on, don't wait for me."

"You'll miss your entrance!"

Colin ran upstairs to the top floor, but there was no sign of

Mrs. Oldham in the wardrobe room. She was probably still in the pub. He returned to the dressing-room and shut the door. Harsh scrapings of music came from the loudspeaker, as the final bars of the overture sounded. His mind was made up, and anyway it was too late now to get down for the opening number. He struggled out of his costume, took off his wig and rapidly wiped off his make-up. It was being reckless, he knew, and no doubt he would be on the carpet tomorrow, perhaps sacked from the show; but he didn't care.

He left, unobserved, using the emergency iron stairway which ran down the outside wall at the back of the theatre and came out into a narrow, deserted passage. Within a few minutes he was boarding a tramcar and speeding towards Leith Walk.

At about the same time, 'Josie' and 'Netta,' on finishing their Spanish dance, left the wings and crossed behind the backcloth to reach the exit door. As they did so, they again caught sight of the two men who had been standing inside the stage door a few minutes ago—obviously the Management, for no ordinary visitors were allowed backstage. Whatever the previous performance had lacked, one could at least make a favourable impression with a show of good manners and charm, and a little politeness now might well be remembered in the future. Seizing their big chance, 'Netta' and 'Josie' bestowed their warmest smiles, and voiced a "Good evening!" in the most caressing, honeyed tones imaginable. They didn't wait for a reply, but 'Josie' was heard clearly to say "How nice of them to come round!" as, flushed with success, they opened the door leading from the stage. They were blissfully unaware that their efforts appeared highly suspect to the 'Management,' who happened to be a couple of plain-clothes detectives.

Jock's lodgings were in a depressing quarter on the dismal fringe of the city, where it merged into the seaport of Leith. As the tramcar rattled away, Colin crossed the broad main road and approached the seedy-looking commercial hotel on the corner of Regal Terrace—a sinister row of stone houses which rose from the pavement like a high, menacing cliff. On the opposite side of the road, a line of faded prefabs stood on a dreary piece of waste land whose acid and gritty soil produced only coarse grass and stunted laurel bushes. Behind the prefabs, a sluggish stream lay in a deep gully below the wall of a factory. Colin looked in dismay at this sordid aspect, and wondered why Jock was living in such miserable surroundings. Perhaps it was to save money, or perhaps it was a normal environment—he knew nothing of Jock's background and upbringing, except that he had been born in Glasgow. Even so, this appalling squalor was not in keeping with Jock's fastidious cleanliness, and the tall houses looked so dirty and uninviting. He felt almost like turning back, and now that the initial excitement of his impulsive dash from the theatre had cooled, somewhat doubtful about his reception. During the tour Jock had never asked him to his rooms for tea or supper—and it was the usual practice in the company to visit one another—and he had always been very secretive and guarded. Although this was an errand of friendship, Jock was likely to resent anyone intruding upon his privacy, and might possibly consider it as prying. But if he were really ill, one couldn't just leave him to get on with it.

Colin glanced towards the prefabs, wondering whether they were included in the numbering of the Terrace. A group of children were playing in the gutter, savagely yelling while a small carroty-haired boy tore along the pavement with a dilapidated perambulator, in which a terrified baby was screaming its head off. He watched, alarmed, as the pram gathered speed and approached the main road with every indication of being dispatched along the tram lines on a lone journey to Leith. Fortunately disaster was averted by the timely emergence from the hotel of a solidly built man, whose hind quarters received the full impact of collision. The boy was soundly castigated, and with the still lustily howling baby returned, slowly, to his companions. Bereft of entertainment they directed their attention to Colin, suspiciously eyeing him before concluding that he was harmless enough and a suitable object on which to practise their devilries.

Rashly he inquired: "Which side is number twenty-three?"

This was greeted with giggles; a girl, older than the rest, tossed her head, and with an attempt at parody imitated his voice, twisting his English accent into an ultra-refined Scottish equivalent. The words were barely intelligible, but the derogatory implication was unmistakable. As he moved away, the others joined in, taking up a merciless chant and following him along the pavement, their shrill voices repeating the words and sounding to his ears like some outlandish foreign tongue. They swarmed after him, stopping only a few paces behind as he came to the front of No. 23 and looked up at the hideous chocolate-brown wall and rows of dirty windowpanes. The door, with the figures 23 painted on the fanlight, opened directly on to the pavement, and several milk bottles were lying about, one of which had rolled into the street. He looked round at the children who were now silent, and their tough, monkey-like little faces glared back at him. He pressed the bell-push and waited. After a long pause the door opened and he was confronted with a pair of frightened eyes and the thin, white face of a small boy in grey flannel shorts and tartan shirt. The boy stared at him for a moment, then glanced at the group on the pavement; his frail body stiffened and his face became set.

The older girl began calling out in a hoarse, mocking voice: "Wullie Mackintosh, we'll hae no tae do wi' ye—sneakin' tae yer mither aboot Jeannie Moffat and Andy Trabert's futher. Mrs. Machonochy says yer mither's no guid hersel' and——"

A piping voice interrupted: "Wullie Mackintosh's mither loves a black man!"

Colin started at this surprising statement, which came from a spotty-faced girl in spectacles. The gang joined her in chanting: "Wullie Mackintosh's mither loves a black man! A black man! A black man!"

Suddenly fearless with rage, the boy in the doorway rushed out and began attacking the girl in spectacles, seizing her hair and kicking at her shins. A shrill uproar started. The girl fell to the ground with the boy writhing and grappling on top of her. The others closed in to haul off the attacker. Colin hastily went to the rescue, receiving a few stray kicks before grabbing at the tartan shirt and raising the boy to his feet. Holding him firmly he dragged him towards the doorway; the boy's shirt was torn and one narrow, bony shoulder was scratched and bleeding. Reaching the entrance, he saw one of the grubby urchins dart forward and pick up the milk bottle in the road. With a faulty aim it was hurled and sent splintering against the stonework of the portal, and the glass crunched under his feet as he entered the house. Quickly he shut the door. Willie Mackintosh stared at him, then backed away along the dark hall.

"It's all right. I won't tell your mother," said Colin. "I want to see Mr. Macmillan." As he spoke, his eyes were taking in the cheerless appearance of the hall. Worn linoleum covered the floor, and a sombre red paper lined the walls. Except for an ancient gas bracket with a cracked globe there was no ornamentation or signs of furnishing. At the far end a narrow window let in a glimmer of light on to the bend of the staircase, which rose steeply and turned under an archway leading to the next floor. At the foot of the stairs he could see a half-opened door, from which came a sound of voices—a man speaking angrily and a woman tearfully protesting.

Expecting at any minute to hear drunken curses and the smashing of glass or china, Colin urgently repeated: "I want to see Mr. Macmillan. Which is his room?"

The boy opened his mouth, gave a startled look and disappeared into the room. Instantly the man's voice lashed out: "Get out! Will ye keep awa' when I tell ye!" Footsteps approached, and Colin drew back as Willie was roughly pushed into the hall. In the dim light he could see the tall and lanky figure of the man, dressed in sailor's trousers and a white singlet. "Go into the kitchen and stay there," he ordered harshly. Silently Willie pointed a finger at Colin, and the man turned round, his eyes fierce and searching in his lean and pale face. A mass of dark, curly hair fell over his brow, and his hollow cheeks were shadowed with an incipient growth of beard. His mouth was firm and determined, his nose long and straight. It was a handsome, cold face, still youthful but looking drawn and anguished.

"What do ye want? Who are ye?" There was no trace of drunkenness here.

"I came to see Mr. Macmillan. Where is he?"

"Ye canna see him now, he's ill."

"Yes, I know. That's why I've come."

"Who are ye?"

"A friend of his," Colin answered impatiently. "Where is he?"

"He's up yon." The man indicated the staircase, then spoke to the boy. "Take him up." Willie remained silent and unmoving. "Ah, blast ye, will ye do as I say?"

As the boy flinched and made for the stairs, Colin hastily intervened. "Don't bother, I'll find it myself."

Ignoring this, the man grasped one of the boy's arms, and with his free hand examined the torn shirt and abraded shoulder. "How have ye done this? Have ye been fighting? Have ye?"

"No," said Colin, "those hooligans in the street did it. It's not his fault. They were jeering at him."

"Why? What were they saying? I'll no' have them saying things aboot the bairn."

"I don't know. It's no business of mine."

"Was it aboot yer mither, Willie? Was it? Was it? Will ye answer me, damn ye!" Mutely the boy tried to release himself. The man let him go. "I'll no' make ye," he said thickly. "I'll find the truth mysel'." He leaned wearily against the wall, his face bitter and despairing.

Without a word Colin followed the boy up the stairs. Reaching the archway, he looked down into the hall. The man had not moved, and his pale face and white singlet stood out in sharp relief from the red wallpaper behind him.

Willie was now mounting the next flight of stairs. As Colin caught up with him the door of the room below closed. He paused, but could hear nothing more, only the creaking banister and the boy's shoes on the linoleum-covered stair-treads. They came to a dingy landing and faced another flight of stairs. His heart sank. Whatever sort of place had he come to? There were no signs of life anywhere; no sounds of voices or movements from any of the rooms. The thought of Jock lying ill and alone at the top of the house forced him to continue his climb, although by now he felt dread and apprehension, and had to hold firmly on to the banister rail to steady himself.

"Is this it?" he asked, reaching the second-floor landing. The boy pointed to the nearest door, belonging to the room at the back of the house. "Thank you." He waited for the boy to go, but Willie did not move. "What's the matter? Why don't you go downstairs?"

Then, for the first time, Willie spoke. "I'm sceered."

"You'll be all right. Go straight down to the kitchen."

"I canna. I'm sceered."

"But you can't stay here. Now, be a good boy—please." He glanced at the tiny slit of window, high up in the wall. Daylight had nearly gone. "Are you afraid of the dark?"

"Noo." The boy stared at him, his enormous eyes solemn and dark in the small, pinched face.

Colin took out a box of matches from his pocket. "Look," he said, "I'll light the gas. You'll be able to see your way down." He descended to the half-landing, turned on the tap of the gas bracket and struck a match. The light flickered in the blackened globe, shedding a sulphurous hue on to the ceiling and only dimly reaching the growing shadows on the staircase. He smiled at the boy, who edged from him and began slowly to go down the stairs, sidling against the wallpaper.

Colin returned to the higher landing and knocked on Jock's door. As no reply came, he quietly entered the room. At first he could see nothing but a window, admitting the hazy twilight through a bedraggled lace curtain. Vague shapes of furniture gradually appeared as his eyes became accustomed to the gloom. Facing him he could distinguish the outlines of a fireplace and a towering overmantel, which surrounded a faintly gleaming mirror. He moved forward and something lightly brushed his leg; he stopped and put out a hand, touching the corner of an eiderdown. Cautiously he leaned over the bed, which stood between the fireplace and the wall, and gently placed his hand on the motionless figure lying there. Jock's head was hidden and his breathing muffled by the rumpled bedclothes. He lifted the sheet and whispered: "Jock—Jock . . ." and again touched him.

With a deep groan Jock restlessly shifted his head, until the insistent repetition of his name stirred and awakened him. "What is it?" his voice came sleepily.

"I wanted to see if you were all right."

Suddenly Jock's eyes were open and flashing, his head hastily raised. "Who are ye?" The question was sharp, startled.

"It's Colin."

Jock struggled into a sitting position, gripping the sides of the bed. "Colin! What are ye doing here? Is something wrong?"

"No. I've come to see how you are."

"But ye shouldna be here. Ye should be at the theatre."

"Yes, I know, but that doesn't matter."

"Ye shouldna be here."

"I was worried."

"Ye shouldna hae come."

"Oh, Jock . . ." Checked by this unwelcoming rebuff, he lapsed into silence. He rose and crossed to the window, drawing aside the curtain, which no longer filtered the light but hung, soiled and rag-like, over the darkened pane. Below him lay a cavern of blackness, and beyond this the backs of tall houses, with rooftops and chimney-pots silhouetted against the sky. A few unshaded windows revealed the drab interiors of ill-lighted rooms. He let the curtain fall and returned to the bed.

"Jock, please be sensible. Whether you want me here or not, I've got to see that you're all right."

"I'm no' sae bad now." Jock sounded more reasonable.

"Only thirsty and a wee bit hot. If ye'll give me some water—on the table there. And will ye put on the gas—it's above the fireplace."

After lighting the gas, he handed Jock a glass of water, and asked: "Did the doctor bring you back in his car?"

"Aye. He's coming again tomorrow. He gave me a shot—something to make me sleep. It hasna worked properly yet. Och, this bed's awfu' uncomfortable."

Colin was about to remark on the sordidness of the whole house and neighbourhood, but thought better of it. It would only start Jock arguing. "Let me straighten you up a bit." He shook the pillows and smoothed and tucked in the blankets. "That's better. All we want now is a thermometer. Shall I take your pulse?" His attempt at lightness failed. Jock stared at him silently, almost, he thought, resentfully. "Jock, what's the matter?" He was aware of an increasing tension, a mingling of anger and misery in the look Jock gave him. "Is there anything I can do?"

"Aye. Ye can stop playing."

He stiffened, chilled by the accusing tone, but continued: "I don't know what you mean. Don't be so silly."

"All right. That's what I am. Silly. Silly!"

"You certainly are, to go on like this."

"I know ye think I'm stupid—I canna help it . . ."

"I think you're being very unreasonable. I've come all this way because you're ill and I'm sorry for you."

"Sorry?" Jock abruptly sat up again. "Is that what ye are? Sorry for me."

"Sorry you're *ill*." He failed to prevent a slight edginess from creeping into his voice. Naturally he was sorry that Jock was ill, but it was extremely irritating to have one's good intentions held up to such doubting and suspicious scrutiny. It would not be the first time, either, in which Jock demanded sympathy and then, on receiving it, cavilled at it, as though some ulterior motive was implied by the offering. "Jock—how can I help you if you won't trust me—when you doubt everything I say? Why can't we be straightforward? Why do you object because I'm sorry? Aren't *you* being rather sorry for yourself, too?"

"Mebbe I am," Jock muttered, averting his gaze.

"But why?"

"Because—because I canna trust mysel'."

"Can't you tell me?"

"No. No. I'll no' tell ye. Will ye leave me alone, I'm no' worth yer trouble." Jock shook his head, despairingly.

"Would I have come here if I thought that?"

Jock looked at him intently. "Ye're no' lying to me, are ye?"

"No."

"Will ye swear that?"

"Yes, of course. Don't you believe me?"

"I have to be certain." Then, painfully: "I canna bear the torture any longer."

He echoed: "Torture? . . ."

"I've had to struggle wi' mysel'—not to tell ye before . . ." Jock paused, then went on in a low voice, as if talking to himself: "I love ye. I love ye terribly. Sae strongly I've no' known sometimes how to bear it . . . I've no' told it ye—I've no' dared to say what I feel . . . ye might have despised me for it. Mebbe it would have spoiled our friendship—I would have lost ye altogether . . . and it hurt to watch ye playing—to listen to ye when ye laughed . . . knowing when ye touched me that I wanted to touch ye back but shouldna . . . I've no right to love ye. My mind tries to resist ye—but my heart goes out to ye."

He stared at Jock's haunted face, feeling strangely moved by this confession, uttered so simply and sincerely in the roughish burr of his voice. And he was touched by the humility in Jock's declaration of love, knowing that it had been born of a long, inner struggle. There was no need to question the genuineness of his devotion, or to find reasons for a continued vigilance over his own heart—always controlled and determined against anything sentimental or promiscuous. Jock needed someone with that strength.

He smiled, and heard him say: "Och, yer sae bonny." And his hands were taken gently and held. It wasn't quite what he had expected, but then of course Jock wasn't feeling very well. They were silent for a moment, and then, as if sensing his thoughts, Jock spoke. "I'm sorry. If I wasna poorly . . ."

"You must go to sleep, Jock."

"But what aboot yersel'?"

"I'll stay here for a while. It's still fairly early." He waited until Jock had sunk back on to the pillows and closed his eyes; then he moved from the bed and sat down in the hard and uncomfortable arm-chair by the fireplace. It was not long before Jock fell asleep and the room was quiet, except for the hissing gas bracket. He looked at his watch. It was half-past nine. He had almost forgotten about the theatre, and in another ten minutes it would be the interval of the second house. Tomorrow he would have to account for his unprofessional behaviour, probably to the stage director or, if they hadn't gone back to London in the meantime, to the 'Management.' It was no good worrying about it, however, and he couldn't go rushing back to the theatre right away. Instead, he closed his eyes and wondered whether Jock would be well enough to return to the show tomorrow.

He awoke with a start, confused at first by his surroundings. The room seemed smaller and lighter, and glancing towards the wall bracket he saw that the pressure of gas had increased and was hissing loudly in the brightly flaring mantle. He had been dozing for about an hour, until something had disturbed him; but on looking round the room there was no evidence of anything being different. The door was closed, and Jock was lying quietly asleep.

He sighed, shut his eyes and then immediately opened them again. He had not been mistaken—the strange, intense silence of the house amplified the slightest sounds. A faint creaking of wood came from the other side of the wall: the soft padding of footsteps mounting the stairs. He heard someone come on to the landing, and then stop. He listened intently. There was a curious, whimpering noise. Quietly he went to the door and opened it. Willie Mackintosh stood in the dim gaslight, frightened and trembling, his white face streaked with tears. "What's the matter?" he asked the boy, who began to sob loudly. He shut the door, in case Jock should be disturbed. "What is it?"

"Will ye come—please—will ye come ..." The boy gulped and shakily moved towards the stairs.

Alarmed, he followed Willie, pausing on the half-landing to question him; but he could hardly understand what the boy was saying ... something about his mother ... his mother was lying on the bed, his father had gone ...

Supporting the trembling little body, he led Willie downstairs to the ground floor. The boy hung back, refusing to enter the room. He went in alone. The woman was lying on the bed, as if asleep, but her head was resting on a bolster, and a large white pillow covered the lower part of her legs. Peering closely, he saw the distorted face and dishevelled hair. A cheap, plastic slide hung loosely from the curls over one ear. Without touching her, he knew she was dead—suffocated, probably, by the pillow. He turned away, feeling sick and faint, and unable to move or think. After what seemed a long time, he was aroused by a tearful sound from the hall. Willie's distress instantly banished his own fears, and he quickly pulled himself together. He mustn't give way to panic. The first thing to do was to inform the police, but as there appeared to be no telephone in the house it would mean going out to get them; and what should he do about Willie? Also there was Jock, upstairs ...

He returned to the hall. Willie stared at him dumbly. The poor kid looked so helpless and lost; he couldn't be left here alone, someone would have to take care of him. Where had the sailor, Mackintosh, gone? He shuddered, thinking of the terrible scene which must have taken place in that room ... while all the time he had been dozing in an arm-chair on the top floor of the house. And the boy ... where had *he* been? In the kitchen—or perhaps actually in that room? Trying to speak calmly, he said: "Your father ..." and saw Willie's frightened eyes look towards the front door. "He's gone? You're sure? Is there anyone else in the house? I mean, besides Mr. Macmillan."

Willie shook his head.

"All right. But you mustn't stay here. You understand, don't you? You'd better come with me, to—to find someone ..." He didn't want to frighten the boy by mentioning the police. "We'll go now." It was the only thing to do, and Jock would have to be left alone. It would waste too much time, getting him to wake up and then trying to explain everything.

"Come along." He held out his hand to Willie. The boy hesitated, then reached out slowly and took it. "That's right. There's nothing to be frightened of now."

They went out into the street. No one was about. The adjoining houses were in darkness, but farther along the Terrace there were lighted windows and from one of the prefabs opposite a radio was blaring. All this was unreal, he thought, he would wake up in a minute. Only two hours ago he was in the theatre, worrying about Jock. And now this ... all because "Wullie Mackintosh's mither loves a black man."

A tram flashed by on the main road, and he quickened his steps. Willie, running to keep pace with him, clutched tightly at his hand.

On the following day, the later editions of the Edinburgh newspapers had given front-page headlines to the Tragedy in Regal Terrace. Mackintosh had been found by the police, walking the beach at Portobello. He had confessed to suffocating his wife with a pillow, after discovering that she was pregnant and had been intimate with a coloured stevedore, who recently lodged in the house. The boy, Willie, had been taken into the care of the N.S.P.C.C. The present lodger, and another witness, both unnamed, had given evidence. To the people of Edinburgh proper, it was just the sort of thing that would happen in Leith anyway; and to the seaport itself it wasn't sensational enough to hold the interest for more than a few hours.

To Colin, it was a great relief to find that his own and Jock's name had not appeared in print. But he was deeply worried, and by something even more disturbing than his innocent involvement with the Mackintosh affair. That had been upsetting enough. Worse, however, was Jock's strange behaviour when the police had come to the house and questioned them. It was all a matter of routine, they were not implicated in any way, and the police had been most considerate on seeing that Jock was ill. In fact, the police doctor had advised him to leave the house if possible, and when he, Colin, suggested going to his own boarding house in Morningside, had offered to take them there in his car. Nothing could have been simpler, and Jock was not too ill to be moved. Why was it, then, that Jock seemed so nervous and apprehensive? Of course nobody *liked* being interviewed by the police—but in this case there was nothing to fear. Jock had looked and behaved as if he were guilty. What was the matter with him? It was odd, too, the way he had spoken when eventually they were alone ... "Why did ye bring them up to my room? They needna hae seen me at all—I couldna tell them anything." Perhaps not; but he might have considered *me,* Colin thought; it would have been very awkward if the police assumed I was there on my own.

He was annoyed with Jock. Even allowing for his illness it was a peculiar way of carrying on, and one could not be blamed for feeling slightly impatient with him. He had done the best he could, giving up his bed to Jock and sleeping on the settee. Fortunately, in the morning, Jock had seemed much better, and after discussing the situation with Miss Andrews, the landlady, it was arranged that they should share the bed-sitting-room—the rest of the house being fully occupied by 'regular' boarders. Although it was a large room, he was uncertain as to whether or not it was a good thing for them to be together the whole time. It would act as a sort of test period—and if you could stand living with someone in the same room for a week, no doubt you could put up with anything—but was it perhaps just a little too soon to begin setting themselves such an exacting task? He hoped he hadn't let himself in for a lot of difficulty and trouble. It was no good pretending he wasn't worried by the signs of uneasiness which Jock had shown last night; and the more he thought about it the more it seemed that Jock was afraid of something. But of what? And why?

On that same Tuesday morning, leaving Jock to recover in bed, Colin called at the theatre, fully prepared for a cold reception and severe disapproval of his conduct. The stage door was deserted and Harry Archer's office locked, so he went upstairs to his dressing-room. There was no one about on the first floor, which was unusual, as most of the company looked in before lunch to collect letters or do some private laundry. He decided to try the next floor, and on his way up almost fell over Duncan, an enormous black cat who lived in the property room behind the stage. It was a rare occurrence to find him invading the upper floors of the theatre, and as Colin called his name he stopped and looked up guiltily. Then, arching his back, and with a bushy tail aloft, he rubbed his way along the wall and coyly teetered out of sight. Something must have drawn him from his backstage quarters, for normally he was a lazy creature and spent most of his time in eating or sleeping, and only the thought of a good meal would have attracted him from his usual abode.

Colin walked down the passage, towards the wardrobe room, thinking he might find Mrs. Oldham there; if any bad news was in the offing she would be the most likely one to impart it. But when he came to the door he found it locked. Pausing for a moment, he looked about him, trying to discover where Duncan had come from. All the doors were shut, including the one which led to a narrow flight of stairs ascending to the roof. Just as he was about to go, he heard someone singing in a peculiar, husky kind of way—a sort of ginny, cigarette voice. It appeared to be coming from a room near the main staircase, one of the chorus dressing-rooms, and on finding its source he opened the door and looked in.

"Who the hell—— Darling!" 'Josie' screeched and swung round, looking like an oriental dancer taken by surprise in the bathroom. His head was swathed in a turban of Turkish towelling, from under which beads of water trickled on to his brow, and a silken kimono, lavishly embroidered with magenta and white chrysanthemums, clung limply to him like damp and faded wrapping paper.

"Come in, dear," said 'Josie.' "I know I look like an eastern brothel-keeper, but it's quite all right, I've been washing my hair. I see you're admiring my robe and can't wait to try it on. Isn't it smart? Especially under the armpits." He lifted his arms to reveal shreds of rotting silk. "I've had it for years. Someone left it behind in a dressing-room at the Chesterfield Hippodrome. Dame Madge Kendal, I expect. But, darling ... what happened to *you* last night?"

"I had to go and see if Jock was all right."

"The poor bastard. How is he?"

"Much better. I had to go, I couldn't just leave him to get on with it. What happened? Was there a terrible row?"

"My dear! Don't you know? I thought you'd seen the plain-clothes men and hurriedly disappeared—disguised as Mary Queen of Scots or someone ... You've missed all the fun."

"It won't be so funny if I get the sack for missing a performance."

"Oh, I don't mean *that*. No, it's *much* worse ... your running off was only a curtain-raiser before the Big Drama."

"What do you mean?"

"Well, dear—" 'Josie' wryly twisted his mouth, "while you were doing your Lady With A Lamp act and leaving a great gap in the first-half finale—which your poor old mother had to fill by kicking up her legs in an extra number ... French knickers by Gamage's and roll-top stockings by the Old Times Furnishing Co. *Well* ... no sooner had I got into the wings and switched off my electric truss, what do I spy? Two sinister-looking gentlemen in the dreariest hats you've ever seen. The very pair that Netta and I earlier on mistook for the Management. Only they weren't the Management at all—they were Lily Law! Yes, dear, detectives! A stage hand told me—and I thought 'My God—my pearls!' quite forgetting they were in the bank and I was wearing only paste diamonds. Anyway, they were standing right by the tabs, watching Tessa ... and honestly, I wouldn't have blamed them if they'd taken her away, she was terrible. Flat as a pancake. There wasn't time to find out what was going on—you know that mad rush for the finale—and poor Netta was white as a sheet and kept moaning 'Oh my God, they're going to close the show,' you know how hysterical she gets ... and then of course when the curtain came down and we all trooped off, it happened." With a dramatic, Madame X gesture, 'Josie' clutched the back of a chair and closed his eyes. "It was simply ghastly. They were waiting for him—and the moment he came off the stage they arrested him!"

"What?" Colin stared incredulously. "You mean they arrested Tessa?"

"No, not Tessa—Butch!"

"My God ..."

"Yes, that's what I thought. Much as I dislike him I can't help feeling sorry for the poor sod."

"But what's he done?"

"Your guess is as good as mine, but judging by that black eye I think he got into a bit of trouble in Newcastle. Of course he's just rent. I mean, all those gold cigarette cases and things, and dozens of nylon shirts ... you couldn't buy them on the salaries *we* get. You can imagine how we all felt. The police came up here to our room and waited while Butch changed. Netta and I had to stay outside in the passage. And that wasn't all. The whole company was questioned—it was like the Inquisition—only much funnier. Everyone suddenly became madly hearty and pipe-smoking— for fear of being arrested, I suppose. Of course it didn't last, once they'd gone ... The second half started late, but we were all so nervous and it went right down the drain. Nobody knew *what* they were doing."

"But what did the Management say? Weren't they in front?"

"No, it was all a terrible hoax. One of the backers was there, that's all. A tiny, shrivelled-up little man, like a gnome. He came round afterwards."

"What did *he* say?"

"Nothing! He took Magda out to supper. Really, some people

have the most extraordinary taste. We were all ignored. But then, what does that type of man know about the theatre? I ask you." 'Josie' removed the turban and shook out his hair.

"Well," said Colin "you can't really call the show 'high art.'"

"No," 'Josie' smiled. "It's more tarty than arty, isn't it? But what a night! You needn't worry about missing a performance; it'll be forgotten by this evening. Now, I'll just brilliantine my tresses and fluff it out at the back—no—perhaps I'd better not, just in case. I'll be discreet—for a change. Why don't you come along to the digs and have lunch with Netta and me?"

"I'd love to, but I must get back to Jock."

"When's he returning to the show?"

"He should be all right by tomorrow."

"Mmm ..." 'Josie' unwrapped himself and hung up the kimono. "Quite a little ding-dong going on, isn't there? You're a sly pair, I must say. But, darling ... do you think it's wise? I mean, Jock is so *very* strange. God knows I'm the last person to deny the call of the flesh—or any other call for that matter, be it Indian Love or just the muffin man crossing the road ... but *do* be careful, ducky. We should hate anything to happen to you."

"You needn't worry. I know what I'm doing."

"Well, you've probably got more sense than most of us, so perhaps it'll be all right."

The subject was closed. Colin had no desire to discuss it with anyone, least of all to admit the uncertainty he felt. Jo was pretty shrewd, and had known Jock from the very beginning of the tour; and at one time 'Netta' had been in the same lodgings. He remembered him once saying something about it, but hadn't attached much importance to it. "Jock," 'Netta' had said, "is a closed book. Always on guard and a bit shifty in a funny sort of way. Rather frightening really. I'm very easy to get on with—but he just wouldn't *give*."

Changing the subject, he asked: "How's Netta?"

"My dear," 'Josie' looked pained, "she's driving me mad with that gramophone of hers. From the moment she's up the damned thing never stops playing. And the same record the whole time. 'The Blue Tango'! She never puts on the reverse side. Out of sheer desperation I gave her Skips Marlowe singing 'Love,

Lovely Love,' and she had it on once and then went back to that bloody 'Blue Tango.' You know, sometimes I feel I'd like to live alone . . . but of course it would be ghastly really. One must have somebody to talk to. Like a piece of chocolate?"

Breaking a thick slab of nut milk, he gave Colin a large portion and continued to chatter, but Colin scarcely listened; he was suddenly depressed and anxious. The news of Butch's arrest disturbed and saddened him, and now these hints and warnings about Jock seemed unduly to magnify his present state of ambiguity, not only in their relationship but in the whole pattern of his own life. He had given little thought to the future, preferring to act impulsively but always independent of other people, and by becoming emotionally involved in what appeared to be a rather dubious partnership, he began to doubt his capacity for dealing with it. He was not sure of Jock, and not even any longer sure of himself. His previous conviction that the world in which he lived could hold something more durable than the transient mode of existence commonly supposed to be the lot of all inverts, appeared as an empty mockery. The all too familiar conclusion—"It can't last. It never does, for *us*"—was a startling reminder that perhaps he was no different from the rest, and that he should take even the smallest crumbs when they were offered, and be thankful.

Glancing at him, he wondered if 'Josie' had always been cynical and hard, or whether an assumed veneer of bravado concealed the same longings and dissatisfaction. It was strange how they had been brought together, he and 'Josie,' 'Netta' and 'Tessa,' all of them—all of them figures in a game of double pretence, each escaping into a 'third' world as it were; but was it to discover themselves or to lose themselves?

"Jo . . ."

"Umm?"

"What made you join this show? I mean, have you always done this kind of thing?"

"I've always been in the business, if that's what you mean. Not in drag. Not at first, anyway. I was a chorus boy—with a bit of dancing thrown in. I was in one or two quite big shows. *Imperial Waltz*—did you see it? And *Rainbow,* and that terrible thing

Hullo—Goodbye! which is asking for trouble with a title like that. It died on us after four nights."

"But did you like the work? Why didn't you stay in the ordinary kind of shows?"

"Quite simply, because I haven't any illusions about myself. Let's face it, when the American 'invasion' came—all those big shows from the States, *Oklahoma!* and *Annie* and the rest of them—it was no good pretending I could look a hundred per cent he-man. Theda Bara, dressed up as a cowboy! I might have got by at the Chelsea Arts Ball—but it was no good for Drury Lane or the Coliseum. Anyway, I happened to meet Netta at a party, and she was just going into *Out of Uniform* for a long tour, and suggested I went for an audition. Of course I got in easily, you've never seen such a tatty collection who applied. Out of uniform was right—they'd certainly never been *in* it! Then I came into this one, and where do we go from here?"

"I suppose," said Colin, "there'll always be shows like this."

"God knows what most of us would do if there weren't. We're not much good for anything else. What a prospect! All of us getting older and tattier and bitchier. It's all right for people like Charlotte and Betty, they've got real talent and can get big money in panto. But what's going to happen to Tessa and Magda, or me, for that matter? Is it worth trying to stay the course? And what about *you?* Still, you're clever with your pencils and paints, you could always go back to that sort of work. What made you join this racket?"

"For the excitement and glamour, I expect."

"Glamour!" 'Josie' laughed hollowly. "It's all right when you're actually on the stage, knocking the audience cold with a bit of glitter and tit, but it's a hell of a life tramping from town to town, spending every Sunday in a railway carriage and eating boiled cod in bed-sitting-rooms practically every night of the week. And yet—" he shrugged philosophically—"we'd be far more miserable doing something else that we hated. At least for a few hours every day we can be ourselves and enjoy it."

'Josie' finished the remainder of the nut milk and put on his raincoat. Together they went downstairs, without meeting anyone on the way, and walked to the nearest tram stop. Before crossing the road, Colin waited with 'Josie,' who was going in the opposite direction, and as the tramcar drew up 'Josie' parted with a loud "See you tonight, girl," which considerably surprised the waiting queue of people. Colin hurried from sight as quickly as possible.

Riding towards Morningside, he began musing over the past, recalling how this fantastic life had started, launching him into a masquerade which led deeper and deeper into a shadowy world of conflicts. It seemed as if he had always realised the 'difference' of his nature—even as a youngster at school, when he had entered into strong emotional attachments with older boys. And then in his late teens there had been his first serious 'affair.' . . . It had ended tragically. John was killed in a car accident; and perhaps because it had been the perfect friendship, the perfect love, he had remained too exacting in his ideas of what a love relationship should mean and be. It had driven him into an arid region of unfulfilment; but he had also managed to escape the temptations of promiscuity. Why, then, had he drifted into this shallow and aimless way of life? Was it because no one had come to replace that love? Was it a desire for adulation and homage, to redress the deficiency of more intimate attentions? Perhaps. After all, one couldn't suppress every form of expression, and the feminine side of his personality had to take some form or other. It was saner to face up to what one was, rather than to go mad by kidding oneself that one wasn't!

A colourful life . . . and colour was a strong influence in everything he did. On leaving school, he wanted to be an artist, and although there had been opposition from his father he had eventually persuaded his parents into letting him go to an art school. He also pointed out that, whatever he did, it would be interrupted by his National Service call-up—not knowing then, of course, that he was to be rejected as unsuitable. He would have liked to be a stage designer, but was forced to admit that, commercially, it was an uncertain profession, and by no means easy to get into without the right sort of connections. Instead, he found himself designing textiles and wallpapers, without knowing that later he would embellish a stage far more colourfully than its scenery.

His passion for the theatre was rewarded in another way. Through a fellow student, he met a young man named Kenneth Stubbs, who spent most of his time in the overwrought, backstage atmosphere of the opera house. His mother was a singer of minor roles at Covent Garden, and used the pseudonym of 'Maddalena Verdi,' which she had sentimentally adopted after an early success in *Rigoletto.* Her velvety mezzo had roughened a little over the years, but she was a good actress and useful for serving-women, faithful old nurses, proprietresses of Bohemian inns and the occasional angry priestess—all indispensable characters in the operatic repertoire. With Kenneth, he enjoyed many evenings in 'Mum's' dressing-room, where, making a great deal of noise, the three of them would hilariously try on her wigs and costumes much to the annoyance of the serious-minded prima donna relaxing on a chaise-longue in the next room. He remembered one night, when Mrs. Stubbs had a wait of two and a quarter hours during a performance of *Götterdammerung,* they had whiled away the time by giving their own potted version of the *Ring;* and just as his friend's mother had embarked on an unflattering but very funny impression of a typically Teutonic Valkyrie, the prototype of this heroic figure arrived on the landing outside. The outraged, blazing Brünnhilde had stormed into the room and, with a crescendo of sound even more violent than the closing scene of the opera, hurled threats, abuse (and her helmet and spear) at the astonished offenders.

It was Kenneth who had also introduced him to the 'underground,' as some people called it, and his first entry into the gilded realm of unconventionality was somewhat startling. An invitation for 'Mr. Stubbs and Friend,' bidding them to the showrooms of Osric Steinberg, the interior decorator, had arrived by way of an embossed card, so ornate in its Gothic traceries as to be mistaken at first glance for a printer's advertising sample of an illuminated missal. Heavily drenched in perfume, its aroma of chic decadence had lingered most unsuitably in the bag of the elderly postman who delivered it.

On arrival at the showrooms, near Sloane Square, they were conducted by a coloured manservant in brocade knee-breeches to the main *salon* where Osric awaited his guests. Standing on the

Aubusson carpet, under a crystal chandelier, and surrounded by an elegant assortment of friends and reproduction Louis Quatorze furniture, he ecstatically received each visitor with outstretched jewelled hands and cries of delighted welcome. These effusive greetings were equally reciprocated by his intimates, but those outside the admiring coterie—strangers like Colin and a few others who were making their first appearance in the 'royal' circle—were confronted with a problem of social etiquette unknown to the pages of Emily Post or Lady Troubridge. On entering this sumptuous room, and with no precedent to guide him, how was the novice to act when introduced to a host who was magnificently and authentically dressed as Madame Dubarry?

Recollecting this first of many parties, Colin smiled. He remembered being taken upstairs, later that evening, to Osric's private apartment, where the owner's bedroom resembled a frivolous, Fragonard bower of pink and white roses, velvet bows and chubby, plaster cherubs. All the rooms in the house were exquisitely appointed, including the bathroom with its stylised *chinoiserie,* its lacquered bathtub and its imitation Ming lavatory bowl with a seat of hand-painted water-lilies, and a cover which, when raised, formed the gorgeous fan-like tail of a peacock. After such excesses of decorative art it was a relief to find that the kitchen was purely functional, that the gas cooker was not made of bamboo or the refrigerator disguised as a Chinese pagoda.

It was at Osric's house where he had first seen Claud Loveday, seated at a harpsichord and rather drunkenly playing a Handel minuet, which provided a suitable 'period' atmosphere for a costume ball given to celebrate Osric's forty-second birthday. "Don't tell anyone that I'm forty-two!" Osric whispered to his friends, who had no intention of doing so, as they very well knew that he was nearly fifty. Away from all the nonsense, Claud was a really brilliant pianist and could have had a successful career on the concert platform, but he preferred the less austere conditions of party-playing, and a glass of gin within easy reach. He often saw Claud at these parties, and remembered one of them in particular—it was his first appearance in 'drag.' Someone had egged him on into wearing one of Osric's 'costumes,' and after a few potent drinks he had been brave enough to descend the staircase in an Edwardian ball dress, complete with ostrich feather fan and a rhinestone tiara. With his slender figure, fair skin, and gold curly hair swept up on top of his head he became the focal point of the party. Stirred by the triumphal entry, Claud had fittingly accompanied him with *The Merry Widow* waltz. Someone had offered a glass of champagne; another had claimed him in the dance. Osric was furious at not having worn the dress himself—his own grey lace panniers were a mistake and definitely ageing.

Osric and Claud had been, in their different ways, the moving agents in the next and present phase of his experience in the 'gay' world. He had to get away from the restrictive atmosphere at home; although his mother encouraged his artistic inclinations, his father remained sceptical about his choice of career, and stipulated a time limit for his period of study. If he failed to make good immediately on leaving the art school, he would be faced with the prospect of having to take some dreary office job—and he was determined never to do that. But unless he had a job and money, it was impossible to leave home right away. Something had to be done, as living at home was becoming increasingly irksome, and not the least of his troubles was the regular visits of his sister and her husband. Geoffrey was weak and harmless enough, but Laura had grown more insufferable and smug than ever, self-consciously virtuous in her role of a wife and mother. She had done her 'duty' by producing two brats, and imagined herself the perfection of womanhood. And as for little Susan and David, no other children could touch them—which seemed a pity, when so obviously they were an ideal target for a quiverful of arrows or a round of machine-gun bullets. He had also to contend with Laura's thinly veiled insinuations about his 'arty-crafty' friends. To use 'Josie's' apt description, she was "just a great big send-up." He simply had to get away from it all. Find a job and live in one room, if necessary.

Without hesitation he had gone to Osric, disregarding the slight coolness of his reception, the cause of which he knew only too well: he had never really been forgiven for usurping his host's crown at that party. However, with a certain amount of flattery and some admiring remarks about the new décor in

the spare-room, he succeeded in gaining Osric's attention. The
fashionable interior decorator was very happy to recommend a
course of action: Colin must at once call on Bronwen Morgan,
"an absolute genius at weaving, she's done some fabulous mate-
rials for me . . . a real find . . . the Duchess of Something is *always*
writing about her . . . but poor Bronwen—well . . . not *exactly*
poor—she can't get new designs fast enough. You might be just
the person she needs to keep up with her output." Thanking
Osric, and visualising a woman in mittens and a tall black hat,
sitting at a spinning-wheel in the hearth and perhaps listening to
her mother playing the harp, he set out to find Miss Morgan at
the address Osric had given him. He found Miss Morgan sitting
behind a large desk in an unromantic third-floor office just off
Bond Street. She was Armenian, wearing neither mittens nor
hat; and apart from her adopted name there was nothing Celtic
about her, either in her rasping voice or in her shrewd, slanting
eyes which had gleamed at him through the thick lenses of her
diamanté-studded spectacles. Above these eyes her hennaed hair
was the colour of dried blood, styled in a coiffure which could
have been set only under a jelly-mould. She wore a black woollen
dress, which also served as an ash-tray while she chain-smoked.
On the desk in front of her were bales of material woven into
or printed with outlandish designs in strange colours. When he
entered the room she was examining the various textures with
her nicotined, claw-like fingers, and she frowned suspiciously at
him before she spoke.

"You are Mr. Colin Ford? Yes, Osric has just telephoned—
always he is sending young men to see me. Always they say they
have talent and always I have to tell him they are no good. No
good at all. They are artistic and pretty, but—no talent. Sit down,
darlink." She sounded rather cross and continued fingering the
material. "It is disgusting," she hissed. "Look at this. Repellent!"
A long, grey snake of ash dropped from her cigarette on to the
bale of cloth. "It is no good at all. There is no *talent* in this design.
It is hideous. What does it mean? You tell me."

Somewhat apprehensively he drew his chair nearer to the desk
while she hovered like a vulture over the offending design. "It—it
looks as if it might be seaweed," he suggested.

"Seaweed!" she cried hoarsely. "Never! As a child I was taken to the Black Sea and to the Caspian, but I never saw anything like this. Never!" Her eyes flashed and, dragonlike, smoke curled from her lips.

"Well—" he began.

Impatiently she pushed aside the cloth and lit another cigarette. "If you can design something better—which would not be difficult," she cut him short, "I might give you a trial. But—" she stabbed the repulsive seaweed with a long index finger—"I want talent. Show me your designs."

Most of his work was for the theatre, but the rich colours of a drop curtain caught her eyes. She thought it showed talent. He must do something for textiles and let her see it—but quickly, because she had to get back to the factory before the end of the week. He had produced the designs for her within the next two days; and she emphasised that if she decided to employ him he would have to work in the factory with the other designers. Fairly certain that he was going to get the job, he excitedly telephoned Osric to thank him for his help. Osric was delighted, but for reasons which he did not impart; neither he nor Bronwen had mentioned that the factory was in Liverpool—and would thus exile Colin from London and from any participation in the social gatherings at the Steinberg *salon* in Belgravia.

He went to Liverpool the following week. His mother tried not to show that she minded his leaving London, and his father was nonplussed but silenced over the sudden departure. He had taken a step towards freedom and independence. At first the novelty of new surroundings and work interested him, but after settling down to a steady routine the monotony of factory life soon made him restless. His colleagues were all much older than himself, a closely knit little group who, he felt, resented his intrusion. Petty jealousies dominated the designing-room and were fanned by Miss Morgan's enthusiasm for heir new artist. He was her golden-haired boy—possessed of such talent and originality! Fortunately he had kept his head and remained suitably modest as befitted a newcomer, but it did nothing to dispel the atmosphere of resentment. He kept to himself, at the risk of appearing standoffish, but he was not particularly happy—only grimly determined not to give in and return home defeated. One day his chance would come and he would seize it. Often he was lonely, especially during the long winter evenings when the thick sea mists seeped into the city from the docks. He would sit by the gas fire in his room and try to write amusing, gossipy letters to Kenneth and reassuring lines to his mother, who anxiously inquired after his health and comfort.

To put her mind at rest he had invented a home-from-home in which he was almost one of the landlady's family. It was just as well that his mother couldn't see or even visualise Mrs. Liffey, who had for years lived in a state of perpetual pregnancy and never tired of discussing her latest condition or previous confinements and miscarriages. Ideal accommodation had proved impossible to find, and as the house was reasonably clean and the food plentiful he had remained there, shutting himself off as much as he could from the exuberant but exhausting life of the Liffeys. They lived noisily and full-bloodedly on the ground floor—arguing and quarrelling and crying in an atmosphere of beer, whisky and Irish stew.

He was bored and lonely. He missed London, and Kenneth, even Osric, and longed for the backstage excitement of Covent Garden and the glittering *salon* of Maison Steinberg. For six months he had been starved of everything colourful and extravagant. His nature seemed to crave it, but confining it to regular *motifs* on a piece of fabric was not enough. He wanted to do something drastic, even outrageous—and quite unexpectedly the opportunity arose. Nearly every evening he had gone to the theatre or cinema, but with the former it had always been to see straight plays or musicals. Variety programmes didn't appeal to him, and it was only by chance that he happened to pass the Globe Music Hall, in a narrow side street. The theatre looked like an ancient Moorish palace, flanked by fish-and-chip shops. Normally he would not have bothered about the place, but the posters outside had made him stop to look at the photographs displayed near the entrance; they were fantastic pictures of the artists in the show, and bore such names as Terry Horsham, Bobby Williams and Harald Bronson—not to mention one of Jo Raye, dressed as the Queen of Sheba—all of whom he was later to know so well as

'Tessa,' 'Netta,' 'Magda' and 'Josie,' glamorous members of *The Merrie Belles*. He bought a ticket and went inside.

The show was even more surprising than the photographs. He admired the magnificent dresses and tried to ignore the dreadful scenery, which seemed to consist of bits and pieces from old pantomimes. The theatre was packed and the audience enjoyed every minute without turning a hair. One thing astonished him, however, when the curtains parted to reveal a grand piano and a pianist in regal velvet and diamonds whom he could have sworn was Claud Loveday. The long, aristocratic face and the mannerisms were the same, and when at the final curtain the company doffed their wigs there was no doubt about it.

Out in the street he consulted the programme again. The item was listed as 'Concerto. At the piano—LYDIA.' The thought of seeing someone from the 'old' life sent him hurrying round to the stage door, but on asking for Claud he was told that visitors were not allowed backstage. Disappointed, he was about to turn away when the inner swing door opened and a member of the company appeared, holding a wig and still wearing the finale costume, an off-the-shoulder crinoline gown. The strong light from a bare electric bulb emphasised the heavy, mask-like make-up, with its enormous false eyelashes, blue lids and exaggerated carmined mouth. The mask impression was further accentuated by the hair, flattened by the wearing of a wig.

"Any messages, George?" a rather husky voice inquired of the doorkeeper.

"Nothing tonight," the man answered.

"Ditched again." Then, as the doorkeeper went into his office: "Did you want to see anyone?"

"I—I wanted to see Claud—Lydia—" he began, stopping as the door opened again and another painted face, softer and rounder, peered out.

"Hurry up, Jo," said the newcomer. "Oh—sorry . . ."

"It's all right, Netta, he wants to see Claud. He hasn't gone yet, has he?"

"I shouldn't think so." Then, as somebody passed in the corridor behind, he called out: "Give Lady Loveday a shout, will you. Someone to see her."

"What name?" Jo asked.

"Ford. Colin Ford," he said, looking calmly at the two young men and fully aware of their critical gaze.

"I expect he'll be down in a minute," the round-faced boy said. "Come on, Jo, do you want to catch pneumonia? Good night." He gave a friendly smile and turned away.

Jo continued to stare, faintly amused, a wry smile twisting his mouth. "Are you a friend of Claud's?" he asked.

"I've met him before." He was polite but guarded.

"Oh." Jo sounded bored, and with a brief nod left him.

The orchestra players came out, followed by some stage hands, but there was no sign of Claud. A few minutes later, a grey-haired woman in a blouse and skirt and wearing a red hat poked her head round the door and frowned crossly at him. Over one arm she carried a dress of shimmering blue sequins. "Are you Mr. Ford? Mr. Loveday says will you wait in the pub—the saloon bar. It's on the corner. The Clarence Arms."

"Thank you."

"I wish they'd tell people about not having visitors," she grumbled, "the times I have to go up and down those stairs. There's enough to do without that." She crossed to the doorkeeper's office. "George—you forgot my Guinness tonight."

"Sorry, Mrs. Oldham," said George, "but I had a lot of phone calls in the interval. Couldn't get out."

"There ought to be a call-boy in a theatre this size—even if it is only a Number Two date."

"What do you mean by that? It's as good as any theatre in the country."

"Oh, is it? It's in the wrong position to start with—stuck down a back alley."

"It was good enough for Ellen Terry to appear in."

"Oh well, if you're going back as far as *that*..."

He left them, still arguing, and entered the Clarence Arms. When Claud appeared he was irritated to see that Jo and his friend were with him, and also a rather silly-looking boy with a pinched face and fair crimpy hair. Claud introduced them as Jo Raye, Bobby Williams and Terry Horsham. Offstage, Terry was just recognisable as the pink-and-white creature who had sung in a piercing soprano and thrown artificial roses into the front-row stalls.

"What are you doing in a dangerous city like Liverpool?" Claud inquired.

"I work here."

"My dear boy, how ghastly. The last time I saw you was in Belgravia, coming down a staircase and looking exactly like Lily Elsie. No doubt you're surprised to see *me,* looking like—well ... the Abbé Liszt in drag, perhaps. But tell me, what do you *do* up here? What? You don't—do you? In a factory with weavers? Yes, I will have another gin. Thank you. You should be moving in more glamorous circles. I mean—having seen you descending those stairs at Osric's, I expected you to be in Society by now. I must explain," he turned to the others, "that Colin was wearing an Edwardian ball dress."

"He'd look marvellous in drag!" Bobby exclaimed.

"Indeed he did," Claud went on, "much to our host's *chagrin* —delicious word ... poor Osric was looking his age in dove grey, which I think is such an unfortunate colour. Oh—now it's closing time. Shall we see you tomorrow, Colin?"

The next evening he sat in the front row of the stalls, and again each night for the rest of the week. By the Saturday he knew the show so well that, in an emergency, he felt he could have stepped quite easily into Bobby's or Jo's shoes. If only he could be up there with them! But how did one get into a show of this kind? He supposed that auditions were held, but when? And where? He would ask Claud. After all, Claud had more or less suggested that he should be doing something like this. The more he thought about it the more he became obsessed with the idea. He had got to know some of the company and liked them very much; they were cheerful and amusing; the show appeared to have a good reputation and there was nothing unsavoury about it. He would lose very little by giving up his job.

Claud was quite helpful when the subject was broached; but of course it wasn't all that simple, he explained. Dozens of people had tried to get in and failed—for reasons best known to the Management. It would mean going up to London and per- haps hanging about for several days before one got even as far as the office boy. ("Remind me to tell you about that office boy!" Claud said.) Gaiety Tours Ltd. was a hard nut to crack, especially for someone without experience. "Good luck to you, dear boy. We may yet see you in fairyland," were Claud's parting words.

A few days later he was waiting to see the business manager of Gaiety Tours at their suite of offices in Old Compton Street. He sat in a small, overheated room, and gazed at the rows of theatrical posters on the walls. In one corner, near the window, stood a large table with two telephones on it, behind which a dazzling chemical blonde accompanied herself on the typewriter with an orchestration of tinkling charm bracelets and swishing nylon. Frequent interruptions from the telephones caused her to pause and speak into the instruments with bored affectation and in a frightfully grand accent.

"Helleow. Gaiety Tours Ltd. Neow, I'm seow sorry, he's eowt. Eow—if you'll heowld on I'll get Mr. Spender on the other laine. Helleow, Mr. Spender—Miss Ceowlchester wants to kneow if she can change her appointment to faive-thirty. Neow, she's down for teow-thirty. Very well. Helleow, Miss Ceowlchester—faive-thirty will be faine. Thankyeow. Goodbay." And back to the typewriter.

Patiently he waited and wondered what was happening in the inner sanctum behind the door marked 'Private.' He speculated on what sort of man Mr. Spender might be; reasonably accommodating, he gathered, with regard to Miss Colchester, whoever she was. The door opened and the office boy, a sleek youth of about seventeen, entered with a tray of used coffee things. He tossed a stiffly bound play script on to the table.

"You can send this back," he said.

"Eow." The typist glanced at it, disdainfully.

"It's no good."

"Has he read it?"

"No. I told him it was no good."

"Is he free?"

"Yep."

The typist picked up a telephone. "Mr. Colin Ford is here. Very well. Mr. Spender will see you neow." She gave a cool nod towards the door.

He rose and went into the other room. Claud had warned him

not to be intimidated by its palatial atmosphere, and not to be nervous with Mr. Spender, who liked a confident approach—but his brisk entry was somewhat retarded by the thickness of the crimson pile carpet, and crossing to the big desk at the far end of the room was like trudging through a field of heather, out of which the furniture seemed to grow. Arriving at the desk, he smiled at Mr. Spender; or, more accurately, he smiled at the top of his head, for the business manager was shuffling through some papers and hadn't bothered to look up.

"Yes?" The head remained lowered, uninterested.

"You wanted to see me . . ." he began.

"Did I?" Mr. Spender at last looked up and stared at him rudely. It was an embarrassing, prolonged stare, but it gave him time to examine the details of the man's face: dark eyes darkly ringed; a coarse skin, greenish-grey in complexion; a sprawling fleshly nose and a sensual mouth; a head of thick, black hair; black hair, too, on the backs of his well-shaped hands, and in his ears and nostrils. A suggestion of brooding power emanated from him— something uncomfortable and disturbing, accentuated by the grating, forceful voice. His age was perhaps between forty-five and fifty. In spite of Claud's instructions he felt his confidence beginning to wane; Spender's almost hypnotic stare was boring into him—the dark-ringed eyes smouldering, probing, calculating, and penetrating him until he was forced to look away, his face flushed and burning.

"A very pretty blush," said Spender, sardonically. "Especially in this profession. Sit down. What decided you to come here? What makes you think you'd be any good to this show? You don't look the right type to me. You're too quiet."

"Mr. Spender—if you'll give me a chance—I could show you . . ."

"Yes. I know," Spender sneered. "I've had dozens of screaming little queens up here, peddling and flaunting themselves, but it doesn't get them anywhere."

"I don't happen to be that sort."

"Oh, no, of course not, you're the quiet type. Shy."

"I'm not in the least shy. I wouldn't have come here if I were."

"We'll soon find out about that. I've never heard of you before.

What experience have you had? None? That's no use to me. It's wasting my time—and yours."

"Look, Mr. Spender—I've been watching the show in Liverpool for the past week—and if you don't mind my saying so, the scenery——"

"Nobody's going to look at the scenery. It took five thousand pounds for the dresses, and that's quite enough. So shut up. What proof can you give me that you're any good?"

"Now? In here?"

"Of course in here, where the hell do you think I mean? I'm not hiring Drury Lane for a five-minute audition."

For the first time he noticed a grand piano by the window, but as he neither sang nor played it was difficult, under these conditions, to know what to do, as it really needed visual appeal to be effective. "I can't sing," he explained, "but I can dance and——"

"Yes, full of talent, by the sound of it. Let's see what you can look like. Stand up. Turn round. Well, I've seen them clumsier, but not much."

"These are hardly the clothes——"

"I was coming to that. What are your measurements?"

"I'm five feet six."

"Yes, yes, but the rest of you? Don't you know? Here——"

Spender opened a drawer in the desk and flung a tape measure at him. "Call them out."

With some difficulty he did so, and Spender jotted down the figures.

"That's all right. No deformities. Small waist and hips. We don't want big hips, it causes too much talk. I shall want to see your legs, too."

"But what about clothes? Do you want me to come back? I mean . . ."

"No, I don't want you to come back," Spender snapped. "I want to see you *now*."

"Oh. Do you mean you want me to . . ."

"My God. You won't have time for all this false modesty in a dressing-room with six people. How old are you?"

"Twenty."

"Done your National Service?"

"No. I wasn't passed fit at the time."

"That's one way of explaining it," Spender cryptically observed.

"Shall I . . ." He indicated his clothes.

"Yes, in a minute." Then, into the telephone: "Send Irving in."

This was going to be worse than he'd imagined; rather humiliating, too, having to undress in front of the office boy. Quickly he glanced round the room, hoping to find a screen or some curtains, but there was no visible place for retirement—unless he squeezed behind the grand piano.

Irving appeared, giving him an oblique, faintly amused look.

"Take these measurements," Spender ordered, "and get him fixed up. I'll give you ten minutes. And remove that silly grin from your face."

Irving obediently took the piece of paper. "All right." Then, speaking impassively: "This way."

He followed the boy to a door behind the desk. They crossed a small lobby and entered what looked like a theatre dressing-room. There was a mirror with lights round it, a table with a make-up box on it, and a row of theatrical costumes and dresses hanging from a rail in a deep recess.

"Now," said Irving, "we'll doll you up so's your own mother won't know you. Or will she? Ha-ha."

He was not sure whether the boy was being friendly or sarcastic.

"Let's see," Irving went on, consulting the measurements, "got a slim build, haven't you? What about this?" A pink, frilled creation was held up for inspection. "No? A bit sickly. Well, there's *this*." The familiar crinoline. "Needs falsies up top to keep it on."

He shook his head. He was not going to wear one of the chorus costumes.

"Hard to please, aren't you? Be quick. If we're too long the boss'll start thinking things. We've had some ripe customers in here before now. Phew! Not that you look that sort."

"Thanks, but I'm here to get a job. I'll wear this." It was a black moiré gown, with a backward-sweeping overskirt—the type of dress described in the fashion magazines as 'dramatic,' and usually worn with long gloves and the minimum of jewellery. It would look well with his blond hair and fair skin.

"Very sophisticated, that one," Irving nodded approvingly. "A bit of make-up and you'll look the goods."

He smiled. The boy seemed more friendly now. He carefully made-up his face; found some gloves in a drawer, and also earrings and a paste wristlet. Taking off his shoes, he stood up in his brief trunks while Irving slipped the dress over his head.

Irving gave a low wolf-whistle and stared at him. "Oh, lovely . . ." he said, "do you look beautiful." And his eyes goggled. "Let's arrange your hair a bit." Moist hands pulled at the curls. "You look a beaut. A real beaut. Oh boy . . . if only you were a girl. I'd go for you in a big way."

"You needn't bother," he said, moving away from the hot, excited look in Irving's eyes.

"You're dangerous," Irving said. "Come on." He led the way back to the lobby. From Spender's office came the sound of music. Someone was playing the piano. "Mavis. The typist," Irving explained. "Wait here. I'll tell them you're ready."

Nervously he waited. It seemed ridiculous to be standing here at eleven-thirty in the morning, dressed in a Paris model (without shoes) and with no idea of what was really expected of him. It was one thing to make an entrance on the stage—with the full panoply of lighting, scenery and orchestra—but quite another to enter an office in broad daylight and impress a business manager and a typist, even if the office boy's reaction had been so convincing. However, it was too late now to back out; Irving had returned and was holding open the door.

"Any special music?"

"What? Er—no—I mean—yes! Yes! Something gay." He thought quickly. *"The Merry Widow* waltz!"

"Right." Irving winked. *"The Merry Widow,* Mavis."

The music floated out to him. Mavis lacked Claud's touch and there was no staircase for him to come down, but now that the moment had arrived he swept boldly and determinedly into the room—to find the crimson carpet blazing in the light of a flood-lamp. The curtains were drawn, and beyond the circle of light Mavis's hair gleamed above the bulk of the grand piano.

Slowly he drifted round the room . . . the music quickened . . . he began whirling, faster and faster, black clouds of silk streaming behind him . . . he called out: "Irving! Dance! Dance!" He glided into Irving's arms. Swiftly, lightly, meltingly they danced. Again the music quickened. Faster and faster they turned. Dizzily, breathlessly . . . Irving's hair fell over his brow and his eyes closed . . . then suddenly Spender's harsh voice shouted over the music: "That's enough! That's enough! For God's sake!"

Abruptly the music stopped. Exhausted, Irving let him go. Mavis had risen and drawn back the curtains. The floodlamp went out. Motionless, he waited as Spender approached.

"All right, Irving, you can save your energy for the Hammersmith Palais. Go and have your lunch and don't be back late. And straighten your hair."

Irving looked reproachfully at Spender and silently brushed the hair from his brow.

"Go on. Get out."

With a set face the boy turned and left the room.

"That's all, Mavis."

The typist followed, her spiky heels leaving an indented trail in the pile carpet.

"When I want to see a double act," said Spender, "I'll send for one. I don't want my office boy used as a stooge."

"I'm sorry. He was only being helpful."

"Yes, and a bit too intimate. Irving doesn't want that sort of a encouragement."

"May I go now?" he asked, not wanting to start an argument.

"In a minute." Spender looked at him critically. "You're not bad. You could be made into something. You're not too damned bitchy. That's generally the trouble with you lot. Let's see your legs."

Feeling like a secretary applying for a job, he lifted the skirt, but Spender showed no signs of pleasure; he merely frowned, as if the legs on view belonged to a chair which was either badly made or else had woodworm.

"Mmm . . . All right. Get dressed." The verdict was noncommittal.

When he returned to the office Spender was seated at the desk.

"I'm willing to give you a trial. Mavis will hand you a contract when you go out. Read it carefully before you sign—you can take it away—and let me have it back tomorrow. You'll join the company this week—the stage director will rehearse you—and if you're any good at all you *might* appear in a scene or two the following date. And a word of warning—as a member of the company your behaviour will be under strict observation. We want no scandal or trouble with the police. There are to be no backstage visitors of *any* sort. No stage costumes or accessories may be worn other than at the theatre. You will supply your own make-up. There will be no indecencies or suggestiveness in performance. And with every costume a jock strap *must* be worn—always presuming that it's necessary. That's all. You can go."

Perfunctorily dismissed, he went into the outer office and collected his contract, politely bidding Mavis goodbye.

"Eow—goodbay." Mavis gave a lukewarm smile, her thoughts obviously elsewhere.

Thankfully he escaped, but on leaving the building he was surprised to see Irving standing in front of a shop window a few yards along the street. The boy must have been waiting for him, for as he emerged from the doorway a signal of recognition was given.

"Got your contract all right?" asked Irving, coming up to him.

"Yes," he answered wryly. "Mr. Spender didn't seem very enthusiastic."

"I shouldn't let him worry you," said Irving. "He always behaves like that. Got a down on everyone, 'specially your type." The boy's explanation was cheerfully frank, with an added apology: "No offence meant."

"I don't understand it. Why be connected with this kind of show if you dislike the people who are needed for it?"

"Shouldn't be surprised if he's fascinated by it, in a funny sort of way. You never know, these days, do you? Lots of people are a bit peculiar. Take my dad——"

"What?"

"Loves pinching bottoms. Even mine. Well, cheerio. Be seeing you." And Irving walked off towards Charing Cross Road.

It had certainly been a very odd morning, he reflected, but

at least he had achieved something. He had only to sign the contract, and by the end of the week he would be entering an entirely new and exciting life, although he was a little uneasy about his parents. He would have to keep it secret, but perhaps it would be fairly easy to do so, away from London; and then if he were found unsuitable he could probably get another job in Liverpool and nobody would be any the wiser. He studied the contract—noting that he would have to become a member of the Actors' Equity Association—and after lunch he went to their offices, where they were most obliging and helpful and did *not* ask him to undress and show them his legs. He signed and posted the contract to Mr. Spender, and caught the next train up to Liverpool.

Bronwen Morgan was furious when he gave in his notice, and all her former acclamations of his brilliance and talent and charm were instantly forgotten. A complete volte-face was effected in a matter of seconds. In a towering rage she stamped around her office, waving her arms, spilling ash on to her bosom, and at one point of her gyrations accidentally setting alight a bale of cloth with a carelessly dropped cigarette end. She accused him of disloyalty and treachery; she pointed out how she had saved him from prostituting his art, how he had flung back into her face her great faith in him; and in the next breath she condemned him as a no-good fake, a miserable little upstart who had betrayed her kindness of heart. In a final hoarse scream of invective—expressed somewhat inaccurately, owing to her loss of control and her ill command of the English language—she called him an 'inversion' and a 'feminine little puff.' Angrily he left her while she was endeavouring to suppress the miniature conflagration which again threatened the unfortunate bale of material. He wondered whether she would have let it burn had she realised it was one of his own designs.

Well, he thought, that was that. All that remained was the settling up with the Liffeys and the sending of a telegram to Claud, announcing his imminent arrival as a member of the *Merrie Belles* company. Whatever was in store for him, it could surely not be more surprising than the experience he had undergone in the business manager's office of Gaiety Tours Ltd.

★

As if suddenly startled, Colin glanced out of the window. The tramcar had gone beyond his stop and had nearly reached the end of its run at Morningside. For the last ten minutes he had been on a very different journey—a visit to his recent past—and it still seemed to him like a story told about some person other than himself. A strange pattern of events, not yet completed, and the way things were going anything could happen. And probably would, too! He hurriedly got off the tram and began walking back to Miss Andrews' boarding house. After last night's nervous tension and lack of sleep, he felt extremely tired, but remembered that he had given up his bed to Jock, and that if he wanted to lie down after lunch it would have to be on the settee. It was going to be difficult, getting used to the idea of sharing a room, and he was also a little uneasy about the hints and warnings which 'Josie' had casually dropped. The implication that there was something strange and sinister about Jock was nonsense. Or at least he hoped it was. Jock's behaviour last night, after the police had questioned them, was rather suspicious, but then that might have been due to his illness—he was overwrought and it could be a natural reaction after weeks of unhappiness and tension. Anyway, he reassured himself, the police had been satisfied with their answers, so perhaps there was no need to worry.

On reaching 'Glen Garry,' he went upstairs and entered the bed-sitting-room. Jock appeared to be asleep in an arm-chair near the window, and he was wearing an old pair of flannel trousers and a thick navy blue jersey. The tension was eased from his face and body; it was the first time he had seen him looking relaxed, and somehow much younger, but as he stood watching him Jock opened his eyes and the familiar guarded expression returned, and the obstinate tightening of the mouth. *Now* what have I done wrong? he thought, waiting for him to speak.

"I didna hear ye come in. Have ye stood there watching me?"

"No. I'm sorry if I woke you up."

"It's all right," Jock murmured. He rose and stared at Colin less resentfully, but still with a kind of pained suspicion. "I was waiting for ye. The doctor said I could get up. I'm feeling better."

"That's good. I've been down to the theatre."

"Oh. Did they—did they say anything aboot—aboot last night?"

"There was no one there—only Jo. They hardly noticed I'd gone. Something else happened at the theatre. Apparently Butch got into some trouble—I don't know what it was—and they . . ."

"Butch?" Jock frowned. "What do ye mean? What's he done?"

"I don't know. The police came for him." Again Colin saw the frightened look come into Jock's eyes. "It's a rotten thing to happen, I know, but there was always something funny about Butch—well . . ."

"What's he done?" Jock repeated tensely.

"Oh . . . you know what he's like. They've probably been watching him—or somebody's reported him."

"Aye. The poor devil . . . the poor devil . . ."

Colin was startled by the note of hopelessness and despair in Jock's voice. "I didn't think you'd feel so sorry for him," he said.

"It—it could have been any one of us."

"Don't be absurd. Butch isn't really one of us at all."

"If it had happened to anyone else, would ye have said that?"

"I don't think it's likely to. We're not such fools."

"But would ye have pity?"

"Yes, of course I would, Jock. What's the matter with you?" Seeing the agitation in Jock's face, he put out a hand and gently touched his cheek, feeling him tremble. And then his wrist was seized tightly, drawing his hand away. "Jock—you're hurting me . . ."

"Ye're a torment to me. I'm sorry." Jock released Colin's wrist. "I won't harm ye. I'll no touch ye again. I shouldna hae touched ye now, only . . ."

"I don't understand you. After what you said last night—I thought I meant something to you . . ."

"Ye mean everything to me." Jock sounded harsh, almost angry.

"You have an odd way of showing it. But I'm not a stuffed dummy, Jock, or someone on a pedestal. You needn't be afraid of me."

"It's not yersel' I'm afraid of."

"Well, then . . . don't look so miserable." Colin smiled, and pressed his hand on the woollen jersey. Jock's heart was beating rapidly. They stared at each other. He felt Jock's hands shaking as they gripped his arms; feel his breath on his face—and then the swift withdrawal as a brisk tapping sounded on the door.

Miss Andrews entered with a loaded tray, and with a pink, gummy smile nodded to them brightly and began laying the table carefully and very slowly. Colin watched her impatiently. Why didn't she go, instead of fiddling about with the cruet like that? But he knew it didn't matter now how long she took. The moment was spoiled. Jock had moved away and was staring out of the window; he could tell by the set of his head and shoulders that he was again on the defensive, that the spell was broken and a barrier between them.

When at last Miss Andrews had gone, he spoke quietly. "We— we'd better have lunch, Jock." It was a harmless enough remark, but Jock's sudden vehemence surprised him.

"Lunch? How can ye think about lunch? Och—will ye try to be serious just for a minute. Mebbe ye canna see it as I do . . ."

"See what?"

"That there'll be no peace for us. We canna be what we are— the police, the landlady, everybody—they'll no' let us alone!"

"That's exaggerating a bit. Of course it's difficult sometimes, but we've always known it and had to face it. We've just got to be strong enough, that's all. Unless you don't think it's worth it."

"Och, no, ye mustna say that." Jock looked alarmed. "But if ye'll take no warning of the harm I might do to ye . . . if anything should go wrong I'll—— Ye'll no' forgive me if I hurt ye. Some-times love can hurt—when it's sae strong as ma own. I might kill ye wi' love."

"I'll risk it," Colin answered lightly. But what, he thought, did Jock mean? It sounded almost as though he were trying to put him off. Perhaps Jo had been right, after all, and Jock *was* pecu-liar . . . it seemed strange, the way he talked about love and yet appeared frightened of making the least move. Was he a bit shy, or funny in some way about sex? There were lots of people like that; ideal subjects for case-books but very tiresome to live with. And if he's a masochist, he thought grimly, God help me! But then masochists didn't kill you with love—they only exasperated you while they tortured themselves. He just didn't know what was the matter with Jock. Probably repression or some sort of guilt-complex—he sighed—and he would have to be very tactful and patient with him. And firm, of course, when he became too difficult.

"We'd better eat while the food's still warm," he said, moving to the table.

"I canna eat anything, thanks."

"Just as you like. I'm hungry."

Jock flung himself down on to the bed and lay staring at the ceiling, his mind and his body in conflict. Love, fear and shame struggled unhappily within him. He could not tell Colin the truth and risk losing him; the boy could so easily hate him. That was the terrible thing. He could see it so clearly. And he loved him . . . It was deep and painful and he almost resented the fact.

Colin awoke from a heavy, dreamless sleep. He looked at his watch, then abruptly sat up. It was half-past five and he had to be at the theatre not later than six o'clock. Meaning to have about an hour's rest, he had lain on the settee after lunch and immediately dropped off; but nobody had called him, either with a cup of tea or to tell him what time it was. Miss Andrews must have gone out, and presumably Jock had felt as tired as himself and gone on sleeping. Quickly he rose and crossed to the bed, but stopped in surprise on finding it empty. The coverlet had been neatly replaced and Jock's woollen jersey and flannels were folded over the back of a chair. His outdoor shoes and raincoat were missing, also his wallet and loose change from the bedside table. But why had he disappeared like this, without saying anything? And where was he? The doctor had told Jock to stay in quietly and not attempt to do two shows this evening, and now like a fool he'd gone out somewhere, not even troubling to leave a message. It was getting late, however, and he couldn't wait for him to come back.

After a hurried wash he went downstairs and found Miss Andrews in the kitchen. No, she informed him, she had not heard or seen Mr. Macmillan leave, and anyway she had been out most of the afternoon and it really was silly of him to disregard the doctor's orders like that. "He'll do himsel' no good," she said, stabbing a griddle cake with a skewer. "Ye canna play aboot wi' yer health and expect no consequences."

Colin left the house and walked to the tram stop, feeling annoyed with Jock and anxious as well. There were two performances to get through, and probably a sharp reprimand from the stage director about his absence last night, as well as the worry of wondering where Jock was and what he was doing. Supposing he was ill and feverish, wandering about somewhere ... or getting drunk on an empty stomach ... involved in a fight, an accident ... perhaps throwing himself into the river ... there were all kinds of alarming possibilities. By the end of the tram-ride he had worked himself up into a thoroughly nervous state, and instead of eagerly approaching the evening ahead of him he entered the stage door feeling depressed and on edge. His low spirits were not helped, either, by the subdued atmosphere which pervaded the dressing-room corridors. Usually, before a performance, there was a great deal of noise from everybody and a lot of running in and out of rooms in various stages of undress; but tonight the marked absence of hilarity seemed strangely disquieting. It was as if the closing notice of the show had gone up—dim murmurings came from behind closed doors, like hushed, whispering voices in church. Obviously they had not yet recovered from Butch's misfortune; although none of them had really liked him, it had affected them all.

He paused at Jock's door, half hopeful of finding him, but the room was dark and empty. Passing his own door he came to 'Magda's' room. He must find out whether anyone had news of Jock. But 'Magda'? ... He decided against it. 'Magda' wasn't particularly sympathetic, and anyway disliked Jock, who had rudely spurned his overtures of friendship. Finally, coming to the last room on the corridor, he knocked and went in.

'Tessa' looked up, rather wanly and minus one false eyelash, which gave his face a peculiar, lop-sided expression. Traces of recent tears had hurriedly been wiped away and he spoke breathlessly. "Oh, come in, dear. You're late tonight." He sniffed and spat into the mascara box. "I feel terrible. I think my voice is going again. I mustn't talk too loudly. I'm so upset about Jimmy ... it's so unfair to *us* that some men can switch about like that ... I mean, I've just been treated as if I were the 'other woman' ... Oh, hell, why won't this thing stick? Aren't you going to get changed?"

"Yes. Tessa, have you seen Jock anywhere?"

"No. Why? Not for the last half-hour—they haven't called the half yet, have they?"

"You mean you've seen him *here?*"

"Yes, dear, of course. At the stage door when I came in. What's the matter? I can't find my ear-rings anywhere."

"He hasn't been in his room."

"Well, I shouldn't worry, he's not on until nearly seven o'clock. He's probably gone out to get a bottle of whisky or something."

"I hope you're right. He's been ill and I'm rather worried."

"It's no good worrying about *Jock,* dear, he's very much a lone wolf."

"What do you mean?"

"Well," said 'Tessa,' peering short-sightedly into a hand mirror, "practically everybody in the company has tried to be friendly with him, but he just doesn't seem to *want* friends. I don't understand people like that. I should think he's a bit cruel, wouldn't you? Still, he can't be all *that* bad, can he, as you've shared a dressing-room with him. I'm sure Magda's borrowed my ear-rings again . . . honestly, she's so spiteful these days . . ."

As 'Tessa' prattled on, Colin opened the door. The half-hour was called through the speaker. He would have to get dressed. Perhaps Jock had come in by now. Once more he noticed the silence in the corridor. "Everyone's so quiet tonight . . ."

"I know, isn't it awful? *They're* here again."

"Who? The Management?"

"No. The police. Oh—of course you weren't here last night when it happened . . ."

"You mean about Butch? Jo told me this morning."

"I suppose they'll question us again. Why they have to, just because Butch . . . And fancy doing it while we're dressed up like this!"

"Were they—were they here when you saw Jock?" He tried to sound unconcerned; Jock might have gone out only for a few minutes. And yet . . . "Did Jock see them?" he asked.

"I suppose so. He must have done."

"Oh. I must go."

As he left 'Tessa,' he saw Mrs. Oldham approaching, her arms loaded with costumes. Beneath a hat of pale pink feathers her face, after bending over a hot ironing-board for the best part of an hour, looked flushed and shining. She saw him and gave an abrupt nod.

"Mrs. Oldham—have you seen Jock?"

"No, I haven't. I've been far too busy in the wardrobe to have seen anyone. All these dresses—I don't know what people do with them—creased and torn and flung down anywhere after the show. The time it's taken—and what with all these stairs . . ."

Colin hurried down to the stage door.

"Aye," said the doorkeeper, "Mr. Macmillan's been gone a guid while—but I saw him yon, wi' the stage director—so he'll no' be gone wi'out telling." He gestured towards the door which led on to the stage.

Thanking him, Colin went to find Harry Archer. He discovered him in the property room, looking slightly dyspeptic and holding a saucepan over a gas ring. The cat, Duncan, stood on the table, with his head almost in the pan. An odour of boiled fish mingled unpleasantly with the smell of paint and size which permanently filled the cluttered and airless little room.

"Yes? What is it?" Harry looked up. "Oh—it's you. I've got a bone to pick with you, and it's not a fishbone, either. If it wasn't for the trouble we've having already you'd be up on the carpet, good and proper. Where did you get to last night?" He turned off the gas and smacked away Duncan's paw as it tentatively hovered over the pan of fish. "Leave it alone, it's too hot. Well?"

"I'm sorry," said Colin. "I didn't want to miss a performance but—but I suddenly felt terrible and couldn't go on."

"Oh. I see." Harry obviously didn't believe him, but something else appeared to be worrying him, and he dismissed the matter with a curt "Don't let it happen again," and began turning out the fish on to an enamelled plate. Duncan greedily pushed his face into it, regardless of the heat.

"What are you hanging about for? If you don't get dressed quickly you're going to miss another performance, aren't you?"

"I wanted to ask you about Jock. Someone said they'd seen him here—but the doctor told him not to go on tonight . . ."

"Yes, and so did I. I sent him home. The knife-throwing act's out and Claud's doing an extra solo instead. You'll all have to be on your toes, or else . . ."

"Jock could have sent a message by me—he needn't have come himself to tell you. We're in the same digs."

"I don't know about that, but he didn't look too good to me. Very nervous. Anyway, he seemed glad to go—tore out of my office in a great hurry."

"Oh . . . What's all this about the police being here again?"

"Just routine." Harry sounded disgusted. "The trouble I have with this show . . . I've tried to hush things up, but if the boss gets to hear about it—or our fine friend Mr. Spender . . . And as for Butch . . . some mothers have them all right, don't they? I have to be a ruddy nursemaid to their children."

"We're not all like Butch, you know."

"No." Harry looked almost sympathetic for a moment. "You're not a bad lot on the whole—but, my God, I'd have far less to worry about if I were handling a tour of *Naughty Nudes* or some such show."

"We'll try not to let you down," said Colin, and without any further mention of Jock returned to his dressing-room. What did it all mean? Was Jock really ill, or shamming? Had he intended to appear tonight, but when seeing the police hastily disappeared? It seemed suspiciously like it, and frightening to think that Jock might have been concerned in some shady business at some time and was now on the run. Perhaps joining the company to escape detection. Whatever it was, he had no desire to become involved himself.

"Quarter of an hour, please."

The voice from the loudspeaker startled him. Preoccupied with his thoughts, he hadn't even started to make up. He had never felt less like giving a performance, but at least it was a good thing that he had so many costume changes during the evening—it would probably keep his mind off Jock. A nuisance, though, that there wasn't a telephone at 'Glen Garry.' He could have rung through in the interval, to find out if Jock had returned to the house . . .

Colin left the theatre with 'Josie' and 'Netta.' Although both performances had gone smoothly enough, and to full houses, they were glad to get away from the nervous tension which had persisted throughout the evening. It was an unpleasant experience, having the police backstage and wondering whether they were all going to be rounded up after the show and taken away in a Black Maria. Unfortunately, it was 'Josie' and 'Netta' who had borne the worst of it, owing to their having shared their dressing-room with Butch. Presumably they had acquitted themselves well during a gruelling interrogation—merely by corroborating their evidence of the previous night (which stressed the fact that neither of them knew anything at all about the accused)—for the police had immediately departed, leaving them to swear that never again would they share a dressing-room with anybody, however small the theatre might be.

'Josie' was still fuming as they walked to the tram stop. "It takes a lot to embarrass *me*—but really, the questions! Even Dr. Kinsey would have blanched. I'm surprised we weren't asked to strip and cough and say 'ah'!"

"The older one was rather nice," said 'Netta' mildly.

"You *would* notice that! His eyes were too small and he had hands like bunches of bananas."

Colin laughed but made no comment. He was glad for their sakes that they had emerged fairly harmlessly from the ordeal, and relieved that he had not been interviewed himself. He couldn't help thinking uneasily of what it might have been like had Jock been there. As it was, he was quite worried enough about his own immediate problems—whether to keep silent or question Jock with regard to his movements.

"Well, we must get back and have our Scotch salmon and cold chicken," said 'Josie.' "Our landlady is a genius at making it taste exactly like dried haddock and spam. It even looks like it, too. Isn't it strange? You ought to see our landlady—po-faced Annie Laurie we call her, if you know what I mean. Colin, are you listening or have you gone into a trance?"

"I'm sorry. I was thinking."

"About Jock, I expect," said 'Netta.'

"Yes, I was."

"Now don't tell me you've quarrelled already," said 'Josie.'

"No. I'm worried about him. He's—he's in the same digs with me, now."

"Oh. I didn't know. I see." 'Josie' nodded sagely. "He's not too well, is he?"

"Is he worse?" asked 'Netta.'

"I—I don't know—I'm just a bit anxious. He—he's so . . ." It was difficult to explain his fears to them.

"He can't be all that bad, if he came out," said 'Josie.' "I shouldn't worry too much, it just isn't worth it. Jock's always been self-centred; he won't thank you for it."

"Don't be silly, Jo," 'Netta' reproved.

"I'm only being truthful. You've got to be realistic about things. If we all faced up to what other people are, and what we are ourselves . . ."

"I don't know what you're talking about," said 'Netta,' "and I don't think you do, either. Don't listen, Colin."

"You take my advice," 'Josie' went on, "and tell Jock not to be a spoil-sport. Tell him that if he doesn't buck up his ideas you'll expose his secret."

"What secret?"

"Oh, *any* secret. Everybody's got at least one. You'd be surprised how it works."

"And what," asked 'Netta,' "is yours?"

"Well—" 'Josie' lowered his voice, "I oughtn't to tell you really—but sometimes I dress up in women's clothes."

"Is that so? Mmm. Very interesting. Why don't you consult your psychiatrist?"

"*Consult* him? He designs my gowns for me! Here's our tram." 'Josie' turned to Colin. "Now, not to worry. If you want us, you know where we are—but don't come screaming through the streets in your nightie—put something on first."

Hearing the front door close, Colin raised his head and stared into the darkness. He had lain awake for a long time, and during the past hour had risen more than once from the settee to peer out of the window. At first he had been angry and disappointed by Jock's absence, then alarmed when the street lights went out and there was still no sign of him. He could do nothing but wait, knowing it would be useless to go out and search. The pubs had closed while he was at the theatre and he could not walk every street in the city on the off-chance of finding him. Glancing at the luminous dial of his watch, he saw that it was nearly one o'clock. Someone had stopped, outside the door, and as he waited tensely he heard him moving away and the sound of the bathroom door opening. Perhaps it was one of the other lodgers; but then he remembered Miss Andrews saying that they all went to bed very early. As he hesitated, wondering whether to switch on the light, the footsteps sounded once more on the landing and the handle of the door squeaked slightly and turned. He pressed the switch. The light dazzled him for a moment, and then he saw Jock leaning against the door panel with one hand shading his eyes from the glare. He seemed to be dazed and startled by the unexpected brightness, and as he moved forward into the room, letting his hand fall away, he swayed and stumbled on the edge of the carpet. Colin stiffened, noticing at once the bleary-eyed expression and flushed cheeks.

"Where on earth have you been?" He spoke sharply and coldly, hoping it would have a sobering effect.

"I've been wi' friends ... wi' friends ... to the pictures ..." Jock's eyes tried to focus on him.

"Don't be silly. You've been drinking."

"Och, I'm no' drunk ..."

"I didn't say you were drunk. I said you'd been drinking."

"Mebbe. Ye canna be un—unsociable wi' friends."

"You can draw the line somewhere. Who were they?"

"That's ma own business."

"All right. You needn't tell me."

"If—if ye're suggesting I havena any friends ... let me tell ye I have sae many friends—that I can do wi'out ye ..." Jock came towards him unsteadily.

"I see. And why did you tell Harry you were going home because you were ill? If you are, it's stupid to go round the pubs. In any case they closed hours ago."

"Och, will ye shut up! Ye're no' ma keeper."

"No. I'm not. But I was worried, and if anything happened to you ..."

"I was in guid company." Jock looked at him, stubbornly.

"Were you?"

"Aye. We went dancing."

"Dancing?" Colin stared at him in surprise. "Where?"

"I canna remember the name of the place. We didna stay long. It was awfu' hot there."

Whoever Jock had been with, Colin could no longer remain disinterested. "But—but who did you dance with?"

"A girl."

"Obviously. I didn't imagine otherwise, in Edinburgh. I hope you enjoyed it. What about your other friends?"

"Oh . . . they were awa' to Leith . . ."

"You mean you went to this—this dance place alone? And just danced with anybody?"

"No. I went wi' a girl from the pub."

"Did you know her?"

"I picked her up. She was a tart."

"I don't think I want to hear any more." He watched Jock suddenly reel towards him, and frightened that he would fall over rose from the settee and put out a steadying hand. Jock seized his arm and swayed against him.

"D'ye think I'm no' man enough to go wi' a prostitute? I could go wi' anyone I want and ye'll nae stop me."

"Did you go back with her? Jock, for heaven's sake stand up. Well? Did you?"

"No." Jock closed his eyes and leaned heavily on him. "I didna go to the dance, I was lying to ye . . . I said it to make ye jealous."

"Who *were* you with?"

"Wi' mysel' . . . och, I'm sae drunk, Colin . . . I couldna help it . . . when ye're lonely . . . it'll no' happen again, I promise ye . . ."

"I think you'd better go to bed and sleep it off. I still don't understand why you went to the theatre, and then avoided me. If you weren't ill, what made you leave like that?"

"That's ma own affair." Jock's mouth tightened.

Colin realised it was hopeless to question him further; it was hardly the time to employ the shock tactics which 'Josie' had suggested. Gently he removed Jock's hand and returned to the settee. He was tired and upset and wanted only to close his eyes and go to sleep. He had had more than enough to contend with and was beginning to feel slightly hysterical. He had made a ghastly mistake in thinking that he could help Jock . . . one couldn't alter people like that . . . he should have listened to the repeated warnings of the others. Lying down, he pressed the switch and cut off the glare of light above him.

Then, in the darkness, Jock seized his arms and drew him up. He struck out, hitting Jock's face. For a moment they fought. Angrily he pushed Jock from him, and heard him stumble against the low table. The water-jug and glass crashed to the floor. "Oh Christ . . ." Jock moaned. "Oh Christ . . . I'm sae drunk . . ." And he stumbled across the room to his own bed.

At nine o'clock Miss Andrews briskly entered with the breakfast tray, arousing Colin with her usual morning hustle. Depositing the tray on the table, she crossed to the window and drew back the curtains with a sharp, rattling sound. Pausing long enough to adjust the position of a chair and straighten a crooked antimacassar which offended her sense of order and neatness, she returned to the table and hurriedly spread a white cloth over it. Her air of determination and haste made the not unduly late breakfast-time of nine o'clock seem like midday; it was her way of hinting that people should be up and about and not lingering in bed.

"Good morning, Miss Andrews."

"Och, you're awake, then? It's late."

"I didn't sleep very well." He yawned and sat up. "Is that sunlight, out there?"

"Aye, it is that. It's a beautiful morning—the wind's a wee bit keen but it's dry." Then, accusingly: "My, it's awful stuffy in here—no wonder ye canna sleep properly, without a breath of God's clean air. The window's shut tight, I wouldna be surprised."

With little clicking noises of disapproval, she lowered the top pane a few inches, and with a suspicious frown surveyed the room, sniffing loudly. He knew at once what she was thinking, and hastily cast a surreptitious glance in the same direction. Fortunately, as far as he could see, there were no empty whisky bottles lying about. He heaved a sigh of relief. It was too early in the day to listen to a temperance lecture by Miss Andrews. Then he noticed that the bed was empty.

"Where's Mr. Macmillan?"

"He's having a bath." Miss Andrews's eyes avoided his own, and after a moment's uneasy shifting fixed their stare high up on the wall, between the picture rail and the ceiling. Her expression clearly indicated that she was about to mention something which she found rather distasteful. "I hope, Mr. Ford," she said, "that your friend will not be making a disturbance every night when he comes in. I made an exception, taking him in and letting him share your room, because he was ill—but I have to think of my regular boarders. It's not my way to suggest things, but—it was awful late when he came in—and while I wouldn't like to say that he was not—well—quite himself . . . I would rather not have the responsibility. All my people have been with me a long time—they know what to expect. It's homely, nothing fancy, and they appreciate it because it's quiet. Aye, that's always been a great source of pride with me—a quiet, homely atmosphere. It may not suit some, but I've had no complaints until now."

"No, of course not," Colin murmured.

"Mr. Galbraith, my ground-floor front, was very difficult this morning. Complained about the noise when your friend came in. Bumping on the stairs, he said, and a great deal of talking going on for a long time afterwards. And something falling to the floor, he said, right above his head . . . I canna think what it could be, but it made him jump and think mebbe there was a burglar about the house . . . the poor gentleman has a weak heart, you know. Well, now, it would never do to have the place talked about, would it? I trust ye'll tell yer friend to be more considerate."

"I'll do my best. I'm sorry we disturbed you. It was just that he was very upset yesterday, about—about something . . . and then, being ill . . ."

"Aye. It's a great pity, a young man like that . . ." Miss Andrews looked at him and her face softened. "Ye're only a wee boy yerself—it's not the right influence for ye."

"Don't worry, Miss Andrews. I can take care of myself."

"Well, I hope ye can. There's an awful lot of temptation

these days for a young person. Especially in the theatrical profession." She shook her head sadly. "I must be away. Breakfast is all ready. Sausages and a wee bit of bacon. Goodbye for now." Miss Andrews hurried from the room, without seeing the broken water-jug lying near the settee.

He put on his dressing-gown and went to the table as the door opened and Jock entered, his hair curling and damp from the steam of the bath. Together they sat down to breakfast, and Colin looked quickly at Jock's face. Apart from the tiredness of his eyes, and faintly dark smudges beneath them, there were no traces of the previous night's dissipation.

"You look better this morning, Jock."

"Aye. Aye, I am." Jock smiled nervously and began pouring out the tea. Then, after a short silence: "Colin . . ."

"Yes?"

"Will ye—will ye try to understand something? I think I was mad last night. Will ye forgive me—for hurting ye like that? I canna remember what I said to ye, but I'm ashamed all right . . . If I frightened ye—ye'll understand it was the drink?"

"Yes, Jock, I know. Let's forget about the whole thing, shall we?"

"No, I canna forget it—ye've every right to hate me or no' speak to me again. I could just crawl away like an animal, out of sight . . ."

"Jock, please don't be so humble, there's no need."

"I'm no good to ye. Something gets inside me . . . mebbe it's the devil himsel'—and I have to fight—ye don't know how strong it is . . . I'm sae frightened I'll no' fight it . . ."

"Jock—look—I think I know what you mean. I know some people find it difficult to—to control. We're not all alike. But aren't you exaggerating things a bit—letting it get out of proportion? Creating a guilt complex for yourself?"

Jock looked at him despairingly and lapsed into silence again. When they had finished breakfast, Colin rose.

"I'll shave now and have a bath. It's a lovely morning. If you like, we'll go out today and have a look round. I've hardly seen anything of Edinburgh."

"Aye. We'll do that." Jock sounded grateful; and Colin, feeling that the situation might be a little easier now, went off to the bathroom.

Jock sat alone at the table. He lit a cigarette, his hand shaking as he held the match, and suddenly felt weak and tired. The bath must have been too hot and its immediate tonic effect was wearing off. If only he could have a drink . . . just a small one . . . and then he'd be all right. But the whisky bottle he'd hidden in the wardrobe was empty; he'd finished it yesterday, before going out and while Colin was asleep. Anyway, he mustn't start drinking again. Not after last night. Although a few drinks did give him courage, he'd gone the wrong way about it by resorting to force. It was a shameful thing to do, even if being drunk was the only solution for releasing the fear which held him in chains—the fear of added guilt to an already burdened conscience. If he could be sure of Colin's love, perhaps in time there would be no need to feel guilty; their happiness and trust in one another would erase all shadows of the past. But until then, what was he to do? And was there just a small gleam of hope in the fact that Colin had forgiven him for last night and seemed to want his company today? They would be together the whole day . . . and nothing must spoil it.

In a more cheerful frame of mind, he began dressing.

With Colin, he had only just entered the bar—both of them relieved to get out of the blustering wind which swept down Waverley Steps—when the swing door opened again to admit a stranger. He was immediately struck by the man's red hair, and by the breathless, eager manner of his entry. Colin had gone up to the bar counter to order drinks, and had not noticed this new arrival. He watched the man, whose gaze swiftly ranged over the tables and then alighted on the people at the bar. He saw him smile and go towards the counter. He stared, in amazement, as the man lightly tapped Colin's shoulder and spoke to him. The look of surprised recognition which slowly lighted the boy's face—turning from astonishment into warm delight—cut into his heart like a knife.

CHAPTER 6

"Colin, this is wonderful! The last person on earth I expected to see up here . . ." Alan Kendrick spoke excitedly, hardly able to contain the intense pleasure he felt at this long-awaited meeting. Entirely forgetting his surroundings and the other people in the bar, he gazed at Colin with almost embarrassing appraisal, absorbing every detail of his appearance with a lively and warm regard. Then, simultaneously, they both started to speak—broke off, and laughed.

"This calls for a drink," said Alan. "What would you like? Gin and ginger ale? Right. We'll sit down. We can talk better."

"Yes, but I'm with somebody . . ." Colin indicated Jock.

Alan looked round and saw a dark-haired man at one of the tables. He was impressed by the handsome, brooding face—although at the moment it seemed to be rather grimly set. He remembered, then, seeing him at the top of the Steps with Colin. "Oh. He won't mind if I join you, will he? What does he drink?"

"Whisky," said Colin, noticing Alan's momentary look of disappointment at Jock's presence. They collected the drinks and moved to the table. "Jock, this is Sergeant Kendrick—I mean Alan. I've never called you *Mister* Kendrick before—it seems funny. Jock Macmillan."

"Hope you don't mind my barging in?" Alan apologised. "Only I haven't seen Colin for years."

"He's an old friend of the family," explained Colin.

"Aye, it's all right," said Jock solemnly, as they shook hands.

"It's amazing, seeing you like this." Alan gave Colin a friendly smile. "I've got hundreds of questions to ask—it's difficult to know where to start. What are you doing now? Are you in Edinburgh for long?"

"No. Only this week."

"How are your mother and father? Are they with you?"

"No, I've been away from home some time—after leaving art

school. I've been designing for textiles—working in Liverpool . . ."

"That doesn't surprise me. I remember you used to draw and paint. Very well, too."

"Yes, you gave me a paint-box. I've still got it."

"Good Lord, it was ages ago—so was our last meeting—ten years at least. I've often thought about you all. What about your sister? Laura. How is she?"

"Much the same," Colin said dryly. "She's married, with two children."

"Oh, *is* she? But what are you doing up here? Are you on business or something?"

"Do you live in Edinburgh now?" Colin broke in. He was not certain as to the best way of explaining things to Alan, and thought it wiser to avoid the subject.

"Yes," said Alan, "I've got quite a good job. I *was* living in London for a time. Look—you must come and have dinner one evening. I'd like you to meet Julia."

"Julia? Is that your—your wife?"

"No, I'm not married or anything. She's a relation of Father's. Julia Douglas. A widow. I think you'd like her. It's a nice house, too. Across the Meadows, behind the Royal Infirmary."

Was there any significance to that "or anything," Colin wondered. But it was silly to jump to conclusions; it was a habit he and the others had, hopefully imagining that nearly everyone else was the same as themselves, and certainly in Alan's appearance there was nothing to suggest it. Although, if it came to that, Jock didn't look obvious, either. But Alan *had* gazed at him in a very affectionate way . . . unless, of course, his regard still retained the 'older brother' solicitude of the past? There was also the fact that he was still, presumably, unattached—and he must be getting on for forty, even if he didn't look anything like it. He seemed younger now than the childhood recollection of him; but then, to a child, anybody over twenty would be considered old. And thinking about it now, Alan had been rather quiet and serious in those days. Very dependable but somewhat grave, in contrast to the present air of boyishness and good humour. Understandably, there couldn't have been very much for him to laugh about during the war.

Looking at Colin, Alan was thinking along similar lines—comparing his impressions of the schoolboy with the grown-up appearance of the young man now facing him across the table. As he had imagined, Colin was remarkably good-looking, almost too much so, if that were possible; but there was something in the calm beauty of his features which he could not identify. It had no connection with the child he remembered, and it was not the expected difference wrought by maturity. In spite of such pleasing physical attributes, there was something missing. Now that the first excitement of meeting was over, he was puzzled and a little worried by it. Nor was he unaware of the silent tension of the dark-haired Scotsman who sat with them, looking so stern and unhappy. Who was he? A friend or just an acquaintance? It was difficult to tell, as Colin had totally ignored his presence after the introductions had been made. He was impatient to know more, for already he was beginning to wonder about Colin and longed to talk to him alone, even at the risk of making an embarrassing mistake.

"Another drink, Alan?"

"Oh—no, thanks." Alan looked at his watch. "I shall have to go now—but you will come to dinner, won't you?"

"I—I can't manage the evenings," Colin answered hastily. "May I come to lunch or tea?"

"Yes, of course. *Both,* if you like." Now why, thought Alan, can't he manage the evenings? Colin's smile told him no more than the unflinching expression on Jock's face. "Here's my card. This is where I work, but my home address and phone number's on the back. Will you ring me in the morning? I can fix an afternoon off and you can come to lunch and tea." He rose from the table. "It's been wonderful, meeting like this. Sorry I've got to rush away, but we'll have plenty of time to talk when you come over. Goodbye, Jock. Thanks for letting me join you."

Alan smiled at them and walked out on to Waverley Steps. He hoped Colin would ring him soon. Glad as he was over this unexpected reunion, its full pleasure had been restricted by the atmosphere of the crowded bar, lack of time and, most of all, the uncomfortable silence of Jock Macmillan. It would be quite different when Colin came to the house.

Entering the club, a few minutes later, he met Gavin on the main staircase.

"I thought you'd got lost," said Gavin. "Did you find your cigarettes?"

"Yes, thanks," he replied casually.

"You've been a hell of a time."

"As a matter of fact I met somebody and stopped for another drink."

"Ah-ha . . ." Gavin looked knowingly at him. "Nice?"

"What do you mean?"

"Just that. Nice. A nice girl."

"No."

"Oh yeah? Never thought I'd see you blush." Gavin sounded horribly coy.

"It wasn't a——"

"All right. All right. 'Nuff said. You're a dark horse all right. Or are you a black sheep?" Gavin giggled.

"Possibly both," said Alan. "Anyway, it's better than being just dirty grey, isn't it?" He smiled pleasantly, amused by Gavin's nonplussed expression, and at the same time cursing himself for having ridiculously blushed like that. At *his* age, too. It was his own fault, of course, that people were curious about him. He *was* a dark horse, and he must consider himself lucky that so far nobody at work had gone beyond a few mild digs about his supposed preference for clandestine adventure. Better to let them think he was a bit of a lad on the quiet; but how long could he keep it up? Already there were signs that Gavin's interest was growing and might later prove embarrassing.

The afternoon dragged on. He found it difficult to concentrate on his work; his mind was wandering and he kept thinking about Colin. He must arrange to have a day off—tomorrow, if possible, taking a chance that Colin would ring him and be free to come to the house. Julia would be home for lunch, but in the afternoon she was going to Rosslyn Chapel with an old friend who was on vacation from Canada. He and Colin would have the whole afternoon in which to talk, and there were hundreds of questions to be asked and answered . . .

"This won't do at all."

Gavin's voice, coming from the other side of the office, startled him. He had forgotten he was there, and he hastily withdrew his gaze from the ceiling and looked down at the desk.

"Idle thoughts, when you should be working," said Gavin, in a mock-serious tone. "Deplorable."

"You're quite right," he replied, pulling himself together. It was foolish to day-dream—and no use denying to himself that he wasn't doing so. In fact, he was almost building castles in the air.

"You look as if you've been smitten," said Gavin. "Very dangerous—at your age. Very dangerous indeed."

"Shut up, Gavin, and let me get on with my work."

"Ah, yes. Work . . . I'll just put the kettle on for some tea." Gavin left the room to get some water.

I must be mad, thought Alan.

But perhaps he *was* 'smitten'? And as Gavin had said, it was highly dangerous at his age. Still, it was a pleasant condition. At the moment.

Colin and Jock had walked the entire length of Princes Street, and beyond the Royal Academy had descended the steps into the West gardens. Here, sheltered from the wind, the afternoon sun was warm, and many people were seated along the promenade, enjoying the first really comfortable day of spring weather. Below them, the deserted bandstand and enclosure seemed dwarfed by the towering Castle Rock, and on reaching this lower level they found themselves alone on the main path which led to the far western end of the gardens.

"It's wonderful here," said Colin. "I've never been to Edinburgh before. We must go up to the Castle—only there won't be time now. Perhaps we could go tomorrow, or—or some time . . ." he finished lamely, avoiding Jock's eyes. He knew what was in Jock's mind; since leaving the bar neither of them had referred to the meeting with Alan, but he could tell that Jock was thinking about the future luncheon appointment. "Let's go up here," he said, indicating a smaller pathway by the fountain. They came nearer to the Castle Rock and discovered a bridge which crossed the railway lines. They walked on and came to a gateway opening into King's Stables Road, low-lying between steep banks and overshadowed by the massive bulk of the Rock. Out of the sun, it seemed dark and cold. The road sloped gently down, towards what appeared to be a bridge, but as they came nearer they could see it was another, higher road crossing over it, and they halted for a moment to get their bearings and decide whether they should continue in the same direction or turn back.

"We seem to be lost," said Colin. "I don't know where we are. I've never known such a place for roads crossing over and under each other."

Jock looked at him thoughtfully, then spoke in a low voice. "Will ye telephone him tomorrow?"

"What? Oh—you mean Alan? Yes, of course. Why?"

"I suppose he'll be wanting to see ye every day?"

"I don't suppose so. But I must go to lunch. After all, he *has* known the family a long time, even if it is ten years since we last met. It would be terribly rude if I didn't go."

"No doubt ye'll have plenty to talk about?"

"Naturally."

"Why didn't ye tell him what ye were doing up here? Mebbe ye thought it was safer not to disillusion him."

"Disillusion him? Really, what on earth do you mean?"

"I saw the way he was looking at ye." Jock was unable to keep the note of jealousy out of his voice.

"That's absurd. I don't know a thing about him. The last time I saw him I was ten years old. You're surely not suggesting . . ."

"I'm sorry. Ye make me say things I shouldna. I canna help my thoughts . . . only ye drive me mad sometimes . . . the calm way ye have of looking at me, as if ye hated me . . ."

"No, I don't. You imagine too much, Jock. We can't stay here, some people are coming."

They moved on. Colin was worried. What did it mean, about his hating Jock? And that remark about looking calm? Somebody had to remain calm, otherwise there'd be no peace at all for either of them. Jock was extraordinary. It really seemed as if he were a little mad sometimes. Neither of them spoke until they came into Grassmarket.

"Will you be coming back into the show tonight?" Colin asked.

"Aye," Jock replied without enthusiasm. "I canna afford to stay out too long."

"No. Providing you feel well enough." Colin was thinking of the knife-throwing act and the risk he would be taking if Jock were not absolutely fit. "Oh dear . . . there's *another* street crossing over this one." Colin looked up and saw the tramcars passing along George IV Bridge. "How do we get out of this place?"

Eventually, after climbing the steep, cobbled slope of Candlemaker Row, they reached the higher level. Colin's feet were aching by this time and he was longing to sit down. "Let's get a tram," he said. "I don't care which one, or where it goes. I'm worn out."

They boarded the first tramcar which approached. It crossed over High Street and swung into Bank Street, and suddenly his tiredness was forgotten as the confining buildings around them opened out to a fine view of the gardens and Princes Street. The car slowly descended the gentle curve of the Mound. To their left the huge pile of Castle and Rock jutted against the sky. On their other side, the East gardens were hidden by the elegant 'classical' proportions of the National Gallery and the Royal Scottish Academy. Bathed in golden, April sunlight, the city lay like a brilliant tapestry between the hills and the river.

Colin was enchanted, and scarcely noticed that the tramcar, instead of taking them along Princes Street, crossed the main thoroughfare and entered the dignified but quieter and less spectacular atmosphere of the 'New' town. Looking out of the window, he caught a glimpse of George Street—Alan's club, he recalled, was somewhere here—and as he was admiring the wide streets leading away on either side, with their sombre lines of grey buildings broken by splashes of green foliage in the squares and gardens, he felt Jock's elbow gently nudging him.

"I think we're going the wrong way." Not particularly interested in this sedate part of the city, Jock was more concerned with the unnecessary expenditure on fares.

"Yes, I know, but let's stay on," said Colin. "It's a good way of seeing things. We needn't go back for tea; we can have it out and go straight to the theatre. All the way, please." The conductor had appeared; he paid for the tickets and resumed his sightseeing from the window. Jock made no further objection, and sat quietly, his eyes on Colin's half-turned head. At least, he thought, they were together. If only it could always be like this ... without suspicion and jealousy eating into him. He ought to be grateful for this small happiness, instead of submitting to constant self-torture and doubt. Now was the time to make a tentative gesture in the right direction—show Colin some indication of trust and affection.

Quickly he glanced round the car. Nobody was behind them, and nearer the front the only passengers were three women, loaded with shopping baskets and parcels, and too intent upon their chattering to notice anything. Gently he took Colin's hand into his own; with a slight start, the boy turned and looked at him.

"Jock, please be careful." Colin spoke softly, casting an anxious look towards the three women. As Jock's grip tightened, he made no attempt to withdraw his hand. The tramcar raced past the Botanical Gardens and soon they could see the Firth of Forth, as the tram began its gentle descent towards Granton Harbour. They alighted in a large square; tall, grey buildings were on two sides, and from the south side of the square rose houses on the slope of a hill. Facing them, by the river, was the entrance to Granton Pier.

The wide pier, bearing no resemblance to the familiar seaside construction, began as a roadway, with low-built sheds and warehouses on the left, and railway lines, carrying coal trucks, on the right. Beyond these trucks, after walking for some time, they could see the water. From the shore, low and wide stone walls extended into the river, curving inwards at their ends, to form an enclosure around the shorter pier. In the lagoon-like area of water nearest to them, small sailing craft of every description rocked gently on the light swell. Exploring further, they crossed between the warehouses and came to the other side of the pier. Walking on the thin slats of wood, through which the oily water could be seen, they had to pick their way carefully over trailing ropes and around stacks of fish-smelling crates. Three ancient trawlers lay alongside, their paintwork worn and neglected, and sadly belying their glamorous namesakes, just visible on the peeling bows ... *Oriana* ... *Fair Maid of Perth* ... *Isabel Jeans* ... They reached the end of the pier, where the railway lines terminated at a coaling station. The trucks tipped their loads into a deep shaft, and the coal was conveyed up a high, tower-like structure, and thence through huge pipes, where it roared down to refuel the holds of waiting ships. For several minutes they watched a vessel being fed from the giant pipes, but presently moved to a quieter position, away from the deafening noise.

"Look—" said Jock, "ye can see the trawlers—away over there."

At first, Colin could see nothing but the immense stretch of river, grey and cold, swiftly running and with isolated patches of stronger current rippling with the yellow light of the sun. A fierce wind rushed at them, and he had to shout to make himself heard.

"I can't see a damn' thing, except water. Oh, yes I can—they must be miles away." The trawlers looked like tiny, unmoving specks in the distance. "I wish we could see them come in, but it'll probably be hours yet."

"Aye." Jock sounded regretful. "But we canna stay here, it's too cold. Mebbe they're going to Leith, anyway."

They were both shivering a little, but almost childishly pleased at having sighted the trawlers. After the vivid, crowded impressions of the city, the peaceful openness of the river had rested and refreshed them. Returning to the square, they got on a waiting tramcar and mounted the stairs to the top deck.

"We'll get off at Princes Street and find somewhere for tea," Colin said. "I'm glad we came down here, I've enjoyed it."

"Aye, it's grand—good to get away from everyone for a wee while." Jock placed his arm along the back of the seat, his hand touching Colin's shoulder. A feeling of intense happiness and elation filled him. His heart seemed too full to confine the almost painful pleasure which surged over him. He was powerless and could no longer resist its force. Without thinking of the danger he was inviting, he drew Colin into his arms.

Amazed, then angry, Colin struggled furiously and wrenched himself free. "What the hell do you think you're doing? You idiot! Do you want to get us arrested or something?" The car jerked into motion. Footsteps sounded on the stairs and the conductor appeared. "Two, to Princes Street." Colin's voice was icy, and the conductor looked at him in surprise, then at Jock's crimson face. Handing out the tickets, he shrugged and returned to the lower deck.

"I'm sorry," Jock mumbled.

"Yes, you ought to be. What's the matter with you? Do you *want* to get yourself into trouble?"

Jock looked away quickly. After a long silence he spoke. "I suppose it's all over now? Finished."

"What do you mean?"

"Ye'll no' want to go on after this. I've spoilt it."

"Don't be absurd. If you behaved properly in public—controlled yourself . . ."

"Not touch ye at all?"

"Oh, don't let's start all that again."

"If I've shocked ye, I apologise. Mebbe I am crude and clumsy . . ." Jock stared straight ahead. "But I'm no' made of stone. I've got a heart," he added.

For the remainder of the ride neither of them spoke. When the tramcar turned into Princes Street they rose and went down the stairs.

Alan lit his pipe again, for the third time. On each occasion, after a few short puffs, it had gone out because he wasn't properly concentrating. It was the same with the morning paper, attempting to read yet another article on 'Home Rule For Scotland.' He abandoned the effort and gave in to the restlessness which had possessed him since getting out of bed. He wondered if Julia had noticed his sudden lapses into vagueness, his wanderings from room to room and his inability to remain still for more than a couple of minutes at a time. Fortunately she was in the kitchen now, seeing to the last-minute details of cooking, otherwise she might have wondered still more at his frequent journeyings to the drawing-room window, and the somewhat excessive interest in the front garden which he appeared to be taking. He was watching the gate and waiting for Colin to arrive. Already it was half an hour past the appointed time, and he was becoming anxious.

Julia wanted lunch promptly at one o'clock, as she had to meet her friend afterwards and catch the bus for Rosslyn. He hoped nothing had occurred to prevent Colin from coming. Quickly he turned from the window as Julia entered the room.

"Well, everything's ready—on a low gas." She sounded triumphant and satisfied. "I hope your friend's not going to be too late. I shan't be a moment, laying the table, and I would like a tiny drink before we eat."

"He can't be much longer. Mmmm—something smells good. What are you giving us?"

"Oh, it's quite a simple meal."

"Yes, but what? Now, come on, don't be mysterious."

"I'll tell you one thing, it's not baked beans on toast."

"I should hope not."

"Nor is it sar—what is that revolting expression you use?"

"Sar-bloody-dines," Alan laughed. This slightly modified relic of Army days always amused him.

Julia hurried off to the dining-room. From across the hall he could hear the tinkling of glass as she began setting the table. Nearly one o'clock . . . perhaps Colin had no idea of time. About to go to the window again, he heard the wrought-iron gate bang and footsteps on the path. As the bell rang, he opened the front door.

"Hullo! Come in. Thought you'd lost your way."

"No. I'm sorry I'm late."

Something was wrong. Alan instantly noted the brief, distracted smile which Colin gave him, and saw that he looked unnaturally pale. "Come and sit down and have a drink." Leading the way into the drawing-room, he indicated a chair by the fire. "Sherry?"

"Yes, please."

Alan handed Colin a drink, and sat down in the chair facing him. "It's good to see you again so soon. Are you sure you're all right? You look very pale."

"Do I? No, I'm all right. This is a lovely room . . ." Colin turned from Alan's concerned gaze and looked about him. "What a wonderful picture." He rose and examined the painting above the piano. "Italy, isn't it?"

"Yes. Tuscany. Not one of the great masters, but pretty good."

Colin then admired the Venetian glass, the silver ornaments and the tapestry chairs. He went on talking, rather brightly now, but to Alan, who was worriedly following his movements about the room, it sounded so obviously mechanical and evasive; the boy was making conversation, for some reason being deliberately impersonal.

"What's the matter, Colin? Is something wrong? You——"

"I'm all right, thanks."

"You look as if something's upset you. I noticed it the moment I opened the front door."

Colin stared at the picture again. "Yes. As a matter of fact I've had a blazing row with somebody, and I'm still rather angry." He was thinking grimly of last night, and of the events which had led to this morning's bitter climax between Jock and himself. Jock had said some extremely hurtful things, finishing up with a crudely expressed insinuation which had really shocked him. Last night he had tried to relent a little and be kind to Jock—forgive him for his behaviour on the tram, and overlook the carelessness of his knife-throwing at the theatre, which had ruined the speed and neatness of the act—but Jock had presumed on that kindness and had taken it for granted that it meant an assent to the intimacy which had been refused on the return journey from Granton. Because it was denied to him, he had become angry and sullen; thinking only of himself, with no understanding for other people's feelings. And he had told Jock that he didn't feel well and had a splitting headache, which was quite true. Now, this morning, Jock had made that unpleasant gibe, clearly showing that he had no respect for any of the finer affections. That was the truth. It might be wiser to end the whole thing, before Jock became an encumbrance to him. He was not quite sure how this could be achieved without harming their professional association—and he didn't want that to happen, when they worked so well together—but somehow he must get Jock to see that it was better for them to be no more than just friends. After all, Jock wouldn't be any worse off than he was now—in its present state, their relationship could hardly be called satisfactory from his point of view.

Thus, wrapped in his thoughts, Colin had almost forgotten Alan's presence, until suddenly he heard him speak.

"You must be miles away."

"Oh . . . yes . . . I'm sorry. I was thinking."

"Rather black thoughts, judging by your expression."

"No, not entirely."

"I shall have to get you out of this mood. What can I do to bring back your normally sunny nature?"

"I don't know, Alan."

"Just keep quiet and mind my own business?"

"No—I didn't mean that. I——" Colin broke off and looked at Alan. The clear, grey eyes, meeting his own, were puzzled and questioning. Did he suspect or know anything? In the old days Alan had always been sympathetic and understanding; but his concern had been for the problems of a child. It would be quite a different matter to confront him with a subject which many people hesitated to mention, let alone even imagine themselves remotely connected, and although Alan was no fool and probably far from narrow-minded, he would hardly welcome such frankness during his guest's first visit and only ten minutes after entering the house. Besides, there was the possibility that Alan might think it easier to drop him, rather than to be saddled with an embarrassing situation. And he had no intention of letting Alan do that.

Hastily finishing his sherry, Colin put down his glass as Julia came into the room. Alan's absorbed scrutiny made him feel uncomfortable, and he wasn't altogether sure whether it was entirely sympathetic or frankly curious. He felt as if he were being summed up; and hoped he wasn't being unfavourably compared with any preconceived notion that Alan might have formed.

The slight feeling of restraint between them persisted in spite of Julia's agreeable presence and conversation. She warmly greeted Colin, accepted a sherry from Alan and talked lightly and pleasantly until Mrs. Morven appeared and announced luncheon. If she were aware of Alan's silence, and Colin's rather forced responses, she gave no sign of it, and cheerfully led the way into the dining-room. She usually found that most people thawed out a little over a meal, and to forestall the possibility of a too slow de-freezing always omitted the soup, a beverage which seemed to stop some from talking. Today, however, once her culinary efforts were admired the subdued atmosphere about her table almost defeated her. In the drawing-room her first impression of Alan's friend had not been one of shyness or timidity; he was a little reserved, perhaps, but appeared quite at ease. Now, as the meal progressed, he seemed to withdraw into himself. His replies to her questions were polite but brief.

"There is no warmth of personality here," she thought. "His aloofness is not even definite enough to be arrogant . . . he is not even rude or ill-mannered, but cold . . ." Yes, she suddenly felt that, when he had looked at her with his calm, blue eyes. They were a beautiful shape, fringed with long lashes; two beautiful, cold stones. It was not often that she wholeheartedly disliked anyone, but with this young man she experienced a curious feeling of hostility, and it puzzled her as to why this should be. She knew nothing about him, beyond the few details Alan had given her. He had known Colin as a child, and the boy's mother had been very kind during the war. Although Alan rarely talked about himself, and she had no wish to probe into his life, he had spoken affectionately of the Ford family, who had obviously meant a great deal to him at that time. It was shortly after his marriage had broken up, and he must have been miserable and unsettled, in the Army and away from home, needing the warmth of a kindly, family atmosphere. Thinking about it now, she wondered whether that early, disastrous marriage had put him off from ever marrying again. As far as she knew, there had been no one since then to claim his attention. But he appeared contented enough. Except today . . . She had never seen him so downcast, and was convinced that Colin was in some way responsible for it. Probably Alan felt that the boy was letting him down—and it certainly seemed so, after the enthusiastic accounts she had heard of Colin, praising his charm and cleverness as a child.

Well, true or not, she had never found it so difficult to entertain anyone; even Harry's relations would be preferable—for if they only argued or criticised they did at least have something to say. She hoped Alan's mood of depression was a temporary one and would soon lift; but she must leave him to settle it by himself. Rather guiltily she felt thankful at having to go out this afternoon, and was greatly relieved to see Mrs. Morven enter with the coffee; another ten minutes and she would be away from the house. Picking up the silver pot, she smiled across the table and gave what she hoped was a convincing portrayal of an unruffled hostess.

"Coffee for both of you? Colin? Alan?"

But, except for the murmured politeness of acceptance, the silence persisted. She quickly finished her cup, excused herself and left the room.

Alan was annoyed with himself. Lunch had been a failure, and poor Julia must have wondered what on earth was wrong. He had badly let her down by his morose behaviour, and the exasperating thing was that even to himself he could not explain the exact reason for it. He had just felt himself sinking lower and lower into a state of depression, and it wasn't entirely due to Colin's equally low spirits. He could understand Colin's mood—he had arrived with it, after quarrelling with someone; it was only natural and could partly excuse his odd attitude during lunch. What puzzled him was his own reaction to this second meeting, which, despite the adjustments that had to be made in accepting Colin as a different personality from the one expected, could still have been a delightful occasion of discovery and friendliness. Somehow it was not working out as he intended. There was a sense of failure about it, and perhaps it was his fault for expecting too much from Colin. It was unreasonable to demand complete reciprocation from everyone just because he was, to put it bluntly, particularly ripe for it—although in another ten years, he thought ruefully, he would be positively mellow, and then perhaps it would be too late. But there *was* a lack of communication between them, and it was nothing to do with Colin's discomposure over a quarrel, or the difference in their ages. Neither was it due to shyness on the boy's part, for there had certainly been no trace of it yesterday. Of course the obvious answer might have been that Colin wasn't what he thought him to be—but somehow he felt this to be unlikely.

It was only now that it suddenly occurred to him that he had not made clear his own position. Until he did so, it was only natural for Colin to remain guarded. But how could it be done, and without in any way suggesting that he suspected Colin? While there was still an element of doubt, he did not want to offend or embarrass him. Perhaps a subtle hint of his own propensities— but given in such a way that Colin could either accept it, reject it or fail to perceive it, as he pleased. It was a chance worth taking, and if the outcome proved successful their mutual knowledge and their sharing of the same difficulties might result in a closer friendship or even, he dared to hope, something deeper. Whatever happened it couldn't be worse than the troubled half-hour he had just undergone.

They left the table and went into the hall, meeting Julia as she came downstairs. Apologising for having to rush away, she said goodbye—with a fleeting, anxious smile at Alan—and hurried off to see her friend, who was joining her at the bus stop in Nicolson Street. Profoundly thankful to get out of the house, she welcomed the opportunity to have a few hours of easy conversation. There would be no lack of *that,* with Norah. No uncomfortable pauses or long, baffling silences when you were with *her.* Norah would, perhaps, lower her voice a little in the quiet interior of Rosslyn Chapel, but it would not prevent her from talking altogether.

Alan waved to her as she closed the wrought-iron gate, trying as he did so to give a reassuring impression that all would be well. He shut the front door and looked at Colin.

"What would you like to do, Colin? Look over the house— or—or just sit down and talk? You've only got to say."

"I'd like to see the house."

"There are no State Apartments, so it won't take long."

They began their tour of inspection. As they went from room to room, Alan felt himself becoming more relaxed and easier in his mind; Colin seemed to be taking an interest in everything and slowly losing the remote, abstracted air which had been so disconcerting during their meal. Alan carefully avoided any personal questions, and concentrated on the task in hand. He was delighted to observe Colin's obvious pleasure and admiration as they entered each room, and with a growing confidence he finally ushered him into his own room on the first floor. He watched him look with approval at the antique tallboy and the small writing desk which stood against the plain, parchment-coloured walls; at the old brocade curtains framing the tall window; and at the books which filled the alcoves on either side of the fireplace. With its muted tones of colour the room was almost severely simple, relieved only by the damask rose glow of a wing chair, and by the warm, bright motley of books in the alcoves. Colin went over to the window and looked down into the garden, his eyes instantly attracted by the statue of Apollo beyond the yew trees.

"Rather unexpected, isn't it?" Alan stood beside him and gazed at the stone figures of the Sun God and his two companions—those prim maidens, who with baskets of sculptured fruit on their heads, stared rigidly towards the house as if in strong disapproval of their friend's unabashed nakedness.

"It makes me think of art school," said Colin. "We never stopped drawing figures of Apollo."

"I should think you enjoyed being there."

"Yes, but I didn't stay very long. I wanted to get a job."

"The one in Liverpool? You're designing for textiles, aren't you?"

"Yes . . ."

"Plenty of scope there, I should think."

Colin turned from the window and glanced about the room. "You don't mind if I look at your things, do you?"

"No. Go ahead. Anything you like." Alan noticed the evasion, but hopefully continued: "It makes things much easier if you're able to do what you really like—and, God knows, life can be difficult enough. The main thing is to be happy. Trite but true."

"Yes." Colin examined the bookshelves: uniform editions of the classics, volumes on travel, plays, dictionaries of various languages.

"You do like it there, then?"

"Oh, yes."

Slightly puzzled by Colin's non-committal replies, Alan doggedly pursued the subject. "It must be interesting, working in a place like that."

"Oh—I—I suppose it is, really . . ."

"You don't sound very sure. Are you going back there?"

"Back?" Colin looked startled.

"I mean, when you leave Edinburgh."

"Oh. I see. Well, no, not immediately. At least . . ."

"You're not working there any more?"

"No. No . . . I've—I've left there now. It was rather a dead-end job."

"I'm sorry to hear that. Still, if you've got something else . . . I didn't know whether you were on holiday or not. When you mentioned not having any free evenings, I thought——"

"No—I—I'm staying with someone—with people . . . I have to be in—in the evenings . . ." Colin's voice trailed off lamely.

"Yes, of course. Are you with that friend of yours—the one I met yesterday? Jock."

"He is staying in the same house." Colin took down a book and slowly turned the pages, his back towards Alan.

"I thought he seemed very reserved."

"Did you?"

"It—it wasn't he that—that you had a row with this morning?"

"Yes. It was."

"Oh. I hope it wasn't anything too serious?"

"It was all very stupid and not worth talking about."

"I just wondered, because I don't like seeing you miserable."

"I'm not miserable."

"I don't like people being hurt."

"I'm not hurt, Alan. Why do you think that?"

"Sometimes friends *can* hurt one, even unintentionally."

"Oh, it's no good worrying about Jock," Colin spoke bitterly.

"Then he has hurt you?"

"He's annoyed me intensely, I know that."

"Is he very difficult to get on with?"

"Quite impossible sometimes."

"That must be awkward. I mean—if you have to see a good deal of him . . . or haven't you known him very long?"

"Only a few weeks."

"Oh. But you like him?"

Colin hesitated. He was not quite sure what answer to give,

and not certain whether Alan was just showing a kindly interest or trying deliberately to find out the real truth of the situation. Those remarks about being 'hurt' were not the kind that people usually made when you told them that you'd had a row with somebody. "Yes. I like him. Why?" he asked. "He's a friend. One must have friends."

"I know. It's very important to have the right friends."

Oh dear, thought Colin, what is all this leading up to? Alan sounded so very serious. He remembered that tone, years ago . . . Alan explaining things to him, always kindly and gently firm. Carefully putting him right. Good God . . . was that happening now? Was Alan trying to give him wise, 'fatherly' advice? Warn him about the dangers of forming the wrong kinds of friendship? It would be dreadful if he started lecturing on 'healthy' living and 'clean' thoughts and the benefits of games in the open air . . . for a moment an absurd picture entered his mind, of Alan suddenly producing a cricket bat and rushing him off to the nearest recreation ground. It vanished, however, as swiftly as it had come. Whatever he was, Alan was no 'hearty.'

Colin began to examine the books in the other alcove, and presently Alan spoke again.

"Would you like some music? I've got a record player here. My tastes are pretty varied—but I won't inflict you with Gregorian chants or anything like that. Something restful, I think, don't you?"

The delicate, misty notes of 'Summer Night on the River' filled the room. Colin stopped his perusal of the shelves, and listened. It was a lovely sound, like a soft sighing in the still air . . . the murmuring of strings, and a songbird fluting in the distance . . . A harp rippled, whispering across the cool water which shared its secrets with the trailing willows on the river's bank. But even as he listened to this mysterious night-music of summer, his eyes went again to the books, and suddenly making a discovery he became only half aware of the flowing stream of music around him. His interest was at once aroused. Alan's small library contained a wide range of authors, but in the best sense it was a 'conventional' collection—writers one would expect to find: Dickens, Thackeray, Austen, the Brontes, and many others among the 'giants' of literature—and it was surprising to see in their midst (flanked by such respectable pillars of English tradition as Trollope and Kingsley—which included *The Water Babies*, of all things!) several recently translated novels by André Gide.

"I see you have some Gide."

Alan, kneeling on the floor by the record player, rose and went over to him. "Yes. Have you read any of them?"

"Only *The Coiners*."

"What did you think of it?"

"I liked it."

"Some people think Gide's overrated—too subjective and personal for genius. They get so worked up about it, too. It's the same with Walt Whitman. But if they're stating the truth about things—about themselves—why shouldn't they be? And in music . . . protesting about Tchaikovsky because it isn't like Bach."

"Perhaps Bach is an emotional experience for some people . . . the thrill of 'pure mathematics.'"

"Yes." Alan felt that they were diverging from the more interesting part of the conversation, and sought to draw Colin's attention back to it. "I have the Gide Journals and *Corydon*, if you'd like to look at them. They're in my case, under the bed."

"Have you?"

"Yes."

"Adam Bede. I've never read that." Colin peered at the books again.

"I'll get them out. Or perhaps you don't want to—I mean . . ." Alan was aware of the note of desperation in his own voice. He was bungling the whole thing, like an inept juggler, and instead of Indian clubs or plates he was tossing authors and composers into the air; trying to keep Gide, Whitman and Tchaikovsky spinning, while casually disposing of George Eliot and Bach. If he wasn't very careful he'd be dropping the lot. Already he was feeling frustrated and unnerved by Colin's detached, casual manner. "I'll see if I can find them——"

Colin interrupted: "Why do you keep them in a case?"

"Why? Well—it's full of books, there isn't room on the shelves . . ."

"Alan . . ."

"Yes?"

"Is it because you don't want—other people to see them?"

"No. I don't keep books hidden just because they're . . ."

"Those sort of books? Alan, I know just what you're trying to get at."

"It's fairly obvious, isn't it? Well?"

"Well what?"

"Look, Colin—I'm sorry. I don't want you to feel embarrassed. It's my fault for bringing it up. It's quite true, what I was 'getting at'—and you're no fool, so I won't pretend otherwise. Somehow, now it's come out, I don't mind your knowing. I think you're intelligent enough not to hold it against me. Let's change the subject. I won't bore you any more with it. Don't let it worry you—I shan't become violent or anything like that."

"It doesn't worry me in the least." Colin looked at him, coolly.

"Well, it's a relief to me that you can take it sensibly. Some people would——" Before Alan could finish the sentence, Colin began laughing softly. "Colin—what on earth . . . What are you laughing about?"

"Oh, Alan—if only you knew how solemn and serious you sound. Like one of your straight, sensible talks when I was small. 'Now you know all about the bees and the flowers—and that little girls are different from little boys—so there's no need to feel ashamed or worried, just forget all about it for a few years.' . . ."

"I never said anything remotely like that to you." Alan looked puzzled and indignant.

"No, of course you didn't, but I'm sure you would have—a few years later. And very considerately. Practically taking the blame yourself."

"Colin—what are you talking about?"

"You're just the same, now. But there really isn't any need. I am a little older, you know."

"I don't quite follow you. If you mean I'm taking the blame now—of course I am."

"Yes, and you're still trying to explain that although I'm now adult, and capable of understanding adult truths, it isn't really anything which should concern *me*."

Alan stared at him intently. "You're—you're not saying this to make me feel less uncomfortable?"

"No."

"I'm not getting it wrong, am I? I mean—you are telling me that—well—I don't have to ask outright, do I?"

"That's three questions in one," Colin smiled. "Don't look so worried. It's a plain answer in a plain wrapper: 'Yes.' I thought perhaps you'd guessed, anyway."

"Yes, I think I had, but I wanted to be quite certain before saying anything."

"I'm glad you took the chance, Alan, because I wasn't at all sure about *you*. At least, not until you began talking about Gide and Whitman."

"You must have wondered what on earth I was going to say next. In fact, *I* did, too—I was horribly nervous." Alan gazed delightedly at Colin, and smiled warmly. "This is wonderful. You know, you *did* have me worried—you seemed miles away when you arrived, and I thought I'd said or done something to annoy you. Only I couldn't think what it was. Look—I don't know why we're standing—shall we . . ." He indicated the wing chair. They both sat, he on the floor, at Colin's feet. The Delius record had finished, but neither of them noticed that it had stopped. "How long have you known about yourself?" Alan asked.

"Oh, always," Colin replied matter-of-factly.

"Oh. But—but there must have been a first time, when you discovered that—well . . ."

"I can't remember, it's such a long time ago."

"Good God. And you're—what? Only twenty now."

"You sound surprised. Didn't you know anything at that age?"

"Yes—but—perhaps I wasn't as sensible as you. I was married, at that age, trying to be conventional. It didn't work. We were divorced. Not because of that. She went off with someone else."

"And what did *you* do?"

"Oh . . . wallowed in doubt and got on everyone's nerves. It was during the war—just before I knew you."

"And when you knew me—were you . . ."

"Do you remember Bill Burton?"

"Yes. Of course . . . Big Bill . . . was it he?"

"The first. And luckily for me, it was Bill. He was killed, later, in Italy." For a moment, Alan's face was clouded. "But what about *you*, Colin? You haven't told me anything. Has it been bad for you?"

"Oh, I get by." Colin laughed.

"I don't doubt it. You're not exactly a plain, dull boy, are you? Is it indiscreet to ask whether someone . . ."

"I don't know, Alan. Is it?"

"It's for you to say. Or would you rather not?"

"Well . . . there's nothing serious . . ."

"No?"

"No. Really. Why do you look so doubtful?"

"It seems so unlikely. Not even anyone in the offing?"

"Alan, you're very inquisitive."

"Yes, I know. But I'm interested. After all, I've known you almost since you were first out of the nursery. You used to tell me all sorts of things."

"Not things like that, I hope."

"Colin. Stop kidding. You needn't mind saying anything to me. Now, come on."

"But there's nothing to tell you."

"You're just a teaser."

"What do you mean by that?" Colin stiffened, annoyed. He knew Alan was only speaking lightly, but the phrase irritated him by its unpleasant reminder of this morning's incident at the boarding house.

"Be serious just for a minute, Colin. You must know how pleased I am to see you again. It's not just a casual encounter—especially now, after finding out about each other—and naturally I want to ask questions. You can trust me, surely? I'm not asking you to give a detailed account of your love-life—but I couldn't help noticing how upset you were when you came here. I know you had a quarrel this morning, and you rather edged from telling me anything when I asked you about it . . . I guessed it must have been pretty serious, and I wondered . . . Is it Jock?"

"Jock?"

"Are you in love with him?"

Colin stared at Alan, who was now kneeling in front of him.

"In love with Jock? No. No, I'm not. I don't know why you had that impression. We just had a row, and he said some rather nasty things, and we both lost our tempers. I told you, he's impossible."

"Oh. I see. But Jock——"

"It's not worth worrying about," Colin quickly cut in. He had no desire to spend the afternoon in discussing Jock's short-comings. Alan meant very well, and obviously wanted to be helpful, but his disconcerting frankness sometimes became a little too intense and personal. He was not unaware, either, of the relieved, eager expression on Alan's face. It was not difficult to interpret that look—there was something so ardent and warm about it. He really did look very attractive and boyish, kneeling like that on the floor, his eyes so clear and shining ... utterly different from Jock's sombre, brooding stare, with its sudden darkenings of pain and flashes of cruelty. Jock only knew the torments of love. Alan might be passionate, but it would be a gentle passion—perhaps becoming a trifle dull and sentimental after a while—but it would at least be restful and uncomplicated; not too demanding or filled with jealousy and suspicion all the time. He toyed with the idea.

"Miles away again?" Alan asked quietly. Once more that baffling sense of Colin's remoteness assailed him. Although Colin's eyes were on him, they seemed so distant, almost as if they were looking right through him.

"I was thinking."

"What about?"

Colin shrugged. Why did people always want to know one's thoughts? One had only to be silent for a moment, and they asked. Did they really expect a true answer? Or did they just want to be reassured that one hadn't forgotten they were still there? "Oh ... life ..." he replied, somewhat vaguely.

"That sounds rather serious for one so young. Has it been very hard for you?"

"I can cope with it. Anyway, Alan, don't let's get all gloomy and introspective. Couldn't we go into the garden, while the sun's out? I've hardly had any fresh air today."

"Yes. All right." Alan looked at him gravely. "You're a funny kid." Then he smiled and rose to his feet. They left the room and went downstairs.

At half-past four they had tea in the drawing-room. Colin had to leave at five o'clock, and as the time for his departure approached he again grew silent and preoccupied. Several immediate problems were facing him; and they had to be solved or disposed of without procrastination. Firstly, there was Jock. Well, he had more or less decided about that . . . Then there was Alan. In one way, there was no real difficulty there. Alan was practically waiting for him to fall into his arms. But of course it might be a little unwise to be over-hasty, before everything was sorted out. And there was so little time left. Only a few more days and then he would be off to Glasgow, and after that they had some dates to play in the Midlands. He might never get to Edinburgh again. And ought he to tell Alan about his being in the show? Perhaps it was silly, not wanting to mention it, but until now there was no point in doing so. Then again, even knowing about each other, would Alan really understand? As yet there were no indications that Alan had any special liking or interest for this particularly 'gay' aspect of their world. One never knew about people—how they would react. It wasn't the sort of thing, either, that could casually be inserted during ordinary conversation . . . "Oh, by the way—I'm appearing in a twice-nightly drag show, you must come and see it. What was that you were saying about the Forth Bridge? . . ."

Promptly at five o'clock, Alan stood at the door to see him off. "I shall see you again, won't I, Colin? Couldn't you possibly manage an evening? Except for lunch hours, I shan't have any more free time during the day."

"Well—no, I can't, really. It's a bit difficult . . ."

"You're very mysterious about it. Still, if you can't . . . I understand, if it's some sort of work or study you have to do . . ."

"In a way, it is. I—I can't explain now."

"I'll take your word for it. I hope it's something with good prospects. What about tomorrow, for lunch? One o'clock, on the corner of Hanover Street. It's opposite the Royal Academy."

"All right. Thanks."

"Don't be late."

"I'll try not to be, this time."

"And Colin—I *am* glad we've met again."

Colin shut the wrought-iron gate and waved goodbye. Then, walking thoughtfully, he set off for the theatre, wondering in what sort of mood Jock would be, and whether tonight's performances would be less hair-raising than the previous two—in which he had been at the mercy of his partner's erratic aim and temperament.

After a stimulating outing with her friend, Julia returned home to find Alan in a more cheerful frame of mind. She was pleased, too, that his friend had gone, although she had to admit to herself that Colin must somehow have been instrumental in putting Alan into a good humour again—he seemed relaxed and happy, and spoke of meeting Colin tomorrow for lunch. Perhaps she had misjudged the boy? There might have been a valid explanation for his apparent unresponsiveness. She hoped, if only for Alan's sake, that it was nothing more than a temporary phase—and seeing him now, restored to his old self, she reflected that surely it must be that—for if it were not, she would indeed have cause to acknowledge the almost instinctive mistrust she had felt when the boy's cold, blue eyes had unflinchingly looked into hers.

"Did you have a nice time this afternoon?" asked Alan.

"Oh, yes. Lovely. Regular 'trippers.' It was like a charabanc outing. We 'did' the Chapel, had a high tea, and bought souvenir postcards. Views of the Chapel—photographed from ground-level. It makes the little place look as big as Canterbury Cathedral. But it really is charming. And what about you? What time did Colin go? Did you give him tea?"

"Yes. He left at five. I—er—I'm sorry about the lunch . . ."

"Yes, my dear, so am I. I couldn't think what was wrong. I began to wonder if I'd lost grip—whether it was *me,* or the food or something. And I really did try awfully hard."

"No, it wasn't that at all. I was just as puzzled. But he *did* tell me that he was upset—he'd had a terrible row with someone before he came here. He got over it, later on."

"Good. I'm so glad. I did think for a while there was something seriously wrong—although having a row *can* be serious— but I was rather concerned about *you*. I've never seen you look so miserable. But if everything's all right now . . ."

"Yes—yes, I think so. Thanks." Alan hastily turned away and knocked out his pipe into an ash-tray. And then he wondered if by this action he had given himself away; whether Julia had noticed the deliberate movement he had made in order to conceal the sudden embarrassment he felt at talking about Colin.

Later that evening, on returning with Julia from the cinema, Alan sat for a long time in his room before going to bed. He had time now to think about Colin's visit and all that it implied. It was a great relief to feel that they need no longer conceal everything from each other, but there was still an elusiveness about Colin, not easy to define, and the more he thought about it the more doubtful it seemed that the conquest he envisaged would take place without further tantalising evasions. Almost despairingly, he wondered if he were in for another bout of emotional upheaval. He had been too long without love, and now, as he grew older, he was finding that it was not the heady, intoxicating experience which sweeps confident youth to the heights. There was far too much anxiety about it—especially in his own world, where one had to compete with so much promiscuousness and disloyalty. Perhaps he was unduly pessimistic, but Colin had given the impression that he was . . . Was what? Flighty? Unreliable? Shallow? . . . Of course, he was only a kid; probably going through a phase; conscious of his power to attract people. But this quarrel with Jock . . . what exactly did it mean? He was not altogether convinced by Colin's emphatic denial that Jock was of any consequence to him—and unless he could be quite sure about this, it was stupid to get into such a state when there was not the slightest chance of receiving anything other than disappointment and a bitter reminder that he was too old to play Prince Charming. With gloomy and unnecessary exaggeration, he all but likened himself to the pitiable creature who had tried without success to interest the young soldier at the bar counter yesterday morning.

CHAPTER 7

"Curtain going up! Curtain going up!"

Colin was late getting down for the opening number. The announcement came from the loudspeaker above the door which led on to the stage. Sometimes there was a couple of minutes' grace, and perhaps tonight he'd be able to make it without resorting to the undignified method of joining the dance after the curtain had risen.

Hurrying behind the backcloth, he saw Jock talking to one of the scene-shifters, and as he came near to them Jock turned away and walked off in the opposite direction. He knew Jock was deliberately avoiding him; first of all, upstairs, there had not been the usual knock on the dressing-room door, to see if he were ready when 'Overture and beginners' was called; and now he had rudely been cut dead. It was too much to stomach, especially when he had decided not to refer to this morning's quarrel, and if possible try to establish a less exacting but still friendly basis for their relationship. He had felt sure that Jock would probably be ashamed of himself and come grovelling to him—he always did in the end—and then he could have told him how important their friendship was, how they should trust one another for the sake of their work, and not be harassed by the emotional incompatibility which seemed likely to persist with the present unsatisfactory state of affairs. He had intended to be very kind and considerate to Jock, and show him that something real and lasting would result from it. But if Jock was going to carry on like this, they'd never get anywhere.

Quickly he took his place on the stage.

"Only just in time," said 'Josie.' "I thought you'd fallen down a trapdoor. Here we go again . . ." and as the curtain rose he widened his eyes, swayed his hips and energetically clicked away at the castanets.

After the opening number Colin had several changes of costume, and it was not until the cabaret scene that he came face to face with Jock. He emerged from the curtained archway and stood in front of the red baize board. A brilliant spotlight was on him, and in its glare it was impossible to distinguish anyone else on the stage. Only when Jock came close to him, to tie his wrists, could he clearly see his face. It was grim and unsmiling. The reassuring nod and the few whispered words which he generally gave were absent; Jock didn't even look at him, but hastily fastened his wrists to the hooks, much too tightly so that they hurt, and took up his position for the first throw. Colin suddenly felt scared; far more so than last night, when Jock's aim had been so erratic but fortunately wide of the mark. Now, he felt an instinctive warning of danger. There was something purposeful in the way Jock tied his wrists and then turned away without a glance. His heart pounded rapidly. He closed his eyes and waited. In the brief silence of the whole theatre, which always preceded the first knife-throw, he could hear Jock breathing.

Then came the ominous drum-roll. He heard a sharp 'crack,' and the board vibrated behind him. A burst of applause sounded from the auditorium, repeated almost immediately as the second knife pierced the red baize, so close to his shoulder that he could feel the coldness of the steel through his costume. The next knife would land near the tips of the fingers of his right hand. This throw nearly always frightened him as much as the climax of the act, where he risked his head within the three points of a triangle. There was so very little space between the ends of his fingernails and the edge of the board. Nervously he opened his fingers as wide as possible. He started violently when the expected knife pricked the baize just to the right of his waist. For some reason Jock had changed the order of throwing. But why? Had he forgotten the hands? Would he go back to them? Another knife landed below the previous one, at his thigh—and as this outlining of the body continued, he realised that Jock was deliberately prolonging the pauses between each throw—stretching the tension and delaying the return to the hands, which he knew was an anxious moment. Instead of the three final aims at his head, which were quite dangerous enough, it would mean five difficult throws one after the other. He felt sick and cold. If Jock didn't hurry, he'd probably faint before the finish of it, and he was convinced that one of the knives would be too close . . .

Then suddenly he heard the savage splitting in the board, and felt a twinge of pain at the top joint of his middle finger. He was not sure whether it was the blade or a splinter of wood which had pierced the skin, but he could feel a trickle of blood running down into the palm of his hand. Again there was a long pause before another blade swished through the air, and he held his breath, waiting for a further stab of pain—but this time it had safely cleared his other hand. With an effort he remained still, staring at the rows of blurred, white faces in the darkness beyond the orchestra pit. Did any of those people out there, comfortably relaxing in their seats, guess what he was going through? Perhaps they did, for now there was a stir of expectancy, a few nervous giggles as Jock slowly prepared for the climax which literally crowned the act. This time, his slowness was all part of the performance and calculated to raise the spectators' fears that perhaps there *might* be an accident and it *did* seem as if the 'negro' was hesitating a little before throwing the knives. But Jock appeared to be taking too long over it for his liking. Now! he thought, as the poised daggers glittered in the powerful shaft of light . . . The drum thundered again, and the last three knives were flung in rapid succession. The sound of quivering metal hummed about his head.

The agony was over, until the next performance. Through the crashing chord from the orchestra a roar of applause seemed to roll on to the stage like a huge, breaking wave. For a second he thought Jock was going to walk off, leaving him pinned to the board. Seeing him bow briefly to the audience and move towards the wings, the inward panic of the last few minutes changed to icy fury. How dared Jock do that? Entirely ignore him, as if he were nothing to the act, a mere assistant who came on and handed him things . . . he was shaking with anger. Then, as the loud applause continued, Jock suddenly turned and approached him. The cords were quickly untied, his blood-stained hand seized, and he was drawn down to the footlights to receive—and nobody could fail to observe it—an even louder demonstration of enthusiasm. Someone shouted from the invisible heights near the roof, and he flashed a dazzling smile to the gallery. They ran off, through the narrow opening behind the proscenium arch, but the audience insisted upon another appearance before finally letting them go. 'Tessa,' whose song immediately followed, came on as usual, back centre, directly they left the stage for the first time—mistaking the ovation for their second call as a tribute to his own entrance—and was livid at having to wait in the background before beginning his number.

In the wings, Colin snatched his hand from Jock's and angrily turned on him. "What the hell do you think you're playing at tonight? Look what you've done to me!" He held up his blood-smeared hand.

Jock stared at it, surprised. "Och, I'm sorry—I didna realise . . ." He sounded genuinely concerned. "Let me——"

"Don't touch me! Luckily for you it isn't worse. And don't tell me you couldn't help it. You've gone deliberately out of your way to be vicious. And look at my wrists, too!"

"If that's what ye think . . ."

"Oh, get out of my way!" Colin stormed off towards the exit door, so enraged that he forgot to wait for the first-half finale, where the entire company came on to do a brisk conga with 'Charlotte' and 'Betty.' Jock stared after him, oblivious to the hurrying, backstage activity, his eyes glinting fiercely in his darkened face. Those who were not on the stage gathered behind the canvas flats of the cabaret set, waiting for 'Tessa' to finish his song before they danced on, one behind the other, in the rhythmic, jerking movements of the conga. 'Josie' and 'Netta,' always quick to sense any kind of drama that was taking place, had heard with considerable trepidation Colin's harsh accusations, and seeing the dangerous look in Jock's eyes wisely refrained from calling his attention to the already forming line of dancers.

"I *knew* something was going to happen," 'Josie' hissed to the agitated 'Netta.' "Those knives—it was like a slaughterhouse tonight. Did you see that blood?"

"Don't!" 'Netta' shuddered.

"It was like a terrible, primitive sacrifice. Do you remember that film, *The White Captive?*" But before 'Netta' could reply, and as if to illustrate the jungle rites of that particular epic of the screen, they were swept into the tribal-like abandon of the conga. 'Tessa' was nearly trampled underfoot by the swaying, kicking dancers as they jerked past him through the centre archway. He quickly adjusted the ostrich feather head-dress, which had slipped down on to the bridge of his nose, and staggered after 'Netta' on the tail-end of the line. Half-way through their circling of the stage, 'Netta' heard a desperate sighing from behind. "What's the matter?" he asked in a loud whisper. "What *is* it?"

"My shoe's come undone."

"*What?*" 'Netta' found it difficult to hear or talk. The orchestra was blaring away, roars of laughter came from the auditorium as 'Charlotte' and 'Betty' zestfully performed some lunatic variation of their steps, and he was out of breath from the strenuous kicking and lunging of the dance. 'Tessa' was pulling on him and wobbling about in a very peculiar manner. What on earth was the silly cow doing? Under his breath he counted: one two three four five—kick! One two three four five—kick! And then from behind him a diamanté-buckled shoe skimmed across the stage and came to rest, miraculously upright, in front of the footlights. 'Tessa' clutched him tightly, swaying like a derailed coach at the end of an express train. With the remaining shoe he finished the dance, uncomfortably bumping up and down and emitting little gasps of terror as the pace became more furious. The curtain fell. As if mesmerised, they watched the heavy, weighted folds of velvet descend on to the shoe. When it rose again the shoe was lying on its side. Anxiously 'Tessa' waited, ready to spring out and retrieve it the moment the curtain came down.

As the tasselled border touched the floor he moved forward, but abruptly stopped when the curtain unexpectedly began to rise again. Gauging the warmth of applause, the stage manager had risked another 'curtain.' 'Tessa' gulped and stared, open-mouthed, at the strip of floor near the footlights. The shoe had disappeared. A roar of delighted laughter came from the audience, and in dismay he saw the glittering buckle and the painted high heel, caught in the elaborate fringing, rise into the air and perilously tremble at the edge of the proscenium pelmet. Once more the curtain fell. Loud cheers and a few piercing whistles signalled the landing of the shoe, which did a dainty little jig on its own before subsiding beneath the swinging loops and tassels brushing the floor. Ignoring the amused comments of the others, who were hurrying off into the wings, 'Tessa' went down on his knees and fumbled along the bottom of the curtain, sneezing violently as clouds of dust blew into his face. His efforts at rescue were, however, not quick enough, for the iron safety curtain was already descending on the other side of the crimson velvet. Hastily he drew back out of harm's way as the hydraulically operated curtain, with peculiar hissings and clankings, slid down and sealed off the stage from the auditorium. It also very effectively pulped the heel of poor 'Tessa's' shoe and crushed the diamanté buckle beyond all recognition. Miserably he returned to the dressing-room and had a good cry.

Until the moment arrived for their act in the second performance, Colin avoided seeing Jock. Now, raising one arm as he stood in front of the board, he felt Jock's hand slide into his own, and with a gentle pressure hold it for a moment before tying his wrists. Jock looked at him pleadingly. "Don't worry, I'll be verra careful," he whispered. Colin stared coldly ahead into the darkness of the auditorium. Jock needn't think he was going to be forgiven as easily as that—or get round him by lovingly squeezing his hand. And as the knives swished and quivered, his increasing annoyance almost obliterated his nervousness. This time it seemed that Jock was feeling the strain more than he, and was hastening to get the whole thing completed as quickly as possible. He could see the sweat shining on his face and chest, and noticed, as they took their call, that his hand was shaking.

In the wings, they separated. Jock put on his dressing-gown and sat down, apart from the others. Colin moved from the proscenium wall to a place behind the tabs, where he had an uninterrupted view of the stage, and stood watching 'Tessa,' whose forced top notes sounded like a rare tropical bird in distress. He looked like one, too, with the curled plumes trembling above his head.

"Really, she gets *worse*," 'Josie' whispered from near by; and then, with a hasty glance over his shoulder: "What's the matter with Jock? We were quite worried about you tonight. Poor Netta nearly had Chinese diarrhoea in the first house when those knives started coming so close. Was it an accident? Or intentional—some new vice you've both thought up?"

"I don't know," Colin shrugged. They left the wings, to join the line of dancers near the centre archway. Out of the corner of his eye he saw Jock leaving the stage.

It was after midnight. The last tram had long since departed from Morningside, and the only sounds in the dark, empty street came from the wind playing on the overhead wires and rustling through the trees and bushes in the garden. Lying in bed, Jock listened to the faint, singing music of the wires—an eerie whispering, as if some phantom tramcar signalled its approach but never arrived. Closer to him, in the house, were the tiny creakings and rattlings of ill-fitting windows and doors, the scurrying of mice behind the walls, and the sudden gurglings from the water-tank in the roof over the bathroom. Below, in the 'ground-floor front,' the springs in Mr. Galbraith's bed loudly twanged as he shook with a violent fit of coughing. The mean old devil had complained about other people making a noise, and now he was choking and spluttering loud enough to disturb the entire house.

Jock turned restlessly and lay on his back. He felt tense and unhappy, physically and emotionally frustrated; and he hated himself for his weakness, for allowing it to dominate him and force him to seek refuge in drink—an escape from misery, but one which now no longer promised release from the yearnings of his heart and body. No wonder Colin was disgusted by his behaviour ... but the boy drove him to it ... treated him like dirt, laughed at him, used him, tormented him to a pitch of frenzy and then upbraided him for complaining. He thought of last night, when they had come back from the theatre. Colin had shown an unexpected warmth and friendliness. Then that sudden freezing ... plunging him into misery and anger. He couldn't go on much longer like this. He had reached breaking-point.

The half-hour bell clanged from a distant clock-tower. He sighed loudly and switched on the bedside lamp, listening hopefully for the sound of footsteps. Colin should have been back by now. Through the thin wall dividing their dressing-rooms he had heard him arranging to go out to supper with 'Josie' and 'Netta.' Jealously he had listened to their gay laughter. Of course it was stupid to resent Colin's friendliness with those two—and at least it did mean that Colin was not seeking other company . . . meeting Alan Kendrick again . . . He couldn't forget the confident, proprietary air with which Alan had proposed further meetings and hinted at a renewal of their friendship—if it could be called that, after a silence of ten years.

At the click of the gate-latch he was instantly alert. He heard the front door being opened and then quietly closed. Colin entered the room and stopped short, obviously surprised at finding him awake. "I couldna sleep. I wondered what had happened to ye, and . . ."

"I had to walk back. There weren't any trams." Picking up his toilet things, Colin went off to the bathroom. When he returned he was annoyed to see Jock still sitting up, and as he began to undress he was conscious of the watchful, silent tension which accompanied his movements. He glanced at Jock, and saw him guiltily avert his eyes. Turning away, he put on his dressing-gown and took out his pyjamas from under the pillow.

Jock spoke in a low voice. "Colin—I've got to speak to ye—just for a minute, if ye'll listen . . ."

"Can't it wait until the morning? I'm tired now, it's late."

"Aye, but it's no good to keep putting things off. Please come here."

Surprised by Jock's firm tone and words, Colin looked at him warily before slowly crossing to the bedside.

"Will ye sit down?" Jock placed a hand on the eiderdown, near the edge of the bed. Colin sat, without speaking, and stared at the window curtains on the other side of the room. He felt Jock move a little, and glancing down saw that he had not taken his hand away.

"I'm sorry aboot tonight, Colin—if I frightened ye. It'll no' happen again. I hope ye won't always hold it against me."

"No, but be more careful in future."

"Aye, I will."

"Quite apart from placing me in danger, if you don't properly concentrate the whole act just falls flat. It's one of the best things in the show and we don't want it cut." Colin turned and faced Jock. "We work together so well, Jock, it seems a pity to spoil it with—with personal complications . . ."

"What do ye mean?"

"All this jealousy and suspicion—rows and endless arguments . . ."

"If ye're thinking of this morning . . ."

"It's not only that. There never seems to be any peace between us. Never will be if we go on like this."

"Is it my fault that we quarrel? Is it always me who's in the wrong? Ye've not always been fair to me, Colin . . ."

"I don't know what you mean."

"Aye, ye do, all right. Ye take a great pleasure in tormenting me."

"Don't be ridiculous."

"Mebbe it amuses ye to have somebody on a string, dancing for ye?"

"What are you driving at?"

"If ye want it plainly, I'll tell ye. In case ye've forgotten last night—and what I said to ye this morning . . ."

"Is that all that matters to you, Jock?"

"No. Ye know verra well it isna. But I've told ye before how it was—I've no' lied to ye aboot it—and ye made me believe that ye understood how I couldna always be—well . . . sae patient all the time." Jock took hold of Colin's hand and gently pressed it. "Ye have me worried a lot. I've no' known where I am wi' ye—or what ye expect of me. And when I've tried to reach ye it's always been wrong. A stupid, clumsy mistake. And ye make me ashamed and angry wi' mysel' . . ." Jock tightened his grip, his voice becoming tenser as he went on. "But ye drive me to it. Don't ye see? I've told ye I'm no' cold-blooded, but ye've no' heeded it—ye've no'——"

"Jock, I *have* tried—but you must admit you've been difficult. You go from one extreme to the other. And all this drinking—the other night, for instance, when you came home and practically started a fight . . ."

"I was verra unhappy."

"What did you expect me to do, after you'd made up that stupid story about going to a dance? No, the fact is, however unfair I've been—and I don't consider that I have—*you* haven't been particularly straight about everything. I've always felt that you've been hiding something. Why did you go out drinking that night?"

"I've already told ye. I was upset and miserable. I wanted to be on my own—to think."

"Is that why you came to the theatre—and then disappeared? Harry Archer told me he'd sent you home because you looked ill. Was it his idea or did you tell him you weren't well?"

"I might have done. I don't remember. Why are ye sae interested, now? I'm back in the show and it doesna matter."

"Did you know the police were at the theatre again?" As Colin spoke, he felt Jock's hand stiffen.

"How should I know? I was only there a few minutes. What is all this? Why are ye trying to cross-examine me?"

"For God's sake keep your voice down. I don't want any more complaints from Miss Andrews. Every time the police are mentioned you go up in the air. Anyone would think——"

"What would they think?"

"All right, since we've come to it we might as well have it out. It's been worrying me ever since that awful night at Regal Terrace. Why are you frightened of the police, Jock? It's no good pretending you aren't, because I've noticed it."

Jock slowly withdrew his hand. For a long time he stared at Colin with troubled eyes, his face stern and unhappy. "It'll do no good to tell ye—but if I don't ye'll no' let it rest. As ye've rightly guessed, I've no liking for the police."

"But they haven't got anything on you, have they?"

"Not now they havena—but once ye've seen trouble it's as well to keep awa' from it."

"What trouble? You're not involved in anything, are you? Besides, they only came to ask questions about Butch—and none of us had anything to do with *him*. You never spoke to him, even."

"No. But there's a danger—I mean—if they knew . . . Och, it's sae hard to tell ye . . ."

"Jock . . . Is it something to do with Butch? *Is* it?"

"No."

"Well, then—really . . ."

"Only in a way. Ye see—I—I've been inside, Colin . . ."

"Inside? Prison? Oh. I see . . ."

"No." Jock shook his head. "I don't think ye do. And I'll no' give ye the chance to ask—I'll tell ye. I was caught wi' somebody."

"You were *what?*" Colin stared at him incredulously.

"Now perhaps ye understand why I couldna touch ye wi'out feeling guilty—why I wanted yer love but was afraid to make a mistake . . . it was the only chance I had to be happy and forget what I'd done . . . and ye wouldna let me . . . ye wouldna let me . . ."

"Jock. Please. I'm terribly sorry about it, but I think it would be better not to say any more. You've been absolutely honest about it, and I appreciate it——"

"Oh, ye do?" Jock was suddenly angry and contemptuous.

"There's no reason why it should spoil our friendship."

"Friendship?"

"Of course. I want us to remain friends."

"Aye. Now ye know I'm no' fit for a lover ye'll keep me as a friend." Jock spoke bitterly. "Ye're not even disgusted by the thought that I might have contaminated ye. No, ye're relieved at the excuse ye now have to drop me. It'll leave ye free to have me off yer conscience while ye run around wi' that Alan what's-his-name."

"That's quite untrue." Colin rose and looked down at him coldly. "And now, if you don't mind, I'm going to bed. You'd be a lot happier, Jock, if you weren't so self-pitying and jealous."

"Ye're as hard as nails." Jock gazed at him steadily. "What do ye hope to get out of Alan? Are ye sae fond of him—or is it because he has more money than me? Ye don't answer, do ye? Or mebbe ye like to flirt—tease him as ye did me. That's what ye're doing all the time. Playing a clever game."

"I'm getting rather tired of this conversation."

"Well—when ye've started something wi' me ye'll finish it. See how ye bloody well like this, ma bonny . . ."

Colin struggled furiously as Jock pulled him down. In the powerful embrace he could only cry out weakly. Unable to release himself, he tore at the pyjama jacket. Jock had now raised himself and was on his knees, swaying over him. He tried to get away, and felt himself slipping over the edge of the bed. He touched the floor, grasping at the blankets as he fell. Before he could get up, Jock had left the bed and was gripping his arms, forcing him to rise. Again he struggled wildly, aware now that Jock was holding him closely and no longer fighting or even conscious of the battle between them. Angrily he attempted to free himself from the pressure of Jock's hands and arms; but his efforts were useless against the superior strength and force. Out of breath, and holding himself rigidly, he tried to place one foot behind Jock's heels, hoping it would make him stumble and lose his balance. With a quick movement, he extended his foot, only to find his action impeded. But suddenly he seemed stronger than Jock, and tore himself away. Guilty and confused, Jock turned from him, helpless to avoid the embarrassment in which he was inevitably trapped. For a long time they were both silent. Shocked, and alone in their thoughts. Hard, unyielding anger, and a deep, welling shame. After a while Jock spoke gruffly. "If I've hurt ye at all, I'm sorry—but I'll no' forgive ye being sae cruel. Ye don't care, do ye, that I've shamed mysel' because of ye. That's all I can say. I canna bring mysel' to speak any more of love to ye—ye have none to give. One day ye'll wish ye had, but mebbe then it'll be too late."

Colin lay on the settee, feeling miserable and near to tears; but presently his anger reasserted itself when he remembered how Jock had reviled him and taunted him with those scathing remarks about himself and Alan. What right, he thought indignantly, had Jock to accuse him? Considering the way he had behaved in the past, Jock should count himself lucky to have anyone taking notice of him. He had certainly forfeited any further claim to sympathy. Staring into the darkness around him, he began to feel a little calmer and was able to think more clearly. About one thing he was quite decided—Jock would not be sharing this room tomorrow. No doubt he'd create a scene over it, but that couldn't be helped. Or he might even be glad to leave. It would be peaceful without him, and perhaps he'd at last get a good night's sleep. He mustn't forget that he was seeing Alan tomorrow—seeing him *today,* for it was long past midnight. Thank God Alan was sane and dependable . . .

Beginning to feel drowsy, he closed his eyes. Outside, the wind had stopped, silencing the whispered music of the tram wires and the faint, papery rustle of leaves; but a sudden coldness gripped him. In the quietness of the room he could hear Jock weeping. For some minutes, lying perfectly still, he listened; then, when the deep, shuddering sobs had died, he was glad that he had not gone to him. He would not lower himself further; he would not crawl as Jock had so often done; he would not betray his own honesty by a show of concern and sympathy, which he no longer felt. Everything was over and done with.

He drifted into sleep before the small voice of conscience could be heard.

"Shut the door," 'Josie' ordered, removing his coronet and wig, and disdainfully surveying himself in the mirror as he gave his head a good scratch. 'Netta' did as requested, also taking off his wig, which after mid-week invariably managed to resemble an abandoned and derelict bird's nest. "I look really *old* tonight," 'Josie' went on, suddenly letting fall the top portion of his crinoline gown. "It's no good saying otherwise."

"I wasn't going to, darling."

"Cow," 'Josie' said mildly, and stepped out of the wire-framed skirt. "The whole lot of us'll be old bags by the time we get to Glasgow. Rehearsals all morning and afternoon tomorrow! And I wanted to see the Castle—it would happen when I've left it until the last day."

"Supposing Jock comes back tomorrow night? It's absurd to make changes until we know for certain. If he's ill again . . ."

"Well, we don't *know* that, do we? In any case Harry Archer's furious and probably won't *have* him back."

"Poor Jock."

"I'm not at all surprised—when you think how peculiar he's been lately. Last night, for instance, throwing those knives about. It's a wonder Colin wasn't killed in full view of the audience. I was almost prepared to go into black today—pass me that tin of cream, doll." 'Josie' began blandly to wipe off his make-up.

"Has Colin said anything to you?"

"Not a word. As far as I can see he doesn't appear particularly worried."

"Surely he must know something? They're sharing digs."

"I knew it would be disaster. I said so at the time, and so did you. *You* know what Jock's like—you were in digs with him yourself for one week. Very intimate and cosy."

"Very. He spoke about six words the entire time. It was lovely. Just the sort of companion for a wet week in Stockport." 'Netta's' expression became pensive at the memory. For a few minutes they cleaned their faces.

"Oh—I'd love a gin now." 'Josie' slumped against the chair-back.

"No chance of that, the pubs are closed."

"If we were on the Continent everything would be so much easier. No stupid restrictions about drinks or worrying about other people. One could be oneself—completely natural." Patting on a little sun-tan powder, 'Josie' went over to the basin and washed his hands and armpits with a tablet of Highland Heather soap. Although not so chic as French Fern it was the next best thing, and someone had told him it was all the rage just now at the H.L.I. barracks.

"Perhaps," said 'Netta,' reverting to the previous subject, "they've had another row. I expect Jock's gone drinking again."

"Oh well, if he wants to drown his sorrows . . . we can't do anything about it anyway. What I want to know is, if he doesn't come back, who's going to take his place? There's nobody in the company to fill it—you or I couldn't throw those daggers, that's quite certain."

"My dear, I can't pick up a paper-knife without feeling faint."

"No. And I'd refuse to black my body all over unless I could look like Josephine Baker. I've an idea there's going to be a lot of heart-burning when they begin rearranging the show."

"Oh, I do hope they won't let Tessa sing any more!"

"Or Magda—worse still."

"Much worse! But we've already lost Butch, and if Jock . . . They'll *have* to get some new people."

"Not at *our* expense!" 'Josie's' eyes glinted with the promise of a battle royal. "We've been in the show right from the beginning. I shall insist on having a solo dance—and you could do your 'Pierrette' number." He paused, frowning, and then asked suspiciously: "I suppose Colin can't sing?"

"I don't think so. I've never heard him."

"Oh. Well, that's all right . . . Hurry up, dear, we don't want to miss seeing him before he goes. It's been a bit of a week, hasn't it? What with one thing and another. Not that I'm complaining— things were getting terribly dreary."

"Ghastly," 'Netta' agreed.

"When you think of the old days—something used to happen *every* night. Do you remember in *Out of Uniform*, the time that Johnny Larkin went haywire in the interval one night and screamed 'Knives and forks! Knives and forks! Mad woman covered in muck!' . . . God knows why . . . and ran out into Portsmouth High Street with hardly a stitch on?"

"Yes! Lena Larkin! She was always doing things like that. What about in Plymouth—she went out in drag after the show and a Rear Admiral or someone tried to pick her up—only the wind blew her wig off and she had to run for it. For her life, I mean—not the wig."

"Wasn't it Plymouth where Tony Orlando forgot to stop in time during his strip-tease, and the curtain stuck and they couldn't black out the lights?"

"No, dear, Chatham."

"Do you remember poor old 'Tottie Faye'?"

"Yes, and do you remember Eric Whatever-it-was?"

"Who could forget? And 'Helen' Twelvetrees . . ."

"And 'Claudia' . . ."

"'Baroness' Griffin . . ."

"Camp . . ."

"Glorious . . . Dead, I expect."

"Must be."

"All that drink."

"And drugs."

"And sex."

"Oh dear . . . isn't it sad, when you think? . . ."

CHAPTER 8

Outside the main post office, Alan hastily said goodnight to Gavin and began walking home. In a moment of weakness during the afternoon he had accepted Gavin's invitation to attend a meeting arranged by the Caledonia Discussion Group—which, judging by the name, should have been warning enough. For three hours he had sat in a badly ventilated basement room, trying with diminishing success to look and sound intelligent about such vital matters as Reason and Unreason in Kant (expounded and explained in twenty minutes by an eighteen-year-old student of the University). Was Richard III Guilty? (No. He was completely misunderstood, according to Miss Fiona Drummond, who silenced any dissenters by the alarming authority of all her seventeen years.) Is Television Harmful to the Young? (Yes, if it became a habit and encouraged laziness, but then again, educationally, it could be a great source of enlightenment—handled properly—in backward countries. The advanced Scots must be tolerant about it, warned young Iain Lennox, modestly concluding his twelve-minute dissertation.)

And so it went on, intensely solemn and humourless—with a short half-way break for refreshments; but by then Alan was even flatter than the buttered bannocks which Fiona's mother had supplied and, from their primitive appearance and taste, obviously cooked over a bonfire. The coffee was equally revolting and tasted of long-settled dust. Wishing to escape from so much hot air (in more senses than one) he rose from his chair and crossed the room, with the intention of taking Gavin aside and quietly explaining that he would have to go. Unfortunately, Gavin was deeply engrossed in conversation with an austere-looking girl in a hand-knitted dress, who repeatedly shook her head and kept saying in a determined voice, "I don't agree. I don't agree at all. You're quite wrong." Rather anxiously he waited for a suitable opportunity to speak, but Gavin refused to be intimidated by the austere girl and calmly went on talking. If they didn't stop soon, he thought, it would be too late. He would be trapped. Somewhat furtively he glanced at the door, wondering whether he could unobtrusively edge towards it and slip out while nobody was looking. However, it was not to be; Iain Lennox, mistaking his apprehensive expression, touched his arm and whispered, "It's outside at the end of the passage if you want it," and before he could assure him it was quite all right and that he *didn't* want it, Gavin suddenly turned round and ordered him to "come and talk to Ursula." With terrible foreboding his heart sank as Ursula fixed her eye on him and said with slightly sinister implication, "I've been watching you. You've got a very interesting head." To prevent her going any further, he quickly offered her a cigarette. "I don't smoke," she declined loftily, making it sound as if he were trafficking in reefers.

He was thankful when Fiona clapped her hands and announced that they would now have some music and would everybody please sit down. This was more to his liking, and he settled in his chair, carefully ensuring that he was sitting well behind Ursula and out of range from her keenly inspecting eyes. "What's it to be, this week, Murray?" Fiona asked the University student. And "Oh, lovely!" she responded, as Murray informed her. There were little sighs and murmurs of appreciation from the Group. His own pleasurable anticipation was instantly extinguished at the mention of the composer's name. Boris Kalavinsky. And the 'cello concerto, of all things! Nothing, unless it were the same composer's violin sonata, could be more hideous than this experimental work of advanced atonality, in which the solo instrument was made to writhe and choke like some doomed animal trapped at the bottom of a very nasty drain. It was Kalavinsky's farewell to music, for shortly after completing the concerto he was found dead in rather peculiar circumstances in an hotel bedroom in Bucharest. This had led to minor repercussions in Rumanian musical circles, not in any way due to his position as a composer, but for the simple reason that the coveted professorship he held at the Conservatoire automatically fell vacant on his decease. As a respectful afterthought, however, subscriptions were raised and the money used to perpetuate his two most 'significant' works by way of a rather turgid gramophone recording. It became a collector's piece among ardent discophiles—and here again it was not the importance of the composition, or the limited number of records in existence, which accounted for its success. Its claim to posterity rested upon the third movement of the concerto, where the 'cellist, waging a losing battle against the tyranny of the score, was heard giving vent to his grievance in an utterance (presumably Rumanian) which to all intents and purposes sounded exactly like "Oh, bugger this!" The recording engineers had not troubled to delete the now famous interspersion—but even acknowledging their limited acquaintance with the English language, they must obviously have been aware that the soloist was far from enjoying his task, and that his oral and instrumental tones were definitely not ones of pure ecstasy.

Surely, wondered Alan, as Murray opened the lid of the gramophone, they were not going to have the whole concerto? It was half-past nine already and the damned thing took over an hour to play. The first movement alone lasted for thirty-five minutes, and the *andante,* although shorter, seemed twice as long because of its tedium.

"I think," said Murray, eyeing them all solemnly, "we'll wait until the end before criticising and discussing. In that way we can absorb the work as a whole without interrupting the fluidity of the composer's conception and intentions. I warn you that it's a very difficult work, but for those who are prepared really to listen with open, receptive minds it will be extremely rewarding." Murray finished his introduction with a satisfied smile, and Fiona nodded approvingly. Then the first movement of the concerto began.

After about ten minutes or so, in which Alan had gazed stonily at the wire-mesh grille set in the walnut panelling of the gramophone, he cast a dubious glance at the members of the Group. He saw at once that their reactions to Kalavinsky's dismal outpourings were not the same as his own. On him, the effect of this excruciating dirge—one could not term it 'music'—was, apart from the isolated occasions when he shook with inward laughter at some of the more violent passages, one of acute boredom. But apparently this was not so with the Group. As if taking part in a seance and listening to the medium's voice coming through the loudspeaker, all had their eyes closed and all were sitting in attitudes of intense concentration, their heads raised ceilingwards and their hands clutching the arms of their chairs. And while they were thus transfixed, a serious mechanical defect in the gramophone brought the concerto to a sudden and premature halt—rudely shattering the trance-like state of the company. There were subdued moans of disappointment, increasing in volume and despair as Murray, Iain and Gavin failed in turn to rectify the fault.

"Oh dear," bewailed Fiona, "we shall lose the thread of the whole thing. It's terribly interesting, that movement. The way it builds up, then suddenly . . . Didn't you notice? The music was almost *silent* . . . do you know what I mean?"

"It's definitely *got* something," Ursula affirmed, "but one would want to hear it again. I do feel that the 'cello tone is a little *thick* sometimes, but that may be purely a personal opinion . . ."

"Oh, but I think that's intentional," Fiona protested. "I mean, the 'cello *not* being absolutely *plastic*—there's tremendous *strength* and *tautness*—how can I express it? A sort of *inner conflict* all the time. I mean, when you listen to the accompaniment going *one* way and the 'cello going the *other*—it's a sort of challenge, you see? Perhaps, musically, it's unorthodox—at least to the *purist* . . . and really that's *so* old-fashioned, isn't it? . . . but I *do feel* that the basic structure is sound and that we were right in choosing it for discussion. After all, we pride ourselves on being fairly advanced and tackling things which . . ." She gave a superior smile and gazed contemplatively at a Picasso reproduction hanging above the fireplace.

At ten o'clock the gramophone still refused to function, in spite of Murray's assurance that "we'll get it going in a minute." And at ten-fifteen, when an intricate piece of mechanism clattered down inside the machine, he informed them that he would have to telephone the radio repairs shop in the morning.

"How tantalising," said Fiona. "I do want to hear the rest of the concerto. Perhaps we can fit it in next week, although we've got an awfully full programme and Stewart Fraser's promised to bring his oboe."

"I saw him yesterday," said Iain.

"How is he?" inquired Ursula.

"Oh, he seemed all right. Considering."

"That's rather surprising. When you think," Ursula looked somewhat doubtful.

"Oh, I don't know. Not really—when you know him as *we* do," Fiona added to this rather mystifying conversation. "Anyway, you must all come next week. And you, too, Mr. Kendrick, of course. We like to welcome any friends of members."

The thought of Stewart Fraser's oboe and Kalavinsky's concerto all in one evening was too much for Alan. He politely murmured his thanks and inwardly vowed never to set foot in the place again.

"Well?" asked Gavin, a few minutes later, as they walked towards Waterloo Place. "What did you think of it?"

"Don't you dare suggest anything like it again."

"But I thought you'd be interested. Highbrow stuff and all that."

"I've never heard so much cock in all my life."

"Oh." Gavin sounded hurt. "Being a bit sweeping, aren't you? I think it's a good thing for people to get together and talk about worth-while subjects."

"I'm sorry, Gavin. They mean well, I'm sure. But, quite frankly, *what* do they mean?"

"Well . . ." Gavin began, and then stopped, thinking it wiser to leave the question unanswered.

After parting from Gavin, Alan turned into North Bridge. He felt he needed fresh air, and decided to walk back to The Meadows. It had been a wasted evening. In fact, the whole day had been unsatisfactory, including the luncheon date with Colin, which had not proved entirely successful. What should have been an enjoyable occasion had been marred once again by his uneasiness over his feelings towards Colin. The first shock of disappointment he received was the discovery that Colin wasn't really listening to him as he talked; and later he was even more disturbed to find himself inwardly criticising the boy. He knew it was foolish to expect too much from someone of Colin's age, but what dismayed him was the suggestion of ruthlessness beneath the cool, calm façade. One or two things Colin had said strength-ened this impression, and by the end of their hour together he was forced to admit that however much the boy's good looks attracted him he could not blind himself to the less favourable aspects of his personality. He had particularly noticed Colin's habit of sheering from any direct questions about his presence in Edinburgh; it was all very mysterious. Despite their frank conversation yesterday afternoon, he still knew nothing about him—his real character eluded him. There was something arti-ficial in that cool, vague manner which, had they been strangers to one another, might perhaps seem understandable; but all this beating about the bush was quite unnecessary. He must have it out with the boy.

Occupied with these thoughts, it was a sudden shock to see Colin waiting at a tram stop only a few yards along the pave-ment. Two people were with him and they were laughing and talking together, and as he approached he saw the startled look of recognition on Colin's face. His eyes went quickly to the boy's companions, noticing at once their effeminate appearance and mannerisms. One of them was obviously made up and overpow-eringly scented. Whatever was Colin doing with these types?

Colin hastily recovered himself and greeted him calmly. "Oh, hullo, Alan. I didn't expect to see you this time of night."

"I'm on my way home."

"Yes, so are we—but not all in the same direction. I was waiting until their tram came. Oh—this is Jo and Bobby. Alan Kendrick."

Rather embarrassed, he shook hands with them and was sur-prised by their firm clasps. At least that was one point in their favour; he had expected a limp and dainty toying of fingers. All the same he was slightly uncomfortable from the way Jo eyed him up and down.

"Do you live in Edinburgh?" Bobby asked politely. "It's an interesting place, isn't it? Historically."

"Oh dear . . ." Jo laughed and pulled a face.

"Well, it *is*. What's so funny about that?"

"Here's your tram," said Colin.

"See you at the theatre, tomorrow. Don't be late, rehearsal's at ten-thirty. 'Bye!"

Rapidly they were borne away.

"I must get back," said Colin. "Are you coming the same way?" He noticed that Alan was looking at him strangely, and hurriedly went on. "It's still awfully cold in the evenings. I suppose you're used to it—or don't you feel it?"

"Are those two particular friends of yours?"

"I know them quite well. They're not *close* friends, if that's what you mean."

"I hope not. They hardly seem your type."

"You needn't sound so disapproving, when you don't even know them."

"Colin, what is all this? I don't understand . . ."

"All what?"

"About rehearsals—and seeing you at the theatre . . ."

"Oh—well . . . they're in the show at the Palace."

"Good God. I might have guessed from the look of them. How on earth did you get in with them? They're not your class— at least, I shouldn't have thought so. Do you *have* to watch them rehearse?"

"Really, Alan, I'm not still a child. I don't have to account to you for everything I do. You must get out of this habit of lecturing me."

"I'm sorry. But you can't expect me not to be interested . . ."

"Yes, I know, but you criticise too much."

"I see. If you don't want me to know . . ."

"What *should* you know, anyway?"

"That's just it. Look, Colin—if we're to be friends, let's be quite honest with one another."

"What do you mean?"

"It's fairly obvious that you've avoided telling me certain things. And it worries me. Surely, by now, you can trust me? What is all this mystery?"

"Mystery? Really, I . . ."

"Well, isn't it? You've told me absolutely nothing. Not a word of why you're here or how long you're staying. You can't see me in the evenings—and yet you find time to go about with those— those travesties from the theatre."

"You've no right to say that. Just because Josie and Netta——"

Unthinkingly, from force of habit, their names had slipped out.

"Is that what they're called? I might have known it."

"And what of it? Good heavens, nearly everyone gets called names like that—it's just an amusing bit of camp."

"I don't find it very funny."

"Aren't you being a bit priggish? Jo and Bobby are perfectly harmless, hard-working people and you can't expect the theatre to be like a Sunday school outing."

"That isn't the point. They may be all right personally, but I hate anything that publicly stresses that sort of thing. It's difficult enough for us as it is, and it gives a false impression. The majority are going to judge us all in that light."

"Oh, nonsense, they love the show. Don't be so old-fashioned. I'm surprised at you."

"I'm only telling you what I feel, Colin."

"In other words, you don't approve of me?"

"I don't like seeing you mixed up with that type of person."

"All right, Alan, you've delivered your little sermon. You might call it 'But for the Grace of God . . .' Or is your own conscience so clear?"

Stung by Colin's words, Alan was silent.

"From what I remember, you've changed a great deal, Alan."

"I'm afraid we both have."

"You couldn't expect me to remain ten years old indefinitely. Oh, I know you're disappointed in me, but you'll have to accept me as I am."

"Perhaps I could do that if I really *knew* what you are. I mean that seriously, Colin."

"It sounds as if you wanted me to 'confess' something."

"I'd like to feel that you can tell me anything you want to."

They had reached the gate of 'Glen Garry,' and Colin stopped. "This is where I'm staying."

"Will you have lunch with me tomorrow?" asked Alan.

"Yes, of course. Thanks. One o'clock, at the same place? Good night, Alan."

Colin quickly went into the house. Alone in his room, he sighed with relief, pleased to find that Jock had definitely gone, taking his belongings with him. The bed was re-made, and on the table supper was laid for one. This morning he had breakfasted alone and then gone out early, leaving Jock still asleep. That was the last he had seen of him, for Jock had not turned up at the theatre tonight. He had just crept away, before he could be told to go . . . it had spared them another unpleasant scene, anyhow.

He sat down and began his meal; but although it was pleasant to be on his own, and to be rid of Jock, another problem remained to be faced. It really looked as if Alan were going to be rather tiresome and difficult. No doubt it was well-intentioned, all this questioning and lecturing, and appeals for shared confidences, but there was just a little too much of the guardian or the welfare officer in his manner—and in time it would probably grow worse; that strong, reforming streak in a person could so easily become over-earnest and deadly dull. Already, tonight, there had been a hint of it in that censorious pronouncement on poor 'Josie' and 'Netta,' and there was no reason to suppose that Alan, upon receiving further disclosures more closely affecting him, would waive his disapproval and calmly accept the situation. What, then, should be done about it? At this stage it wasn't going to be easy to put Alan off the scent and at the same time keep him interested and attentive. Alan wasn't so soft as he had first imagined! Sometimes, of course, it was better not to appear so readily available—it lowered one's worth—but in this case there was no time left for such tactics. And when he was away from Edinburgh, would Alan still be as keen? Only, perhaps, on receiving a binding promise which allowed him exclusive ownership.

It needed thinking about, especially after hearing Alan's comments about people's behaviour and his obvious dislike of anything at all 'gay' on the stage. Either he would have to give up the theatre altogether, or else devise some means of holding Alan's interest while they were apart—and without revealing that he was on tour in the revue. How could it be done? He would be expected to write letters, and he would be getting replies, but what explanation could he give for a different address every week? Perhaps . . . it might work . . . he could tell Alan that he had a new job which entailed travelling round the country. In that way, he would have plenty of time to decide about the future, without missing any chances of promotion in the show—and it wasn't unlikely, now that changes were being made—then when the tour ended he could pop up to Edinburgh to see Alan. After all, if Alan had managed to go without seeing him for ten years, a few months' more waiting wouldn't harm him. He would settle the matter tomorrow, during lunch. But now, he really must get some sleep; he wanted to be quite fresh for the morning rehearsal. Jo had said that it would probably be somewhat electric, with sparks flying in all directions.

The bed seemed extra luxurious and springy after the hardness and discomfort of the settee, and just for a moment it reminded him of Jock—he was probably at home, in Glasgow, by now. On Monday, he would be there himself; but it seemed unlikely that they'd bump into each other. Unless Jock came to the theatre and tried to make trouble . . . he wouldn't put it past him . . . not that he'd get anywhere, if he did. Having walked out on the show, there was no chance of being taken back. No doubt someone else would be engaged to fill his place, although the thought of facing a new knife-thrower was rather alarming. After the recent experiences with Jock, it would take time to regain confidence, however skilful another partner might be. Of course, there was a possibility of the act being dropped and replaced by something quite different—he could be shot from a cannon, or just perform a simple dance with a skipping rope. Both, if necessary. How did one train to become a human cannon-ball? Perhaps courses were held at the Tower of London during ceremonial salutes . . . a full class could be fired across the Thames on the Queen's Birthday . . .

For nearly an hour Jock had waited, leaning against a tree trunk and out of sight from the road. Only a narrow strip of tufted grass lay between the near pavement and the rooty ground on which he stood, but the shadows of leaves and branches concealed him, and the line of trees made an effective screen against the light of the street lamps. Facing him, on the other side of the street, were the large, grey-stoned houses which this morning he had examined while slowly walking the length of The Meadows. By a stroke of luck he had seen Alan emerge from a wrought-iron gate and walk briskly away. Tonight, it had been a simple matter to find the house again.

He had been in a miserable state the whole day; angry and bitter over last night's scene with Colin, whose steel-like hardness goaded him and finally drove him to violence. Everything between them was finished, but there was still no peace for him and no lessening of jealousy. Something compelled him to come here and wait, although he had no clear idea of what he would do or say when the moment arrived. He had been drinking a good deal, too, with the vain hope of finding comfort or even exhilaration—anything to dispel the unhappiness which gnawed him. All it had produced was a dull feeling of resentment and belligerence, already fading as the effect of the whisky wore off. He felt tired, now, and his hand was smarting after badly scratching it on the bark of the tree. In the darkness he had stumbled over the twisted roots, and to save himself from falling had clutched at the rough wood of the trunk.

He looked at the luminous dial of his watch. It was nearly eleven-thirty. No people or cars had gone by for some time. Supposing nobody came . . . He couldn't wait here much longer. If he left it too late, he'd never get a hotel room anywhere. Anxiously he looked across at the house. The porch light was still on, which meant that somebody had yet to come in. It was unlikely that a Scottish householder would keep it alight all night. He was beginning to feel cold; the wind had risen and was blowing from the east. But suddenly he was alert. At a distance, on the opposite pavement, he could discern someone quickly walking, and as the figure drew nearer—a man in a raincoat—he saw the unmistakable red gleam of his hair. Saw, too, that he was on his own.

"What are you doing here?" Alan was surprised at seeing Jock, who came up to him as he reached the gate. At once he noticed his tense, strained manner.

"I've got to see ye."

"What about?"

"I think ye already know that."

"Oh? Do I? Is it urgent? It's a bit late now, wouldn't tomorrow . . ."

"No. It canna wait till tomorrow."

"How did you know where I lived?"

"I knew the road but wasna sure of the house—till I saw ye leave this morning."

"Oh . . . Why didn't you speak to me then?"

"I had to make up my mind—decide aboot ye, first."

"What on earth . . . Look here, what is all this about? What are you driving at?"

"It's aboot yersel' and—and Colin . . ."

"I see." Alan could think of nothing better to say, although from his point of view it was an appropriate statement. He *did* see, now, and clearly. If there had been any doubts in his mind about the exact relationship between Jock and Colin, they were instantly dispelled. There was no mistaking Jock's meaning, in the accusing tone of his words. He could at last understand the reasons for Colin's evasiveness, his avoidance of certain questions, and his vague excuses for not being available in the evenings. But why hadn't Colin told him the truth in the first place, instead of making him believe that no serious attachment existed? In fact, the boy had appeared to be encouraging him; but perhaps it was merely to arouse Jock's jealousy. He had certainly succeeded in doing so, if Jock's present behaviour was anything to go by. But somehow, even in his own disappointment, he felt no resentment towards this obviously hurt and angry young Scotsman. If he could, he would try to ease Jock's mind a little.

"There's nothing between Colin and me, Jock. There never has been. I've known nothing whatever about him since he was a kid—nothing at all, until a couple of days ago. Believe me, I'm sorry if things have gone wrong between you. It would have been better for all of us if Colin had told me the truth—I don't mean he's exactly lied—he's just avoided saying anything at all."

"I'm no' surprised," Jock said bitterly. "That's his way—he'll lead ye on and play wi' ye."

"Did you expect him to be with me tonight? Is that why you waited—in case we came back here together? You needn't have worried. This house isn't mine, and I don't live on my own. But I did see him tonight, quite by accident. I walked with him as far as the boarding house. We didn't have a very satisfactory conversation." Alan suddenly noticed Jock's hand. "How did you get that?"

"I scratched it a wee bit, on a tree."

"It looks like a deep cut."

"It'll be all right."

"I shouldn't leave it too long. Put something on it."

"Aye. I'll do that," Jock mumbled. "I'm not sure if I have anything . . ."

"Well—you'd better let me fix it for you; it won't take a moment. I've got a proper first-aid box. Come inside, only don't make a noise."

Alan opened the gate, and Jock followed him up the path to the front door. They entered the house, and Alan switched on the hall light and turned out the lamp in the porch. Julia had gone to bed, and the rest of the ground floor was in darkness.

Jock stared with interest at the pictures and furniture. "It's guid taste ye have here. It must be verra valuable."

"Yes, some of it is."

"And it's no' yours? Ye were living in London before this, weren't ye? On yer own?"

"Yes. In a furnished flat."

"Since a bairn I've nae had a home. I canna remember much aboot it. Och—it wasna like this—I was better awa' from it. A back street in Glasgow." Jock's face clouded, and then he asked quietly: "Ye said the other day that it was yer auntie who lived here. Does she know aboot ye?"

"I don't think so. It's very unlikely. She's not the inquisitive type, anyway. I think we'd better see about your hand, it's getting late."

They went upstairs. Alan had his own bathroom, adjoining the bedroom at the back of the house. He washed his hands, and then, while Jock rinsed away the blood, opened the first-aid box and took out a neatly shaped dressing. The job was completed in a few seconds.

"That'll keep it clean. I should wear it as long as possible."

"Aye, I will. Thanks."

"Right. I'll see you down to the door. Sorry I can't do more for you, Jock, but at least you know how things are now. You can be

clear in your mind that I've no intention of becoming a dangerous rival." Alan opened the bathroom door. "I hope it will work
out all right. I shouldn't do anything about it tonight, though,
unless—unless you can't avoid seeing him." He saw Jock looking
uneasy and miserable, and wondered why he didn't move.

"I'll no' be seeing him again. I couldna stand it any longer. I've
left the boarding house."

"But why did you come here and watch the house?"

"Mebbe to satisfy mysel'."

"If it's all over between you, what's the point in doing that?"

"I canna tell. I canna tell what I've been doing today."

"I'm really sorry, Jock."

"Aye."

"Let me know if I can do anything. I know it's not much good
saying 'Don't let it get you down' ... Where are you staying
now?"

"Oh, it'll no' matter. I'll find somewhere."

"But ... Good God, do you mean you haven't anywhere to
go?"

"I'll find a place. I was going to, only—well, I've been drinking
and ..."

"You won't get anything at this time of night. Isn't there anyone—friends you could go to, who'd put you up?"

"I've no friends in Edinburgh. Mebbe I can get a lift to Glasgow. I could find somebody there. But I'll no' go to relations.
It'll only make trouble." Jock stared at him sombrely. "I'd best be
awa' now."

"No ... Jock—that's damned silly. You might be wandering
about all night. You—you can stay here, if you like."

"I've caused ye enough bother, wi'out ye having to take a
stranger in."

"We're not really strangers, Jock. You're welcome to stay. If
you don't still feel badly about me ... I'll quite understand if you
don't want to, of course ..."

"It's kind of ye. Aye, I'll stay. I wasna very keen aboot being
out all night. But I—I havena got any clothes wi' me—my case is
at Waverley Station."

"That's all right, you can borrow something of mine. Would

you like to wash now? Might as well—as you're in the bathroom. I'll be in the next room. Oh—er—would you like anything to eat?"

"Och, no, thank ye verra much."

Alan closed the door and went into his bedroom. Altogether, he thought, it had been a very strange evening. The Discussion Group, the chance encounter with Colin, and now this unexpected development. He hoped he hadn't made a mistake by asking Jock to stay. He really knew nothing at all about him; but seeing him looking so miserable, he couldn't let him go off with only a vague hope of finding shelter and the possibility of having to walk most of the way to Glasgow. And after all, they had something in common; both of them had been led a pretty dance . . . He undressed and, using the basin in the corner of the room, cleaned his teeth and washed. He put on his pyjamas and found another pair for Jock—blue silk ones which he bought in Italy on his last visit. Presently Jock appeared, carrying his jacket, his shirt sleeves rolled up; already he looked fresher and less strained, and his hair curled damply. He had probably put his head under the tap, for there were wet patches on his shirt.

"All right?"

"Aye. I feel better."

"There's a comb on the dressing-table, if you want it." He watched Jock glance round the room before going slowly over to the table. The jet-black hair glistened under the light, springing into thick curls as he ran the comb through it. "Pyjamas, on the bed."

"Thanks." Jock picked them up. "Where do I have to go now?"

"What?"

"To sleep, I mean."

"Well—that's just it. I'm afraid it's got to be in here, there isn't another room ready at the moment. If you think it'll be too cramped, I'll sleep on the mattress, on the floor. I can find some spare blankets, although it won't leave the bed very comfortable for you."

"No—no, ye mustna do that. Ye've had enough bother. I'll be all right." Jock hastily looked at the bed. "It's a fair size. I hope I'll no' keep ye awake."

"I shouldn't think so. Well—we'd better turn in, hadn't we?" Alan got into bed and pressed the switch which put out the light over the dressing-table. The shaded lamp beside him cast a subdued, glowing circle over the bedclothes. He closed his eyes. He could hear Jock moving about quietly, taking off his clothes and folding them and placing them on a chair. It seemed odd, having someone else in the room with him, after being on his own for so long. Odd, but somehow friendly, in spite of the strangeness of the situation. A sharp jolting of the bed hastily aroused him, and he opened his eyes. Jock was swearing under his breath.

"Och, I'm sorry. I stubbed my toe."

Alan sat up. Jock's face was partly in darkness, but the warm, shaded light gleamed rosily on his body. He had not meant to stare; and neither, he thought, had Jock intended any deliberate exhibition. Both were held in surprise, immovable for a second. His astonishment at this sudden, intimate glimpse of nakedness changed into frank admiration. Unguarded as he stood, there was a vital strength and beauty in Jock's magnificent physique; a fine sculpture of limbs and trunk—compact and restrained, for all its suggestion of power—and possessing, in its completed maleness, a natural and unoffending simplicity. Then Jock bent down swiftly, picked up the pyjamas and turned away. After a moment he came back to the bed, clad in the blue silk.

"Sorry if I embarrassed you. Staring like that."

"It doesna matter," Jock murmured.

"You reminded me of a statue. Hermes. Anyway, you're in pretty good shape."

"I have to keep fit."

"How old are you, Jock?"

"Twenty-seven. Why?"

"I just wondered. Hadn't you better get into bed?" Jock slipped in beside him, and Alan continued: "Shall I turn out the light or would you like to talk for a bit?"

"Aye, if ye like."

"I think I would. Let's have a fag, shall we? I don't know why it is, but lately I've taken to smoking in bed. A bad habit."

"Mebbe it calms ye."

"You think I need it? Perhaps you're right. What about you?"

Jock drew hard on his cigarette. "I havena slept well for a long while."

"Yes, I can imagine that. Has it—has all this business hurt you very much?"

"Aye. Bad enough."

"Jock—what do you do for a living?"

"I—I've been all sorts."

"Yes, but now? You are working, aren't you?"

"I was until yesterday."

"Oh. That's bad luck. Do you think you'll get something in Glasgow?"

"I'm no' certain. I havena really thought yet."

"Have you been in Edinburgh very long?"

"Well—no, I havena . . ." Jock looked away uncomfortably.

"Was it a good job? What happened, though, did you get the sack?"

"I left it. I'll no' go back."

"Was it because of Colin?"

Jock turned and stared at Alan, looking at him suspiciously for a moment. "Has he told ye?"

"Nothing at all—either about you or himself. Anyway, I won't pretend that I don't want to know."

"Mebbe ye won't like it," Jock replied grimly.

"What do you mean?"

"Och, I suppose the harm's done now—it canna matter any more. But I'll tell ye, I've got nothing to hide for mysel' . . ."

"Hide?"

"Ye have to do the work that's best fitted for ye. I'm no' sae proud of it, but it's a living like any other. It needs skill . . ."

"Well, go on. You can tell me, surely?"

"Aye, but ye mustna think I had any influence on Colin. I've been working an act in a show—a knife-throwing act . . ."

"Oh, I see. That must take a bit of doing. And you've left the show? What show is it?"

"It's a touring revue. I expect ye've heard of it. At the Palace Theatre."

"The Palace—— Oh . . ."

"I know it isna everyone's taste . . ."

"I've heard it's good of its kind; but you certainly surprise me, Jock. Funnily enough, when I saw Colin tonight, he was with two of the boys from the show. He told me he was going to a rehearsal in the morning. I didn't connect it in any way with you—although I don't see why he should want to go if you've left it, and if you've both finished with each other. How long have you known him, Jock? Did you meet him up here—or did he come up to see you? He said something about not having a job, but of course I didn't know he was here because of you . . ."

"Och, no, ye havena caught on." Jock sighed and shook his head. "I thought ye'd be quicker than that, wi'out my telling ye. Have ye no idea at all? Have ye no' wondered why he hasna told ye? Well, I knew he wouldna, because he thought it would spoil his wee game. Ye've got a shock coming."

"Jock—what the hell . . ."

"Aye, he's in the show all right. Part of the act. We worked together. A few weeks now it's been."

"Good God." Alan stared at Jock in amazement. "You mean he's your partner in this knife act? But—but what does he do?"

"Stands in front of a board," Jock answered briefly.

"And you throw knives at him? It's incredible, I can hardly believe it. It seems a strange thing for him to want to do. I know it's your living—but for him to give up a good job just to become a knife-thrower's assistant . . . Where's it going to get him? It sounds a bit dangerous to me. No wonder he didn't want to tell me. My God . . . Of course, in a way I can understand his being attracted by the stage. But—*this* . . . well . . . I don't know . . . What about his parents? I shouldn't think they approve."

"He hasna said. I doubt if they do."

"What'll happen to him, now that you've parted? Has someone taken your place?"

"I don't know. I expect he'll stay on in the show. Mebbe they'll just drop the act and he'll stay in the chorus."

"He'll *what*? Let me get this straight. Are you—were you a separate act in the show?"

"We had to do other things as well."

"What sort of things?"

"I had to sing and dance—black myself up as a negro."

"And what does Colin do? Sing and dance as a negro, as well?"

"I canna see him doing that. He's in wi' the others."

"You mean dressed as a woman?" Alan spoke sharply. "Well, is he or isn't he?"

"Aye. But he's always been different from the rest——"

"Like hell he has! The little fool! And you're attracted by that sort of thing, are you, Jock?"

"Ye'll leave me out of it." Jock angrily stubbed his cigarette in the ash-tray. "I've told ye before, I've no' influenced him. I've no' wanted him to be friends wi' any of them. If ye understood anything aboot him ye'd know that ye canna have any effect on him—no matter how hard ye tried. And I shouldna worry yersel', because he's no' worth it."

Alan was silenced by the bitterness of Jock's words. He watched him turn away and lie down with his back to him. His own anger gradually subsided, and as he lay staring at the window curtains on the other side of the room he experienced a curious feeling of relief. The truth was out, and however dis-illusioning it might be, there was no longer any need to deceive himself. It had been a narrow escape. He had hovered on the edge of a fool's paradise, unwilling to accept the warnings of his better judgment. Colin was lost to him, but his deepest regret was for the utter waste of talent, the wanton throwing away of so much promise; and somehow it was impossible to believe that this embracement of a rather dubious form of glamour could ever really satisfy him, whatever the need for expressing this dual aspect of his nature. He realised, though, that there was nothing in his own experience or inclinations which would make him capable of a full understanding; it was something beyond his comprehension.

He lay still for a while, listening to Jock's quiet breathing. He turned and looked at the dark head beside his own on the pillow. Jock had suffered far more than he.

"Jock . . ." He spoke softly. "Jock . . ."

"Aye. What is it?"

"I don't know. At least—I just wanted to say *something*. Any-thing. To break the silence. I know you're feeling bloody miser-able."

"Och, I'll be all right," Jock murmured.

"That's fine. I'll put out the light."

In the darkness, Alan could hear the faint ticking of his travelling-clock on the bedside table. A scuffling sound came from the garden—a cat-fight by the pond. A mad squalling and scrambling up the stone wall followed. Then silence. A long time passed and he was still awake.

"Are ye asleep, Alan?" Jock whispered.

"No. Can't you get off, either?"

"It's being in a strange bed. Ye have to get used to it."

"Do you find it uncomfortable, sharing like this?"

"I didna mean that. It's fine, thanks. But I was thinking, if I moved, mebbe it would disturb ye."

"No, you can move, Jock. There's plenty of room." Alan slid his hand over the space between them. "Where are you? You must be almost on the floor." He felt Jock shift and draw nearer, turning on his side, and he rolled over to face him. Their heads were close and he could feel Jock's warm breath on his neck. "You're like a hot-water bottle, Jock."

"Aye, I'm a bit warm. So are ye." Jock lightly placed a hand on Alan's shoulder.

"Jock . . . This is a funny situation, isn't it? We might easily have been at daggers drawn."

"Aye, it's strange."

There was a long silence. Alan was conscious of the hand still touching his shoulder. "I shouldn't think you ever feel the cold, Jock. Your hand's like fire." Their fingers brushed. Jock tightly clenched his fist; his arm pressed against Alan's chest.

"I can feel yer heart beating," Jock whispered.

Alan made no reply. Jock's nearness and warmth was disturbing. He drew away, breaking the contact between them.

"I think we'd better get some sleep."

"Aye . . . I think mebbe we'd better," Jock replied slowly.

They turned from each other, lying quite still in the darkness. The sudden tenseness died, and they were alone in their separate thoughts.

As 'Josie' had forecast, sparks had begun to fly—and barely ten

minutes after the entire company had assembled on the stage. In
fact, the atmosphere became so charged that Harry Archer was
forced to take the rehearsal with the safety curtain lowered; thus
depriving the theatre cleaners of free entertainment while they
swept up the litter dropped by last night's audience. But apart
from confining the noise to one place, and not letting it be heard
from the auditorium or even, as seemed likely in this case, from
the foyer and the street outside, Harry had already been driven to
desperation by the unceasing exchange of pleasantries between
the various worthy ladies in the stalls, boxes and three circles.
Nothing could stop their chatter as, like a flock of sheep on a
hillside, they scrambled up and down the steep rows of seats.
Conversation was not restricted by distance, and height did not
preclude those in the gallery from talking to their fellow workers
down below in the stalls. Occasionally they paused to glance at
the stage and loudly comment on what was taking place there,
but very little surprised them, for the spectacle of 'Josie' prac-
tising high kicks, 'Betty' and 'Charlotte' trying out some new
'business' for their comedy ballerina act, and 'Magda' descending
the staircase while singing a contralto aria from *Carmen* was part
and parcel of the mad carryings-on of all theatrical people.

Poor Harry was confronted with the task of deleting certain
items from the show, replacing them by others, and firmly ignoring any complaints about unfairness and favouritism. "I don't
care," he said to 'Magda,' who had been the first to create, "I don't
care *what* you sing, whether it's *Carmen, Samson and Delilah* or
'Nellie Dean'—but you are *not* singing more than two numbers
in the first half." And during a pregnant pause, in which the whole
company inwardly crowed, 'Tessa' inadvertently let out a nervous
giggle. Like a tigress, 'Magda' rounded on him, slapped his face,
and with a ringing cry of "Bloody little castrato!" stormed off the
stage like a prima donna at La Scala. 'Tessa' dissolved in tears and
had to be taken behind the backcloth to recover. The next incident occurred during the alterations to the cabaret scene. Claud
was to take the place of the now defunct knife-throwing act; but
not without protest from 'Josie.' "I don't want to be difficult," he
said, "and we all know Claud plays brilliantly—" he gave a quick
smile in reply to Claud's sub-acid "Thank you, darling!" and went

on: "But don't you think it's a little unexciting? I mean, we've got the audience all worked up over the Can-Can, then there's a rest while Magda's on . . . if we follow that with a piano and go into *another* song, by Tessa, isn't it going to seem rather like a concert recital? It wants plenty of action, something that builds up to the finale. Perhaps I'm wrong—I'm not the producer, but . . ."

"You most certainly aren't!" said 'Charlotte,' bristling. "If I remember rightly, Peter and I do our Apache number *somewhere* in this scene. Or has that been cut, too?"

"Oh, I'm sorry," said 'Josie,' "it was an oversight; of course I didn't mean——"

"*Oversight?* It's out-and-out sabotage!"

"Now, now, now," Harry interrupted soothingly. "Look here——"

"I will *not* look there!" 'Charlotte' snapped. "Nor will I have someone out of the chorus suggesting the running order of the show. Peter and I have been stars for twenty years, and there is a clause in our present contract stating quite clearly that the production is built round our personalities. We have every right to use what material we like, and *when* we like."

"Anyone would think you owned the show," said 'Josie' haughtily.

"And they wouldn't be far wrong, considering we're the principal backers," replied 'Betty.'

"Yes," said 'Charlotte,' "and now perhaps we can get on with the rehearsal. There's still the second half to go through."

"All right, kids," said Harry, silencing the murmur of voices which had broken out at 'Betty's' surprising information. "Pay attention. Before we go any farther, let me tell you that there'll be more rehearsals next week in Glasgow. We shall be having some new recruits and they'll need breaking in—or should I say breaking down?" Not a sound greeted this little sally. "We've got two shows tonight and I don't want to overwork you. So, if we can get through the second half without interruptions, I won't call you for this afternoon. With any luck we should be finished by one-thirty. Any questions? All right. Get cracking."

One-thirty . . . Colin heard this announcement with dismay. He was supposed to meet Alan for lunch at one o'clock. It was out of the question now to ask Harry if he could leave early. Alan might not wait half an hour for him—and it would probably be more than that; even if he got away promptly at one-thirty it would take about ten minutes to reach Hanover Street. Perhaps he could telephone Alan's club . . . hastily he searched his wallet for the card. There was no sign of it; he must have left it in the jacket pocket of his other suit. The number would be in the telephone directory, and if he missed the luncheon appointment he could ring Alan at work, but it wouldn't be the same as seeing him and being able to talk freely. The best way would be to go to the club and try to see him privately or, if there were other people in the office, have tea together in the lounge. What a damned nuisance it was that he couldn't ring him now, but Harry was keeping them all so busy and there just wasn't time enough to get to a phone. He could kill 'Magda' and 'Charlotte' for holding up everything and making them run late.

The rehearsal dragged on. 'Magda' had returned, remaining icily aloof from the others and singing "Softly Awakes My Heart" with a scowling, venomous expression on his face. 'Tessa's' voice cracked on an ear-piercing note in the middle of "My Hero," and Claud played nearly everything in the wrong key and said he wouldn't go on tonight unless the piano was retuned. At five minutes to two Harry dismissed them, remarking that they were bloody terrible and all in the wrong profession.

"Where are you off to?" asked 'Josie,' as Colin began to hurry from the stage.

"I've got to telephone someone."

"Well, be quick, then we can have lunch."

"Just a minute, boys . . ." Harry detained them. "Peter and Charles are trying out a new sketch tonight, which they want to rehearse this afternoon—in private. There's also a small part in it for someone else, and I thought perhaps one of you might like it."

"*How* small?" said 'Josie.' "I can't see *them* giving much away."

"I don't know. But I want a quick answer. How about you, Colin? A little compensation for the loss of the knife-throwing."

"Well—I . . . What time do they want to rehearse?"

"Directly after lunch. They're having sandwiches in their dressing-room. You'd better go and see them now."

"Oh dear . . . will it mean the whole afternoon?"

"I expect so. They'll want to get it as good as possible."

"Well, I don't know if I can—I was going out to tea . . ."

"If Colin doesn't want to, I don't mind doing it," said 'Netta.'

"Neither do I," said 'Josie.' "I mean—if it's going to help out . . ."

"And it might lead to something bigger, later on," said 'Netta.'

"We shall have to toss for it, Nett. Fair's fair. We can't *both* do it," said 'Josie.'

"All right, Harry," Colin rapidly decided, "I'll do it." After all, he thought, why should he be left behind in the rat race? It was well known in the theatre that if you dropped dead or merely fainted there was always somebody ready to step into your shoes. As likely as not they'd untie your laces before loosening your collar. Even his two friends appeared to have no conscience about seizing a part from under his nose. "I'll go and see Charles, but I must make a phone call first." And he dashed away.

"I expect it's a *very* small part," said 'Josie.' "Hardly worth doing."

"Yes," agreed 'Netta,' "and it's not like having an extra solo dance or song. Poor Colin . . . he'll miss the knife-throwing and not having a dressing-room to himself . . ."

By the time they had gone through all the disadvantages of appearing in a sketch with two comedians and having to share a crowded room at least three flights up from the stage, they were quite sorry for Colin. But they felt much better themselves.

Meanwhile, Colin had gone to the stage door and found the office locked. He would have to telephone from the call-box upstairs—leave a message for Alan, who was probably still at lunch alone and very late. But it couldn't be helped; he would try to get on to him later this afternoon. Passing the star dressing-room, he heard voices from within, and at the same moment the door opened and 'Charlotte' looked out, holding a sandwich in one hand.

"Ah, Colin . . . I asked Harry to send someone along. I'm glad it's you. Come in. Peter and I want someone for our new sketch. It's a nice little part—not much dialogue—but you'll be *seen* . . . Have you had lunch? No, of course you haven't—Peter, give him a sandwich. No, not those—they're my smoked salmon. Ham . . . that's right. Now then. I'll just give you a brief outline . . ."

Colin rehearsed until nearly six o'clock, and after swallowing a cup of tepid coffee from Peter's flask, it was time to get ready for the six-thirty performance. He telephoned the club, but Alan had just left, and whether it was for home or otherwise nobody seemed to know. What a hellish day it had been—except for the part in the sketch, and God knows he had earned it after sacrificing so much. He must speak to Harry, too, about having a separate dressing-room as usual, and perhaps his name on the posters. And tonight he would take 'Josie' and 'Netta' out to supper, just to show that there were no ill feelings.

Julia sat alone in the drawing-room, waiting for Alan to return home from the club. She was worried, and almost for the first time in her life felt nervous. Ever since this morning she had tried to reason with herself, convince herself that her imagination was carrying her away in the wrong direction. She was in a difficult position, facing a problem which, if wrongly handled, either through ignorance or lack of delicacy, could so easily destroy the warm and uncomplicated affection between Alan and herself. Although for many years she had selfishly enjoyed her independence and freedom from hampering personal ties, and respected any like desire in others, she now realised that this experience of freedom had been two-edged. While it had caused her to reject all tiresome 'family' relationships—and it must be conceded that there was no real love lost on either side—it had also had the effect of making her slightly inhuman. For years she had been so intent upon cultivating her independence and arranging her life to exclude what she called the 'inessentials' that she had, eventually, become too cut-and-dried and impersonal. In her wish to remain autonomous and preserve her insularity, she had respected the privacy of others; she had 'minded her own business'; to such an extent, however, that now, confronted with a problem requiring a more intimate approach, she found it extremely difficult to break a habit so deeply ingrained. She hated the thought of interfering, prying into something without any real knowledge to substantiate her reasons for so doing.

Was it wise, she wondered, to say anything to Alan? She would run a grave risk of putting him against her for ever, if she had mistakenly assumed something which did not exist, could not, in fact, have any part in his life. Even so, if she had not made that accidental discovery this morning, there had recently been something in his manner to suggest that her suspicion might be correct. She had been aware of it the other day, observing his state of nervous tension during lunch; then later, his over-anxiousness to conceal the fact that he was worried about the unfavourable impression made by his young friend, Colin. That was quite understandable, of course; from the little he had told her about his previous connection with boy's family, there had been enough to indicate that his affection for them was warmly returned—and by Colin in particular. But that was a long time ago, and although the boy had obviously turned out something of a disappointment, it was hard to believe it as being the main reason for so much agitation and strangeness in Alan's behaviour. Unless he were excessively sentimental, he could not expect the boy to look upon him with the same childlike and almost filial regard which had been natural in the circumstances at that time. If not completely sure of the dangerous ground she was treading, she was inclined, nevertheless, to think that Alan's feelings for Colin went far deeper than this. And how long had he been leading this secret life? Had it always been so, and was it in any way responsible for his broken marriage? Although he had divorced Myra for being unfaithful, her conduct might have resulted from some failure on his part to express all that she demanded from a husband. One could not be certain about that; according to many, Myra went to extremes in everything she did. However, it was no good dwelling in the past; the immediate situation and her own reactions to the matter concerned her far more.

How was she to deal with it? Certainly not by adopting a high-minded moral attitude and registering shock and outrage and disapproval. To be honest, she felt none of these things—only a sense of dismay in the fact that by some unkind twist of fate Alan was made to bear the penalties of being 'different.' She hated to see him suffer, and she wanted desperately to help him; but she could not do so by direct inference. If he thought she were trying to probe into his private affairs, he would probably suspect (although wrongly) that her lack of curiosity during the last few months had been merely to lull him into a false state of security. He would distrust her, draw farther away from her—perhaps leave the house and have nothing more to do with her. It was a horrible thought.

She checked herself. She was leaping to conclusions, forgetting that Alan was a kind, gentle person, and that he might equally be distressed for her sake. Perhaps it would be better to leave things as they were. He was adult; he was free to do as he pleased—she had made that clear when offering him a home—but in no way had he abused her hospitality or taken it for granted. Her own life had been enriched by his companionship. Everything about him couldn't suddenly become different, just because of this chance discovery. Today was the same as yesterday; last week—the preceding weeks and months. The mere fact of knowing it *then* or *now,* didn't matter. He had not altered—she must remember that. Neither had he deceived. By her deliberate eschewal of personal questions she could not expect a real intimacy between them. Thus she had made things needlessly difficult for herself.

Sighing deeply, she frowned and lit another cigarette. The ash-tray on the table beside her was brimming with stubs. Alan would be home soon, and she was no nearer to finding a solution to the problem. It was all very well, remaining silent, but what of her own peace of mind? To be the unsuspected owner of another's secret was in itself bad enough; but in this case the real danger existed in the fact that she possessed only a half-knowledge. By its power to invite speculation, her anxiety would doubly be increased. Taking such a thoroughly selfish attitude was, however, no help to Alan. It was unfair, especially if there were no real grounds for her supposition. She *could* be mistaken about that overheard conversation . . .

This morning, Alan had carried up a breakfast tray to Jock. She had not yet seen his friend, but was interested by the description Alan had given. Jock was rather reserved, he said, and smilingly added that he was also extremely good-looking. Replying that she could wait without undue impatience for his appearance downstairs, she went on with her breakfast and was still at the table when he hurried off to say goodbye to Jock. A few minutes later she went up to dress, but remembered that she hadn't asked Alan whether or not he would be in to dinner tonight. Quite unthinkingly she approached his door, then heard voices and saw that it was open. She stopped, not wanting to barge in on them, and the words came to her clearly from the open doorway.

". . . Had ye planned on seeing Colin at all?"

"Yes, today. For lunch."

"Och, I shouldna. It'll nae be any guid. He'll have ye on. There's no use in worrying yersel'. He's a cruel boy and hasna consideration or love except for himsel' . . . Aye, if ye'll heed me, Alan, ye'll do best to cut him out. Finish wi' him."

"I don't know what to do."

"He'll take care he's no' hurt. He'll no' be the one to suffer."

Fearing that Alan might discover her standing there, she quickly went to her room. She could not have faced him at that moment.

And now, hours later, she was still uncertain—wondering whether she had mistakenly attached too much importance to those few minutes of overheard conversation. Jock had merely warned Alan against seeing Colin again, and it confirmed her own opinion about the boy's possible worthlessness. She knew, also, that Alan hated the thought of hurting anyone. But she had sensed an emotional implication in Jock's words, an underlying concern; and he had mentioned 'love'—everything he had said appeared, on reflection, to be slightly ambiguous. Even if she had allowed herself to imagine things, it was a strange way of talking for one man to another. The more she thought about it, the more deeply involved it seemed. Who *was* Jock? If he could speak so frankly to Alan, it was obvious that he must have intimate knowledge of what was taking place. Although how was it that until now his existence as a close friend had in no way been evident? She had discovered very little when meeting him this morning for the first time.

Alan's description of Jock had led her to expect someone of personable appearance, but she had not anticipated that it would do him less than justice. Handsome features and a finely built body would have impressed her no more than the sight of a typical film star or athlete, and although Jock possessed these in outward form, his real attraction came from within. She was aware of a strange magnetism—something deep and mysterious and sad—something darkly still in his brooding eyes and proud face. And he seemed completely unconscious of his looks . . . no hint of conceit or vanity, no deliberate use of physical beauty to create effect or disarm by sheer perfection of form. In spite of his reserve, she instantly felt more at ease with him than she had with the coolly poised Colin. Whatever his private life might be she found herself curiously stirred and moved by the look of unhappiness in his eyes, and by the answering smile he gave her— lighting the almost stern expression on his face with a warmth that conveyed a genuine response to her friendly greeting. His quiet attentiveness pleased her and she experienced no difficulty in talking to him; stimulated and encouraged by his interest, she felt a renewed enjoyment in the familiar performance of show- ing her china and glass collection to a stranger.

More satisfying than anything was the fact that he had begun to relax in her company; even if it had not been enough to make him talk about himself, it dispelled that first impression of suf- fering. Apart from his natural reserve, there was no shyness in his manner towards her—nor did she feel that he was putting on an act for her benefit. She would have known at once had he been insincere. But there were still the other, unspoken things which she might never know . . . Several times, during their hour together, she had tried vainly to see in him some evidence of the problems and difficulties which beset Alan. In her failure to do so, she had hastily concluded that she was quite wrong in her original assumption. Only later did she begin to doubt again and wonder whether this was oversimplifying the matter. However ignorant she was about such a complex subject—not of its exist- ence, but of its modes of expression—it was foolish to suppose that a marked, visible sign always distinguished the invert from the heterosexual. Apart from extreme instances, how could one be certain? Only because of Colin and an underlying hint of growing emotional attachment was she less doubtful about Alan, but with Jock it was impossible to be sure. His warning to

Alan, concerning the boy, might be prompted by an understanding friendship—and in offering such advice it was not essential for him to have been in a similar predicament.

It was not until he was leaving that she saw him glance at the photograph of Alan, which stood on a small table near the drawing-room fireplace. As she reached the door, to show him into the hall, she stopped as she saw him turn back to look at it. For a moment he seemed unaware of her presence; he remained staring at the photograph for a long time, as if committing to memory the likeness of its subject. When he turned and came towards her, his face was shadowed and serious, but she noticed the quick change of expression in his eyes—the moment he saw her watching him, a warm light had suddenly gone out. Once more he became the reserved young Scotsman whom, just an hour ago, she had first seen and wondered about. Quietly he thanked her and said goodbye, making no reference to his departure for Glasgow or indicating in any way that he would be seeing either her or Alan again. From the front steps she watched him go down the path and out through the gate. Briefly he paused on the other side of the wrought-iron tracery and diffidently raised a hand in salute. Before she had time to smile or wave in acknowledgment, he had gone. She closed the front door, feeling completely baffled.

"Well, what did you think of Jock?" Alan handed Julia an extra-large gin and tonic and then sat down in the chair facing her. Normally she would have refused such a big glass, and she had already had one stiff drink just before he came home, but she still felt in need of something to brace her—and she suspected that he did, too. During dinner he had appeared worried and depressed, and unusually quiet, and was now only slowly beginning to relax.

"I liked him very much." She stared at the piece of lemon and the quickly surfacing bubbles. "We got on awfully well."

"Oh . . ." Alan sounded faintly surprised. "You didn't find him difficult?"

"Not a bit. I expected him to be rather reserved—he was at first, of course, but we were soon chatting away quite cosily. He wanted to know all about my china and glass. I think it was a genuine interest, not just being polite."

"When we came home last night he had a good look at everything in the hall. Said it was in good taste. He—he hasn't had much of a home life. A Glasgow slum."

"I should never have guessed that. Not by looking at him, anyway, or by hearing him talk. But I always find it difficult to 'place' a Scottish accent, even after all these years. Sometimes it's cultivated deliberately to sound outlandish!"

"I'm glad you liked him."

"I wish there'd been more time. We were getting on splendidly and I believe he was really enjoying our little talk—then, of course, he had to go. Quite suddenly he shut up like a clam and became terribly reserved again, almost a stranger. It seemed so odd, having thawed out like that." Julia paused to light a cigarette, and then went on: "When I first saw him, he gave me the impression of being unhappy. After we started talking I thought I must have imagined it—but it came back again. In fact I was rather worried . . . I hope I didn't upset him in any way."

"No, it couldn't be that. He's a bit moody sometimes." Alan lapsed into silence, thinking about Jock. For a while neither of them spoke.

Julia recalled in her mind the fleeting glimpse of the strange, intensely glowing expression in Jock's eyes—a light which seemed to transform his whole face and for an instant pierce the armour of reserve. It had been extinguished as suddenly as it had come, and at that moment she had realised that she was out of her depth and unable to reach him; there were secret places she could not enter. By his swift withdrawal behind a stern mask of pride and suffering, she knew he had not meant her to see his true, innermost self. She was left to wonder at that unguarded moment. It was only an hour ago when she had understood, with a sudden shock, the possible significance of that brief display of deep feeling.

She glanced at Alan, who was abstractedly watching the spiral of grey smoke from his cigarette. "Are you seeing him again?" she asked.

"Jock? I—I don't know. He said he'd write, but I don't suppose he will . . ."

"It's a pity he has to go back to Glasgow. I liked him, Alan. I felt he was a genuine sort of person. Someone you could trust. I imagine he's had a pretty hard life—quite a few disappointments. And I enjoyed talking to him—I'm sure it took him out of himself for a little. It certainly did *me*—with such a handsome young man. Quite flattering for an old lady."

"Oh, nonsense," Alan smiled. "You'd make a hit with anybody."

"No, but seriously, my dear, it's not altogether nonsense. One can so easily get out of touch with young people. It's not often, nowadays, that I get the chance to be with them. I suppose in a way it's my own fault, I've always been rather self-centred and lazy—too disinterested really to get on well with the younger generation. And I'm beginning to realise I've missed a great deal. Of course, if Harry were still alive, I might be different. He was at ease with people of any age. Yes ... eventually I might have become very motherly and cosy!"

"You're just as nice, as a chic, rather dashing aunt!"

"Oh, but I've always been dashing *away*! I'm not really a homemaker."

"What do you call all this luxury and comfort and beauty?"

"Nothing more than a 'collection.' A museum. Inanimate."

"That simply isn't true. I've never been so comfortable and contented anywhere, for years."

"Haven't you? Well, 'comfortable,' perhaps—I've never skimped over beds and chairs, when a great part of one's life is spent either sitting or lying down—but I have sometimes wondered whether you've been happy here. You've been used to your own place and it's never the same in somebody else's house. I love having you here, but I can't help thinking it's a purely selfish enjoyment. And it's no good protesting," Julia went on, as Alan tried to interrupt. "I haven't put myself out in the slightest. You must have noticed that. It's been bothering me lately, and I feel I haven't done enough for you. I'm inclined to forget that you're a quarter of a century younger than me—that you must want something rather more lively at times. Perhaps it's discouraged you a little from bringing your friends here——"

"Good God, no! You needn't think any of those things at

all. I'd gladly bring hordes of people—except that most of my friends are in London. And out of working hours, I like to get away from everyone at business. That's why I didn't want to 'live in' at the club."

"I can understand that; but I do want to be quite sure that you're all right, that you're not finding things—difficult—because of me . . ."

"Thanks, Julia. It's all right. You needn't worry."

"I do sometimes, you know, Alan. You haven't been your usual cheerful self lately. There—there isn't anything wrong, is there?"

"No. Of course not." Alan finished his drink and put down the glass, conscious that he was again trying to appear casual in the same way as when he had emptied his pipe the other afternoon.

"Perhaps I *am* worrying too much," Julia said, "but I was beginning to think that I might be responsible in some way—because I *have* rather taken it for granted that you'd want nothing more than a comfortable house and good food to keep you perfectly happy. And now . . . well, I wouldn't say anything at all, Alan dear, if it weren't so obvious that something's upset and depressed you."

"I'm terribly sorry, Julia, I know I get a bit moody at times, but it's certainly not your fault. Nobody could be nicer to live with than you, and I really mean it. Anyway, it'll pass off. I expect I'm tired, or haven't got over the winter yet. Or perhaps it's just middle age coming on. Sighing for one's lost youth . . ."

"For heaven's sake don't do that, my dear. You're not yet forty. Enjoy yourself while you're in the 'prime'—if that doesn't make you feel feel a piece of Scotch beef. No, I think you're too much of a worrier." Julia smiled. "Try not to be. It really isn't worth it."

"But just now you were . . ." Alan began.

"Yes, I know. I should have said I was *concerned* about you," corrected Julia. "I'm pleased that there's nothing wrong here."

"Bless you, nothing at all. And no business worries either, thank God. Not that I'd burden *those* on you, if there were."

"Whatever it was, Alan, I'd try to help and understand."

Alan looked at her, suddenly feeling hot and tense. Julia knows, he thought. Or at least suspects something. He thought he'd been particularly discreet, but he must have given himself away at some time—made himself obvious over this business with Colin. That was what it was. And what *does* she know, he wondered in alarm. She had seen Colin only briefly, and the boy had been very subdued; giving, in fact, an impression of complete detachment. She had never expressed any opinion about him, either. Jock would have revealed even less to her, he was sure. He must be mistaken over the implication of her words; but now that she had spoken, how was he to reply? He knew that her concern was genuine, and he could not fob her off with a vague answer. And yet he hated the idea of lying to her.

Then, before he could say anything, Julia continued: "Alan, dear—I would like you to understand something. It's not fair to you, letting you feel that I know more—more than you'd really care to tell anyone—because I don't. If I'd thought everything was all right, I wouldn't have spoken. But now that I *have*—well ... it might become painful for both of us if we allowed any misunderstanding to—to spoil our nice, easy relationship ... Oh dear ... I'm putting this so badly, making it sound so formal. You'll think I'm just an inquisitive, interfering old woman."

"No." Alan shook his head. "I've made things uncomfortable for *you*, expecting you to put up with my dreary moods and not even murmur. I'd fully deserve it if you bashed me over the head."

"I'd much rather put out a helping hand," Julia said quietly, "if I can do it, Alan, without embarrassing you."

"Julia ..." Alan stared at her, unhappily.

"You mustn't mind my saying this. It upsets me to see you hurt and miserable—forced to keep something bottled up inside you, because you think there's no one who'd understand. Believe me, *I* know what it's like. There have been times when I've experienced utter blackness and misery—and, without Harry, had no one to turn to. You can't *always* be self-sufficient. In the end it makes you inhuman. You find yourself living in a world where even the most ordinary, simplest affections are denied you. I thought *I* could exist like that, entirely on my own; but I was wrong. It's an arid, lonely business—I've discovered that. Of course, at first, I revelled in the idea of complete independence and freedom—going my own way and not caring a damn what anybody said or thought. I wasn't going to become cluttered with other people's emotional and domestic problems. They all seemed so petty and trivial and—and *messy*. Well, it was certainly a drastic step to take. 'If that's the way she wants it, let her have it,' they said. No half-measures, either!

"Unfortunately, it was a very long time before I realised how rootless I'd become. By then it was almost too late; I was getting old and there was nobody who could be bothered to find out how mistaken I'd been. You really can't blame them, I suppose. But the important thing, for both of us, Alan, is to not lose all feeling of 'communication'—do you know what I mean? So many of us have failed to help one another. We put up barriers, and for lack of courage we leave things unsaid and undone. We want to sympathise and understand, but something prevents us—and we let the opportunity go by. Sometimes just for the want of a single word, a single action, which might make all the difference in the world."

Julia paused, and then said gently: "Alan, dear, don't you think we're needlessly making things difficult for ourselves?"

"I don't know, Julia. If it meant a helping word or action, I know you'd give it. But it might not be worth while, and then you'd wish you hadn't."

"No. Never that, my dear. I don't pretend to know everything, and I'm not going to criticise. But I would like you to trust me. I realise it isn't easy for you—there must have been times when you've despaired of anyone ever understanding or sympathising. Or perhaps you've never expected it? Sympathy, without any real understanding, is useless. That's why I need your help just as much, Alan. It's a dangerous thing to possess a—how can I put it? A half-knowledge ... especially when you have, or hope you have, an orderly, practical mind. Anyway, to come to the point—I couldn't avoid seeing why you've been so worried and upset these last few days. It is because of Colin, isn't it? I know you were very fond of him, a long time ago—I gathered that, when you spoke about his family—and I could see you were disappointed in him the other day, in the way he'd changed. To be quite truthful, I didn't like him. He seemed so cold and calculating. I felt he didn't care about anyone except himself—that he wouldn't hesitate to let you down if it suited him."

"Yes, I know, Julia. He *has* changed more than I expected. I was disappointed—almost shocked, in a way . . . at least at first, because I couldn't understand it. Then I thought it must be something to do with his upbringing; nobody at home troubled very much about him. He didn't get on well with his father, and his mother was rather vague and easy-going. He had to leave home and strike out on his own. I suppose it's made him hard."

"Do you still feel that he's worth helping?"

"I—I don't know what to feel any more."

"He has—let you down, hasn't he? And let down Jock, too."

"Jock? What do you mean?" Alan looked surprised, but his tone was guarded.

"Alan, dear—I told you I wasn't going to criticise, and I'm not. I don't blame you at all for—for feeling deeply about someone in this way. If it's how you're made, what else can you do? I'm worried only because of the unhappiness this boy seems to have caused. It's a poor return for any of the love you can give him—and I don't think you'd want to do that lightly or casually. You're not that sort of person."

"I don't know what to say." Alan frowned and stared at the carpet. "Except that I'm sorry. I shouldn't have dragged you into this—come here under false pretences . . ."

"You've done nothing of the kind."

"Julia—do you *really* know what it means? The kind of life I've been forced to lead—the pretence—the lies I've had to tell? . . ."

"I can imagine. But I want to understand, Alan."

"About Colin?"

"Not only that."

"You mean Jock?"

"Yes. Alan . . . this morning, quite accidentally, I overheard Jock talking to you about Colin, warning you against him . . . I was naturally upset . . . I hadn't even seen Jock then. It's been on my mind the whole day."

"Jock's had a pretty raw deal from Colin—I expect you've guessed that by now. I didn't know anything about it until last night. But the whole thing's over and done with." Alan spoke grimly.

"There hasn't been any trouble between you and Jock, because of that?"

"Not really. I think he was jealous at first, until he found out that Colin cared nothing at all, and that I hadn't—hadn't got anywhere, either. I've tried to kid myself it would work out, even when I knew how hopeless it was to go on."

"I know so little about it, Alan, but it is possible for you, isn't it, to—to achieve a lasting, permanent love with someone?"

"Yes, I think so. For some of us. It could have been for me— once. During the war. He was killed. It was the first person . . . the first time I'd ever—— We never thought about it as being wrong. It *wasn't* wrong, when it meant so much to us, when it made bearable the whole wretched business of existence during the war. And since then I haven't wanted to change myself . . . but please don't think that I've been leading a life of 'vice,' or anything like that—because I haven't. I've no wish to go from one person to another, endlessly seeking new sensations. Those are the kind you mostly hear and read about, but there are thousands of us who want only to settle down happily with someone—to have that chance, like anyone else. But you can see how difficult it is, when we're driven underground . . . it makes everything seem so furtive and sordid." Alan sighed and shook his head sadly. "I suppose I'm asking too much. I don't want to become embittered, but . . ."

"Perhaps," Julia said gently, "you've been searching in the wrong direction. I mean Colin. In spite of everything I think you still feel something will happen to change him."

"I've wanted to help him."

"Does he need it? He appeared to be very sure of himself. By the way—did you meet him for lunch today?"

"No. He didn't turn up. Naturally I was disappointed, and a bit angry too—only it wore off, and then I started making all sorts of excuses for him, but it wasn't any good. In the end I almost felt relieved that he hadn't come."

"Do you still feel that, now?"

"No. Just empty. The whole thing seems such a wretched waste."

"For him, perhaps. But there are—others—who might need and deserve your help far more. You may not realise it yourself, my dear, but you have a very generous and compassionate heart.

You must guide it in the right direction. You've never really given up all hope, have you, of finding happiness?"

"No. No—never. But, Julia—if Colin . . ."

"I don't mean Colin. He hasn't been hurt. *You* have—but you also have the capacity not to let it defeat you. An inner strength, call it what you like . . . Someone else may need that strength to lift them out of despair and loneliness. Only don't leave it until it's too late."

"Julia—what . . ."

"Yes . . ." Julia stared at him calmly. "You can help him, Alan. Give him your friendship. He's desperately unhappy, I'm sure of that. But this morning, for a moment, I glimpsed something of his real self. It puzzled me, then, but now I can see what it was— what it could mean to him if someone could show just a little understanding, a little care for what happens to him. I'm positive he felt a genuine gratitude. Oh, he didn't say anything—it was shining from his eyes . . ."

"Because you'd shown him sympathy and kindness, Julia."

Julia shook her head. "No, my dear, it wasn't gratitude towards *me*." She looked at the photograph on the low table, then rose and lightly touched his shoulder. "I'm going to make some coffee. I shan't be long."

Picking up the empty glasses, Julia left the room.

Alan stared thoughtfully at the closed door. It had never occurred to him that Jock—— No, it was impossible. It couldn't be that. In her desire to help, Julia was perhaps reading into the situation more than it allowed. He had done nothing in particular to earn Jock's gratitude; nothing which would merit, according to Julia's interpretation, such a deep expression of regard. All he had done was to bandage Jock's hand and offer him shelter for the night. Anyone else would have done the same.

Then suddenly he remembered that momentary closeness, when they had lain side by side, very near to each other, and Jock had touched him and felt his heart beating. But that was nothing; Jock had been drinking and was in an emotional state anyway. It didn't add up at all. Besides, if Jock had wanted it that way, why had he chosen to go this morning, leaving no address and only a doubtful indication that he would write at some time or other? Probably they would never see each other again . . .

He closed his eyes, suddenly shaken by the thought that he couldn't get Jock out of his mind. He was worrying about him, and not only because he was sorry for him. It was kind of Julia to say he had a compassionate and generous heart, but nowhere near the truth to imagine that it was entirely selfless. His inflated egoism had led him to believe that he could succeed with Colin; and now, although he did not consider any such chance with Jock, his desire to see him was not completely altruistic. To be honest, he dreaded the thought of being alone again, without a single understanding friend. Already he was aware that as he grew older it was becoming more difficult to form intimate friendships. It wasn't enough, being ever hopeful and increasingly optimistic as, day by day, one's chances grew less and less . . . He must also face the fact that Jock might not welcome any further intrusion—he had suffered deeply and possibly his reserved nature condemned him to nurse his wounds in private. He was a secretive and mysterious creature, who could become locked in an obstinate, silent unhappiness. Without holding any brief for Colin's behaviour, it was easy enough to guess the effect Jock would have on the boy's youthful impatience and scorn. And as for himself . . . he couldn't deny the curiosity and interest he felt in Jock's conflicting personality. But if he were to seek him out, would it be in vain and result only in a rebuff?

He was torn between the impulse to go to Glasgow and the cautious inclination to remain where he was and not recklessly stick out his head to be kicked again so soon. Surely Jock would eventually write to him. If he didn't . . . would that be enough to convince him that any kind of friendship with Jock was an impossibility? There were all sorts of reasons why he might fail to get in touch; he could be too busily occupied with work; too proud to ask for anyone's help; unsure of expecting anyone really to care or bother about him. All these things. Or simply that he had found consolation in others. And why not? It was a common remedy—to obliterate the past with new interests; not to look back. But could that be Jock's way of forgetting? And if he *were* miserable and lonely as hell . . .

Julia returned to the room.

"The coffee will be ready in a few minutes." She sat down and for a moment appeared preoccupied. Then, answering his inquiring look: "I've been thinking. About Jock."

"Yes. So have I," said Alan. "Wondering what I should do."

CHAPTER 9

"All down for the finale! All down for the finale!"

The voice on the loudspeaker cut in sharply over the fainter, slightly distorted relay from the stage—the familiar sound of a comedy double act, punctuated by bursts of laughter and applause. In the usual manner, a noisy and colourful procession wended along the corridors and down the stairs. The conversation had not altered, but the hair styles and costumes were different; coronets and velvet were out—sequins and nylon were in. Calf-length skirts for the singers, and short, ballerina dresses for the dancers had replaced the heavy crinolines and the weighted trains of regal silk.

"My feet are killing me," 'Netta' complained.

"If you try to squeeze them into size three instead of seven, what can you expect?" 'Josie' glanced unsympathetically at 'Netta's' heels, which were hanging well over the edge of the fashionable sling-backs.

"It was much better when we had long skirts," said 'Netta.' "It didn't matter what your feet looked like. Still—" he became more cheerful, "we have got decent legs. Have you noticed Magda's? Like matchsticks—and those dreadful old lavatory shoes she wears . . ."

Opening the door, and heedless of the SILENCE notice, they chattered their way on to the stage and stood behind the back-cloth to await their entrance cue for the finale. In a few seconds the entire company had gathered, busy with hurried, last-minute titivations before the almost traditional parade and line-up. There was grumbling and dissatisfaction, too; certain changes in procedure had not been to everyone's liking. While it appeared very effective from the front, the introduction of *two* staircases on the stage had nearly caused a riot among the cast. It was nothing less than class distinction for the principals to have a separate staircase to themselves, and it was a slight to the hard-working and indispensable chorus. They had been segregated. It was a downright affront; and 'Josie' had not been slow in voicing his opinion about it. In spite of his objections, however, the new routine had come to stay.

"I could *kill* Magda," he hissed. "That awful smug look she puts on—just because she comes down the other staircase."

"Never mind, dear," said 'Netta.' "She's the first one on and nobody claps much."

'Josie's' eagle eyes suddenly spotted someone. "There goes Madame. Let's send her up. Ssss! Ssss!"

Colin, in mock disdain, tossed his head and gave a backward kick with one leg. The 'cowboy,' walking behind him, hastily drew away.

"Mind where you place that heel!" 'Josie' laughed, and then added, "She nearly put a stop to Larry's ambition."

"I wish somebody would," said 'Netta.' "I'm tired of hearing all those stories about himself. I don't know why he bothers to tell *us* what a great big normal man he is and how many girls he seduces at week-ends. Oh, my God—we're nearly off—come on . . ."

Breathlessly and somewhat late for their entrance, they scrambled up the rickety steps to the head of the staircase. With dazzling, fixed smiles they made their descent to the centre of the stage—no mean feat when the stairs were so awkwardly spaced. The deep treads and too high steps necessitated exceptional poise and balance. It was agonising for 'Netta'; but 'Josie,' who led the way, had brought it to a fine art, combining movement with ventriloquism as, vividly smiling, he continued to talk from the corner of his mouth without disturbing a muscle. "We'll go out to supper tonight . . . What did you say?" as 'Netta' murmured inaudibly. "I can't hear you."

"Ayshedyaysheshaymumamuma," was all 'Netta' could manage as he precariously tottered behind.

"Careful, girl," warned Cyril Cushion, who followed him. Cyril had replaced 'Butch,' and he was a giggler, needing very little to set him off.

Arriving safely at the footlights they curtsied and drew aside, leaving the floor clear for the 'stars' of the show. They were supposed to turn, with a welcoming gesture towards the other staircase, as these brilliant luminaries appeared—but this spurious act of homage had long since palled, and after a year of twice-nightly performances on tour they had abandoned all pretence and found it more amusing to talk among themselves or distract the audience's attention by smiling straight at them across the orchestra pit.

'Magda' was the first one down, and reached his position near the proscenium arch before the audience became fully aware that the principals were entering to take their call. Next came 'Tessa' in a cloud of pink drapery, grimacing to the wolf-whistles from the gallery. The applause swelled as Colin appeared, ablaze with sequins, preceding Larry, whose jeans were so tight that he could hardly walk.

"Annie Oakley's taking her time tonight," observed 'Josie,' referring to Colin's deliberately slow descent. (He varied the speed, according to the warmth of the reception.) An appreciative cheer went up as 'Lady Loveday' followed, soignee and expressionless as a top-class mannequin. Then, finally, 'Betty' and 'Charlotte,' the undisputed Queens of Comedy. Securely in the public's affection for nearly twenty years, they had nothing to fear—as backers, they had reaped a tidy harvest from the show, quite apart from their weekly salaries and a percentage on the box-office takings.

Wigs were doffed; illusion dispelled; and another performance had ended. With the falling of the curtain the audience returned to reality. On the other side of the footlights the process was slower and, with few exceptions, not wholly convincing.

'Josie' and 'Netta' changed quickly, beating Cyril Cushion in the race for the wash-basin. Then, clashing with perfumes, they hurried down to the next floor and burst into Colin's dressing-room.

"We're going out to supper. Are you coming?"

"Darling! Heavenly! Yes! Where?"

"There's a place round the corner. One of the stage hands told me—the tall, blond one . . ."

"I'm sure his hair's dyed," said 'Netta.'

"Anyway, it keeps open late, which is something."

"It sounds terribly smart. Café society, dear, that's me. I'm nearly ready." Colin picked up a powder puff and dabbed his face. "Just the teeniest touch of Corelli . . . a new box . . . madly expensive but fabulous . . . There! Now I can face the world with confidence. Are my lips red enough?"

"You're not going to put on lipstick?" 'Netta' asked.

"It won't be *obvious*."

"You're getting dreadfully camp," said 'Josie.'

"I can't go about looking drab. Oh—I nearly forgot—a dab behind the ears. 'Tweed.' . . ."

"Very hearty. Who do you think *you're* kidding?"

"Angel . . ." Colin replaced the stopper in the bottle. "It was a good house tonight, wasn't it? Once they'd warmed up. Went very well."

"Larry was a bit off, wasn't he?"

"My dear, I was livid, I could have *screamed* . . . I don't know *what* he was doing with that lasso—kept missing me—I practically had to jump into it myself, he was so wide of the mark. Then he dropped the revolvers twice. It was sheer torture, standing against the board, waiting for him to fire . . . *What* we have to do for a living, my dear . . . Oh, Larry's impossible! And so conceited! There's no pleasing him, either. Of course it's all bluff, the way he pretends he's not gay. I'm quite sure that if—— Oh dear, who's this coming in?"

Larry, overpoweringly dressed in American-style clothes, swaggered into the room. "Excuse *me*," he said, adopting a simpering voice. "Is this fairyland? Pardon my intrusion . . ."

"Your *what?*" 'Josie' looked at him scathingly.

"Well, Larry, what do you want?" asked Colin.

"Nothing you can give me, kid," Larry drawled.

"Have you come to apologise?"

"Apologise? What the hell for?"

"You certainly messed up the act tonight, didn't you? You were all over the place."

"So what?"

"It doesn't matter about me, I suppose? I'm just the stooge, while you play about, trigger-happy . . ."

"Scared, eh? Anyone could've dropped something . . ."

"You weren't concentrating. There might have been an accident. Of course, if you want to break up the act . . . only you'll soon find yourself out of work; there aren't many who'd risk taking over from me."

"Someone should have shot you up long ago, ducky. A pity that knife-thrower didn't pin you before I came along."

"I don't know what you mean!" Colin stiffened angrily.

"Don't listen to him, dear!" 'Netta' implored anxiously.

"Huh! I'm not going to. You needn't get swollen-headed, Larry. You're not the star of this show, or ever likely to be. It only needs a few words from Harry Archer to the boss, and you're out."

"Caught in your own lasso," 'Josie' added.

"And who do you think *you* are?" Larry's eyes narrowed unpleasantly. "Top of the bill? The lot of you put together wouldn't get as far as a pavement act outside the Palladium. I've never seen such a bloody bunch of fairies."

"Why—you bum cowboy!" 'Josie' grabbed furiously at Larry's hand-painted tie.

"Strangle me, would you, you fruit!"

"Your mother should have done it at birth!" 'Josie' pulled with all his might. There was a rending sound as the tie split beneath Larry's collar.

"All right!" shouted Larry. "I'm going to beat you up!"

"No! No! Stop it! For God's sake . . ." cried 'Netta,' attempting to draw 'Josie' away. "Jo—Colin——— Oh, why doesn't somebody *do* something?"

Colin shrugged contemptuously. "Really—such childish behaviour."

'Netta' let out a terrified scream as 'Josie' hurtled towards him. Receiving the full impact, he staggered and fell. 'Josie' landed on top of him. Together they lay on the floor, a tangle of legs and arms.

"And as for you . . ." The dishevelled Larry threateningly moved near to Colin. "You'd better look out. One of these days it'll be your turn—you little pouff!" He strode from the room, slamming the door.

"Well!" 'Josie' rose to his feet, and with one hand pulled the limp and exhausted 'Netta' from the floor. "Charming!" Then accusingly to Colin: "You didn't lift a finger to help!"

"Darling, what could I do? You were like a couple of mad things. It's so foolish to lose control, dear. Much more effective if you're calm. I mean, when you're not the fighting type . . ." Colin started to laugh. "It really was rather funny. If you could have seen Netta's face when you landed on top of her . . ."

"It wasn't a bit funny," said 'Netta.' "I might have been knocked unconscious."

"Well, you weren't, so it's all right," said Colin.

"That isn't the point," said 'Josie,' shortly. "You might at least sound as if you cared."

"I do. But really—what do you expect me to do? Have hysterics?"

"No you don't. Not one bit. I don't know what's come over you lately. I don't understand it at all. You've become hard."

"You have to be hard in this game," said Colin. "Now come along, if we're going out to supper . . ."

"I'm not sure that I want to."

"Oh, don't be so silly. Surely we're above such petty quarrelling?"

"Well—I might come and look at this café," 'Josie' grudgingly replied. "Only it had better be good."

"It was *you* who said it was, darling—and I'm starving," said 'Netta,' who had quickly recovered and didn't want the rest of their evening spoiled. They left the dressing-room and walked along the corridor. Mrs. Oldham, looking resigned under a toque of purple feathers, approached them, on her way to the wardrobe.

"Good night, dear," they chorused.

"I'm glad you think so," she replied enigmatically.

"What's the matter, Mrs. Oldham?" asked 'Netta.'

"Haven't you seen the call-board yet?"

"No," said 'Josie.' "Not more rehearsals, surely?"

"I don't mean rehearsals," Mrs. Oldham said. "No need for *that*. The notice has gone up."

"WHAT!!" They looked at her in blank astonishment.

"Two weeks. Closing Saturday fortnight," she informed them.

"Oh, my God . . . but why? *Why?*" 'Josie' demanded dramatically; the others were too stunned to speak.

"Business, I suppose. It hasn't been good lately. Running costs are high, you know. Can't go on for ever. It's the same everywhere—bit of a slump just now. Of course it may pick up . . ." Mrs. Oldham sounded doubtful. "I suppose we're lucky to have had so long."

"Oh dear . . ." 'Netta' at last found voice. "Only two weeks. Then what are we going to do?"

"It's monstrous!" exclaimed 'Josie.' "We must get on to Equity at once!"

"They can't stop us closing," said Colin.

'Josie' went on: "We had a full house tonight, didn't we? And last night."

"Yes, second house. They're all right—but nobody comes first house. I've always said it's too early." And Mrs. Oldham shook her head.

"What a time to be out of work!" said 'Josie' in disgust. "It's too late now to get into a summer show, and there'll be nothing doing again until the autumn—if then."

"Perhaps the management will send us out again later," said 'Netta' hopefully.

"I shouldn't bank on it."

"Well, there it is," Mrs. Oldham pronounced. "I must finish tidying up."

"It's ghastly," said 'Josie.' "What a night! I *knew* this theatre was unlucky—I sensed it the last time—and look what happened then!"

"We'd better go," Colin advised, "or we shall be locked in."

Gloomily they went down to the stage door. 'Tessa' and 'Magda' were standing near the call-board. 'Tessa' was sniffing loudly and dabbing his eyes with a handkerchief. "Isn't it dreadful?" he gulped. "What are we going to do? I'm sure there's no work about and I haven't saved a penny . . ."

"Pull yourself together, dear," said 'Netta.' "It isn't the end of the world."

"I wish to God it was," 'Tessa's' eyes began to stream again, "then we wouldn't have to worry any more."

"You'd better have supper with us. Wipe your face."

"Yes, come on," said 'Josie.' He turned to 'Magda.' They were all in the same boat now and must console one another. "We'll all go. Magda? . . ."

"Thanks—but I prefer to get drunk," said 'Magda.' "I've got a bottle of gin at my digs—if the landlady hasn't been at it already."

"Just as you like, but where's it going to get you?"

"Where's anything going to get any of us now?" 'Magda' glanced at them bitterly and then abruptly pushed through the swing doors.

"She really is a silly cow," said 'Josie.' "She'll only make herself ill and be sour and bad-tempered tomorrow."

They left the theatre in silence, each occupied with his own thoughts. The future seemed uncertain and perilous; the prospects of ever working again appeared remote. What they had all secretly dreaded had perhaps come at last—the vogue for this particular kind of show was waning. For a while its colourful extravagance appealed to the public; they accepted it as an entertaining novelty, a change from the usual touring revues. For a time they remained amused and indulgent, but eventually the original purpose of all such shows—the presentation of ex-services talent to a wider, peace-time audience—had become meaningless. The supply of genuine ex-service performers had run out long ago, and in many instances their places were taken by players of little experience and colossal nerve, but who otherwise would never gain admittance to the professional stage. It was hard for those who, like 'Josie' and 'Netta,' had worked most of their lives in the theatre—beginning as ordinary chorus boys or dancers and getting no farther in their careers while new, up-and-coming youngsters (of a more virile school of training) readily adapted themselves to the muscular requirements of American musicals. The chances of resuming their former positions were small indeed, for it was a dubious recommendation to admit that one had been out in a 'drag' show, however successful it might have been. They were 'branded'; and already the touring circuits, warned by the unfavourable publicity recently given to certain, sensational 'exposures' in the Press, were getting cold feet and refused to book such productions for their theatres.

Colin, who had never known the desperate, heart-breaking struggle of trying to find work on the stage, was the least affected. It had been good fun, he thought, although his hopes of becoming a 'star' artist never materialised; but what with one thing and another he felt a change was indicated. Besides, all this tiresome business with Larry was so exhausting—the man was just an egotistical bore, consumed with monotonous self-appraisal; and if Larry expected him to play second fiddle he was greatly mistaken . . . he was a dead loss, too, as far as any personal relationship was concerned. Really, people were so disappointing and unreliable; one couldn't go on for ever, giving out all the time and receiving so little in return. When the show finished he would have a good holiday, perhaps in the South of France or somewhere like that. He would look up Kenneth Stubbs as soon as he got back to London—it would be fun to go away with him, and Kenneth was easy to get on with, never arguing or opposing, and always ready to fall in with his plans . . . yes, he was very fond of Kenneth. In any case, he could probably stay at the Stubbs' for a bit, while he looked around for a job; it would be much more agreeable than going into a furnished room, and of course it was out of the question now to return home. Regarding work—well, he could always take up his drawing again. If, as seemed likely, Gaiety Tours had nothing to offer him as a performer, he would tackle them about the possibility of becoming a stage designer. Claud Loveday, too, might be able to help him again with some useful contacts. There was no reason why he shouldn't succeed. After all, he was young and healthy and good-looking. There was something precious and wonderful about youth—only it didn't last for ever. It was terribly important to make the most of its advantages, and that was exactly what he would do. Nobody should hinder his purpose, either . . .

'Josie,' rather grimly, was musing on life. Where did he go from here? He had no illusions about it. As he once said to Colin: "We'll just go on getting older and older and tattier and tattier," and as far as he could see at the moment the process could continue equally well away from the theatre as behind the footlights. In fact, without the consolatory glamour and trappings of the stage, it was in danger of rapid acceleration. What the hell was he going to do? No money and, let's face it, nothing that was likely to revolutionise the West End—either in a playhouse or on the pavements of Piccadilly. Anyway, *that* sort of thing wasn't his line at all. Whatever people thought (and he'd always pretended to be an outrageous, bold cow) he had been unwontedly and unwillingly respectable for years. So—he must find a job. There were other branches of entertainment besides the stage. For instance there was—well . . . what, exactly? Skipping all high falutin ideas, he did know somebody working in a seaside fun-fair, and they were always wanting people during the season. He could picture himself standing by a decorated stall, gaily persuading visitors to try their luck at a game of chance. It might be quite an experience. What was the name of that film—the one where the girl assisted in the rifle range and was nearly strangled on the Big Dipper one night by Orson Welles? . . .

'Netta' was anxious, of course, but quite willing to plump for anything at all, providing he and Jo were not separated. They had worked together for so long, sharing the joys and woes, that to part now would seem like losing a limb. Imagine wanting to do something, and suddenly finding you couldn't . . . that's how it would be without Jo. About as useless as one half of a cross-talk act. Still, perhaps something would turn up for them both. In the paper this morning 'Your Lucky Star' had said "Leo is in the ascendant. Important friendships will prosper. A good time for business and for laying plans. Most favourable day—Saturday. Lucky number—7. Colour—Red." Not a bad horoscope and Jo's had been much the same. Things could be far worse, and they'd had a pretty long innings. He'd even been able to save a little money each week, which was more than some of them had. Just as well, too, for Jo was wickedly extravagant, what with sweets and cigarettes and expensive bottles of scent and tablets of soap. The money would come in handy for them both and help to tide them over if they struck a bad patch. Altogether he was better off than most. Colin, he was sure, never saved a penny—he was always buying clothes and books and God knows how many pairs of shoes in the past year. As for poor Tess, she hadn't a bean. Heaven only knows what would become of *her* . . .

Poor 'Tessa' was indeed wondering about the future—but

his vision was blurred in a haze of tears. Rather uncertainly he wavered from one possibility to another, vaguely dismissing each as they burst like empty bubbles before him. He just wasn't good at anything. It was too awful to contemplate. What was there for him? Perhaps he could work in a shop . . . only he always got hopelessly muddled when it came to dealing with money— had to work out everything on paper, and then it usually came wrong. Or could he go into domestic service? It was dreadfully confusing, though, especially when you had to have some sort of order and routine, and know how to make beds properly and lay the table for dinner parties, and serve food. He was always breaking things, too . . . and also he wasn't very strong. He couldn't do a job where you had to lift things; nor could he be outside, in the winter, because of feeling the cold. Oh, life was so cruel and unfair—and it wasn't as if he were asking too much. Apart from having somebody strong, who could protect him, all he wanted was to sing and to look lovely . . .

"This is the place," said 'Josie,' advancing to the restaurant door. Flanking the entrance were plate-glass windows filled with a miniature jungle of semi-tropical plants and half-lowered Venetian blinds. Just visible through the greenery, pink and amber lights glowed from birdcage shades of white-painted metal.

"My dear . . . Tondelayo . . ." 'Josie' threshed his way through a tangled curtain of beads. "It's like being in *White Cargo.*" They came into a large room filled with tables, all spread with gay-coloured cloths and raffia mats. The chairs were starkly Scandinavian, but along the walls and beneath the bold pattern of 'contemporary' paper were comfortable *banquettes* upholstered in deep blue. A smaller room, also for diners, adjoined the main part of the restaurant; climbing and trailing plants, hanging baskets of flowers and *jardinières* brimming with exotic vegetation gave it the appearance of a conservatory.

"It looks cheerful enough," said 'Netta.' "Where shall we sit? It's rather full."

"There's a table there—those people are just going." 'Tessa' indicated the corner nearest the door. The previous occupants moved away and they sat down, 'Josie' and 'Netta' on the *ban-*

quette and Colin and 'Tessa' on the chairs, facing the wall. While
'Netta' pored over the menu card, 'Josie' gazed serenely across
the room, feeling like a rich shipping magnate's wife who had
just loosened her furs at the Savoy.

"We might as well make the most of it and have a good meal,"
said 'Netta' reluctantly and somewhat dismayed by the prices.

"Yes. Fish and chips tomorrow and probably the soup kitchen
when we're all out of work," said 'Josie.'

"Oh dear ... the menu's in French," 'Tessa' complained.
"What's this?" He pointed to an item on the card.

"Moules marinière," said Colin. "Mussels."

"Sea food," said 'Josie,' "and nothing to do with sailors."

After much deliberation they ordered from the waiter. 'Josie'
resumed his surveyal of the other diners, mostly middle-aged
couples. Absently he smiled in the direction of a bald-headed
gentleman, but the man's eager expression was intended merely
to attract the waiter's attention, and on catching 'Josie's' eyes he
gave a frightened start and dropped his buttered roll on the floor.
Presently their waiter returned, skilfully balancing four plates on
his arms, and then for a minute or two they silently concentrated
on their food.

"Ummm ... delicious," 'Josie' murmured, spearing a tender
button mushroom with his fork. "If only we could eat like this
every day, instead of having those dreadful things our landlady
dishes up."

"Shepherd's pie, or if it's not that it's cottage pie," said 'Netta.'
"They both taste exactly the same. Filthy."

"I've a good mind to go to a decent hotel for our last week, and
do things in style," said 'Josie.' "I'd love to have breakfast in bed
and ring the bell for the chambermaid to run my bath."

"Yes," sighed 'Netta,' "and a 'loo' to yourself, without having
to queue for it. We can never get into ours, first thing. Then when
we do, someone always comes and rattles the door-handle."

"I always go at the theatre, it's more peaceful," said 'Tessa.'

"It's all right *this* week," Colin agreed, "but some of the backstage loos are so awful and primitive."

'Josie' confirmed this with an agonised glance towards the
ceiling. "My dear, I shall never forget that one at—where was it?

Oh, I can't remember . . . but you had to pull the chain and run out quickly because the floor always got flooded."

"Terrifying," said 'Netta.' "So was that one where you had to pull up a handle thing at the side, and if you pulled too far it came right out and took hours to get back again."

"The worst experience I ever had," said 'Josie', warming to the subject, "was during the *Out of Uniform* tour. Don't you remember, Nett? Wolverhampton . . ." A spirited discussion on theatre lavatories took them well into the next course of their meal. With their stomachs satisfied, and feeling more relaxed, they forgot for the time being the depressing reality of their uncertain future. Over coffee, 'Tessa' and Colin became absorbed in a talk about films and film stars; 'Netta' began enthusing about holidays abroad (he had spent ten days in Paris five years ago) and 'Josie,' half listening but with occasional interjections of "Glorious" or "Marvellous," casually noted the various activities going on around them. The customers appeared rather a dull lot, but one of the waiters looked interesting. Then, just as 'Netta' was plunging into a lurid description of a gay bar in Montmartre, his idle gaze ceased its wanderings among the tables and became fixed in the direction of the 'conservatory' room. Smothering an astonished "Oh!" he dug 'Netta' in the ribs with his elbow.

"Ouch!" 'Netta' jumped slightly. "What are you doing?"

"Sshh! Over there," 'Josie' whispered.

"What? Where?" 'Netta's' eyes searched the hanging baskets and pots of ivy, as if about to discover a new and rare species of plant life.

"Lower!" said 'Josie' through clenched teeth.

"I can't see anything—those people are in the way."

"You fool—*look!*" 'Josie' ordered.

"Do you mean the camp hat that woman's wearing? It's like a—— Good God . . ." 'Netta' clapped a hand over his mouth. "My dear . . ." he murmured behind his fingers.

"What's going on?" Colin asked, noticing their barely suppressed excitement.

". . . it wasn't nearly as good as *Mildred Pierce*, when Joan Crawford . . ." 'Tessa' stopped in mid-sentence and stared at the others.

"Oh, nothing," 'Josie' said hastily. "Just a hat . . ."

"Where?" 'Tessa' turned in his chair and received a hard kick under the table from 'Josie.' "Oh! You beast! My leg . . ."

"Shut up and finish your coffee."

"You needn't snap at me."

"Really, you two . . ." Colin turned and looked across the room. Several people were leaving the restaurant, and a smiling waiter was ushering them out, bowing to each of them as they went. Negotiating her passage through the tables, like a ship on the Panama Canal, the large woman in the camp hat sailed with fluttering pennants of tulle towards the entrance. As if released from a guiding tug-boat, and rapidly gathering speed, she left the escorting waiter and steamed bulkily forward into the night. The bead curtain rattled about her like a violent rainstorm in the Pacific. Colin barely noticed her departure; he was staring at the remaining two people who had paused to speak to the waiter. They were Alan and Jock. Both of them smiling; and Jock laughing, with Alan lightly holding his arm as they turned and left. So that was it . . . The shock of seeing them together like this froze him in a grip of anger and resentment. For a moment he could think of nothing but his own outraged feelings; then, coldly and scornfully, he dismissed them. Alan and Jock were welcome to each other as far as he was concerned. It wouldn't last, anyway. Jock was far too unstable and easily went off the rails—he'd soon grow tired of Alan's schoolmasterish ways. Really, it was ludicrous. He wondered whether Alan knew the whole truth of Jock's past. Probably he did by now; Jock would love wallowing in an orgy of confession, and Alan would see himself as a shining crusader, coming to the rescue and 'reforming' him. The pair of them had looked so smug, too. No, it couldn't possibly last. He thought also that Alan had aged a bit and put on weight . . .

In silence the four of them finished their coffee and asked for the bill. A few minutes later, in the street, 'Josie' at last spoke. "Well! What about that? Your red-headed friend, too. I didn't know he knew Jock. How long has it been going on?"

"Going on?" Colin tried to sound casual.

"My dear, it's obvious. Did you introduce them in the first place?"

"Yes."

"Oh well . . . and I suppose your friend whisked him away. You should have kept your eyes on Jock. Of course I thought something had happened, when you had all that trouble with him last year. I told you he was a dark horse. It wouldn't last."

"Don't be so cruel, Jo," said 'Netta.' "It's enough to upset anyone. Colin was very kind to him. Jock only left the show because he was ill and got drunk."

"And since when," 'Josie' asked, "have you stood up for Jock?"

"It's not that at all, but you're trying to rub it in that Colin couldn't hold him . . ."

"Really, dear, don't be idiotic. We all know what Jock's like. It's no good being sentimental and weak about it. Face up to life, darling! Even if it's death."

"I think it's a great pity. When you think of all the wasted love . . ."

"Don't go on about it, dear. You sound like a James Barrie heroine . . . lost in the woods or something."

"Don't you *mind*, Colin?" asked 'Netta.'

"I should worry," said Colin. "Plenty more fish in the sea. Nobody keeps *me*."

"*Yet*," 'Josie' added.

"Is this the right way?" asked 'Tessa,' as they approached a street corner. "Where do we go from here?"

"We just go on and on and on, dear." 'Josie's' lips stretched into a smile on his white-mask face. "And if we're lucky we find what we're looking for."

"Oh . . . do we?" 'Tessa' sounded unbelieving.

"Come along," said 'Josie' briskly. "Don't just stand there like a tart. My sense of direction says 'straight on.'"

"I hope you're right," said 'Netta,' "because it's getting late and I'm tired. All I want is bed. You know, that staircase puts years on me. I felt my ankles going again tonight."

"Perhaps you'd like them to install an escalator," 'Josie' replied dryly.

"Oh, I *love* coming down those stairs." 'Tessa's' eyes were moist and shining. "The orchestra, the lights, the applause . . ."

"Hah!" said 'Josie.'

"It's all very well to scoff," said 'Netta,' "but you couldn't do without it. It's the only thing that really keeps us going."

"The Big Parade!" 'Josie' suddenly laughed.

"What are you laughing for? What's the joke?"

"The whole thing, Nett. The whole, gay pageant."

"Never mind, dear, we can stand it."

"We always have," said Colin. "Oh, do stop laughing like that!" But 'Josie' continued to laugh louder than ever.

"She's getting hysterical now." 'Netta' shook 'Josie's' arm. "Jo! Do be sensible. If only you could see yourself . . ."

"I can!" exclaimed 'Josie.' "That's why I'm laughing—it's much better than weeping. Anyway, darling, if *we* can't laugh about it, who can? At least, not in the same way . . . and remember, we're the Merrie Belles, aren't we?"

Linking arms, the four of them, like a team of dancers, stepped forward in unison along the road. Ahead, there were lights as far as their vision could reach—bright, shining globes stretching into the distance. Hopefully they went on, their eyes seeing only the brilliant lamps above them. Perhaps it was just as well that they could see no farther.

Lying comfortably with his feet up on the settee, Alan lit a cigarette and gazed lazily about the quiet, peaceful room. He was pleasantly tired and relaxed; this was a favourite hour, around midnight, after returning from an evening out. A drink or two, a good film, a satisfying supper, and a walk home in the coolish air. No coming back alone any more, no regrets or frustrations to keep him awake when he wanted to sleep. It was wonderful, not to have a care in the world . . .

He smiled to himself as he heard Jock padding about in the kitchen, arranging the tea-tray and waiting for the kettle to boil—very much at home, as if he had been living here for years—and it seemed inconceivable that nearly a year ago he had hesitated to ask Jock to make his home with Julia and himself. But Julia had urged him to do so, and she had been right. Even more gratifying was the fact that she got on so well with Jock, who had quickly responded to the warmth and affection around him, shedding his reserve and, with the security and pleasures of home life, gaining a new confidence. His unhappy past—and Jock had withheld nothing from him about his former life—ceased to trouble him. Mentally and physically he had become more balanced, more attuned to the quieter intimacies of companionship. Between them both there was perfect accord, devotion and respect. It was, Alan rejoiced, everything he had wished and waited for; the final proof he had been seeking—that their world was not always the empty, despairing place of ill-fated or unattained love.

Presently Jock came into the room, bearing the tea-tray, which he put down on a low table beside the settee. Kneeling on the carpet, he stared inquiringly at Alan.

"I've been thinking," said Alan.

"Have ye?" Jock gave him an amused, quizzical look.

"Aye—I mean yes . . ." They both laughed, and Alan went on: "Pleasant thoughts. About us. How lucky we are. I know *I* am, anyway. It seems almost unfair and greedy to have everything I want."

"Och, I'm sure ye havena sae much as me." Jock shook his head wonderingly, as if amazed by his good fortune. "I wish I could tell ye . . ."

"No regrets?"

"No. None at all . . . Would ye like a biscuit wi' yer tea?" Jock hurriedly proffered the tin, suddenly shy at having to find words for what he felt.

"No, thanks, I've already eaten too much. Jock . . ."

"What?"

"Oh . . . just 'Jock' . . . I like saying your name."

"Ye daft fool." Jock smiled broadly and stirred the tea in the pot.

"I had a letter from Julia, today. She's staying with Norah, in Montreal, until the end of the month, and hopes to take a look at New York on the way back. Are you comfortable on the floor?"

"No." Carefully balancing his cup, Jock raised himself on to the opposite end of the settee and sat with his legs up, facing Alan.

"What time are you on tomorrow, Jock? Early?"

"Midday. I can lie in till ten."

"Lazy lives you clubroom stewards lead."

"If ye'd like to change places . . ."

"Not really; although it must be quite amusing sometimes."

"Aye, on occasion. Ye learn a lot aboot people. It's verra strange—but awfu' interesting."

"It certainly is. Ah well . . ." Alan yawned and stretched. "Nearly half-past twelve."

"Ye can have the bathroom first, while I clear up these things."

"Right. Make sure the back door's locked."

"I will." Jock picked up the tray and looked down at Alan. "I forgot to ask ye before, but did ye notice what was on at the Palace this week?"

"Yes, Jock, I did. Only I haven't said anything because . . ."

"Ye've no cause to mind. Och, sometimes I think of it, but it all seems unreal. I've no hankering for the life again. As a matter of fact, I went by the theatre yesterday and saw the pictures outside."

"Oh . . ."

"He's still in it."

"I don't worry about it now, but I can't think where it's going to get him in the end—what he gets out of it," Alan mused; and then, seeing Jock's smile: "What are you smiling about?"

"I was wondering what he'd say if he knew aboot us being together. He'd be awfu' put out to learn that he'd done one worthwhile thing wi'out knowing it. If it hadna been for him I might never have seen ye again. Never been sae happy as I am now . . ." With a warm look of regard Jock left Alan and took the tray into the kitchen.

Alan switched off the lights and went upstairs. He undressed, whistling softly as he moved about the room. After returning from the bathroom, he took off the bedspread and wound the alarm clock; he could have an extra half-hour in the morning, as Jock wasn't getting up early. Putting on his pyjamas, he crossed to the window, drew back the curtains, and opened it wide at the bottom. In the light of a full moon the garden seemed to wait, mysterious and silent, bathed in silvered whiteness and deep shadows. Beyond the yew trees, the sun god Apollo stood undaunted by the cold gleam of Selene, his rival.

He stared at the brilliant moon-circle, whose radiance

dimmed the galaxy of stars in the night sky. Behind him he heard the door open, and in a moment Jock was standing at his side. "A wonderful night, Jock," he whispered, as if fearful of disturbing the stillness about them.

"Aye, it's beautiful," said Jock.

"The inconstant moon. I'll not swear by it . . ."

But as Jock's friendly, comforting arm rested warmly on his shoulders, Alan left the sentence unfinished. He knew, however much the moon might change within her orbit, that his love would not prove likewise variable. It was lasting and complete.